BETRAYED

by

Cara Louise

BETRAYED

Published by Cara Louise Books.

www.caralouisebooks.com

ISBN - 13 – 978-1500810528
ISBN – 10 - 1500810525

DEDICATION

This book is dedicated to the bravery and resistance of the people of Palestine.

Cara Louise 2014

PROLOGUE

Department of Archaeology, International University of Jerusalem. Cache 5. Cave 7. Ein Gedi. 21/6/01. Ref: BT A1003. Priority A1.

Fragment 1

I found my little sister with her linen robe around her neck. Her skin was as smooth as the alabaster of the Egyptians' finest jars and her eyes stared up to the sky like glassy stones, sightless, thank Astarte, for the vultures were already circling overhead. They would have rich pickings indeed this night.

My sweet, long-haired, doe-eyed sister had seen but eight turns of the sun. Now she was dead.

There was not a mark on her body, save a faint bloom of purple on her thighs. Her spirit had fled before the bruises could form. If the Habiru had slit her throat with a sword I could have borne it better. For though there were no outward signs of death, that smooth, almost naked body told its own story with a horror unmarked by

4

blood. I knew what they had done to her, those murdering Habiru. There was nothing to ease my pain, for I knew what hers had been. Her wounds were inflicted from within.

I stood and gazed at her, seeing only that one still cold body, though all around me was a sea of death. The stench of it drifted on the desert air and the breeze brought no relief, only acrid ash and smoke. All was burning, burning.

I could not weep. I only stared. I had woven the linen of her robe myself, with flax we had gathered with the other women from the fields. Fields that now lay awash with blood, strewn with the broken corpses of our people, every family dead - save one.

I had searched those fields for her. I had seen the little boy who tended his goat outside the city walls with his stomach sliced, the old woman next door with her head lying a little way from the rest of her body, the leper who would beg no more by the city gates.

Cold fury began to spread through my veins like liquid fire. I threw back my head, and tore the combs from my hair. I felt it tumble to my waist like a waterfall of silk, and I screamed. I screamed to Astarte, to Baal, to Dagon, and I screamed against the terrible One God of those blaspheming Habiru who denied all other gods. Then I screamed revenge at their leader, who had led them to swarm like locusts across the plain to devour our city, that murdering bastard, Joshua.

I do not know where the Gods were that day. Perhaps even they had turned their faces away from the slaughter of an entire city. Only the vultures answered my cries.

I dropped to my knees and scraped at the burning sand, tearing my nails. I had to bury my sister.

It was nightfall by the time I had finished. I stood up, my hands bleeding, feeling the skin on my face streaked with the tracks of dried up tears. There were no more tears left to fall. I had cried them all. Only an ocean of desolation remained. I looked around me at last. There was nothing left.

Jericho, my city, was dead.

Chapter 1

"What the...!" I grab the top of the seat in front as the driver of the *sherut* twists the wheel and slams on the brakes.

The screech of the tyres rips through my headache as the taxi-bus slews across the tarmac and comes to a halt in the dust at the side of the road. Then there's this awful moment of silence before a deafening babble of Hebrew and Arabic fills the bus and it seems like everyone's yelling at once, like some free-for-all on the Jerry Springer show.

The driver opens his window and leans out. Two young soldiers in khaki and bottle green stride towards us, with machine guns. Israeli Defence Force. My stomach somersaults. The driver shows them his ID. If only I could make sense of this torrent of conversation. Why the hell did I choose to study dead languages? I can translate Ezekial but out here in the real world I can't even order a pizza.

One of the soldiers turns to point further up the road and, thank God, his machine gun swings away, but as relief pours through me I notice beads of sweat are trickling down my back. My lovely linen suit is going to look less like Liz Hurley's latest and more like Peggy Mitchell's tea-towel. The babble of the Jewish women and the Palestinian workers sharing the *sherut* stops and along with the rest I strain forward to see what's happening. The gleaming streak of the main highway from Tel Aviv to Jerusalem shoots out of sight but by the roadside I can see a twisted heap of metal, black smoke spewing upwards to stain the perfect blue of the sky. My stomach turns into a gaping pit of fear.

The driver has some knowledge of English.

"Excuse me, what's going on?"

I'm shocked at the hate in his eyes.

"Hamas. Bastards."

My Israeli neighbour points out of the window. "Bomb, lady. They blow up a car. Three people, Israelis, dead."

My fingers, still gripping the top of the seat, suddenly feel cold, despite the fact we're in temperatures of over 32° and the air conditioning doesn't work that well. Of course I knew what I was travelling into, I read up on the modern background of Israel before I came out and the TV for months has been full of coverage of bombed out vehicles and buildings and battles in the streets as tensions between Palestinians and Israelis erupt like festering boils across this most hotly disputed, holy land on earth. But terrorist bombing is something that happens in the media, safely contained. I mean, you read about bombs going off in the 'papers, see the wounded carted off on stretchers bright with blood, but it's on Sky News, not right in your face. It happens to other people on a two by two screen. Now here it is, staring me straight in the eyes and I can't turn it off. This isn't supposed to happen and reality sickens me as I catch the stench of petrol and burning rubber drifting on this alien scorching air.

In the seat behind me, an old Jewish woman

dressed in black begins to shriek, crowlike, and jabs a claw at the Palestinian workers. The shrill stream of venom is splitting my head apart.

"She call them scum," my neighbour explains. He seems to have taken me under his wing, probably thinks I'm a tourist. When you're working abroad you resent being classed as one of the herd. You feel you're something special, though really you'll always be on the outside.

"Palestinian scum," he says. "Vermin. She say go back where you come from." I get the feeling he's enjoying this translation.

A sudden scuffle at the back makes me jump. Everyone else simply turns round, and I feel such a stupid bloody foreigner. A young Palestinian has leapt to his feet and is yelling back abuse, but luckily he's restrained by his colleague. I don't know what I'll do if a fight breaks out on the bus. I never bargained for this. I run my hands through my hair. It's gone limp and the gel sticks to my fingers. I could leap out but I don't know if I'd rather be stuck on the *sherut* surrounded by simmering hatred or outside with those too young soldiers, so casual with their guns, and that smoking burnt out wreck.

I think suddenly of Sarah's brother - she's my old room mate from uni. Darren with his spliffs hidden under his bed from his mum and bottles of Clearasil lined up with Nirvana CDs in the chaos of his bedroom. He's no older than these kid soldiers with the power to kill slung over their shoulders.

"He say he come from here," my neighbour continues to translate. "He tell her get back to

9

Auschwitz. Get out their stolen land."

The smell of petrol and burning tyres stings my nostrils and as I stare at the column of smoke staining that alien cobalt sky, I realise three people have died in this mangled heap of wreckage, three people who were chattering, dreaming, looking to the future as we are now. We followed them such a short way behind as they sped to their split second death. If our *sherut* hadn't been delayed by traffic outside the airport, it could have been our vehicle blown to a charred and smouldering wreck. That horrible pit devours more of my stomach. I should never have come.

If only we could drive on and leave it behind, that smoking heap with its three charred bodies which I can't help but see in my mind's eye, but the *sherut* stands still for what seems like an eternity while the soldiers check the driver's papers, and the Palestinian youth and the old Jewish woman trade insults across the seats.

Thank God! At last the IDF soldiers wave the driver on.

The Palestinian stops shouting and sits down. The old woman presses her face against the glass and yells a final stream of abuse as we pass the smouldering wreck.

Across the aisle, is an old Palestinian man, his eyes watery and face heavily lined beneath his *kiffayeh*. He just looks resigned. This is all so shocking to me. To him it's a way of life.

The *sherut* leaves behind the black stain of death on the sky.

I breathe a sigh of relief, then I notice something shaking. At first I think it's the engine vibrating through the seat, but it's me. I'm trembling like the last leaf on the tree. This is no good. I take a swig of Evian and scrabble in my bag. Pull yourself together, girl. Come on, you're Charlotte Adams, MA, ancient Semitic translator *par excellence.* But the contents of my bag have got all shaken up and the face looking out at me from the mirror is now shattered by a spider's web of cracks.

The motion of the bus lulls me into an uneasy doze. I keep expecting to hear a huge explosion. The *sherut* comes abruptly to a halt. Is this it? Another bomb, with our names on this time? My nails have ripped the acrylic of the headrest in front. But we've only stopped at traffic lights.

I try to disguise the rip I've made, I don't know why. This is hardly the time to be worrying over accidental acts of petty vandalism. I stare, stupid from tiredness and the heat, as we pass a road sign announcing some health and beauty resort and the benefits of Dead Sea mud. It's as if I'm watching everything from a distance, as though on a cinema screen, and do you know, it's mad, but I keep expecting a bearded figure to come strolling out in widescreen against the backdrop of those rolling foothills of Judea up ahead.

I'm the last passenger to be dropped off. I should be excited, I suppose. I mean, here I am, arriving in this exotic city teeming with history and colour, land of passion and extremes as the Blue

Guides say, about to take a mega-sized leap in my career, but I feel fit to drop and can't seem to muster a gram of enthusiasm. The driver's trying to point out a few famous landmarks, but I all I can see is parked cars, any one of which could hold a bomb.

Jerusalem seems a frenzy of traffic, a cacophony of screeching horns, where drivers lean right out of their windows to yell greetings or abuse. I've no idea which. Dead languages are a whole lot less threatening. The *sherut* is a little haven now, as the world outside recedes further and further from mine. Teeming pavements speed by. Arabs in flowing robes, Jews in skull-caps, girls in barely existent skirts clinging to the arms of Israeli boys in jeans - pavements full of strangers. What have I done? But it's too late to turn round now. Even if I hate this new life, I can't go back. As Dr. Amesbury at SOAS used to say, when we complained about the workload we had for semantics. You'll just have to like it or lump it. This is a great opportunity, a groundbreaking career move. So why do I feel like a kid at Brownie camp for the very first time, crying alone at night and desperate to get back home with Mum? Maybe I'll feel better when I've had a good night's sleep. Charlotte, who are you kidding?

My apartment is in a small block just outside the old city, in a quiet road off one of the busy main avenues of East Jerusalem. The driver helps me up two flights of steps and chases away a little Arab boy who appears from nowhere as I collect the key from the concierge.

"Pretty lady! I carry your bags! Only twenty shekels! OK, ten shekels. Special price just for you! How old are you? You very young and pretty, lady!"

I'm a limp, sweaty wreck. Tea-towel material. But I feel find myself laughing as the driver cuffs him round the ear and the boy runs squealing up the stairs, pretending he's badly hurt.

"I am Abdul, lady," he calls from a landing as I pay the driver. "You want something, you ask for me. You American, lady? You got hair like Nicole Kidman. Hey, you know Tom Cruise? I give you really good price!"

"Thank you, Abdul." Well, at least I've made my first acquaintance in this new city, and he tells me I look OK, even it is just some snotty kid after easy dollars.

I feel even better when I see my flat. It's light and airy and spotlessly clean. The living room's furnished in wicker and soft cushions and the balcony has this picture postcard view across honey-coloured Jerusalem and a striking hill. I suppose it could be somewhere famous but sightseeing is not on the agenda right now. I am so relieved to yank off these elegant crippling shoes and sink into the settee. I'm absolutely shattered.

What the ...? Something jerks me out of my sleep, drags me away from dreams of confusion, of explosions and pits opening up in the around, and at first I can't remember where I am, then I scramble to locate the phone.

"Hello? Oh, Dr Schlott. Yes, thank you. About..." I glance at my watch. Have I really been asleep that long? "...two hours ago. Yes, it's a lovely flat. The journey?" That smoking wreck. Kalashnikovs through glass. Blood seeping through blankets. Bodies on stretchers. Or parts of bodies.   "Yes, the journey was great. No problems at all. Yes, I'll be there in the morning."

I drop the phone back onto the table. My hands are shaking. I think I'll light a Marlboro. I bought some at the airport, even though I'm trying to give up. They're just for emergencies. Well, if this isn't an emergency, I don't know what is. If my *sherut* hadn't been delayed at the airport, I could have been caught in that blast. I could be one of those bloodied remains that keep flashing before my eyes. But I'm too damn tired to remember where I put the cigarettes.

My suitcases are still by the door. I don't feel like unpacking, but I'll have to sort out some clothes for tomorrow. This job is the chance of a lifetime and I can't turn up looking like something the tumble dryer's spewed out.

Oxford dictionaries, Body Shop sun block and aloe vera gel, brand new selection of frivolities from Knickerbox and M & S sensibles, Jackie Collins three in one blockbuster ... no one from the uni. shall catch me reading that.... one of my secrets. I shovel everything onto the floor until finally I find a suit to press. It's never been worn. Everything is new. I gave all my old things to a charity shop. There is nothing here to remind me of the past.

Dr Schlott shows me though the Archaeology Department. It's amazing! The whole place is completely brand new, gleaming glass and chrome everywhere and enormous windows that look out over this incredible view of domes, minarets and mosques. A planet away from the British Museum. Top of the range computers and labs to match. I can't believe I've fallen on my feet like this. How on earth did I manage to land this job! There must be dozens of far better qualified, more experienced translators than me in the field. Am I good enough to be working here?

"We've only been up and running for a year," explains my new Head of Department. He has this funny little habit of pushing his glasses higher onto his nose but they keep sliding down again. "The whole building was purpose built. I think you'll find our research facilities are more than equal to those you had in London."

"I'm sure."

This place is a palace! When I think of all the noise and dust and workmen everywhere while they built the new south portico at the BM, and the stupid scandals about illegally imported mahogany pilfered from the rainforest and red wine banned from the opening as porous French limestone was sneaked in on the cheap!

"Let me introduce you to Ingrid, Charlotte. She's our departmental secretary. If you need help just ask her. She's a treasure."

The "treasure" is deeply tanned and blonde in

that sickening Scandinavian way, you know, like a photographic negative. She's about my age but cocktail stick thin and gorgeous with barely a lick of make-up. She doesn't spend half an hour in front of a mirror each morning. Her smile is friendly enough, but I bet she's sizing me up too.

"Welcome to the New International University. You are the new ancient Semitic translator, ja?"

That tan and figure make me feel like a beached whale. "Pleased to meet you, Ingrid."

"How do you manage those dead languages? I could never get my tiny brain round those cuneiform signs."

She's thinking I look fat in this suit. I know she is.

"Don't be taken in by that dumb blonde routine," laughs Dr Schlott. "Ingrid was the top graduate of her year from the modern languages department at Heidelberg. As well as English and German, she speaks Hebrew and Arabic and, I'm told, can swear like a trooper in half a dozen others. Come on, I'll show you your office."

Office? Olympic swimming pool, more like. At the B.M. I shared a fishbowl with half a dozen other junior guppies. Honestly, I can hardly believe I've fallen on my feet like this. This place is oozing money out of the woodwork. I hope they aren't regretting signing me up.

"I'm looking forward to starting work on the tablets." I tell Dr Schlott. It's fortunate to have the funding for such a project."

Dr Schlott frowns. His fingers tighten around a pen. "Well, it's one thing to have the funding for

16

setting up an establishment - quite another to keep it running. Anyway, that's not your problem."

I've said the wrong thing. On my very first day. Trust me to stick my size 4 heels right into it.

"Perhaps you could tell me more about the project I'll be working on?" I wonder if I should sit down and claim my new desk.

"Yes, we didn't want to reveal too much until you finally arrived. The work is highly confidential until we know more about what's in these tablets. You know what a ... ah... commotion was caused by the discovery of the Dead Sea scrolls."

Intriguing.

He walks over to a glass case in the middle of the office. "Here is the cache of fragmented clay tablets which was excavated from a cave in the vicinity of Ein Gedi in cliffs above the Dead Sea."

"By one of your teams?"

"Yes, by Dr Ben Travers. You'll be working closely with him on this."

"The Dr Ben Travers, from the Colorado project?" I try not to swallow and make sure I don't look too impressed, like I chew up groundbreaking world authorities along with my cornflakes each day.

"That's right."

I have this sudden desperate urge to start biting my nails. Dr Ben Travers is one of the top biblical archeologists in the field. He's published countless articles in archeological journals and written two major textbooks. His credentials make mine seem like a mediocre report from nursery school. Charlotte tries hard and has made progress at fingerpainting.   I hope I'm going to be up to this job.

Dr Schlott has finished cleaning his specs and gives me one of those "meaningful looks." You know, a thin glaze of smile over a great thick emulsion base of warning. "We want all top people. A lot of money has been invested in creating the International University and we need to prove we're worth it."

"Of course." I flash him my cool reassuring smile but as soon as he's left this office, I'm going to chew my nails down to the quick. Why on earth did they employ me?

"So they're all in fragments?" I ask, leaning over the case. "Presumably they were damaged at some point in the cave?"

"No, they appear to have been written on broken pieces," explains Dr Schlott. "The writer was using rejected materials. We believe this cache may have lain undisturbed for over three thousand years. Since about 1230 BC, to be precise, when the Israelites invaded Canaan."

"I understand Joshua's name appears in the script?

"Yes, that was easy to pick out. Though of course we didn't have an Ancient Semitic specialist till now, so we only have a very cursory knowledge of what the fragments say. That's where you come in. The British Museum gave you excellent references."

Yes they did. They certainly owed me.

"I shall enjoy working on something so unique. It's not often a find like this turns up."

"We're hoping these fragments will prove comparable to the Dead Sea Scrolls in importance." Dr Schlott frowns slightly and paces to the other side of the office and back. I get the feeling there's something he's not telling me. "You see, this is a brand new university. We have some top research staff here. But we're newly established in a highly competitive field. We need to show we're up there with the best and that our scholarship is on a par with any similar establishment in the world. Frankly, we need to attract funding to survive. Your role in translating the tablets is a very important one."

So this showpiece university isn't quite as it's cracked up to be. It has cash flow problems. That nasty little worm of unease starts nibbling at my innards again. If the NIUJ goes under I'll really be screwed.

Dr Schlott glances at his watch. "Look, I have a meeting this morning. I'll leave you to start getting acclimatised. Anything you need, ask Ingrid. By the way, please make sure you always lock your office door when you leave. I know I don't need to tell you how valuable this hoard is."

As soon as he's gone I start chewing my thumbnail. Any new venture has teething troubles and they wouldn't be taking on new staff if things were that bad, would they?

I lift the lid of the case and pick up the topmost fragment. I always get a buzz from the smell of ancient clay and the call of old messages which are sealed from most people but speak to me from centuries long past. I am a lucky ungrateful cow. This cache could really be something. Far better scholars than this jumped up translator barely out of SOAS have slaved for years on mundane texts without ever getting such a chance. I wonder what they reveal about Joshua. It'll be fascinating to find out if these tablets back up what the Bible says, or if they'll give the religious establishment a good kick up the rear. I mean, look what a storm the Dead Sea scrolls created. If this is half as controversial, the Pope could be in for a heart attack. But people don't like it when their cherished beliefs are shattered. Sometimes they fight back. And sometimes they get some pretty nasty characters to pack their punches for them.

Does Dr Schlott realise what he could be letting himself in for? More to the point, do I?

I really need to put the fragments into order before I can start translating properly but from what I've seen so far they contain some pretty strange stuff. Like this bit here. Goodness knows what this could unleash. Surely Joshua didn't... hang on, Charlotte, wait till you see it in context first. It can't be what it appears. One thing I am sure about, these fragments aren't trade documents or accounts but some kind of tale, myths, legends perhaps, or even letters. Hey, what the hell's this?

"Hello. Thought you might like a break."

Ingrid's at the door with two mugs of coffee. Suppose I'll have to be polite. I really want to see what those fragments say. What a sickeningly skinny, nauseatingly suntanned...

"Thanks Ingrid. Just what I need."

Ingrid perches on the desk. My desk. She has long, long legs, with aerobic class muscles and not one teeny dimple of cellulite. "So what do you think?

"Sorry?"

"The university. First impressions."

"Fine. Certainly as good as I'm used to."

"Schlott's a bit uptight at the moment, you might have noticed. He's not attracting the funding he needs. It's a new venture, having an International University in the heart of Jerusalem and the investors want to see results before they stump up more cash. He has high hopes of these tablets - and you."

I suppose she's wondering if I'm good enough for the job. I keep my professional smile pinned firmly in place.

"Have you worked here long?"

"Since it started, last summer. Hey, you like night clubs?"

I sip my coffee slowly. Sarah and I used to go out all the time,
once.

"Not really my scene."

Ingrid looks disappointed. "Well, anytime you want to see the nightlife, just ask, ja?"

"Is Dr Travers not in today?"

"Not back yet from the States. Family problems to sort out. You like Brad Pitt?"

"He's OK, I suppose."

"Dr Ben looks just like him."

This is one of the leading archaeologists in the world we're talking about here. The thought of actually meeting him, let alone working with him, is enough to turn me into a quivering heap of creme caramel, and she's only concerned that he looks like Brad Pitt! I don't think Ingrid and I are eating the same piece of cake.

"His ex-wife's a real pain though."

"Brad Pitt's?"

"Dr Ben's. The number of calls I've had to put through to him from her. And I've seen the e-mails. The names she calls him you would not believe."

Now I know where to come any time I want the low-down on departmental gossip. But Ingrid could be useful for keeping my eye on what's going on around here.

"Hey," Ingrid glances at her watch. "Time for lunch. I'll show you the canteen. We can have lunch together.

I'd really rather grab a sandwich and bring it back to the office than sit listening to Ingrid's archaeological version of "Neighbours," especially as I suspect she's working out what role I'm going to be playing, but even though I'm dying to see what's in those fragments she could be useful for monitoring any financial problems, and besides, I'll look a really snotty cow if I refuse.

At the self-service unit I carefully select a prawn salad and orange juice.

"Is that all you're having?" Ingrid has piled her

tray with a lavish selection of falafel, sweet potato salad and pitta bread, topped off with a sticky baklava for desert. I wish I could be as carefree about stuffing my face in public as her. "You won't get fat on that. Try some of this." She breaks off a piece of pitta bread and shoves it in my face.

"No thanks. Really. I'm not that hungry." I wish I'd got out of this now.

"What sort of food do you like? You can get whatever you want in Jerusalem. Chinese, Turkish, Armenian, Egyptian..." Ingrid stuffs a huge portion of pitta bread into her mouth. Houmous and cress ooze from the edges. I stare at her in amazement then look down at my plate and fix my eyes on a scalloped tomato.

"I'm not very adventurous."

"English pies and chips, huh?" she says with her mouth full. I smile weakly, but inwardly cringe. As if!

Ingrid's enjoying her food and she doesn't care who knows it.

"Jerusalem is a great place to eat. You wait till Dr Ben gets back. He'll drag you to every Arabic restaurant in town and make you scoff till you drop."

I prod at a leaf of lollo rosso. Suddenly I'm dreading meeting Dr
Ben Travers.

"You don't eat much." Ingrid's eyes accuse me across the table . "You on a diet?"

"You mean, I look too fat?" It's out of my mouth before I can stop myself. I see Ingrid pause between bites.

"No, you have a great figure. I didn't mean... I wish I was like you. I could do with losing half a kilo. So, what brought you to Jerusalem?"

"The job. It's a very interesting opportunity."

"No boyfriend in England?"

A peeled prawn sticks in my throat. How many more questions do I have to endure?

"No."

I've answered too quickly, too firmly. Ingrid's finely plucked eyebrows shoot up like an F16.

Fortunately she realises she's not going to get much out of me and launches off into tales of lurid lesbian goings-on in Forensics. I look at the sticky, honey-coated baklava lying in a sugary pool on her plate and watch as she stuffs it in her mouth without a thought. She disposes of it in just three bites and stands up. "I have some shopping to do before I go back. Nice to have lunch with you, Charlotte. See you later."

I am left staring at her plate, at that little syrupy pool with its flaky pastry driftwood and floating islands of sugar, just asking to be scooped up on a finger or lapped up on my tongue. I feel guilty, as though I'd snatched up the plate in both hands and licked it clean in front of the whole massed ranks of the university on graduation day and I shove back my chair. I have to get out of this dreadful canteen with its sickening, tantalising smells of food.

I light up a cigarette on a terrace which overlooks the city and relax against a wall. So much for emergencies but it does the trick and I'm glad to be out in the sun. Before me lie all the domes, minarets and church spires of Jerusalem, shimmering in a sea of golden stone. Above the roar of the traffic I can hear singing from the Jewish *yeshiva* nearby and the sounds of the *muezzin*, calling the faithful to the mosques. London was never like this. I bet it's dull and grey and rainy there. This is truly a vibrant, golden city and though I've had my doubts - still do - suddenly I find myself showered in sunlight and I'm glad I came.

I'm halfway through translating the first fragment when that need for a caffeine kick, or something, digs in. I started out all fired up by knowing I could really make my mark on academia here, and barely able to wait to see what this cache contains. But it's nothing like I expected. I thought it might be a collection of legends like the tablets found at Ugarit, or political correspondence like the Amarna letters. Not this.

This is a first person account, someone's own story. A rather too personal story for my liking. I'm not comfortable with it at all. Damn, I feel cheated. Up till now, I've always been able to rely on my work to lift me away from my personal life, even at the worst times. Especially at the worst times. These ancient texts have always opened a gateway of escape into other places and times; the cuneiform worlds pulling me from mine and all its pain.

But this is no trade correspondence, nor exploits of jealous gods.

It's the death of a sister.

The traffic outside sounds like someone's laid into a wasps' nest with a stick and I can feel a headache coming on.

I need another cigarette and fumble in my bag. Where the hell did I put that packet?

I've done a thousand miles of running, but I'm still too close to home.

Fragment 2

I cannot believe what you have done. Rahab. My older sister. My mother, as I was to Tarasch. Tarasch who lies cold beneath a pile of scorched stones. It was the best I could do.

Rahab, the traitor. Rahab, the living, while Tarasch lies dead. Though you raised me and fed me, and drove the demons from my dreams when our parents were gone, you are part of me no more. Rahab, I curse you and spit upon the memory of your treacherous face. My sister no more.

I have ripped my gown from neck to waist. I have beat my fists against my breast till deep bruises stain my skin. I am purple from shoulder to shoulder, as though the Sea People from Sidon and Tyre had splattered me with their sea creature dye. Purple is the colour I see before my eyes when

I close them at night. Purple are my dreams, and Rahab, all I see is your face. Your beautiful, hated face.

You were the one I looked up to. I wanted to be you. Rahab the Priestess. Rahab, Server in the Temple. Priestess of Astarte, Asherah, Anat. I was so proud of you. I boasted to my friends that you served the Goddess amid the Stones on the hill. I played games in the dust outside our house. The ring of stones I scraped from the around was the Sacred Circle of Anat. The crushed flowers were my offering, the goat boys the priests. When I laid in the dust, closing my eyes against the scarlet of the sun, I was Rahab, the priestess. Rahab, the most beautiful traitor of all.

Fragment 3

I was born at Jericho. It wasn't much of a town, compared to Meggido with its palace filled with ivory and lapis lazuli, standing proud for all to see above the plains of Esdraelon. Nor to Beth-Shan, visible for miles above the lush green plain of Harod, where the soldiers of the Pharaoh keep watch from the walls. But Jericho is my home.

Jericho was my home - till it was betrayed by that

bitch.

Our parents were killed when I was seven turns of the sun.

Father went out hunting one day and never came back. I was playing in the doorway when the men returned. One of them held out a strip of cloth, brightly coloured, red, blue, green. I remember turning to my mother. The inside of the house was dark and smelt of the goat skins laid on our sleeping platform. All I could see was the whiteness of her face and her eyes grown suddenly huge with the fear that seeped through the darkness of our house, spreading through my stomach and grasping at my guts.

"Mummy, why have they brought Daddy's belt," I heard myself ask, Why has Daddy not come back."

I don't remember them telling me what really happened. In the days and years to come I crouched in the dust of the roads of Jericho and held the other children spellbound with stories of my father. My dead father, who strangled three mountain lions with his hands before a giant dragon with two heads leapt down on him from a rock. My father, who struck down a whole tribe of the giant Anakim, before their leader finally ran him through with a magical sword. My brave, strong father who was chosen to dwell with the Gods in the land of El, hurling thunderbolts beside

Baal from on high.

I think I told so many stories I forgot what really happened. Perhaps it was better that way.

Mother died shortly after. The plague spread through Jericho like wildfire. My sisters and I were spared. Tarasch was barely as old as the grapes that had almost ripened on the vines. Our brothers lived too. Hadad was able to totter on his own and Timnal was already working in the fields with the men. I don't think our mother ever recovered from the shock that day when they silently handed her my father's belt. Perhaps she was glad to surrender to Reshef when he called from the Underworld, to slide softly away in the arms of the plague God, to be restored to my father's side.

So Rahab became my mother. She held me in her arms when I cried, as I did for baby Tarasch. We became little mothers when the plague took our own. Rahab cleaned up my knees when I skinned them chasing goats down the hillside. Rahab stirred the cooking pot that sat in the ashes of our fire. Rahab brought in the flax and spun it for our clothes.

And Rahab opened the door to Joshua's spies.

Chapter 2

You know, the passion and violence screaming off this clay just hits me in the face. They invented writing in this part of the world but this girl certainly packs a punch. These fragments are really getting to me, not surprisingly, I spend all day with the girl and her story. But I have to get a grip. I mean, they're only old bits of clay and everyone in them has been dead for eons. Their stories aren't important any more, except to scholars like me. These tablets are no different to any others I've worked on.

You should never let your personal turmoil affect your professional life. Life is a bitch but you can't let her scratch the eyes out of your career when she's already ripped your private life to shreds. You just have to keep it together somehow. Employers don't give a toss if you're screaming inside so long as you trowel on a bright face along with your Max Factor Radiance Glow and get on with the job they're paying you for. That's the score.

It was my work that kept me going through the Jonathon affair, the one thing that kept me sane. Actually, I was surprised how sympathetic they were at the BM when it all came out, but I prided myself on doing my job well, on not letting anyone see through the cracks that I was bawling my heart out inside. I've become expert at switching off and losing myself in work. I threw myself so much into my job when everything else was collapsing around me that the BM probably got a lot more out of me than all those lucky sods I saw every day who seemed to be floating through life on a even keel of stability while I was crashing against on the rocks.

I have to make it work for me now. I *need* to succeed, and it's not just because of the sacrifices Mum and Dad made so Sally-Ann and I could go to uni. One of them has to pan out, make it all worth while. But let's face it, besides my career, I don't have much else. I'm crap at relationships, all of them. I can't afford to screw up now, just because of what's in these tablets. I'd have nowhere to live in England if I went back. I could certainly never stay under the same roof as my mother again, not after everything that's happened, and I can just imagine Dad's face if I turned up on his new family's doorstep, shoving memories of something he can't cope with right under his nose, as welcome as a dog turd.

Fury spits off this page. I thought I understood anger. I've stared at hate in the eyes of someone I thought was a friend. Betrayal is like toothpicks jabbing under your fingernails. I can't help but admire her guts. Maybe it's better to scream and curse like this, rather than bottle it up, pretend you're coping, then cry alone in your room every night, and worse.

But I don't want to dwell on what's past. I check my deciphering of the first fragment. My old Sunday school teacher would be clambering out of her grave if she could see me translating this! Not Joshua? A murdering bastard? He was her hero, for heaven's sake. For some women it's Colin Firth or George Cluny. Mrs Lawrence would have been out there hurling her knickers at Moses and Joshua. Personally, I always thought it pretty tough on the Canaanites. After all, Canaan was their home. They'd lived there for centuries minding their own business along with their flocks. Then along comes a scruffy band of nomads claiming some upstart new God has told them it's theirs for the taking, and no mercy. When you look at what Israel is doing to the Palestinians today, not much has changed. Religion has a lot to answer for, if you ask me.

At Sunday school Joshua was some kind of Bronze Age Mel Gibson, and at that age I hadn't learn to question the propaganda they shoved down our throats along with milk and ginger biscuits at break. It was only later, when I went to The School of African and Oriental Studies, I realised how so much of what we take as gospel is just what someone else wants us to think; how what's left out is as important as what's put in.

There are two other names here, as well as Joshua's. Tarasch and Rahab. Names are always a good starting point. I can search other ancient texts to see if they turn up elsewhere.

One of the first things I need to do is check these fragments are authentic. I doubt someone of Ben Travers' calibre would be fooled but there are plenty of people out to make a quick buck by forging relics and I'd be failing in my job if I didn't verify linguistically that this is as it appears. I hope to God it is. Imagine having to tell the great Dr Travers his find is a fake.

I sip my coffee and take a look at the map. Jericho, slap bang on the border with Jordan, has always been a site of strategic importance. You can understand those nomads, can't you, fresh from the desert, staring hungrily across the river at the lush Land of Milk and Honey, to the oasis of Jericho, with its date palms rising from a sea of burning rock. No wonder they looked at Jericho with a jealousy they could justify by blaming it all on their God.

Now here's a likely reference - Egyptian alabaster. Canaan was a vassal state of Egypt at the time and there was an Egyptian garrison not from Jericho. And this bit here about the Phoenicians with their purple dye. They would have been among the stream of foreign traders passing through on the main trade route from Egypt to Mesapotamia. The script is written in Canaanite, with a liberal sprinkling of Egyptian and Amorite words, which is exactly what I would expect from a writer positioned at the hub of diverse civilisations. She's obviously familiar with Akkadian, the cultural and diplomatic language of the time, so this means she was from the well-educated classes, probably temple-trained, I'd guess. I sit back and pick up my coffee but it's turned cold with a revolting scum on the sides of the cup. This is a complex script. If it is a forgery, someone's done a pretty thorough job.

Never mind the emotional contents. This is exciting stuff. I'd never have got the chance to make my mark with material like this in England. I still can't believe my luck getting this job. Maybe the more experienced translators in the field aren't so useless at relationships and have partners and kids to stop them jetting off to foreign soil. Though I've this nasty suspicion that the NIUJ is running short of cash, and muggins here has been bought on the cheap.

Yet if these tablets are genuine, and nothing so far suggests they aren't, this cheapskate translator is looking straight at a unique account of the battle of Jericho. The Old Testament is the only other source and that was written centuries later. When the Hebrews swept into the so-called Promised Land with their Me Only God, the world was changed forever. These texts could contain material that changes history too. The archaeological record is too scanty to back up the Bible account. Kathleen Kenyon found evidence of burnt walls but they pre-dated Joshua by over three hundred years, though the orthodox dating system is being radically disputed. Maybe I'll discover something new here. Wow! I could find myself at the centre of a brand new academic row! A bit of controversy could really boost my career. Dr Schlott wasn't exaggerating. This find really could rival the Dead Sea Scrolls in importance. It's priceless.

I can hardly wait to see what the rest of the fragments contain. If they confirm the Bible account, the churches will be smug and satisfied. But what if they don't? I might find something that really upsets the applecart and brings down the wrath of the whole Judeo-Christian establishment on my head. Who was that author found hanging from Tower Bridge a few years back? It came out that his research led him to something the Vatican wanted to hide.

But I'm being stupid now. Aren't I? I swill the revolting dregs of coffee round in my cup. There's no need to get paranoid. I push the cup away then walk over to the window and gaze out at all that honey-coloured stone, its antiquity capped with those ubiquitous TV aerials stabbing the sky from every roof.

Maybe I should be on my guard. I'm not safely ensconced in a back room of the British Museum now. This is the heart of Jerusalem, a city torn apart by political and religious unrest. A land of passion and extremes, as the cliched guidebooks say. People will go to any lengths to preserve their faith. I saw that within one hour of my arrival. One moment, that's all it's takes, to change your life, or end it, forever.

I pull down the blinds, shut out the city. I have a job to do.

I need another coffee from the office. There are chocolate biscuits in the machine. Milk or plain. Orange, peppermint or raisin. The sort where the chocolate's thicker than the biscuit. But I will control my eating habits. I will. I take my coffee and run. I have two names as well as Joshua's to go on now. Tarasch and Rahab. So I run a search to check if they occur in any other ancient Canaanite texts. I try the British Museum data base, the American Schools of Oriental Research and the Middle East Archives of Tel Aviv. Nothing. I guess these two ended up as minor figures in the drama which unfolded at Jericho; just two of the millions forgotten by history. Rather sad really, to think so little comes from a life. But if these fragments do turn out to be the next best thing since the Qmran scrolls, perhaps Rahab and her sisters will spring back to life.

This is really going to be exciting. I was stupid to let it get to me the way it did. I was just tired and stressed. I'm so lucky to have landed a post like this. Cache 5 could be one of the most incredible archeological discoveries of all time. It's a brilliant opportunity. A perfect chance to put the past behind, to forget the devastation Jonathon has wreaked on my life and the tragedy of Sally-Ann. You know, I'm even eating properly again. I let Ingrid persuade me to try a Jewish mousakka for lunch, but drew the line at baklava. At last I have my eating habits under control. Dr Hewitt would be well pleased with me now. I must remember to send her a postcard. It's thanks to her I've managed to get back to something like the normality which most people take for granted.

Time to open a new file. My translation is going to make very interesting reading. Hey, I might even end up with an honorary PhD for this. There was no need to react to those fragments as I did.

I have everything under control

I'll have to stop and find a Bible. I need to find

that story about Joshua sending his spies, and I could do with a break. My shoulder muscles feel like lumps of rock cake. Ingrid points me in the direction of the Educational Bookshop and I head out for Salah el-Din. Am I glad to be out among the racket of people and traffic. It's a welcome change from the isolation of my work, cooped up on desolate mountains with vultures for company. After coming out of the bookshop with a copy of the New International Bible, I wander down to the Old City. I don't want to go back yet. It's nice to be out amongst people again, even if I don't know anyone hear Rap music blasting out of a car than those mournful bloody wails of gulls.

The Moslem quarter is full of the most amazing smells. Thyme, cinnamon, coffee, hamburgers, donkey dung. I feel safe here too. Hamas and Hizbollah are hardly likely to blow up their own, are they. The souks sell everything from rugs to rice and I have to keep leaping to one side to avoid being squashed by heavily loaded donkeys. But it's so hot, and those donkeys might look picturesque but they certainly leave a stink. I find a cafe in the shade and order a coke. There are some tasty looking stuffed dates on the counter but I can't eat them because they're frying chips close by and they might be splattered with fat.

Ignoring the smells of food all around me, I leaf through the Pentateuch until I find Joshua.

Oh, I can't believe it. It's here, on the very first page and I wasted all that time scouring the

Internet for Canaanite history. I am so thick. Rahab has never been forgotten. She's right here in the Bible. The prostitute of Jericho who hid the Israelite spies.

I wonder what the other Canaanites thought about that. I know all about deception. I trusted Jonathon. I went out of my way to help him all I could. It was me who looked at his artwork, when he was just a temporary security guard at the museum, and encouraged him to apply when the illustrator's job came up. Yes, I know all about betrayal, and I feel the pain of Rahab's sister, still burning through the centuries from those fractured bits of clay.

"Ben, give me that! I don't know why Dr Schlott keeps you on."
Ingrid looks like she's about to pull a muscle, trying to grab some bit paper from this huge, grizzly bear of a man who looks more like a cross between Hulk Hogan and a St Bernard than Brad Pitt, if you ask me.

"Now, now. Say please."

Ingrid manages to snatch it off him and catches sight of me, as I hover in the doorway like some stupid kid about to see the headmaster.

"Stop fooling around and come and meet our new ancient Semitic translator. What will she think, seeing you torment a poor secretary like this?"

Actually the new ancient Semitic translator doesn't know what to think. I mean, I imagined the redoubtable Dr Ben Travers to be some kind of bespectacled academic type, well on the way to wrinkliehood and a pension, whatever Ingrid said. cope with, but I just don't do frivolity. Not at work, as Ingrid and Ben have been carrying on. I get the distinct impression there's something going on between these two.

"Poor secretary!" he scoffs. "Charlotte Adams, I gather. Ben Travers. Very pleased to meet you."

He's beside me in an instant and I feel like I've hit by a force nine gale. His hand is three times the size of mine, with skin like an emery board and a grip that's surprisingly gentle and takes me by surprise. Like Ingrid, he's that sickening Hollywood bronze. I suppose they make a good couple. If I worked outside in that sun, I'd look like a leather shop-reject. That Ivy League smile comes rather too easily for my liking and there's something unsettling about those deep blue eyes. I don't rate him along with Brad Pitt, though I suppose he is quite attractive for his age, if you like that sort of thing. Antonio Banderas is more my type.

"Don't take any notice of Ingrid. Whatever she's told you about me, I deny it all."

"So how do you like the place?"

"Great. The city is beautiful and I couldn't wish for better facilities." No reason for him to know I've never even had an office to myself before.

"Ah, we'll show you the real Jerusalem, won't we Ingrid? Gee, look, I'm sorry I wasn't here when you arrived." He runs his fingers through that sun-streaked bird's nest and looks suddenly embarrassed. "I er.. I had family problems to sort out back in Denver." He springs away from the desk and it's all I can do not to jump back half a mile. "Hey, how about we go into your office and you can fill me in with the work you've done so far on 'you-know-what'." He lowers his voice and gives me this look like he's David Duchovny and just found aliens under the bed.

"You mean the fragments?"

"Ssh." He looks under the desk. "You never know who could be listening. Our Glorious Leader hopes great things may come."

What the hell is this man on? Why can't he be well... more like I imagined him?

"Serve him right if Dr Schlott hears him carry on," says Ingrid. "I'd fire him on the spot."

"May I call you Charlotte?"

"He will anyway," says Ingrid.

"I'm looking forward to seeing what you've made of cache 5 so far."

With his hand on my elbow, he sweeps me back to my office before I have time to catch my breath. The cheek of it. Who does he think he is? Still at least, I've escaped the Ben and Ingrid Show. I've never been good at that sort of thing and feel much more sure of myself back on my own territory, with my desk providing a reassuring barrier between me and Dr Ben Travers.

"Hey, you sure have been one hell of a busy lady." Ben flips through the sheaf of papers I hand him. "You've done all this already?"

"I don't mess around."

"No," he looks up. "I can see that. I know

you're an excellent translator. Your CV and references are very impressive. I noticed, though, you didn't finish your PhD?"

I fix his questioning gaze with a steely look of my own. I have no intention of going into this.

"Sorry." He holds up his hands. "No business of mine, I know. I just would have thought, with your academic background, it would make sense to..."

Shut up. Just shut up. I stare at him, unflinching.

"OK, OK, none of my business. Let's get back to the tablets. Now, according to this note of yours, the fragments you've translated so far were written by a girl?"

"Yes. She witnessed the fall of Jericho."

"Wow! No one's ever found hard evidence of that story, despite all the excavations.

Do the fragments back up the biblical account?"

"Completely, so far. If the tablets are genuine, of course.

"If they're genuine?" He frowns. "Do you doubt it?"

"My findings so far would suggest they are."

"Of course they're genuine. I dug them out of that cave myself. Do you think if there was any doubt..."

I knew this would happen but I'm not going to let his reputation stop me from doing my job. I might be just an upstart translator, but it's my career on the line here too and nothing is going to stand in my way. "Dr Travers, I'm not casting any aspersions on your ability as an archaeologist. It's just part of my job to..."

"Good. Then don't. And don't call me Dr Travers. We're going to be working together on this so you'd better get used to Ben. I'll call you Charlotte, of course. Unless you prefer Charley?"

I treat him to another of my ice queen stares.

"Look, you've got my translation and notes on the earlier fragments there. Why don't you go off and read them before we discuss it further?" If he thinks he's going press my buttons he's got another think coming. He might be a world class archaeologist but I damn well know my stuff too. "I'm just checking my final draft of the next three at the moment. If you want to come back in an hour, I should have them ready for you."

"OK. I know when I'm being got rid of."

"I didn't.."

But I find myself staring at the door as it crashes shut behind him.

"Facinating. Absolutely fascinating." Ben turns over the page.

I sip my mint tea and stare unhappily at the plateful of sticky Jewish *friandises* which Ben has insisted I try. How the hell did I let him persuade me to come to Cafe Azziz to go through the fragments? It's far easier to cope with him from behind the security of my desk, but I can't afford to offend him. I pick at a date then, certain that Ben is too engrossed in the text to notice, and glancing around to check no one else will, I shove the whole sweetmeat into my mouth.

"Here, have another." He pushes the plate towards me without looking up. I chew at the sickly *datte fourree,* feeling guilty and miserable. I should have made some excuse. Ingrid was right. He is a bully who won't take no for an answer. Why can't he just leave me alone? He doesn't understand. No one does, except Dr Hewitt.

"This is intriguing."

He's already on Fragment 8. I reach for an *armandine.* I know I shouldn't. I'm going to pay for this. But I can't help myself. It's been a stressful morning, having to deal with this irritating..."

"Shit!"

I quickly lick my fingers clean. "What's wrong?"

"Let me finish this." He comes to the end of Fragment 8 and tosses the pages down on the table. "The blasted Ark of the Covenant! If word gets out, we'll have every headcase from here to New York on our backs - and every professional in the field will piss themselves laughing!"

"I can't help what she says. I've only translated it word for word."

"The Ark is the kiss of death for serious archaeology. Put this stuff out and you'll have all the UFO spotters, crop circle crazies and New Age pyramidiots hammering at our door!"

"I'm sure you're exaggerating."

"Look, maybe you're not aware, but this is a new university and Schlott's already having problems..."

"I know. He needs to attract investment. But surely, everything this girl has written not only confirms the Book of Joshua but provides us with a fascinating contemporary...."

"I know. It's amazing stuff. All I'm saying is the first mention of the Ark of the Covenant will attract God knows who."

"It might attract the kind of investors the department needs."

Ben throws his head back and laughs. "Hey, Raiders of the Lost Ark is showing at the Palestinian Palace. How about..."

I bang my mint tea onto the saucer, spilling some onto the table. "You should be pleased my translation suggests your find is genuine."

Now it's Ben's turn to bang his cup onto the table.

"Why are you always so keen to question the authenticity of Cache 5? I do know my clay tablets from my arse, Miss Adams."

"You know as well as I do, there are hundreds of Bedouin tribesmen in the Holy land trying to..."

"Make a fast buck. Sure I'm aware of that. But I've had nearly twenty years of experience digging all sorts out of..."

"Dr Travers. I'm well aware of your expertise. But I have my job to do as well."

"Yes, I'm sorry. I know you have."

This is a turn up for the books: So the great Dr Ben Travers actually does apologies.

"Hey look. I don't want us to get off on the

wrong foot. Have another *datte fourree*. I told you they're the best in Jerusalem."

I can already feel a sickening lump in my stomach and I'm starting to hate myself for this.

"No thanks. Anyway, you'll be pleased to hear the language used in the fragments backs up completely the authenticity of your find. Take the use of the word *Habiru*, for example. Only the invaders called themselves *'Children of Israel'*. The other peoples of the Levant would very likely have referred to them as *Habiru* which indicates a stateless people."

"I know bloody well what it means. I am familiar with the Amarna letters."

"Of course. And as Canaan was a vassal state of Egypt at that time, inevitably Egyptian words crept into Canaanite and vice versa. The point I'm making is that a forger would probably used the term *Israelite*, not *Habiru*."

"So Miss Adams. My team's findings have your expert linguistic seal of approval."

He's grinning at me now! I've had enough of this, and him. I have to get out of here. Those *friandises* feel like concrete congealing in my stomach. I can't cope. I have to get rid of them.

"I should be getting back. I've got work to do."

I get to my feet, trying to look cool, but I knock the table and spill the rest of my tea.

I lean on the sink and look at myself in the

mirror. I am disgusting! I hate myself. No amount of foundation or concealer can hide that ugly creature which looks out from inside. How could I? No one forced me to eat all those cakes. Not Ben Travers, just me. I could have said no. I should have had more control. I am greedy, pathetic, self-indulgent and fat. People would treat me with contempt if they knew what I was really like. The nearest thing to a human pig!

In the glass I can see the rows of doors behind me. Every cubicle is empty. No one is around. It would be so easy to get rid of it all.
I should just go back to the office. But I'll have to deal with those fragments. I have tried so hard to be detached but sometimes I just can't seem to stop it. It's like all the plugs have come out and her grief pours into mine. I thought I thought I had left all that behind, but the memories come flooding back and I feel like I'm drowning. There's Sally-Ann, laughing from the photographs which still stand on our mantelpiece, a shrine to a perfect daughter. Sally-Ann, smiling from her graduation at Oxford with a first. Sally-Ann voted top student in her year from her journalism course. Sally-Ann voted Best Newcomer at the British Press Awards. Sally-Ann - the slim pretty one. Not like the dumpy, ugly duckling younger sister, I can hear them whisper. Always Sally bloody-Ann.

I know it sounds like it but I wasn't jealous. No, really I wasn't. I could never live up to her. But I loved her. Even now I miss her so much. Why did she have to die? Sally-Ann would have been there for me through the Jonathon affair. I know she would. She was strong. Not like poor Mum, too wrapped up in regrets. Dr Hewitt listened though. No one else did. My mother would never have understood. She didn't even guess for a long time, not even when my ribs began to show through, she was so wrapped up in her own loss. She just made me sweet tea when I came home after fainting at sixth form. Sweet tea? What use is that when your sister dead?

I went on binging and throwing up, right through my "A" levels and university. No one guessed. I was sneaky, you see. I'd buy twenty bars of chocolate at a time, but from different shops. I'd come back from the supermarket loaded with carrier bags, hide them behind the bins then carry them upstairs one by one. My whole life revolved around mindlessly stuffing myself with whole loaves of bread, pots of jam, packs of biscuits and litres of lemonade. If I had no money, anything lying around the kitchen would do. Then I'd be so disgusted at my painfully overstuffed stomach, I'd bring the whole lot up. I never put on a pound.

I thought it was cool to be thin. I thought people stared at me in the street because they wished they'd beaten the bulge as well. I just didn't realise until it was almost too late. Until Dr Susan Hewitt and her light bright clinic at Harley Street saved my sanity and my life.

Yes, Mum, I'm OK now, no thanks to you.

Someone pushes open the door. It's the girl who works in Accounts. I take out my lip pen and carefully reapply the line as she disappears into cubicle. As soon as she's gone, I shove it back in my bag[and grab an armful of paper towels from the wall. I am determined now. It's all right. I'll only do it this time. It's all under control. Once won't hurt. The cubicle at the end will do, less conspicuous if anyone else comes in.

I arrange the towels on the floor. Six from one side to the other, six from the toilet to the door. Three more ensure that awkward curve round the bowl is covered too. I kneel down and arrange my clothes so nothing touches the floor. I am about to shove my fingers down my throat when I notice there is no toilet paper and rummage through my bag to check I have some tissues. I do, but I also find a postcard. The one I bought to send to Susan Hewitt, to tell her how well I'm doing, how I'm really on top of my problems. I look from the shiny picture of the Via Dolorosa to the water in the bowl. Then I scramble to my feet, shove all those stupid towels in the bin and straighten my clothes. No, I'm not going back to all that. A few sticky Jewish sweetmeats aren't going to wreck all that effort, both Susan Hewitt's and my own. I want to write and tell her I've not let her down.

I put the postcard back in my bag, splash cold water on my face, and back to work. I shan't give in now.

"You are kidding?"
"No, Dr Travers. I am not." Hermann Schlott

looks at Ben icily over the top of his glasses. "Miss Adams has carried out sterling work on these fragments and it's time we made some of it public."

"OK,OK, a cautious preliminary piece in *Archaeology Today,* but not a load of spiel on the Net."

"Ben, I'm sure you're worried about nothing." I can hardly get a damned word in edgeways. All this stupid departmental bickering gets right up my nose.

Dr Schlott scoops up his copy of my translation and stands up. "Your objections are noted, Dr Travers."

"But not heeded. You're going ahead with this anyway." Ben scowls. "Just don't blame me when you get every headcase turning up at Archaeology on the trail of the long lost Ark."

"Dr Travers. I think you've been watching too much Harrison Ford. Meeting closed."

"Son of a bitch!" mutters Ben, as soon as Schlott has gone. "This is going to bring us one hell of a lot of trouble. And I don't know about you, but I've got enough of my own."

Yes, I have, but you'll never find out about it. Unlike some, I don't go shouting my mouth off. Nor will you find the departmental secretary reading my problems on the office e-mail.

Anyway, Dr I'm-so-wonderful, some of us have our life under control.

"Ah, the very people." Ingrid stands up as we walk through the door to the office. "Ben, a fax for you, and a letter for Charlotte."

Ben takes one look at the fax and screws it into a ball. "Bloody woman!"

I take my envelope from Ingrid. The handwriting is straight out of my nightmares. How did he find me here?

"You sure don't know how lucky you are, Charlotte, to be young, free and single.

Never get married. I've been divorced five years but Maddy still hangs round my neck like a lump of granite. Take my advice. Stay problem free."

I leave him ranting as I take the letter into my office and sit down. The paper is shaking in my hand and I'm all churned up inside. Bastard! How has he found out where I am? My fingers feel contaminated just holding the thing.

Dearest Charlotte,

How could you leave without even saying goodbye? You know there is something truly special between us. There always will be. It is meant to be. I know you didn't mean the things you said in court. Why have you gone so far away?

Ugh! I could really throw up now. I'm not reading any more of his trash! And I'm not going to cry. This letter is being ripped into tiny pieces and going straight in with the rubbish. But I don't even want his filthy fantasies to soil my bin.

I fumble in my handbag, for my lighter, set fire to the paper on my window ledge, then blow the ash towards the roofs of Jerusalem. But a sudden breeze throws them back.

Damn you, Jonathon! Damn you to hell.

When I get back to my flat, Abdul is hovering on the landing.

"Hey, Missus pretty lady. You got anything you want me to do? I give good price specially for you."

I'm too tired for this, not today. "Thank you, Abdul. I'll let you know as soon as I need something done."

I just can't sleep properly tonight. My room is hot and sticky and though I threw off the covers ages ago I'm still drenched in sweat. My dreams are full of blood, fire and people screaming, and whichever way I try to run, ash blows back in my face.

Chapter 3

"I said this would happen, didn't I!"

Ben stalks like an irate Tom cat towards the pile of faxes, e-mails and letters on Ingrid's desk while she pulls a face at me behind his back. Thank God I'm not at his beck and call whenever he throws a strop. Men can be worse than toddlers. I wonder if he's got a thing going with Ingrid. He certainly treats her like his wife.

Ben scoops up a handful of papers, brandishing them in the air. "I warned Schlott this would happen. Bloody Ark of the Covenant! I told him it would attract every headcase going!"

He thrusts a piece of paper under Ingrid's nose. "Look at this."

If he treated me like that, I think I'd deck him.

Church of the Second Coming.
Dear Sirs,
With reference to the feature on your website, would you kindly keep us informed as to the discovery of the Ark so we may prepare for the return of the Messiah who will arise shortly afterwards.

"It's no laughing matter, Charlotte. We've gotten enough work without being snowed under with junk mail from

Loonsville."

"Quite."

"And this one! We're supposed to be running a serious archaeology department. 'FAO Officer of the Ark.' Who in hell's that that supposed to be?"

I have to stifle a giggle and it's even harder when I notice Ingrid is struggling to keep a straight face too.

"Warning! The finding of the Ark will herald the end of the world! Stop all investigations before it is too late!"

"Are you hoping to find the Ark then?" asks Ingrid.

"Course we're not! Nutters! The lot of them. And all banging on our door, just as I said."

"No one's banging on the door, Ben," I point out.

"Not yet. They soon will be. Thanks to Schlott!"

"Ssh, Ben," says Ingrid. "He might come in any minute."

"Bah, I'm going to find him." Ben turns towards the door, still leafing through the wad of correspondence. "'Flying Saucer Review, Anglican Ark Brotherhood... What the hell... Martian Pyramid Society?
Jesus!"

Ben storms out, clutching the offending correspondence like a weapon, and Ingrid and I just explode like a couple of cluster bombs. This isn't doing much for my image. We must look like a pair of naughty schoolgirls.

Ingrid wipes tears from her eyes, leaving smudges of mascara, and it's nice to see she's not perfect either. "Martian Pyramid Society! If Ben's not careful, they might come for him and whisk him up in a spaceship."

"If the Anglican Ark Brotherhood don't get to him first."

"At least it'll make a change from his ex-wife," laughs Ingrid. "Poor Ben. No wonder he's paranoid. "But I reckon he stands a better chance dealing with Martians than Maddy."

"So why is she always on his back?

"Usual thing. Money."

I thought they were divorced."

"They are. She's even married again. But she's still after more."

"Well, if the pyramidiots whisk him off to Mars, it sounds like they'll be doing him a favour. At least he'll be out of her clutches."

"I wouldn't bet on that."

"I'd better get back to work, and leave you to yours."

"Ja, Ben can complain, but it's me who'll end up dealing with it all. Hey, Charlotte, I'll give you a call if the Martians turn up!"

"Don't bother," I say over my shoulder. "Just refer them to Dr Travers. Tell them he's the Ark Officer."

Let Ben Travers deal with aliens and idiots. He deserves all he gets.

I make myself a mug of coffee and sit down at my desk.

I've been thinking a lot about that Canaanite

girl. I mean, imagine all those emotions she must have gone through after finding her sister like that. I know how it is. Pictures you don't want to see flash through your mind, like you're on the ghost train and scary creatures leap out at you from the dark. Then they all go away, and you're left in a vacuum that nothing will fill. At least she had her fury. Emptiness is the worst.

Two police officers turned up on the doorstop that night when Sally-Ann's car hit a Sainsbury's lorry head on. The woman was professionally sympathetic - she had obviously done this before - while her colleague who looked barely out of college, kept turning his helmet in his hand and studying the carpet.

I remember staring at a porcelain cat which Sally-Ann had given Mum one Christmas. I can still see every painted whisker and every tiny claw. I don't know how long I crouched on the floor in front of the mantelpiece. I didn't cry, not then, just sat and stared at that cat. I suppose I went straight into shock. We all did. The tears came later, then recriminations which hardened into bitterness. Just like the pear drops we ate as kids from the corner shop. They're sweet when you pop them into your mouth and later they taste like acid. My mother blamed my father for letting Sally-Ann drive the car, which was ridiculous because no one ever stopped her doing whatever she wanted, while, me - I was Miss Goody Two Shoes, always so eager to please I'd change my colours to suit everyone else if I thought they'd throw me a few scraps of approval.

It makes me cringe to think how I was such a sickening little drip. My father retreated behind a stone wall of silence. Poor Dad. I don't blame him for what happened after that. He was just a weak man, I suppose, as most of them seem to be at the core. Nothing had prepared him for tragedy and he had no idea how to cope. You had to keep a stiff upper lip where he came from. Counselling was never for the likes of him and he told the police woman where she could shove it.

Six months after Sally-Ann's death he walked out. I wasn't surprised but it hurt all the same. How it hurt. He seemed to want nothing to do with me, as though the very sight of Miss dumpy daughter reminded him of the gorgeous one he had lost. Imagine how that made me feel. My mother, bless her, made her shrine to Sally-Ann on the mantelpiece, lived in the past and in the shadow of what might have been, unable, or unwilling, to see what was happening. I simply wrapped up my pain, my emptiness, in a tight ball inside and and struggled to carry it alone.

So, you see, I can understand the grief of the Canaanite
girl. I know what it's like. That gnawing feeling inside, like rats that won't go away. You know you'll never see her walk through the door. Not ever. And you can't come terms with it. You scream inside that you can't go on, and you're desperate to turn back the clock. If only. How many times has that been said since time began? It's beyond cruelty. Such a bright spark of life, snuffed out, never coming back.

I could cry for that girl, really I could. I just wish I didn't feel like my ball of pain is coming unravelled after all this time.

Why am I so inept? It's time I learnt to keep my emotions in check. It was all a long time ago. For her as well as me. Her sorrow has long crumbled into dust. I was fifteen at the time of the crash. Probably about the same age as her. I should be over it by now. I'd never have coped if I'd witnessed the horrors she saw at Jericho. I am pathetic and weak. If I saw one dead body I'd go off my head. I'd never have survived in the wilderness, without supermarkets full of Mars Bars and Galaxies to get me through. I wish I was strong like her.

I pull the latest translation towards me and feel sick. That disgusting old man. I know how Rahab's sister must have felt. Dirty, soiled, ashamed. No matter how she tried to tell herself it wasn't her fault. Maybe women's experiences haven't changed all that much through the years.

Jonathon had seemed just a normal friendly guy. I went out with him several times for a drink, along with the rest of the crowd from Western Asiatic. Just as a friend. That's all it was. I didn't know that twisted bastard was following me home. Drawing portraits of me at night in his scummy little bedsit. Things went missing, my lipstick, my pen, letters from my handbag. How was I to to know he was creating his own sick fantasy world in his room? When the police told me what they had found, I felt dirty and disgusting, yes, soiled, like she did, as though it were me, not poor bloody Jonathon to blame.

These words I've translated leap off the page and taunt me. *My face burnt with shame.* Her words, not mine. But that was exactly how he made me feel. Well, how are you supposed to feel? Is it any worse whether someone's invaded your body or your mind?

Suddenly, tears are streaming down my face and my mascara's not up to the job. I daren't let anyone see me like this. I dab my eyes with my sleeve, making a total mess of both, and honestly, I don't know if I'm crying for myself, or for a girl who's been dead for these last three thousand years.

"Are you glad I dragged you out of your office?

"It's very interesting," I say, as Ben and I reach the observation point on the top of the tell. "And a lovely view."

Actually, it's amazing. You can see for miles across the Jordan plain and I can't get over the fact that I'm really here, at this famous site where the story in the fragments began. I mean, it was right on this hillside that the Canaanite women gossiped as they baked their bread, and stored their corn, and you can just imagine them fleeing past those walls before Joshua's men. Ben is looking at me sideways, I think he's trying to gauge what I'm thinking, fancies himself as some sort of amateur shrink. Let him. My thoughts are my own. I look across the hillside towards the modern town of

Jericho, shading my eyes from the sun. It's incredible to think this mound was the original Jericho where Rahab and her sisters lived. They could have sat at this very spot. I turn around and gaze out at the barren Jordan valley and the vast wasteland of desiccated hills, where that poor girl wandered alone. I really admire her guts. I wouldn't have lasted a day.

"You're very involved with the fragments, aren't you?" says Ben.

"Of course, it's my Job."

"No, I don't mean that. I've seen the way you get so engrossed. I've watched your face. You're kind of personally involved with our Jericho girl."

"I don't really know what you mean." I prefer Ben when he's being a rude aggressive pig. These little glimpses of perceptiveness
concealed beneath that macho hide are disturbing. This is supposed to be to be a new life for me. The last thing I want is someone prodding around in my mind.

Ben points to the sloping banks that surround the tell. "You can see why Watzinger, Garstang and their buddies got so excited, thinking they'd found the walls destroyed by Joshua."

"The way the stones have rolled down the hill, it does look like that at first," I agree. "But they were desperate to find evidence of the Bible story. They couldn't know when they started, the tell contains settlements stretching back nine thousand years."

"That's one of the problems with archaeology. People tend to find what they want to, not what's actually there."

"Do you?" Touché! My turn to get personal.

Ben laughs. "I hope not. But you never can tell."

"Kathleen Kenyon blew all their theories to pieces, though, didn't she?"

"When she found that crumbled wall of mud bricks dated to the Middle Bronze Age, instead of the Hebrew conquest in the Late Bronze Age? I wonder if she was disappointed too."

"By the way, how did the damage occur to the topmost fragments?" I ask.

"It wasn't my team, if that's what you mean."

"I wasn't suggesting..."

"A goat boy found them. He was trying to yank them out the hillside to sell when some of the roof caved in. The fragments on the top were damaged by falling debris."

"Ah, I see." I needed to ask but he's so defensive about anything he thinks is critical of himself or his beloved team. Still, I got the answer I wanted out of him. But there's something else that's been on my mind, though I'm not sure how he'll take it, and the last thing I want is for him or anyone else to think I'm sympathetic to the pyramidiot brigade. Still I guess this is as good a time as any to ask.

"And what do you make of David Rohl's new theory, that the orthodox dating of Bible history is incorrect?" I hold my breath. Will he think

I'm a nutter?

"Very interesting idea. If he's right, then those walls down there, which were destroyed and burnt just as the Bible says, do, in fact, date to around 1230 BC, the time of Joshua's conquest. Not circa 1600 BC, as standard archaeology claims."

So he's not a died-in-the-wool traditionalist after all. Maybe I can risk pressing on.

"Now we've found another account of the fall of Jericho, an authentic, contemporary source which backs up the Bible, it means..."

"Our fragments give credence to David Rohl's new dating system, and help prove orthodox scholarship wrong. I know." Ben frowns. "A lot of people won't like that. They class Rohl along with the Martian Pyramid Society, and now here we come, with authentic clay tablets that back up his claims. When you pulled Cache 5 out of that cave, I bet you didn't realise what a can of worms you were digging up as well."Ben is still frowning. "I know you and Ingrid think it's a joke, but it's not just New Age pyramidiots and Second Coming Societies we could be attracting."

But I don't hear the rest of what he's saying. I shield the sun's glare from my eyes and peer down at the excavations. There they are again. I thought I was just being paranoid in the car, and didn't mention it at the time, but two men in a Mercedes followed us all the way from Jerusalem and now their car's parked here too while the

61

pair of them are standing by the excavation ropes. Behind their sunglasses they could be looking at the dig, or at us.

."Sorry. Am I boring you?"

"What?"

The two men start to wander around the pits. I suppose there are any number of people travelling down here from Jerusalem. It doesn't necessarily mean anything.

"I said, am I such a bore that...?"

"Oh sorry, Ben. I was just..."

"...watching those two men. What's up? Do you know them? Bit smartly dressed to be sightseeing."

"I noticed they were behind us on the road from Jerusalem, that's all."

"And?"

"When we stopped for petrol, they were waiting off a side road. As soon as we carried on, they were behind us again."

"Do you think they were following us?"

"Why should they be?" I don't want him thinking I'm paranoid or going off on one about Martian pyramidiots again.

"Sure?"

"Of course, I know when I'm being followed."

"Sounds like it's a habit."

"What do you mean?"

"You make it sound as if you're always

keeping one eye over your shoulder."

"Of course not." Why didn't I just keep my mouth shut.

I start to walk off, telling him I want to take a look at the defensive tower. Why should I care what he thinks?

Glancing back over my shoulder, I notice that Ben is keeping an eye on those two men, as he follows me towards the ruined tower.

When we drive back through Jericho, I watch the Arab men and women, gathered on rattan stools to sip coffee, play backgammon and chat and wonder if it's changed that much from the Jericho Rahab's sister knew, all those centuries ago. The TV aerials, posters of Arafat and traffic in the dusty streets scream of the twenty first century, but when I look at those markets ablaze with aubergines, tomatoes and olives, and great bunches of dates and bananas swinging from the beams, and those sad-eyed donkeys plodding along, I can just imagine myself in Rahab's City of Palms. I wonder if I'd have fared any better there. Probably not.

Ben keeps glancing in his rear view mirror. Then he frowns. In the side mirror I spot that Mercedes again. I shan't say a thing this time.

Ben puts his foot on the clutch and takes the car up a gear. As the road to Jerusalem gleams in the sunlight ahead, he glances at my safety belt.

"Hold on. We're going to take a sharp left."

I grab the dashboard as the Landrover swings into a turning. "Oasis Casino?" I nod at the sign above the building ahead.

"Don't worry, I'm not about to drag you into a gambling den."

"Don't tell me you couldn't do with a win. An academic's salary's not that great."

"Yeah. Though even if I did, Maddy would scoop the lot."

"So why is she always after you for money, if you've been divorced five years?"

Ben tugs on the brake and sits back. "Actually, it's not for her. It's for Tony, our son."

"I didn't realise you had children."

"Just the one. Here." Ben reaches into his wallet and pulls out a photo of a small boy with a cheeky grin and missing front teeth. "That's Tony."

"He looks cute. So he lives with Maddy?"

"No. I wish he did. She has custody, but he spends nearly all his time in hospital now."

"Oh, I'm sorry."

"He has a rare bone marrow disease. He's getting the best treatment we can give him, but we don't have your NHS in the States. It takes every penny I earn. He's only five."

Ben's eyes are glistening as he slides the photograph back, and I look away.

"I wish I could give more. I'd give the shirt off my back, if I could help that little guy. The worst of it is, he's so brave, always laughing and fooling around, when he's not too ill. But me... I just crack up. Enough of my problems. Time to hit the road."

"That was a quick stop."

"Time enough."

"'Primula Porter Corporation,'" I read aloud from an advertising hoarding on the roadside. "'Dead Sea Spa Resort, Massage, Mud Treatments and Beauty Therapy.' Hmm, I could do with some of that."

"You don't need it," says Ben.

I wish.

We've not gone far down the highway when we see the Mercedes pull out of a turning behind us. We both know there's no point pretending.

"I told Schlott," growls Ben.

"They're not exactly subtle, are they?" I feel more relieved that my paranoia is justified, than worried that we're being followed.

"No, and they're Israeli, which, added to the lack of subtlety, gives me a pretty idea who they are."

"Who?"

"Never mind. Let's just say I think rather more 'governmental agencies' might be showing interest in our work here, than the pyramidiot brigade."

"Ah ha. Here's our chance."

Glancing behind me, I see a large truck has overtaken the Mercedes, blocking us from sight. Ben takes a side road and puts his foot on the gas.

"Let's take a little diversion," Ben grins. That'll get up their noses, once they get out from behind that truck." He makes another sharp left and soon we've left the main highway, and the Mercedes, way behind. The road becomes a dirt track where dilapidated housing blocks with broken windows rise up on either side. A roll of old barbed wire lies alongside.

"What is this place?" I ask.

"Somewhere our friends in the Mercedes won't expect us to visit," says Ben, stopping the car. "This is one of the old refugee camps from the 1967 war. Most of the ones at Jericho are abandoned now, though there're still a few Palestinians here."

"That water's filthy. I try not to let him see that I'm shocked at the ragged children playing in the gutter.

"It's not water," says Ben. "It's raw sewage."

No wonder they hate the Israelis so much. I watch the boys fish a battered football from the mess by the roadside and take their game to a piece of wasteland, covered in rusty oil drums, tins and mounds of fly-infested donkey dung.

"You'd think after all the persecution the Jews have been through, they'd let the Palestinians control their own homeland too."

"That's human nature for you," says Ben. "And the wonderful compassion of religion."

"The Palestinians were here first."

"Not according to Zionists. They reckon the Arabs have no right to Palestine because God gave the land to the descendants of Abraham."

"But the Palestinians claim they're descended from Abraham too, and some were probably descended from the Canaanites, who were the original inhabitants of Palestine."

"Until our friend and hero Joshua burnt their

cities and hacked most of them to death."

I don't think Mrs Lawrence would have approved of Ben Travers either. "Oh no, look at that."

"You think this is bad?" says Ben. "You should see Gaza. There are thousands of Palestinians living in conditions worse than this."

"No, over there." I'm out of the Landrover in an instant. I just can't bear to see animals in distress and this puppy's legs are so weak it can barely stand as it forages for food amongst the piles of rotting cabbage and rusty cans. It's a small alsatian cross with great floppy ears and looks round with big brown eyes as I approach. When I scoop it into my arms I can feel its ribs poke through.

"I wonder if it belongs to anyone."

"Belongs to anyone? There are hundreds of strays in Palestine. Charlotte, for heavens' sake, it'll be covered in fleas."

"Look at him, poor thing. I can't leave him here like this. "He's half starved."

"Ch no, Charlotte. You're not..."

I silence him with a look. No way am I leaving this puppy to starve on a rubbish dump.

"I bet when you were a kid, you fed all the stray cats, gave your pocket money to Save the Whales..."

"Not just when I was a kid. What's wrong with that?"

"You can't solve all the world's problems. If you feed every stray dog in Palestine, you'll have dirty great packs trotting behind you."

"I'm not leaving him here to die.'

"You're not bringing that mangy thing in my car."

"Then this mangy thing and I will catch a taxi back to Jerusalem."

"You might look a fragile little thing, but you sure are stubborn as a mule." Ben opens the back of the car. "Here." He thrusts a blanket at her. "Wrap him up in that. And if I catch one flea in my car, you're dead, lady."

"Hey, Miss Charlotte, you've had visitors!" Abdul leans across the landing then scampers down the stairs. "What you got there, Miss Charlotte?"

"He's a puppy." I show him the pathetic bundle of skin and bones wrapped up in the blanket but he's not very impressed.

"Bah! Miss Charlotte, you're not taking that in your apartment?
It's disgusting!"

"Not when he's cleaned up." Then I have an idea. Perhaps I can make use of Abdul's services after all. "Abdul, I might have a little job for you."

Abdul's eyes light up. "Yes, Miss Charlotte. For you, special price."

"You can come and take the dog for a walk when I'm at work."

"That thing?"

"I'll pay you."

"You gonna clean him up first?"

I nod.

68

"Every day? Twenty shekels."

"Ten shekels. He's only a little dog."

"Fifteen."

Abdul drives a
hard bargain.

"Twelve."

"Done."

"I'll give you a spare key. Make sure you're careful with it – or you won't get your money."

"You can trust me, Miss Charlotte. But you give that dog a bath." Abdul scampers up the stairs then stops halfway and swings on the bannister. "Oh Miss Charlotte. I nearly forgot. What you been up to?"

"Up to?"

"You had Mossad snooping round here."

"Mossad?" I try to spin round but my key gets stuck in the lock. I might not have been in Israel long but I know the Israeli Secret Police make Reggie Kray look like Mother Teresa.

"Two men come round here asking questions. I tell them nothing. I say you gone away. I hate Israelis. 'specially soldiers and police"

"How do you know who they were? Did they say?"

"No, Miss Charlotte. But I'm Arab. I know. I smell them rats five kilometres away."

"Abdul, will you let me know if they come back?'

"Sure, Miss Charlotte. Tomorrow you want me walk that dog?"

"Yes, please. But remember, take care of

the key. And don't let anyone else in."

"'Specially not them Mossad bastards. I swear to Allah, Miss Charlotte, you can trust me. I get rid of any Israeli scum for you."

I close the door and lean back against it. Christ! What on earth could Mossad want with me? Could these be the same two men who followed us to Jericho? It must be some mistake. They've got the wrong flat, the wrong person. Or is Ben right? I suppose the sudden emergence of an Old Testament relic is bound to be of interest to the Israeli government: The Israelis are highly sensitive to their isolation in a sea of Arab lands, and when all's said and done, this young Jewish state relies on its religious past to justify its whole existence.

Perhaps Doctor Schlott did unleash more than he bargained for when he posted details of the fragments on the Internet. Or am I just getting caught up in the climate of fear and paranoia which seems to prevail in this city?

Whatever. That door is going to be firmly locked and bolted before I go to bed tonight.

What have I let myself in for?

Fragment 4

It was a bright sunny day. The flax had been gathered and laid on the roofs to dry. They were in trouble, those men from Shiittim.   Jericho was buzzing with talk of the Habiru. The cities they had conquered, the kings they had slain. Evi, Rekem, Zur, Balaamm... Rumours sizzled through the fields as we worked. Joshua had his sights on our City of Palms. He wanted our lush green oasis amid the giant waste of chalk. He wanted to seize all of Canaan, once Jericho was his. We laughed. Conquer Jericho, with our high walls as thick as a man from head to toe? With our great watchtower standing proud on the hill? With our men as brave as any from Canaan to Cush?

The gossip flew. Spies had been sent, spies from Shittim.

Why did they knock on our door? There were other places in Jericho they could have found lodging for the night. Why choose our house? Perhaps the fame of Rahab's face had spread even to the Habiru. Or perhaps they had heard it was the house of a temple whore. We called them Priestess, our most beautiful women, who took the part of

71

the Goddess in the union of man and woman, Heaven and Earth. The Habiru called them whore.

Had they gone to any other dwelling in Jericho, our city might be standing above its ramparts now. Our friends and neighbours might be laughing in the streets which are no
more. The face of our little sister, Tarasch, might be smiling up at the doves as she lay on her back, gazing at the sky amid the flax.

Why, Rahab? Why?

There were two of them, one short, thick-set, with scowling eyebrows that met in the centre of his forehead. The other was tall, with deep eyes and rich hair that fell to his shoulders. I saw the way he gazed at her. I saw the way she dropped her eyes then raised them suddenly to his, the way she did in the temple, when the men came for the Rites. The full force of those lovely dark eyes almost blinded that Habiru where he stood. Sechem, was his name. Son of Nobah. His companion, who seemed content to let Rahab's new admirer talk for both, was Labor, son of Hul.

"Let us in," said Sechem. "We have travelled far. We are thirsty and hungry."

Rahab's eyelashes flickered, taking in his tangled hair, his handsome weathered face and the hard, sun-bronzed muscles of his arm as he leaned against the jamb of our door.

"Rahab!" I tugged at her sleeve. "These might be the strangers we were warned about! The men sent from Shittim by Joshua to spy on our land."

"Joshua's fame has travelled fast," said Shechem.

I scowled at him, folded my arms and blocked the doorway where he sought to enter. I did not like the way his eyes ran over my sister's face and her gown.

"All Canaan has heard of Joshua." Rahab's voice dropped to a whisper. She pressed her hands together and twisted her fingers below her breast. "They talk of how he is possessed of a strange new God, who will destroy all his enemies before him."

"In Baal's name, send them away," I said. "If they are the spies, they will get us into trouble."

"All strangers are owed hospitality," said Rahab. "It is the way of our Gods. And if they are from Joshua, we dare not anger their One God."

"We need shelter," said Labor, growing impatient.

"Lady," smiled Shechem. "Joshua did send us, but we mean you no harm. In the name of our God, give us water and some of that delicious stew I smell steaming on your fire."

"In the name of your God..." I heard the tremble in

her voice. I saw her fingers tighten into balls. "Your God who gave Moses the power to slay all the kings of Midian?"

Labor glanced behind. The goat boy and his friend who sold bread were watching from across the street, whispering, intent on something, watching the men who sought entry to our door.

"Rahab," I said. "This is dangerous. Send them away. They are spies. Go!" I stepped forward and made to shoo them away as I did the birds from our crops. But Rahab caught my wrist.

"Their God is dangerous too." She stepped aside. "Come. You may enter and be welcome to our house."

In the street behind, I saw the two boys pause. They looked at one another, then ran off.

"Rahab, this is madness!" I whispered, as the men spread their cloaks and settled by our fire. "The boys have seen them enter our house. If our King hears of this..."

"Hush." She laid her hand on my arm. Her eyes were wide and I could see the fear. Fear I had seen in the eyes of an antelope, backed up against a cliff, before the mountain lion pounced.

"We must not offend their God," whispered Rahab.

"Do you know what He did to the Midianites?"

"The Midianites?"

"Their women slept with the Habiru," said Rahab. "They tempted the men to break the laws of their One God." Her nails dug into my skin and her voice held a croak, like the frogs that squat in the Jordan mud. "The One God was angry. He told their leaders they must take revenge."

"So what did they do?"

"The Habiru killed every Midianite man and boy. Then they slaughtered every woman who was not a virgin." Her voice was low and hoarse with fear. "Sister, their God is so powerful, they were able to destroy the whole Midianite people."

"Rahab, what about our Gods?" I was cross she could dismiss them so easily, those Gods she was supposed to serve. All because she was scared of some upstart in the heavens. "What of Baal, Astarte, Dagon? Would you anger the Gods of Thunder and Fire?"

She turned away. She went to the jars beneath the raised platform of the house and brought water to the men by the fire. Then she stirred the stew and smiled at the spies from Shittim

Chapter 4

Honestly, Ben's face is such a picture as he looks up from the print-out. I know exactly what's coming.

"Come on, Charlotte. Are you sure you've got this right?"

Men are so predictable.

"Absolutely sure."

Who does he think he is anyway, questioning my skills? I don't like this any more than he does.

"The fragments are chipped in places. I'm not a linguist, but I know sometimes words can be..."

"Ben," I stab the page with my finger. "Fragment 22 is not chipped. And there is no ambiguity. That is the only possible translation."'

Ben lays the print-out aside but I know he won't let this rest.

"To be honest," he says, "I'm not sure what to make of it. Up to now, the fragments have contained a pretty straightforward account. But this is stating the Ark did have some sort of... well..."

"Supernatural powers?" I suggest.

"Of course not. Some sort of ... Come on, you're a professional too. This could make a laughing stock of us."

Much as I'm enjoying seeing Dr God's discomfort, I don't want to be classed as a loony Arkist either. It's vital I get academic recognition. This is a crucial stage in my career. I can't afford to become an outcast. Yet neither can I pretend the fragments say something else. I'll have to tread so carefully here.

"We know the Ark was just a wooden box, but perhaps we should take into account the veneration it received?"

"It had religious and mythological significance, that's all," says Ben. "Half the peoples of Mesopotamia had the same sort of sacred receptacles."

"Of course, though only this one appears to have induced so much fear - unfounded, naturally."

"You keep something hidden away and of course stories build up around it. But even in the Bible, apart from the odd plague, parting of waters..."

"...boils, festering sores, itches, tumours, blight..."

"Yes, Yes, I know all that, but for God's sake, it was just a holy relic."

"Quite."

I don't want to push the point but Ben knows full well what the the Bible says. Let's face it, Joshua made sure his own people were kept well away and everyone seemed terrified to death of the thing. Not that I believe in ancient powers any more than Ben does, of course, but where there's smoke there must be some weeny spark of fire.

"We know the Bible is totally unreliable."

"We do indeed," agrees Ben. "Look, I've got a lecture. I'll leave you to it and we'll discuss it some more later."

There we go - typical man. Confront them

with something they'd rather not face and they're off. I know he hasn't got a lecture. I heard him tell Ingrid earlier. He's an established expert in his field. He could get any job he likes but I'll never get ahead if my name becomes synonymous with magical madness. Yet there's no getting away from the fact that the Ark is portrayed as something pretty powerful in the Bible and the fragments are backing that up. This would be so much easier if the fragments were a load of trading accounts.

Why is life never simple?

Just look at this stuff. Samuel 4: verse 18, for example.

When he mentioned the ark of God, Eli fell backwards off his chair by the side of the gate. His neck was broken and he died.

It wasn't the Ark that killed him. He scared himself to death, silly old fool, just hearing it mentioned.

But there's loads of this sort of reference, like 1 Samuel 5: verse 10.

As the ark of God was entering Ekron, the people of Ekron cried out,
'They have brought the ark of the god of Israel round to us to kill   us and our people."

And what came next could hardly be put down to mass hysteria. We're talking a bit more than pot smashing here.

...death had filled the city with panic; God's hand was very heavy   upon it. Those who did not die were afflicted with tumours, and the   outcry of the city went up to heaven.

Surely there had to be something that kicked off the stories in the first place. I take the Bible with a hefty sackful of salt, as all secular scholars do, but the fragments are authentic source material. Why would this Canaanite girl make the story up? Unless it's her interpretation of something she couldn't explain.

But what exactly? Looking at this account in *Samuel,* it sounds like radiation, but that's exactly what the fringe brigade claim, with their spaced out technologies from Egypt or whatever. Where's the Marlboro? I'll really have to watch out here. The last thing I need is to start sounding like a pyramidiot, or I'll be carted off straight to academic obscurity. Welcome, Charlotte Adams, to to the Loony Ark Bin! Get your P45 here. These fragments are either going to ruin my professional credibility - or cause an absolute sensation when they're released. Who's that at the door?

"Come in."

"Charlotte," Ben strides up to my desk.

What does he want now? "Lecture cancelled?" I smile at him sweetly.

"What? Oh er, yes. Listen, I've been thinking. I don't think you should show this to anyone yet."

"I'll have to show it to Dr Schlott."

"Especially not Schlott. I think we should see where the fragments go from here before anyone else gets to know about it."

"But he'll soon be asking how much more I've completed."

"Stall him. Look, I'm sure it's nothing to worry about, but those men who followed us to Jericho, I've seen them since then, hovering around the university. I think they're from Mossad."

"I know. They went to my flat, asking questions."

"Why the hell didn't you mention this before?"

I shrug. "I didn't want you to start worrying."

"Worrying? Charlotte, this is the Israeli Secret Police we're talking about here, not the Mickey Mouse Fan Club."

"It's not as if we've done anything."

"Done anything? We don't have to do anything. The Ark of the Covenant is probably the most sacred relic of all time. The State of Israel is founded on religion. Of course the government is going to be interested in this."

"I'm starting to feel like Indiana Jones." I puff my smoke into the air and try to sound humorous.

"Next they'll be thinking we're on the trail of the Ark."

"Maybe they already do," says Ben quietly.

I pause, my cigarette in the air. I don't like the way he said that.

"That's ridiculous."

Maybe Dr Schlott's right and Ben Travers has been watching too many movies.

"There's a reason they're keeping an eye on

us. I'm not saying it's because they think there might be something in the tablets that may lead to the Ark - or to whatever the girl claims was contained inside, but..."

"They're welcome to it. Listen to this. Samuel 6: verse 19.

...God struck down some of the men of Beth Shemesh, putting several of them to death, because they had looked into the ark of the Lord."

This suggests that people could be killed merely by looking inside." Jjust imagine what that kind of power could do in the wrong hands, or what some people might do to get hold of it, whether it exists or not, which it can't do, of course.

"Charlotte," we could attract some pretty heavy people with this stuff. Not so far from Raiders."

"That's ridiculous." I treat him to one of my you've-lost-the-plot looks, politely, of course. Can't risk upsetting someone of his repute.

"I'm not saying I think there's anything in it...

"Of course not."

"But listen, if... and I'm only talking 'ifs' at this stage... the fragments reveal a destructive energy source, something that seems to have been lost along with Solomon's Temple, plenty of organisations would love to get their hands on it. The Israelis, every third world tin pot dictator, governmental defence organisation, multi-national... And Charlotte, you haven't been in Israel long enough to see what Hamas and the Islamic Jihad are capable of. Car bombs are..."

"All right, all right. I get the picture."

Oh no, Dr Know-it-all. I'm such an innocent. I can't possibly have seen a car bomb, can I?

"You're forgetting the other property of the Ark mentioned in the fragments, Ben. According to the girl, it was also able to heal and rejuvenate."

"That doesn't hold such negative possibilities of attracting the wrong kind of interest. Look, all I'm saying is try to hold off Schlott for a bit. Tell him you're having to work around the damage or something. Just till we see where the fragments go from here."

"I'm not making any promises."

"Let's keep what's in these latest fragments between us. At least, for now."

I make sure he sees me pull a disparaging face as he leaves. He should be telling me it's a load of superstitious crap, and nothing to worry about, not suggesting there might be something in it.

"There, let's see if that fixes it."

I hope this hippy technician knows what he's doing. He flicks his hair over his shoulder and scrolls through the menu.

"So can I start using it again?" It's been a really frustrating morning. There's something wrong with my computer and I can't get a thing done till Yusef sorts it out.

"Just let me check." He frowns and toys with the worry beads round his neck.

For goodness sake, how much longer?

Yusef takes off his heavy framed glasses and wipes them with the end of his shirt. "Sorry, Miss Adams, It's going to take longer than I thought."

This is going to be one of those days. "Is it a virus."

"I'm not sure at the moment."

"How long will it take?"

He wipes his hands on his jeans. "Can't say just yet. Maybe all day."

Great. Just great.

"I suppose I'll just have to leave to you to it."

I sit down and pick up the broken tablet 23, but with Yusef tinkering about it's impossible to concentrate. After a while I give up. There is one thing I'd like to do which doesn't involve the computer or the office, but I haven't got a car and I'm not sure how accessible it is. I sit and drum my fingers on the desk. Sally-Ann used to get so annoyed when I did that. I don't want to ask Ben for advice, but he does know the terrain better than anyone so I suppose I'll have to go and find him.

He's about to leave the main lecture hall, amid a stream of under-graduates and smiles when he sees me.

"Hi. How's it going?"

"It's not. There's a fault on the computer so I can't get on with anything."

"A virus?"

"Seems that way."

"Who's working on it for you?"

"A young guy, hippyish, with long hair and glasses. Yusef."

"Ah. If anyone can fix it, Yusef can. He might look a bit of a space cadet but he's a hot-shot with computers. Apparently the government tried to recruit him when they caught him hacking into their defence computer, but he hates politicians and chose us instead."

"Look, I was wondering, I don't have a car but is there any way
getting to the cave at Ein Gedi? I'd really like to see where the fragments were found. After Jericho, I was able to get a much clearer picture of the world she lived in."

Ben glances at his watch. "Sure. I'll take you. I have a tutorial in an hour but I can reschedule that. I need to go down there to check on my team excavating the clay pit."

"Oh, I didn't mean... I was planning to go on my own."

"Nonsense. You can't do it without a car."

"But I don't want to put you out."

I don't want to be indebted to him either. Or to spend a whole day in his company.

"You won't. Give me half an hour. I'll meet you in the car-park.

I watch him stride off with mixed feelings. At least I'll be making good use of the day, and have an interesting trip into the bargain, but why is it I always feel so uncomfortable when Dr Ben Travers is around?

Despite my resolution to be cool, calm and collected in the presence of Dr God, I'm knocked out by the Dead Sea. I mean, it's like nothing I've ever seen before. The sky is straight from a Club Med brochure and the sea is a slash of shining sapphire, set in this weird arid wilderness of ghostly hills, and not a tree in sight. So this is what it's like at the lowest point on earth.

"The southern side is even more amazing," says Ben. "Full of bizarre salt formations. It's like something out of Voyager." He pulls over and stops the car at a viewing point so we can look out across at the shimmering salt flats that float on the surface. I wish he wouldn't. I feel like a tourist, but I can't get over this place.

Then he laughs.

"What's so funny?"

"Nothing. Just you remind me of a little kid, seeing the sea for the first time. Shame I haven't got a bucket and spade in the back."

"It is beautiful," I reply stiffly.

"Beautiful?" He laughs again and holds out his arms to the sea. "Come on, admit it. It's out of this world, and you know it. You don't always have to ..."

"It's just rather different to the sea back home," I say quickly.

"Sure it is. It's kind of nice to be with someone who's seeing it through fresh eyes. Would you like to take a look at the Qmran caves? They're not far from here."

"Have we got time? I don't want to..."

"Madam, I and my Landrover are at your disposal."

We drive on, find a place to park and climb up the cliff to a yawning gap in the rocks. The cave is so low we have to stoop and crouch in the entrance, but after that hike uphill in the heat, I'm just glad to get out of the sun.

"This is where several of the Dead Sea Scrolls were found," says Ben. "They're kept under tight security in Jerusalem now, at the Shrine of the Book."

"I wonder if our fragments will cause such a stir and end up under lock and key as well."

Ben crouches down on the floor of the cave. He looks too big for the tiny space. "I wouldn't be surprised," he says. "Especially if the stuff about the Ark gets out. Even if it is just wild imagination on the part of some psychotic girl."

"Psychotic?"

"Well, disturbed. After everything that happened to her."

"Her account is remarkably lucid." So he thinks anyone who goes through some sort of trauma is psychotic. Ben might have found the fragments but I'm the one who spends hours every day translating her memories. The more I work on them the more I get to know her. And one thing I am sure about, she wasn't delusional. Ben might be an expert on archaeology but on some things he hasn't got a clue. Just because something awful happens to you, it doesn't mean you're climbing the walls.

"Look, now we've seen Qmran, how about a spot of lunch? I'm starved, and I know a great restaurant a little way down the coast."

"Well.." I am hungry but I dread to think what his idea of lunch is."

"Just something light? Salad, rice?"

"All right." I can't really refuse, can I. He's driving.

As we pulls up outside a restaurant, surrounded by date palms and decorated with blue and green mosaic tiles, I pray to whatever god happens to be listening I'm not going to have to fight off platefuls of camel meat or sheep's eyes in grease. Ben opens the door and as we walk into the cool interior, the Arab proprietor comes rushing up to greet him with open arms and a beaming smile.

"Dr Travers. So nice to see you. And with a beautiful young lady too. Your usual table?"

"Don't worry," Ben laughs, after Mr Khalaf has pulled out a chair for me, wiped the already spotless tablecloth and left us with the menus. "I won't force lots of *friandises* on you again. "I'm sorry about that."

"They were delicious, but..." I stare at the menu in panic. It's all in Arabic.

"How about we go for a selection of salads and side dishes?" suggests Ben. "That way you can try a bit of everything and won't have to put up with me forcing you to eat what you don't want."

Thank God for that. I put the menu down and hope his idea of salad isn't platefuls of squid in fatty mayonnaise or cold manna in cream.

"You didn't force..."

"I know, I'm an overbearing, domineering,

ignorant pig who doesn't know how to treat women." He smiles at me over his menu. "Don't worry. I've heard it all before, especially after all those years with Maddy. Anyway, I did feel a bit guilty when I saw... Damn, I'm putting my foot in it again." He beckons Mr Khalaf across. "OK, we'll have *meqadarra*, baked *rishta* with aubergines, okra with tomatoes and coriander, *ful Nabad*, *tabbouleh*, and the goat's cheese, courgette and spinach salads.

How about you?" he asks, when Mr Khalaf has scuttled off to the kitchens.

"Oh, er...yes. That sounds delicious." I catch myself fiddling with the serviette and link my hands firmly in my lap.

"No, I mean, ever been married? Serious relationship?"

"No."

Mr Khalaf returns with a tray which is laden with amazing looking dishes, oozing fresh vegetables and smelling fantastic, of spices and herbs. I could cry with relief. Dr Hewitt couldn't have recommended anything healthier. When I finally sit back in my chair and declare I can't eat another thing, I notice Ben is watching me.

"I'm glad you enjoyed that," he says. "I felt guilty after the last time."

"There was no need."

"I just felt... oh never mind. Do you want coffee?"

"No, I'm really stuffed. That was amazing, thanks." It was too. Ben Travers is full of surprises. I honestly thought I'd be staring at donkey hoof in oil.

"Good. Shall we get going?"

Ben Khalaf escorts us to the door with profuse exhortations to return as soon as possible, and then we're on our way again along the banks of the Dead Sea.

"At least we haven't been followed this time," I remark, as we draw
into the oasis of Ein Gedi where a number of bathers are floating in the water below.

"Don't speak too soon."

I quickly look over my shoulder.

"Don't worry. We're not being followed. I just meant you're tempting fate by saying that."

"I didn't have you down as superstitious."

"I'm not, touch wood." He taps the dashboard and grins. "The cave where we found the fragments is a bit further on. We'll leave the Landrover at the Nature Reserve and then it's a bit of a hike up the cliffs."

We're both streaming with sweat by the time we arrive at a carefully marked out site in the lee of overhanging rocks. Lizards scuttle off the rocks into the ferns as we approach and I can hear the tinkle of water falling close by. The inside of the cave is propped up with timbers and the roof hangs even lower than those at Qmran.

"I imagined it to be bigger than this," I say, crouching in the entrance and looking around.

"It was, but there have been heavy rock falls and the whole structure's pretty much caved in. No pun intended."

I gaze around at the debris and wonder if she actually lived in here.

Ben points down the hillside. "Just down there is the clay pit where the tablets were made."

I find it all too easy to picture her alone in these dark rocks and find myself shivering, despite the heat, and I'm covered in a film of cold sweat. I turn back to the sunlight and follow Ben to to a shallow depression, with excavations marked out by ropes.

"This was dug out in the early Bronze Age," he tells me. "But it had fallen into disuse by Joshua's time. Our tablets were rejects, broken pieces left abandoned at the site.

"She made good use of them."

"We think she must have lived here for some time, if she wrote all those fragments here before hiding them."

I turn back to that dark cleft in the rock. How could a teenage girl survive alone in such a place? Did she ever find any sort of happiness?

"Perhaps she married a shepherd," jokes Ben, as though he's reading my mind, (God forbid.) "and lived happily ever after."

"Nice idea." Somehow I don't think so. I crouch down and run my hand over this ground which yielded the tablets that have so radically changed my life, three thousand years on. Ben's jokes aren't funny. I know how it feels to be alone in a hostile world. I'm glad when he walks away and I'm left with the lizards and the rocks.

Where will her story lead? I'll find out when I

finish the fragments. A happy marriage and children? I have a feeling it won't turn out that way.

When I follow Ben across to the dig further along the cliff, he's in discussion with a member of his team who are working close by. There are a couple of young women on their knees with trowels, students probably. Both are skinny as rakes with sun tans to die for. I have damp patches under my arms and my face is probably peeling and red.

"Emile, this is Charlotte Adams," he turns towards me. "She's translating the tablets at the university."

"Pleased to meet you." Emile grins and wipes some of the grime off his hand before extending it to me.

"It seems we're popular with visitors today."

"Oh?" Ben raises his eyebrows.

"Yes, we had two men here earlier, asking about the site. They wanted to know if we were looking for any more tablets."

 "What did you tell them?"

Emile shrugs. "That we hope to find more, but the first cave is empty now, and we don't know if we'll be so lucky with these others."

"What were they like?" I'm pretty sure I already know. "

Americans, smart, not dressed for sightseeing."

"Americans?" Annoyingly, Ben and I both exclaim at once. We'll be finishing each other's sentences next.

"A woman came later, about thirty, attractive, with sunglasses and a scarf round her head.

"Emile fancied her," calls one of the rakes. "But she's probably more your type, Ben."

"Maybe a tourist," I suggest. It's beneath me to notice student stick insects.

"Not a couple of Israelis?" asks Ben.

"Two Israeli men were here a few days ago," says Emile. "Asking questions about Cave 7 up there."

"Did they say who they were?" I ask.

Emile shrugs.

"Like hell," growls Ben.

"The woman said she was on holiday. Whatever you're finding in those fragments, Mademoiselle Adams, they're attracting a lot of interest."

"Was the woman American too?"

"No. She spoke French with an accent. Maybe Swiss. Is there a problem?"

"No," said Ben. "But Emile, if anyone else comes round asking questions, tell them the caves have all been fully excavated. There's nothing more to find."

Emile returns to his work and I sit down on a rock. It's so hot out here. I don't know how they can work in it. I take out my sun-block and daub some more on my face and legs. The last thing I need is to end up looking like boiled lobster. I wish I had a tan like everyone else seems to have. Beside all these sunbronzed archaeologists, I look like a lump of veal.

"Well, this isn't what we expected," says Ben. "No doubt the Israelis were our familiar friends from Mossad, but the Americans?"

"And the woman," I add.

"She probably was a tourist. A dig in progress does bring them out of their holes. But I'd like to know who these smartly dressed Americans were."

"Maybe your pyramidiots? Unless you're expecting them to turn up with crystals and beaded headbands."

"They're not _my_ pyramidiots. Look, I've some things to sort out with Emile while we're here. It might take a while."

"No problem. I'd like to take another look at the cave then wander down to the shore. It helps with the translation to get a feel for the landscape"

"You sure you don't mind being left on your own?"

"Not at all." What does he think I am, a baby? Feminism seems to have by-passed Ben Travers. "I noticed there's a spa hotel down there. I might go and get a drink, and maybe get myself beautified with Dead Sea mud." Some hope. No amount of mud could give me legs like Ingrid's, nor her figure.

"There's not time. Anyway, I told you, you don't need all that muck."

"Only joking. But I certainly need a drink."

"Sounds good to me. I'll meet you in the bar when I've finished up here."

I sit in the mouth of the cave for a while, wondering if the Canaanite girl sat in this very spot, gazing at this same view of deep blue sea and sky, framed by barren hills. It's a lonely, beautiful place, this little oasis in the ferns. I'd like to think she found some kind of peace here.

The Regency Shalom Hotel is a gleaming six storey monster of glass and steel rising straight out of the shore. I stroll in through the doors, pretending I'm a tourist, and settle down in one of the deep plush sofas of the reception bar, the kind that swallows you up. An immaculate waiter balancing a gleaming silver tray, serves me a kiwi and mango smoothie on ice, in a tall glass decorated with cherries on sticks and a tiny paper umbrella. I settle back in the chintzy depths of the sofa and let the overhead fans waft me with delicious cooling air. I could really get used to this. On the low table in front of me is a brochure, printed on thick expensive paper in sepia and cream. I put down my drink, guiltily, hoping it won't leave a ring on the spotlessly polished glass, and browse through the list of beauty treatments. I might come back one weekend and utterly spoil myself with hedonist delights, even if I am a lost cause in the beauty stakes.

Aromatherapy Back Massage, with Neroli, Melissa and Sandalwood. I certainly could go for that. My shoulders are always aching after all the long hours at my PC. *Primula Porter Facial Supreme and Extra Special Mud Exfoliating Treatment, with sauna and steam bath, optional.* Or how about a *Detoxifying Dead Sea Body Wrap with Seaweed and Essential Oils.* Or *Slendertone Slimdown.* Now that I could do with.

I peer at myself in the reflecting glass of the large window opposite. My thighs look like they're bulging across the sofa. Is my waist spilling over the top of my belt? No, I daren't go down that path again. I change position so I can no longer see my reflection and put the brochure back. I could never afford their prices anyway. I'm not hard up on the salary the university is paying me, but definitely not in this league. I pick up my drink again, trying not to spear my lips on a cocktail stick, and watch a group of suntanned Scandinavians stroll in from the sun terrace, with Chanel shoulder bags and Gucci loafers. As they disappear towards the Sauna and Treatment Rooms, a fat American couple in Raybans waddles in from the pool. Even I'm not that overweight. I can't help staring in fascination at the wife's wobbling hippopotamus bum. I hope I don't look like that from behind. Maybe I do. Her tan is orange and her eyebrows seem stuck in the wrong position on her forehead. A thick crust of face powder can't hide multiple face lifts. Michelin Man complains loudly that the lobster isn't as good as in the Paris Hilton, while orange tan whines that the sea is not as blue as at Cannes, then mercifully the lift sweeps them away.

I return to the brochure again and study the price list. It's criminal. A single body treatment could feed one of those Arab families in the refugee camp at Jericho for months. Pictures flash across my mind - Palestinian boys fishing footballs from open-sewered streets, newly-laundered washing strung across cockroach-infested walls, dogs scavenging in the same piles of garbage the children use for goals. I toss the brochure back on the table. It's not so attractive anymore. I glance at my watch, then pick up a copy of Marie Claire left on the table and scowl at the pouting super-waifs parading across the fashion pages. I mean, how the hell are real women supposed to look like that - and I'm actually really glad to see Ben when he pushes through the doors.

The sun is sinking behind the Mount of Olives by the time we approach Jerusalem, bathing the city in rose-coloured light. This is really a beautiful place. It's a terrible shame it has so many problems.

"Are you're glad you came to Jerusalem?" Bern takes his eyes off the traffic for a moment.

"Of course. Thanks for taking me to Ein Gedi. It's been a fascinating day. I hope I haven't disturbed your schedule too much."

"Nonsense." He swerves to avoid a motorcyclist on pizza delivery then straightens the wheel again. "I told you, I had to go and check up on the dig. Actually, I had a really nice day too. It makes a change to have the company of someone other than academics and wet-nosed undergraduates."

"So I'm not an academic?"

"You know what I mean."

I know exactly what he means, but to keep him sweet I smile at his sexist remark. MCPs are part of the course. You can't climb the ladder without playing the game.

"Have you got anything planned for this evening?"

"I have to see to my dog. He'll be getting

hungry."

"How about I take you home to feed your mangy mutt, then we go for a drink in the Old City? Just to round off the day."

Oh my God, what do I say? I' m so used to making excuses not to go out in the evenings I've forgotten how it feels. There isn't really any reason for me not to go. He's not that bad, and, let's face it, my social calendar is hardly crammed. I shan't be entertaining Antonio Banderas tonight. More like watching Friends with sub-titles and unsynchronised Hebrew spouting from Jennifer Anniston's mouth. But a drink with Dr God... (Maybe that's not fair. He's been quite nice today.) I mean, is that wise? Perhaps he just feels sorry for me. And there's poor Cruiser. That's it, I can't.

"I really mustn't leave my dog on his own any longer."

"We could stop off for a bottle of wine and have a drink at your place. Don't worry, I won't keep you up talking all night."

Help. I haven't really got any other excuse. I hope I haven't left any underwear drying in the bathroom, or my Jackie Collins book on the settee, or... hell, he'll just have to take things as he finds them. And socialising with the experts is hardly going to harm my career, is it: I take a deep breath. "That would be nice. As long as you don't mind my mangy mutt covering your trousers with hair. He's moulting."

"So long as he doesn't cover me with fleas."

When we arrive in East Jerusalem, Ben parks the Landrover in a side road.

"There's a place round the corner that sells a good choice of quality wine. Come on, you can choose. Just to prove I'm not a total domineering bully."

I'm really not sure if this is a good idea. But Dr Hewitt did say I should get used to socialising again. And it can get a bit tedious on my own every night. Not that I get lonely or anything. I'm still trying to rack my brains to remember if I've left anything embarrassing lying around the flat when a loud blast rips through the air and the whole street shakes. Dust and debris go flying everywhere and people I can't see are yelling close by. Earthquake, it has to be. What am I supposed to do? Run?
Where? Inside or out? A cloud of thick black smoke uncoils like an eel behind a nearby apartment block, and I've barely had time to register what's going on when a crowd of some ten or twelve Arabic youths comes rushing around the corner.

"Oh fuck!" says Ben, and grabs my arm.

The boys hurl rocks and stones behind them. A couple only look about ten and... I've seen this on TV, but it's different when it's for real. A volley of gunshots sends the youths fleeing down the street towards us and at the end of the road I catch a fleeting cameo of soldiers, in the khaki and green of the IDF, raising of their guns in our direction.

Ben and I dive simultaneously into a doorway.

Pressed up close against the warmth of his jacket, I can hear Ben's heart beating like artillery, then I realise it's not his, it's mine. A young Palestinian is dragged past us, bleeding, by his friends, leaving a smear of scarlet across the paving not six inches away from my feet.

Something whizzes past my head and I gag at the stench of petrol as an explosion racks the Israelis' end of the street. Ben is yelling something at me but I can't hear for gunfire.

It could be an earthquake. Everything is shaking, but it's not, it's me. Yet it's bizarre, for I could be killed any second, but all I feel is a deep sense of calm while mayhem fills every atom of this Jerusalem street.

We're not the only ones caught in this madness. There's a Palestinian crouched by the wall across the street, trying to shield a young boy, no older than Abdul, whose face is contorted by sobs of fear. He's trying to drag the boy further along the wall but can't reach the shelter of a doorway without risking the hail of Israeli bullets. Then a huge crash shakes the around and I can no longer see them for dust and smoke.

"Mortars!" Ben's voice sounds hoarse and far-away.

The street falls strangely quiet and suddenly I feel like I'm watching a film but somehow I've got trapped on the screen.

A group of soldiers rushes past our doorway, boots thumping on the concrete, in pursuit of the fleeing youths. Their rocks and petrol bombs are no match for Israeli shells.

When the smoke clears, I can just make out

the Palestinian opposite, still cowered against the wall, whimpering and praying. His son lies limp in his arms, his head lolling backwards. He's not crying any more.

"Brandy. I think we need it."

Ben thrusts the bottle into my lap and fishes in his pocket. His car keys rattle and he has trouble getting the key in the ignition. "How far is your place?"

"Just off Derekh Shkem."

We don't speak as we drive through the city. At one point we're shooting past a building site, when Ben pulls up sharply, parks all skew-whiff, and rushes behind a crane, clutching his hand across his mouth. When he returns his face is an odd shade of puce despite his tan. And do you know? I am so surprised. I thought I had some kind of monopoly on the act of throwing up.

We arrive at my flat and Cruiser, bless him, jumps up at us with excited barks and tries to lick both our faces. He doesn't understand.

"He'll calm down in a moment." I crouch down to give him a hug, and his fur is soft and reassuring.

Ben's face has not returned to its normal colour.

"Sit down," I tell him. "I'll feed the dog. You'd better open that bottle."

I hand Ben a tumbler, and as I turn to the kitchen, I can hear the chinking of glass as he struggles to pour himself a drink.

When I return, the tumbler is half empty. Ben sits with his eyes closed, cradling the glass in his lap, his head resting against the back of the sofa.

I pour some mineral water for myself and sit down. Ben opens his eyes. "That's not brandy."

"Perrier."

"You've just seen a kid killed and you're drinking water?"

Cruiser pads back, having licked his bowl clean, and jumps into my lap. I stroke his head and wonder what you're supposed to do when you've seen a child die.

"Sorry." Ben puts his glass on the coffee table and sits forward, running his hands through his hair.

"No need. Here, have some more brandy." "Does that thing have a name?

"Abdul's named him Cruiser. "After Tom Cruise."

"S'pose that's as good a name as any. Who's Abdul?"

"The little boy who lives upstairs. He takes care of him while I'm at work."

"So, Ms Armour-plating, you're friends with dogs and children."

Ben attempts a smile and pours the brandy down his throat. "Maybe that's where I go wrong."

Ms Armour-plating? Is that how people see me?

"Sorry. Forget I said that. Christ, look at me. My hands won't stop shaking. Not exactly the great macho hero, am I?"

"Nor was Indiana Jones." I manage to force a smile, though I don't know if it's any more convincing than his."

"You're very calm. You're a brave lady, Charlotte."

I don't know what to say.

"I'm a total coward, Charlotte. About everything."

He finishes his second glass in one go and reaches for the bottle.

I sip my perrier slowly. I can't believe what I'm hearing. Not coming from him. Surely this top-rate professional doesn't suffer selfdoubt. He doesn't know me. I'm not brave at all. If he really knew what I was like, he'd be disgusted. I can't even cry for that dead boy. Maybe it'll hit me later. I just don't know what to say. One minute we're going to buy a bottle of wine, the next we're cowering in a doorway with petrol bombs and gunfire whizzing round our heads and I'm just sitting in this weird state of calm when I should be throwing hysterics. I push away the picture of that dead boy hanging limp in his father's arms, but I know that later, it'll join the rerun of all those others.

Ben drops his glass on the floor. Cruiser jumps down and looks reproachful as I get to my feet. Ben searches for something to mop up the brandy stain but ends up cutting his hand on the glass.

"Shit!"

I get a wad of paper towels and sit down beside him. "Let me do it." I hold his hand in my lap and press the towel over the cut until it stops bleeding. "There, that'll be OK. I'll go and get you a plaster." But as I'm about to stand up, Ben's fingers close around mine.

"Wait. Don't go." He tilts my chin towards him."

Oh no. I'm not ready for this. It's the last thing I need. Especially not with someone like him. He's gone through three wives and has probably as much emotional baggage as me. But it's been such a long time and there's something very reassuring and warm about being in his arms. I can feel Cruiser pawing at my leg and I really must pull away, but before I know it my arms are sliding around Ben's back and I'm not sure what the hell I'm doing. My body seems to have forgotten it's me who tells it what to do. I should stop this, now. But his lips are on my mine and, oh no, it's already too late.

Fragment 5

That night came a band on the door. "Open, in the name of the King!"

"I *told* you," I whispered. "Rahab, I said those men would bring us trouble."

"Their God will bring far more trouble than the king," whispered Rahab, pushing aside the goat skins and jumping from our sleeping platform.

"If Timnal was here, he'd have stopped you bringing

103

them into our house." I was on my feet too. Little Hadad and Tarasch were rubbing their eyes, stirring beneath the skins. How I wished my elder brother had not gone on that hunting trip with the men. He'd have put paid to Rahab's madness.

"Hush," I whispered. "Go back to sleep."

Rahab was already at the door.

She pinned on her smile as she opened to the soldiers of the King. "Good evening. What brings you here so late?"

Three of our soldiers stepped inside.

Hadad and Tarasch were sitting up amid the skins, staring wide-eyed at the men. I tried to get them to lay down but in vain. I felt a deep pit of fear open in my gut.

"My apologies, Priestess," began their commander. "Have you seen the Habiru?"

"Habiru?" said Rahab.

"Yes," said a soldier, raising his flame and peering into the darkness of our home. He stepped up to the sleeping platform and pulled back the skins. Hadad and Tarasch stared back. The soldier crouched on the floor and pulled away some jars so he could hold his torch to the blackness of the storage space below. A rat ran out and scurried across his feet. He cursed, then made certain there was no one hiding there, before getting to his feet.

The second soldier tramped away. "I'll check the roof." My heart began to race and a river of sweat ran down my back.

The commander bowed to Rahab then turned away. He seemed embarrassed. "Word has reached the King that two spies sent by Joshua were seen entering your house."

"Spies?" said Rahab.

"Two men, strangers," said the commander. "One short and stocky. The other tall and strongly built. They speak our language, but strangely."

"Oh, yes, two such men came to me," said Rahab. "But I did not know where they had come from. I thought they were traders from Gebal passing through. I gave them water and stew, then as darkness fell, and it was time for the city gate to close, they left."

Hadad threw his little wooden goat at the soldier's head. I held my breath. The soldier rubbed his head and scowled at Hadad.

His companion returned from searching the roof.

"I climbed up and looked around but no one was there, Sir."

I began to breathe again and offered a silent

prayer to Astarte.

"Were they really spies?" said Rahab. "I had no idea they were Habiru."

"They're spying out our land for Joshua," said the commander. "Which way did they go?"

"I do not know," said Rahab. "But they have not been gone long. Hurry." She pointed to the darkness beyond the door. Go after them. You may yet catch them up."

"Thank you." The commander bowed to Rahab. "Sorry to disturb you, Priestess. Come!" He called to his men. "Quick. Let's get after those spies!"

"Rahab, what do you think you're playing at?" I rounded on her furiously. "If they had found...."

But she was already outside, watching the soldiers as they headed for the road that leads to the ford of the Jordan. When when they had disappeared from sight, she climbed up to the roof. I followed, certain my sister must be losing her mind. She pulled back the stalks of flax we had laid out to dry. The two men sat up, brushing dry stems from their hair and clothes.

"You are safe," she said. "The King's men have gone."

"Rahab, are you mad?" I grabbed her shoulders and made her look into my face. "These men are our enemies."

"Little sister, listen..."

"Don't little sister me! You listen! Joshua sent them to spy. He wants to conquer Jericho and from here make all of Canaan his!"

"But.. .

"But nothing! "I wanted to shake her, make her see she was leading us into dangerous territory indeed. "Rahab, do you realise what you have done? They were our men, down there, protecting our city. You lied to them. Yet you keep our enemies safe."

Sechem stood up. He smiled at me, the snake. "We are not your foe."

"You are! And I will scream it from these city walls so all of Jericho will know you are here!" I let go of Rahab and turned to rush to the edge of the roof. Before me lay the sleeping houses of Jericho. Behind me yawned the blackness of space, for our house was built into the walls of the city, high above the plain.

But Rahab caught my hand. "Sister, just listen. Think of your little brother and sister, now lying peacefully below. Would you have them slaughtered where they lie?"

107

"That is why I want you to turn these spies over to our King! Before they get the chance."

"Listen." Rahab sank to her knees and pulled me down on the flax beside her. The two spies sat down too, close by the edge, watching the darkened streets below like hawks."

"Sister, I have seen the signs."

I could see the whites of Rahab's eyes, that frightened antelope look.

"What signs?"

"A nest of mice in the corn, huddled together, safe and warm." Rahab looked up at the sky where a bank of dark cloud hid the moon. "Then a hawk dived from above and devoured them, every one."

"So?" I looked at the spies and scowled.

"Sister, I am a Priestess of Astarte. I can read the signs. That nest is Jericho and Joshua is the hawk. It is destiny. Their One God is more powerful than all of ours."

"Rubbish! You should know better. You are a Priestess of Jericho, Rahab. And if you won't act like one then I will."

I leapt to my feet but before I could run to the edge and scream to all Jericho that the spies were here, a hand clamped around my mouth and strong arms dragged me back down on the flax.

"Don't hurt her." I heard Rahab say as I struggled to free myself from Sechem's grip. I tried to bite his hand but even as I opened my mouth, Labor forced the rough cloth of his belt into my mouth and tied it behind my head so I could only gurgle furiously in my throat. Sechem used his to bind my hands behind my back then tied my ankles with binding from the stalks of flax. I could only lie there and glare at Rahab and the spies.

"We will not hurt her," Sechem stood close to Rahab and looked into her eyes, tilting her chin towards his face.

"I have seen the signs," said Rahab. "I have read the entrails of the lambs sacrificed at the Stones. I have seen the stars of doom rip through the nighttime sky. And I have heard terrible stories of what your God and his people have done."

I tried to wriggle towards the steps but Labor rolled me back with his foot.

"Travellers passing through have told us what happened at Jahaz, Aroer and Heshbon," Rahab continued.

I marvelled that a Priestess could harbour such

fear in her voice. Why didn't she call on Astarte to lend her courage? The Goddess only knew, she needed it badly.

"I know he has promised your people our land," she said. "And truly, though people laugh at the idea of your landless tribes taking the whole of Canaan, in our hearts we fear your God."

Sechem reached out and stroked her hair.

Rahab trembled. "We are melting in fear because of you."

I wanted to scream and spit and tugged at my cords but Sechem had bound them tight. How dare she talk of our people like that to the Habiru!

Rahab's voice grew low and her eyes widened in wonder. "We have heard how your God dried up the Sea of Reeds for you, when you came out of Egypt. How he took the form of a pillar of fire. And what you did to Sihon and Og."

At least those two kings of Jordan put up a fight, I wanted to yell. Instead of handing over their cities without a squeak, as my sister was doing.

"No one can beat us," said Labor.

"Joshua has the power of the new One God behind him," said Sechem. "Sweet as you are, you're on the wrong

side. Your ancient gods are dying. No one can stop the One God and he has promised that Canaan shall be ours."

"I knew that when I heard how you destroyed the Amorite kings," said Rahab. "And the omens said that Jericho would fall the same way. My stomach is sick for fear of you and your God. For I know what he can do."

My stomach is sick too, I wanted to scream. Sick at the cowardice of my sister.

Then Rahab flung herself at the feet of Sechem and clutched around his ankles.

It was a good thing my mouth was bound, for I would have thrown up all my vegetable stew on the flax.

Rahab's long hair tumbled wildly about her face as she looked up and begged him. "Please, I have shown kindness to you by not turning you over to our King. Now promise me, in the name of your God, you will spare the lives of my family and save them from death."

So that was her game. I glared. My wrists were hurting and my mouth was cut.

"Our lives for your lives," promised Sechem. If you don't tell what we are doing, we will treat you kindly and faithfully when the Lord gives us the land."

"Even this one," laughed Labor, and nudged me with his foot.

I thought I would burst. But I was innocent then. Jericho was still standing and Tarasch slept peacefully beneath the goat skins. I thought I was angry, but in half a cycle of the moon, I would know such passion as would pour hot lava through my veins and fire my every cell with rage.

Chapter 5

I feel so stupid, creeping down the corridor like this, but with any luck, I might just sneak past Dr Schlott's office unnoticed. It's a good thing there's no one else around. I'm not very good at this and probably look like Buffy the Vampire the Slayer on a very bad day. So far I've managed to avoid showing Dr Schlott my latest translations but I won't be able to stall him much longer. Good, his door's closed. I hurry past, scuttle round the corner - and bump straight into someone coming the opposite way.

"Oh, I'm sorry." And boy, am I sorry. This encounter is going to sap the dregs of my self-esteem right out of me for a week. She's so thin I could scream. And her face is glowing with that foundation which looks so natural that no one would know it's out of a pot - except beauty editors and paranoid studiers of other women like me. Her hair is blonde and cut short, with precision, and I instantly feel like an eighties reject with all these curls. The handbag is Gucci and matches her shoes. As for the suit, well, I could never justify spending so much money on something like that - all the starving children and stuff - but I can't help eying up the cut. She smiles, without really seeing me, and leaves me standing in a cloud of Chanel, while her Guccis tap-tap on the floor. I am just wondering how many Cadbury's Twirls it would take to make me feel better when - would you believe it - she knocks at

Schlott's door. Hell! I'd better get out of here. I hurry on down the corridor, squirming with shame as my Marks and Sparks court shoes squeak.

I wonder if I can avoid Ben as well as Schlott. I could die at the thought of running into him in this awfully cold light of the morning after. I bet he's wishing he hadn't done it. Why on earth would a successful archaelogist want to sleep with a no hoper, fatty-in-waiting like me? I'll have to make sure I let him know I understand it was just a one off, didn't mean a thing. If he knew what I did to stay slim, he wouldn't touch me with his archaelogy trowel. It's going to be so awkward I could curl up and die. Oh God, and there's Ingrid. Ben laughed when I asked him and told me there's nothing between them. But he would say that. I'm sure she's burning a torch for him. She's been friendly enough, but will all that change? And as for my professional credibility... what if if word gets out? Sleeping with a colleague is not exactly a helpful addition to your CV. I mean, can you imagine the whispers? "There's that slut from Ancient Semitic... she'll sleep with anyone to get on, you know...." Oh God, please let me creep into my office without running into anyone from Archaeology.

What the...? I stop dead in front of the central office. My briefcase drops to the floor. There are two uniformed security guards at the door. Both spin round at the noise, guns at their hips. I am frozen to the spot. The guards relax. My briefcase still lies on the floor and one of them picks it up. Just for a moment I thought...

"Boker tov. Your pass, please."

"Yes, of course." I give him a smile along with my ID. As soon as they've nodded me through, I push through the swing doors and march up to Ingrid. "What's with the testosterone excess?"

Ingrid looks up from her desk. "Sorry?"

"The guards outside."

She shrugs. "Dr Schlott's instructions. He says security is to be stepped up, because of the interest that's been shown in those tablets of yours."

"I see."

I search for my cigarettes and light up the minute I sit at my desk. There's a note left here for me. It's from Yusef, to say he's partly sorted the problem so I can use the computer again. Huh. Great. Apparently, he has an urgent job at the study centre but he'll get back as soon as pos. I chuck it in the bin. So my work doesn't rank up there with Ben's wet-nosed under-grads. Sod Yusef. Sod everyone.

I take a drag on the Marlboro and blow the smoke into the air. Funny, the cigarette seems to be trembling. You know, this was how it all started, with security on the door. Jonathon was on duty in the Gallery of the Ancient Levant. I was always friendly with the security people, used to say "Hi," "Had a good weekend?", "How are the kids?"... you know, like you do. Jonathon was no different. Or so I thought at the time. I even invited him along with the rest of the department when we went to the pub to celebrate Michaela's promotion. Was I stupid or what? I suppose I felt sorry for him really. He seemed lonely. He had told me once he lived alone in a bedsit in Kentish Town. I should have saved my pity for myself. God knows, I was going to need it. We sat in those faded velvet bays of the Rose and Crown on the corner of Museum Street, talking about work and music mostly. We both were Prodigy fans, though that was about as far as shared tastes went. He spent hours alone at night, he told me, lying on his bed, listening to Pearl Jam, Nine Inch Nails and Rage Against the Machine. I guess I should have known then.

We didn't really have much in common. I was a suburbia girl from the posher part of Folkestone, he came from a council estate in Luton. I had read Near Eastern Languages at the School of Oriental and African Studies, he had dropped out of Luton Art College. He was good at drawing, though. Perhaps if he'd stuck with it things might have turned out differently for him, and for Dumbo here. Talk about a bad judge of character. That's me all over. But I just laughed, poor bloody fool, when he showed me his caricatures of Lucy Goldsmith, my Head of Department at Western Asiatic and eventually, when we ran out of things in common, I left Jonathon analysing Arsenal's flat back four with the assistant curator, while I argued with Michaela and Anthony about the relationship of Akkadian cuneiform to hieroglyphs. When I got up to get another drink, Jonathon was gone.

A few times, returning home on dark winter evenings, I turned round in the street, convinced that someone was behind me, but there never was, or so I thought.

After I had praised his caricatures, Jonthon brought me more of his sketches. He really did have talent. When the illustrator's job came up, I suggested he apply. How bloody stupid can you get? Just asking for it, wasn't I? Maybe the defence barrister was right and I led him on. Jonathon had no faith he would even be considered for the post, but applied anyway and insisted on buying me a huge box of Milk Tray when he got the job. Maybe he'd been watching the adverts. I tried to refuse, I mean, *me!* Can you imagine it? With a 21b box of Cadbury's? But Jonathon wouldn't take no for an answer. He'd been good at his work. It was a pity held never learnt to channel his obsessions, instead of nurturing enough chips on his shoulder to rival MacDonalds. The father he never knew, his childhood as a latch-key kid in a damp council flat, his mother who split her time between cleaning work and the pub, the teachers who had put him down... you know the kind of stuff. It had all come out in court, social workers' reports which the defence had put forward as 'mitigating circumstances.' Well how do you 'mitigate' all the terror I went through? I wish some bloody social worker would tell me that. I still see shadows at the end of the road in my dreams. But I just sat there, like I always do, Miss Goody Shoes in in my black Oasis suit, no Chanel or Gucci for me, staring ahead with my hands in my lap, and listened to it all.

I've never been able to take control of my life.

I suppose that's my trouble. It's always been someone else dictating how I feel. When the letters dropped onto my mat, and the phone rang late at night with silence on the other end, when the footsteps crunched behind me in the dark alley to the tube, Jonathon was out there, stoking up my fear and stuffing it into his mouth to feed his hateful pleasure. And you know, that sicko sat at his desk opposite mine, watched me as I worked, and listened as I poured out my anguish over coffee.

I couldn't believe it when the police finally caught him. He had been looking up at the light in my window, from the phone box at the end of the road. Not Jonathon. Not someone I knew. Not someone who had sympathised, as I poured out my heart. That's what really hurt. Like needles under my nails.

I stub out my Marlboro. At least Yusef has fixed my computer enough to get down to some work. I just want to lose myself in someone else's world, and her tragedy puts my stupid, feeble self-pity to shame.

"Mail for you, just arrived." Ingrid pops her head round the door and I instantly feel guilty. Does she know? I feel like I've got a dunce's cap on and a sign round my neck with 'I Slept With Ben' in great black letters. She drops the letters onto my desk and breezes out. I flick through the mail, then freeze. Oh no. This can't be possible. Not here. How could he have tracked me to Israel? I mean, I was only just thinking about him. Have I somehow conjured his presence by my thoughts? My evil genie?

On the top of the pile is the spidery handwriting I have learnt to dread. But as I stare at the envelope, the chill in my stomach inflames into anger I throw the sodding letter on the desk I am shaking with rage. I've never felt like this before. How dare he! How the hell has he got hold of my address? It'·s taken me months to feel safe again. I thought with thousands of kilometres between us, and him behind prison bars, I would never have to hear from him again. Now here he is, sending his sick raving letters, intruding on the new life I have created from the ashes of the one he destroyed for me in London. I came here to escape the memories imprinted on the streets of Bloomsbury. Now he's trying to poison Jerusalem for me too. Well, I won't let him. Not this time. Don't they monitor their mail in prison, for heaven's sake? I'll have to phone the police who handled my case, make sure they damn well stop him writing to me with any more of his filth. I tear the letter into tiny pieces, unread, and drop them into the bin. I'll make that call later. Meanwhile I've got work to do. Jonathon is not going to sink his venom into my life anymore.

I slump back in my chair and look at my watch. Christ, I've been working on the fragments all day with barely a break. I feel like I've just done a marathon across the desert as well. The Hebrews will kill her, horribly, if they find out what she's done. I can just see Joshua's fury, and the hatred burning in his dark eyes which turns into Jonathon's. I'll never forget how he looked when I rejected his perverted professions of love. I denounced him in front of everyone, the clerks, the judge, the journalists and the public gawping from the gallery. That whole damned court.

"You bitch!" he yelled. "I only wanted you to love me! I'll get you back for this!" His curses spat in my ears as he was taken down to the cells, and I walked out of court with flashbulbs popping and my knees like jelly.

I fish in my handbag for my organiser and find Detective Inspector Whitehead's number but when I dial 0044 a recorded message announces that all lines to the United Kingdom are busy. I slam down the receiver. The telephone rings almost at once.

"Charlotte?" I could just melt when I hear that voice. It's like aloe vera on sunburn. Maybe I'm not just a one night stand. Perhaps he does care, just a little, though God knows I don't deserve anyone's affection, and I could cry as a fresh surge of happiness washes away past pain. But it doesn't last long. It never does, does it.

"I'm calling from the airport. Maddy rang. Tony's taken a turn for the worse. I'm having to go to the States. Look, I've got to get through all the security checks before take-off. It's even worse than usual with the recent riots. I'll call you."

I'll call you. Huh. Surely someone of his intellectual calibre could come up with a less cliched brush-off than that. I put down the phone. Suddenly it all comes rushing in on me at once - Ben, the death of that boy, the dread I thought I had left behind in London returning with a toss of a letter on my desk. I feel drained, like one of those Egyptian mummies whose innards have been scooped out and poured into jars, and my loneliness is that of the tomb.

Damn. I've split my best fingernail on the sellotape trying to repair my Book of Joshua. Half the pages are loose and it's battle-scarred with dog-eared page markers and old coffee stains. I love my books when they get like this.

God knows how Ben will react to the Ark destroying whole cities
like Gibeon and Ai. He was pacing up and down like some demented tiger just over a pot breaking. Actually, I don't know what to make of this myself. I'm relying on the publication of this work to catapult my name into the international academic arena. I can't afford be bracketed with the Loony Ark Brigade. But I have my personal integrity too and I just can't see this girl imagining things, whatever Dr Know-it-all says. Psychotic, do me a favour. Sometimes he really pisses me off. He can't know her the way I can. He doesn't work with her words every day.

He's always so certain he's right, but he can't know it it was only religious superstition which made people fear the Ark. Archaeology can only go so far. I mean, how can you hope to piece together whole civilisations from a few tombs and shards of pottery. Talk about jigsaws with pieces missing. More like paint your own.

No archaeologist was in Jericho when the

walls came crashing down, but Rahab's sister was.

The remainder of the fragments are teasing me from their case. Sometimes I forget to eat or drink, or just keep going on coffee. I never worked like this even during my finals. It's like an obsession. I have to know how this story ends. When I go to bed at night, I lie there and see the day's translation all over again, as my mind plays action replays over the ceiling in the dark. Often I forward wind as well, my imagination filling in I what might find in tomorrow's fragment. I have to find out if the Canaanite girl did manage to pull off a stunt like stealing the secrets of the Ark, and I'm dying to know just what those secrets are.

But she might have failed and had to face the wrath of Joshua and his jealous God. Yet she lived long enough to write her story. I really hope Joshua never caught her. It makes my flesh creep when I think of what he did to Achan and his pathetic family. If he caught his handmaid stealing the most sacred secrets of the ancient world... Joshua's fury doesn't bear thinking about. Nor does Jonathon's. I wish Ben hadn't gone back to the States. I mean, I understand about his son, but damn it, sometimes I need someone to be there for *me*. It's been a long time since I've let my guard down with anyone. After Jonathon I've not exactly been trusting of men. Perhaps I'm being unfair. Of course Ben has to be there for Tony. He'd be a right shit if he wasn't. But was he just using me? Why do I have to be so hopeless and weak? Whatever possessed me to jump straight into bed with Dr Ben Travers, of all people! I hardly even know the man. I despise myself. I don't deserve a decent relationship. He probably finds a new toy to play with from the new intake every academic year then drops it when the novelty wears off. "I'll call you." Huh!

What was I doing? Maybe if it hadn't been for the shock of seeing that poor boy... but it's too late now. At least while he's in the States I won't have to deal with rejection for a bit and I can try and get my head together. I'll have to be more cool about it when he gets back. For now, I'm going put all thoughts of Dr Ben Travers out of my mind and concentrate on work.

My Bible is open at the destruction of Gibeon. Ben was right about one thing. If the Ark did possess an energy source able to set cities alight, it's no wonder we've got Mossad and God knows who else on our tracks. The world is such an unstable place, and mine more than most. Any nutter could have seen that web site. Damn Dr Schlott. I swill the dregs of a long cold coffee round in my mug. I hate to admit it but Ben's probably right and we should keep the contents of the remaining fragments to ourselves for a bit, at least until we can show there's no chance of resurrecting some ancient power. Unless... no, I'm not going down that road. The last thing I need is to get sucked into Loony Ark paranoia. But something tells me I should be glad of the extra security outside the door, even if it does smack of Jonathon. Still, at least he's safely banged up in Pentonville.

I haven't been listening to a word Ingrid's

been saying and I think she's realised this too. She peers at me suspiciously over her coffee cup.

"What time did you work till last night?"

I shrug. "Oh, I don't know exactly."

"Seven, eight?"

"Something like that." Actually it was more like ten.

"Charlotte, you've got dark shadows under your eyes as if someone's punched you. And your face is so pale anyone would think you were living in Iceland, not Israel."

"I've never felt better."

"You're working far too hard on those tablets. If Ben was here, I'm sure he'd be telling you off and dragging you away to some Arabic dive for a break."

"Ingrid, I do not do everything Dr Ben Travers tells me." Anyway, I think bitterly, he's taken off, leaving me stranded on this dung heap of emotional detritus.

"How about coming out with me this evening? "I've got tickets for a fashion show in town."

"A fashion show?" I manage to inject a shot of enthusiasm into my voice, but a fashion show? Christ, and here's me on the verge of finding out the secrets of the Ark of the Covenant! But as I stifle another yawn behind the back of my hand, I wonder if Ingrid's right. I have been working too hard and I can feel the beginnings of a headache behind my eyes. Still, maybe if I take a break I'll get back to it fresher and get on even faster.

"It's at the King David's Hotel," says Ingrid. "A special preview of next season's designs. Dior, Armani, Chanel, Westwood... all the top names will be there."

"You're not thinking of buying anything?" It really annoys me to think how much money they make while the rest of us slog our guts out for comparative peanuts.

"Of course not, but we can still look. My friend at the German Embassy gave me the tickets so we won't have to pay a thing. Come on, it'll be fun. See the top models in the flesh and rub shoulders with the rich and famous."

Top models? Oh great, like Naomi Campbell, Kate Moss and that latest twig on legs, whatever her name is. I'm on swampy emotional ground already. I don't want to get dragged right under by having what I can't be paraded under my less than perfect nose. It's all right for Ingrid. She wouldn't look out of place on a catwalk herself.

"I suppose..."

"Good. That's settled. You need dragging away from that computer. It's not natural. Meet you in the hotel foyer at seven."

As I sip my complimentary cocktail in the bar during the interval and look around at the old world grandeur of the King David, I have to admit I'm glad Ingrid persuaded me to come. That parade of waifs slinking along the catwalk hasn't affected me as badly as it once would have done. There was a time I wouldn't be sitting here in the bar at all but sneaking to the nearest loo to throw up. Actually most of the models in that last collection looked bizarre, all got up in sort of metal string and peacock feather creations that you'd never dream of wearing down to Tesco's. Ingrid kept pointing people out in the audience. Media people, faces from Hello magazine and this whole row of Arabic women, swathed in black from head to toe, buying designer evening dressers from Paris and Milan. Ingrid said they just keep them as collector's items to show off to their friends. Sick-making. If there's one thing I can't stand it's women who've done nothing to earn their wealth.

People are starting to move back to the auditorium. The second half will be starting soon. I wonder where Ingrid has got to. She's been ages in the ladies. She doesn't need to spend hours on her face.

Then across the bar I catch sight of that woman. She's wearing a little black dress. Well, she would, wouldn't she. No doubt made by one of the designers on show tonight. It would look like a sack on me, but she looks like a classically understated million dollars. She's holding her wine glass in such a way that her long scarlet nails are on display. Probably false, but what the hell. I glance at my own bitten raggedy things then begin to torture myself with endless counts of inferiority as I watch her make effortless smalltalk.

"Sorry, you'll never guess who I got talking to..."

Ingrid comes dashing out of the ladies and when I next look, my confidence zapper has gone.

"Yusef, how much longer will this take?" It seems like he's been tinkering around with my computer for hours.

He just sits there frowning at the screen. It must be a very interesting problem to engross him that much. I wish he'd get on with it. I can't do a thing till this is fixed.

"Gotcha! " Yusef clicks on the mouse and this weird layout slides down the screen.

"Yes, as I suspected." He spins round on the chair.

"Well? Is it fixed? Was it a virus?"

"No. You've been hacked."

"What?"

"Whatever you're working on is interesting somebody." Yusef pushes his hair from his eyes. "Quite a few people, in fact. I've managed to get a trace on them."

I don't like the sound of this. "Mossad, by any chance?"   Yusef's eyes gleam. "Ah, so you've encountered them already?" "What about the others?"

"Not so easy to identify. Three locations in the States - New York, Alabama and Los Angeles - one in Geneva, and one in Southern Lebanon."

"Can you tell who they are?"

Yusef shakes his head. "Sorry, I'm familiar with Mossad's systems but as for the others, I can only give you the location."

I sit down, as the realisation hits me. "So these people have tapped into all my files so far?"

"'fraid so."

This is serious. Those last fragments told how Joshua used the Ark Ark to destroy the armies of Canaan's greatest cities, even though he was vastly outnumbered. This isn't the sort of stuff we want broadcast. So much for keeping things quiet.

"You sure must be onto something interesting, Miss Adams." Yusef is watching me with interest as he toys with his worry beads. "Can you stop them from hacking into my work again?"

"I can try but I can't guarantee it.

"So unless I don't use the computer I can't be sure of keeping my work confidential?"

"That's about it." Yusef is curious, I can tell, but he doesn't ask questions.

I sigh in frustration and push back my hair. "Then I'll just have to write everything up by hand."

"It would be safer, if you've got things you don't want people to see. But give e a call if you need anything else." "Thanks Yusef."

"Any time." He picks up his bag which is plastered in Greenpeace stickers. "So long."

I turn off the PC and take a block of paper

from my drawer. Damn it. This is really going to slow me down but I can't risk any more leaks."

I've barely started when, the telephone rings. Am I going to get any work done today., for Christ's sake?

"Yes?"

"Charlotte, Hermann Schlott here. I was wondering if you have any more translations for me. I have an investor interested and it would be helpful to see some more."

"I've finished up to Fragment 19," 1 lie.

"Splendid. Would you give them to Ingrid? She can drop them in to me with the post."

I breathe a sigh of relief as I put down the 'phone, but I can't avoid giving him the more outrageous fragments for long. I wish Ben were here. At least then I'd have a partner in crime, and keeping it hushed up it was his idea. He still hasn't phoned. I suppose he's busy with hospital visits - unless... oh sod him. I'm just going to bury myself in work. Ancient Aramaic is far easier to understand than men.

Ingrid comes in with the post, and after I've binned the junk mail, and shoved the student loan reminder to the back of a drawer, I'm left with two and letters. The first is from Susan Hewitt, saying she's glad I'm doing so well. Am I? I wonder. But it's good to hear from her.

When I've finished I look at the remaining envelope, plain white and neatly typed. I hope it's from Sarah. She promised to keep in touch though she's a lousy letter writer and usually sends e-mails. But this has a Tel Aviv postmark.

A single sheet of typing paper slides out. The message is cut from newsprint.   Four words only.

I AM WATCHING YOU.

It feels like someone has kicked me in the stomach. My first thought is Jonathon. This is the sort of thing he would do. But he got eighteen months for stalking me and hasn't served anything like that yet. Besides, this letter is from Israel. What do I do? Bin it? Or keep it in case it's ever needed as evidence? I shove it to the back of my drawer with the loan reminder. Then I sit up straight and carefully reorganise the top of my desk. Paperclips and elastic bands go in their own little holders. The pens I separate into red, blue and black. Then I clean every trace of grime from the desk tidy. I use up a whole packet of tissues until everything on display is perfect.

Then I walk over to the window and stare out across the city; the city to which I escaped. But somewhere out there, someone is playing the same game with me here.

"Miss Adams?"

I turn round on the steps outside the university, wondering who is keeping me from going to lunch, and see a middle-aged Arab in a smart western suit coming briskly towards me.

"Yes?"

"Faisal Hamad Zaid." He stretches out his hand and flashes a broad white smile.

"Do I know you?"

"Miss Adams, I am a business associate of Dr Ben Travers. I understand he is away at present?"

"So what do you want with me? Look, I'm on my way..."

"Miss Adams, please." He places a hand on my arm. "Just a moment of your time. Dr Travers and I have come to arrangements in the past. I am a dealer in antiquities and sometimes I have put very special items his way, at a very special price."

"Oh yes?" I say flatly. I've heard that one before and carry on down the steps."

"No wait, Miss Adams. I know about the tablets you are working on and I have information which may be of use."

I stop and glare at him. I'm really not in the mood, not after that message.

He looks around and when he sees no one else is within earshot, he say in a low vice, "The Ein Gedi Fragments."

"I don't know what you're talking about."

"I may be able to get you more. Be in the Botanical Gardens at..." "I'm not meeting you anywhere."

"Then you will lose the opportunity. There are many other buyers." He shrugs and turns to leave.

Think, quickly. What do I do? It would be awful to miss out on something genuine. It's not unheard of for other relics from a cache to turn up. Local people keep their ears to the ground and when they hear of a major find they sometimes know where to lay their hands on a similar lot. But there are plenty of fakes and I've no intention of meeting this man in some isolated spot. No way will I put myself at risk, especially now.

"Wait."

He half turns on the steps.

"I will meet you, but not in the gardens. Somewhere crowded and public."

"As you wish. Cafe Malkha, on Sultan Suleiman, eight o'clock tomorrow evening." Then he goes quickly down the steps and melts into the crowd that flows down the street.

What the hell have I let myself in for? At least Sultan Suleiman is a busy main boulevard. I'm unlikely to get kidnapped or anything there. But I shall damn well make sure I stay firmly among the crowds. Maybe this Faisal bloke has something to do with the message. I can't be sure of anything or anyone any more, and I can feel that wretched headache coming on as I make my way down the road to the sandwich bar.

This is very strange. Maybe I should go for Dead Sea Mud treatment if this is what it did for Joshua and Caleb. I lay the fragment aside and reach for my Bible. It would be even more extraordinary if the Old Testament also states that they had lived to a remarkable old age and would certainly give credence to this strange story I'm translating.

I flick through the pages to the final verses of the Book of Joshua. According to this, he died at the age of a hundred and ten. Caleb's death isn't mentioned but Judges relates that Caleb was still going strong after Joshua was buried. This time scale doesn't make
sense. I've already underlined a quote from Caleb.

I was forty years old when Moses sent me from Kadesh Barnea to explore the land. God has kept me alive for forty five years... so here am I today, eighty-five years old! I am still as strong today as the day Moses sent me out. I'm just as vigorous to go out to battle now as I was then.

Pull the other one. But the Bible and the fragments correlate
exactly. What the hell am I supposed to make of this?
When I check the ages at death of some of the earlier patriarchs,
things get even freakier.
Joseph - 110.
Abraham - 175.
Aaron - 123.
Moses - 120.

It's mad but I think I'm onto something here.There's a quote about Moses that echoes that of Caleb.
Yet his eyes were not weak, nor his strength

133

gone.

Here are two completely separate sources suggesting that the Holders of the Ark really did have something that kept them young. If that stuff was around today, I bet Mrs Facelift at the Regency Shalom would be first in the queue.

As I scribble down the ages of the Hebrew leaders, I find the further back in time I look, the more outrageous they become. I mean, look at this lot.

Shem - 500.
Noah - 950.
Enoch- 905.

And the list goes on. Of course no serious scholar is going to take the Bible literally, but there's a very odd pattern emerging here. If... and it's a whopping great if.. if there are any grains of truth in the scriptures, it's looking like the Hebrew leaders could have possessed the nearest thing ever to immortal youth. Jesus! This is crazy. And did this teenage girl from Jericho steal those secrets from them? That's what I'm burning to know. Of course it's a daft idea, but it would be incredible if were true. I could try and second clues before I finish the translation. If the Bible says the Hebrew leaders after Joshua maintained their youthfulness in old age then she must have failed. But if the indications are that they aged like everyone else, there's a possibility she actually did rob her enemies of their secret of youth. Well, there's one way to find out. I bet even Mrs Lawrence never studied the Bible with the enthusiasm I've got now. Hey, if I learn the secret, I'll never have to envy Naomi and Kate again. They'll be wizened old prunes long after I'm still a plum!

Seriously though, David, according to this edition, ruled Israel for forty years. It says here he died at a good old age, having enjoyed long life, wealth and honour. That's not bad going, though it doesn't say exactly how old he was or if he stayed young and full of vitality. Hang on, what's this? I grab a pen and underline the passage in black.

> *When he was old and well advanced in years, he could not keep warm even when they put covers on him. So they searched for a beautiful virgin to share his bed, but he had no intimate relations with her.*

So he wasn't the randy old bugger that Caleb was in his dotage.

Then I turn to Solomon. Again the Bible says he reigned for forty years but not when he died. Nor does it give Hezekial's. Manasseh, I work out, was sixty seven. In fact, throughout Samuel, Kings and Chronicles, I can't find any one who seems to have stayed young like the earlier leaders.

Christ! This means the secret might have been lost with Joshua and Caleb.

I glance at those fragments which still lie untranslated in the case. It seems incredible but they could reveal that Joshua's handmaid stole the secret of the elexir of youth and took revenge, for Canaan, on whole Hebrew nation. I can't believe I'm actually contemplating this stuff but my palms have grown hot and sticky and I can feel my heart racing. I'll work all night if I have to. It's worth getting bags under the eyes to get to the bottom of this.

I grab another coffee then return to my desk to think about what I know so far. From what the girl described, the Ark possessed two main properties; one healing and rejuvenating, the other dangerous and destructive. The strange cloud which rose from the Ark at Gibeon, the care taken by Joshua to keep his own people well away from it and the odd silver garments worn by the Holders and priests for protection, all suggest some kind of radioactivity. So do the tumours which afflicted the people of Ekron in the later Book 1 of Samuel. The link between the two properties seems to be the flecks of silver, whatever they are, which, though lethal in the case of the cloud, lent the mud its ability to restore health and vitality. I wonder if any scientist today could explain that, or come up with any substance that might fit the bill.

I walk over to the window and gaze out over the rooftops of Jerusalem. Even the academic foundations of my work feel like they're coming unrooted now. I feel like I'm walking on one of those funfair floors with everything wobbling beneath my feet. I've always laughed at the idea of ancient technologies but I'm beginning to wonder if there might be something to it.

The walls of Jericho fell numerous times before Joshua came along. The Jordan valley lies on a double fault line in an earthquake hotspot. Perhaps the walls were already weakened by tremours, but I wonder if it was just coincidence they crashed to the ground right on cue. If Joshua was able to bring the strongest walls in Canaan crashing down, which scholars will no longer be able to dismiss simply as myth when the our new authentic source material in the fragments is published, perhaps it's not so far-fetched that he also had other means at his disposal.

He had, after all, inherited the leadership of the Hebrews from Moses and the powers that went with it, including the Ark. Moses was been raised in a royal house in Egypt and would quite feasibly have been trained by the priests in their secrets at the very highest level. I remember seeing a TV programme which showed how even the top Japanese technology of the 21st century can't replicate the design of the Great Pyramid, which, by all the known laws of physics, should not be standing. Perhaps it's not such a crazy idea that ancient people, who were just as intelligent as today's, possessed knowlege of powers which were lost along with their civilisations. Christ, I really shouldn't be thinking like this.

I turn away from the window. I must keep my heretical thoughts to myself. Ben's right. Lost ancient technologies give the kiss of death to an academic career, even if they're staring me right in the face.

I sit back at my desk and think of that call from him yesterday. We didn't speak for long. Tony needs a bone marrow transplant and the search is on for a suitable donor. I feel sorry for Ben. Maddy sounds like a woodpecker at a rotten tree, tapping and probing for cash which he doesn't have. I could tell from his voice that the strain is taking its toll and by the time I put the receiver down, I felt really guilty about my selfish needs for reassurance that I'm not just another one night fling.

I run my hands through my hair. I need another coffee. Ben's not the only one feeling the strain. I might have stuffed that message to the back of the drawer but the newsprint keeps flashing across my mind. It's odd that someone is threatening me. You'd think that anyone interested in the fragments wouldn't want to let on they're watching what I do. At least I know Jonathon is safely locked up in jail. Perhaps it was some other sad lonely nutcase who accessed the website. I'm starting to wonder if I attract them. Maybe I do bring all my misfortunes down on myself. But I find it hard to believe such a crude attempt to scare me was Mossad. Surely they don't need to resort to such tactics. Their interest is the Ark, and Dr Schlott needs to raise money. I bet the Israeli government would be more than happy to oblige, in exchange for rights to the fragments. One things for sure, though. I can't pretend much longer I haven't translated as much as I have. I'll have to pass on more fragments soon, but first, I must find out what the rest contain.

I shower, redo my hair and make-up and put on a smart long-sleeved shirt and a fine linen skirt for my meeting with Faisal Hamad Zaid, then leave Cruiser tucking into his Happidog. I'll hear what this so called dealer has to say but I'm not going to take any chances. I doubt if he does have any more fragments. I could kick myself now for not asking Ben about him on the phone, but he was so strung out over Tony, I didn't like to mention the things that are bothering me. Anyway, I'll soon find out what this Arab's game is.

The Cafe Malkha is noisy and crowded. The steel tables and chairs on the pavement outside are all taken and a harassed waiter's trying in vain to serve all the customers shouting for his atttention. There's no sign of this Faisal Hamad Zaid.

It's slightly less crowded inside. I take a a spare table near the door where I have a good view of anyone approaching and can make a quick getaway if I have to.

By the time I've fended off a Morrocan street vendor trying to sell me a watch, an Armenian intent on buying me a drink and an old Ethiopian beggar who keeps says how much she loves Americans, I'm getting pretty fed up. It's now ten past seven. I'll give him five more minutes. I can think of better ways of spending my time.

"Miss Adams?" Two Arab men appear at my table, dressed in jeans and casual shirts. Neither is the man I met on the steps. "Yes?"

"May we sit down?"

"I'm waiting for someone."

"I believe you are waiting for us." The older of the two, slim and neat with a short moustache, pulls up a chair and beckons his burlier companion to sit down.

"Just a minute..."

"You have arranged a meeting with Faisal Hamad Zaid." "Yes, but..."

"It was arranged on our behalf. We would like to talk with you about the work you are doing. It may benefit all of us."

I notice the Arab waiter comes to serve these newcomers at once. The bodyguard, as I guess he is, orders a burger. From the size of him, I'd say he eats them quite a lot.

"So what about these so-called newly discovered artefacts?" I get straight to the point. The first hint I get they're not bona fide dealers, I'm out of here.

"Miss Adams, do you mind if I smoke?"

"Just tell *me* why you're here."

He lights a cigarette and puffs a swirl of smoke into the fug of blue that already hovers over the interior of the cafe. "The notion of further relics was a device to get you to talk to us."

"I thought as much. Who are you?"

"That is not important. We would like to offer you a reward in return for information you find in those tablets. Do you hope to find the Ark itself?""

I nearly burst out laughing. This really is

getting like Indiana Jones. "Of course not. There's nothing in the fragments that would give any idea as to what happened to the Ark."

The two men glance at each other. "We know they tell of... shall we say... a power which can destroy cities. Do the tablets lead to this power source?"

I've had enough of this and stand up. "I really have to go. You're way off the mark. The fragments only relate to the past, not to the present. There's nothing that could interest you, whoever you are, I'm sure."But Beefburger Man is blocking my way to the door.

"Wait," says the negociator. "Please sit down, just for two minutes."

"Two minutes only, then I'll yell the place down if you try and stop me leaving."

"That won't be necessary." He gestures to his sidekick who moves away from the doorway. I can't say I feel exactly reassured.

"You must recognise, Miss Adams, the Israelis are an occupying force in Palestine. They have no right to exist on Arab territory. The Jews must be driven back into the sea. If you help us, if you discover in the tablets a means of..."

"I'm sorry," I say coldly. "I've told you, there is nothing in the tablets that can possibly interest..."

"We have means at our disposal. We can pay you far more than you..." "You're wasting your time." I stand up and glare at Burger man. He glances at his colleague.

"I'm leaving *now.*"

"If you change your mind, you can contact..."

"I won't. Goodbye gentlemen." I glare at this oversized lump in the doorway.

His companion gestures him aside and I push open the door, glad to escape the cigarette fug and feel the cool evening breeze on my face.

As I walk back through the city to my flat, I run through this odd encounter. The Arabs weren't exactly subtle about offering me money in exchange for information about the fragments. Never mind Raiders, this is starting to seem more like some cliched spy movie. In any case, they'd be wasting their time even if I had been the sort to accept a backhander. I mean, I'm the the first person to get excited about the fragments, but even so I can't help feeling that a lot of people are getting very steamed up about a relic which was lost millennia ago and in will doubtless stay that way. I'd love to think the Canaanite girl had succeeded in stealing the secrets of the Ark of the Covenant from under the noses of the priests and guards, but despite my findings in the Bible, I have to admit it's pretty unlikely. Even if she had, there is nothing so far to suggest that her story in the fragments could lead anyone today to the source of its ancient power.

But it's not hard to tell which side of the fence the latest interested party is on. From that remark about driving the Jews into the sea, there's little doubt they belong to one of the radical Moslem organisations who want to see the State of

Israel totally destroyed. Hizbollah, perhaps, Hamas or the Islamic Jihad. According to Yusef, someone has been hacking into my files from Southern Lebanon and I know that all three groups have bases there from which to plan attacks on Israel. Perhaps the group whose members I met tonight sent me the message as a prelude, to scare me into submission before they made their bid.

I cut into an empty side street, where the odours from the back of a Chinese restaurant drift out from a ventilation shaft and mix with those of freshly ground coffee and cinnamon from the rear of an Italian pizzeria. Halfway along, I feel the hairs on the back of my neck begin to bristle. I haven't felt this sensation for a while, not since London, but I recognise it instantly and all my alarm bells start ringing. I spin round. There's no one there. Yet I'm sure someone is watching me. Ben was all too close to the truth when he said that it sounded as if looking over my shoulder had become a habit. I've grown to be an expert on feeling hidden eyes on my back. It's some sort of sixth sense, I suppose, not that I believe in that sort of thing, a legacy, one of many, from Jonathon.

I wait, keeping my eyes on the corner of the empty street, but no one appears. So I start to walk on, then spin round quickly, to see if I can catch them in the act. But I still can't see anyone. I race back to the corner, determined to catch whoever it is. I'm more angry than scared this time and sick to the back teeth of looking over my shoulder. I'll be damned if I let anyone intimidate me again, not even a unit of professional terrorists. I look in both directions along the adjoining street. A few people sit at a table of a grotty looking bar, a gang of children squat over some game on the paving stones and a group of old men are hunched over a backgammon board. No one pays me any attention.

Perhaps I was wrong. I could just be imagining things. I'm jumpy, I suppose. I'm sure the men remained in the cafe and didn't follow me along Sultan Suleiman, for I kept turning back to check. I turn round and carry on walking. It probably is just my imagination - but that was what I told myself before.

Something is wrong. I stop dead in the doorway of my office. My sixth sense again, or maybe it's just paranoia. I can't see anything out of position. Then I catch a hint of a fragrance I'm sure I've smelt before, but I can't quite place it before it's gone. This office is not as I left it last night. I cross the room to my desk and catch just the faintest drift of that fragrance again. Perhaps I'm too jumpy. It could be the cleaners.

My translations, stacked beside my desk organiser, I never leave them like that. I have this ritual of leaving everything neat. If my desk is in order then so is my life. No one else would ever notice but it's one of those funny little things I do. I always make sure the top of the pages line up with the in-tray. Someone's moved them. The bin is empty so the cleaners did come in yesterday, but they never touch my work. I occasionally see the two Filipino women when I've been working late. Maybe a different one came in last night, but I remember passing them on my way out.

Then I notice a smear of black print on the title page and snatch it up for a closer look. It's lighter than all the rest. This is a copy of my original. Why should anyone photocopy my title page and not the whole lot? Or maybe they did. It's easy to confuse masters with copies, especially if you're in a hurry, or trying not to get caught. I've done it myself often enough, slipped the wrong page onto the wrong pile of papers. But the security guards on the door should have stopped any intruders. Unless it wasn't a stranger.

I grab a sheet from the pile and hurry to the photocopier in the main office. The copy which slides out of the machine has the exact same smear as that front sheet of my translation. Both have been copied on this machine.

"What's up?" says Ingrid. "You'll get dreadful wrinkles if you keep frowning like that."

"Oh nothing. Just a bit of a headache."

I return to my office and sit down. Could the Islamic militants have tried to recruit someone else as well? Ingrid, for example, would have ample opportunity to spy. But so would all the other members of the department, a good twenty or thirty including admin. staff. There has to be another copy of my key somewhere in the university which a determined person could get hold of. Then there are the cleaners. Foreign quest workers are amongst the poorest people in the city and I can't imagine it would take many shekels to tempt them to sneak a few photocopies. And there must be plenty of Islamic sympathisers among the students. I think it's time for a chat with the security guards outside.

But the burly Israeli shakes his head. "No, Miss Adams." Only regular staff get in. We got strict instructions about security on this floor."

"What about last night, after working hours?"

"Yitzak and Michah were on duty after seven. But we don'tlet no one without a pass come through. Someone take something?"

"No, but I think my papers have been copied."

He glances at the sheaf of translations in my hand. "We got good security here. Special instructions about this floor. No one gets past us without ID. One of your colleagues want a copy maybe?"

"Not without asking me first. Do keep your eyes open, won't you." "We always do." He folds his arms stiffly.

I go back to my desk, still worried. Perhaps it was someone in the department, maybe Dr Schlott. He could simply have come in when I wasn't there to see if I've finished any more fragments, found them on the desk, and taken a copy. I'm in two minds about asking Ingrid if she knows anything about it. I don't want to sound like I'm accusing her. On the other hand she might have been asked to copy it by Dr Schlott, or seen him come in.

But Ingrid shakes her head. "No. No one goes in your office. No one else has a key. Why? Something wrong?"

"No, it's probably just the cleaners moving things round." I force a smile. Ingrid probably knows where to get hold of a key and is perfectly placed to access my office. It really feels horrible to be suspecting my colleagues like this, as though I'm the criminal here. Perhaps it was simply Dr Schlott. I mean, he is my boss, and has every right to see the documents which I'm withholding from him. I decide to take the bull by the horns and head down the corridor to his office, the translations tucked under my arm as I knock.

"Come in," he calls.

I push open the door.

"Charlotte. Goodmorning. Pull up a chair."

"Dr Schlott, I was just passing and..."

"Ah, that's a nice fat wad of work you've got there. How far have you got?" He holds out his hand for the translations. Damn. How the hell could I have been so stupid as to bring them with me. I'm supposed to be keeping the latest ones from him for as long as possible. I hand them over and fake a smile. I suppose if I don't make it in academia, I could always try Hollywood.

He repositions his glasses on the bridge of his nose and leafs through the sheaves of paper. "You've done all this? Up to Fragment 32?

Splendid! I have one or two investors, who'll be interested to hear about the progress you've made."

Ben isn't going to like this. I've half a mind to tell Dr Schlott about my encounters with Mossad and the Islamic militants, but I'm not sure if I should to wait until I speak to Ben.

"I'll go through these this morning," says Dr Schlott. "I'm looking forward to reading them very much indeed."

I take a deep breath. "So you haven't already made a copy?"

Dr Schlott looks puzzled. "Of course not, this is the first I've seen of them."

"I just thought someone might have been into my office and made a photocopy."

Dr Schlott frowns. "Are you suggesting someone has made an unauthorised copy?"

"If you look at the title page, it's not the same as the rest of my masters."

Dr Schlott rubs his chin. "I have a potentially very important sponsor lined up for this project. I don't want any leaks. I'll speak to security about this, and get new locks fitted on your door."

"Dr Schlott..."

The phone rings.

"Ah, yes. Just one moment." He puts his hand over the receiver.

"Many thanks, Charlotte. I'll speak to you later."

I close the door quietly behind me. God, I hope Ben phones again. I desperately need someone else to talk to about these latest incidents, I don't know who to trust. Ingrid has been a good friend to me up till now. I feel a bitch even thinking it might be her. But the more I think about it the more I realise how little I really know about her, or anyone else in the university, for that matter.

"Charlotte!"

Suddenly I'm enveloped in a bear hug and lifted off my feet.

"Ben!" Surprise, delight and relief all wash over me, in turn. I push the dishevelled hair off my face and glance around the corridor guiltily. It would look highly unprofessional to be caught in a clinch with another member of staff. It wouldn't be a blot on Ben's career but I bet it would be on mine.

"Why didn't you phone? When did you get back?"

"Last night." He grins. "I thought I'd surprise you."

"And Tony?"

A shadow crosses his face and I notice how haggard he looks. "Stable, but he's still very ill. They need to find a suitable donor soon."

"But he's getting the best care?" How come it's so hard to find I something to say that won't sound trite in situations like this?

"Oh yes," he says. "The very best." He looks away and I notice a grimness around the corners of his mouth that wasn't there before. "Look, I've got a lecture to give in fifteen minutes and I need to look though my notes. I'll catch you later."

"You look happier," comments Ingrid as I pass. "Headache better?"

My hand goes involuntarily to smooth my hair and panic sets in in case my lipstick has tell-tale smudges. I really don't want Ingrid to know about me and Ben. "I took a paracetamol."

"You might as well take your post while you're here." Ingrid hands me a stack of mail and goes to answer the phone.

I breeze into my office. Ben is back and he hasn't ditched me after all. I'll be able to talk to him about everything that's happened. You know what they say, nothing is so bad when you have someone to share things with.

Then I see the letter. The same small white envelope and neatly typed address as before. Oh Christ, not again. This time it has a Jerusalem postmark. I slit it open. There are five words, cut in uneven letters from newsprint. The message continues from the last.

EVERY STEP OF THE WAY

Fragment 6

I could do nothing but lie on the flax while my sister helped the Habiru.

"Go to the hills and hide," she said. "If anyone pursues you, they will not find you there. Wait three days

150

until the men of Jericho have finished searching the road. Then go to Joshua, and tell him all I have done for you and the oath you have sworn."

Sechem drew her to him then untied the scarlet cord which bound the tunic around her waist. He held it out. "When we enter the land, tie this in the window giving out across the walls, so our people know which house is yours. Make sure you have brought all your family inside. If anyone is outside, we cannot be responsible. But everyone in the house will be spared. I give you my oath."

Rahab took the cord in her hands.

Labor stepped forward and gripped her wrist. His eyes glinted. "If you tell anyone what we are doing, we will be free from the oath we have sworn to you - and your family will die like the rest."

"Agreed," said Rahab. "Let it be as you say."

"Come," said Labor, letting go her wrist. "The soldiers will be safely at the ford of the Jordan by now. We should be gone. "

Sechem took Rahab's hand in his and raised it to his lips. I writhed on the flax and gurgled my indignation into Labor's belt.

Rahab took a rope from the top of the stairs and led them to the window in the walls. She fastened the rope to a wooden beam and tugged at it to make sure it was fast. "Climb down the walls," I heard I her say. No one will see you. It's much safer than going through the streets where people may spot you."

"Remember, she called softly into the darkness as Shechem slid past the window down the rope. "Tell Joshua to honour your oath to me and spare all my family in the house."

But what Rahab couldn't know when she tied the scarlet cord across that very same window, was that on the fateful day when the Habiru struck, one of our family would not be safe inside.

Fragment 7

All Jericho knew the spies had come and gone. The city was on full alert. Our soldiers watched from the tower and the walls from dawn till dusk, then more would take their place through the hours of night.   We often saw the figure of the King, inspecting the lines, briefing his commanders, or just standing, his short but powerful figure silhouetted against the sky, in full battle dress, tugging at his beard from time to time in the way he always did when he was worried, watching the land between Jericho and the Jordan.

It was a bad time for all our strongest men to be guarding the city. The wheat was ripening on the ear and we needed as many hands as possible to gather it in, lest the wrath of the gods be incurred, and the summer sun beat down too hot, too early and scorch the tender crops, or a plaque of locusts blight our sky. So it was mostly left to us women, children, and those who were too old or crippled to fight. For despite the Habiru, we dared not let our precious crops be spoiled or we all risked death from famine in the winter months.

The temple was busy too. People came and went, petitioning the gods for favour, making the most of the services of the priests and priestesses, depending on whether they favoured men or women. Faced with the threat of the Habiru, life became more precious than ever, and our people united in celebration of our world and the gods who ruled our rivers, fields and hills. Jericho teemed. Everyone was busy.

Everyone was urgent. There was not a child in Jericho but had heard the stories of the powerful One God who promised to slaughter the enemies of the Habiru and deliver all Canaan into their hands. We made rude jokes about the

Habiru and ensured our Gods were kept happy and powerful with an endless stream of blood from sheep and goats. But while we tied our sheaves, drew naughty pictures of the Habiru in the dust and made frenzied love in temples bathed in blood, deep in our hearts, there were many who shared the worry of our King. We had heard what the enemy did in in Bashan, in Heshbon, in Midian. Yet somehow I never thought it could happen to us. Not Jericho.

Some days passed and there was no sign of the Habiru. Then one morning, we rose at dawn, went down to the fields - and found the Jordan barely more than a trickle. A cry went up. Soldiers had gathered on the part of the wall which overlooked the river, pointing with their spears. Even as the previous night had drawn its cloak across the land, the Jordan had been in full flood.

"This is a bad omen," muttered a bent old crone beside me. "The power of Baal is drying up, like the river."

"Shut up, you blaspheming hag." Her neighbour clutched her baby closer to her. "Enough of such talk." The baby began to wail.

High up on the walls, the soldiers reformed their lines and we set to work on the sheaves. But our normal cheerful chatter was subdued that day.

Around noon, a shout rang out from the walls. We looked
up, ready to throw down our scythes and run, if the warning came that the Habiru were approaching.

But it wasn't the Habiru. Two men with camels were wading across the ford of the Jordan, the water barely to their knees, heading for Jericho. The city gates were opened to let them in. It was not long before the news spread down to the fields.

They were traders from Gad. They had travelled down from the town of Adam, in Zarethan, where the waters of the Jordan rush through from the distant mountains. They were tired and sore from their journey but they brought a strange tale to the King. Great chunks of ice, soil and rock had washed down from Mount Hermon and piled up at a bend in the river at Adam, cutting off the flow to Jericho and the dead, salty Sea of Arabah. Not a trickle could squeeze through.

The old crone began to bleat. "I told you. The gods of Canaan will not save us now. The land is doomed."

The woman with the baby said nothing.

"Be silent, old one," I said. "Come, we have wheat to gather in - or we will be doomed, from hunger. Let's do something about it, and forget that donkey-arsed

Joshua." I brought down my scythe and cleaved a pile of
dried up dung
in two. "This is what our King will do to his head. And this," I
kicked at the dung, "is what Habiru are made of."

The women around me laughed and we all set to the
wheat again. But my joke was one of few and the laughter
was muted in the wheatfields that day.

Fragment 8

The King had sent men across the valley. They
returned with news that the Habiru were on the move.
Joshua and his people had left Shittim and were
approaching the banks of the Jordan. The gates of Jericho
were closed. All the wheat and barley in the fields outside
was left to ripen in the sun. No one could gather the crops
outside the walls. We could only watch from the walls, over
the heads of our crops nodding gently in the breeze, as the
enemy appeared, specks on the horizon, and made camp on
the far side of the now pathetic trickle which oozed through
the Jordan valley.

One of the King's men sent to keep watch for the

Habiru lived in our street. We went out to greet him when we heard of his return. Even our grandparents, who lived in the house next to ours, came out, though they were both so old and frail they rarely left their hearth.

"Greetings, Jebal," said my grandfather, leaning on his stick and squinting in the bright sunlight he so rarely saw. "What news of the Habiru?"

The goat boys jostled for a place at Jebal's elbow.

"What's Joshua like?" demanded Bel, the oldest and pushiest of the boys. "Is he really ten feet tall with a beard right down to his knees?"

Jebal laughed and ruffled Bel's mop of hair. "No, he's as big as a Cedar of Lebanon and meaner than a mountain lion in a snare." He bit into a loaf his wife thrust into his hand.

"Actually," he said, through a mouthful of bread, looking at my grandfather's watery eyes and anxious face. "He's neither tall nor short. His beard is cropped and though he's not built like the Anakim, he's strong and his muscles are taut and powerful, like the branches of the olive."

"Is it true he can rip the head off a man with his bare hands?" said Bel.

Jebal chewed his loaf slowly. "I doubt that," he said, "but there's something about him..."

"What?" pressed my grandmother, clutching my

157

arm for support.

"He has a look in his eyes like... like a kind of fire burns there. His own people are reverent when he's near and they say he is filled with the spirit of..." Jebal's forehead furrowed and a shadow darkened his face. He spat the last morsel of bread in the dust as if it had offended him, though I knew his wife had freshly baked it for his return. "Bah! He's just a filthy Habiru, like any other of his murdering tribe." Jebal pushed past the goat boys, marched into his house and slammed the door.

It was not till later that evening we heard from Jebal's wife what he had seen when he spied on the Habiru camp. We were all in our grandparents' house, sitting round the hearth when she came in.

"I've never known Jebal to be so moody," she said, sitting down and taking the jug of goat's milk my grandmother held out to her. "Those Habiru have put the wind up him for sure."

"Are they really that strong?" said grandmother, anxiously.

"Of course not," said grandfather. "Jebal's probably tired, and you women fussing round don't help a man."

Jebal's wife ignored him and drank from her bowl.

"Do you know," she began, "he says the Habiru priests have charge of a mysterious box which they carry on golden poles."

Hadad and Timnal drew closer.

"A box?" said Hadad.

"A box won't kill us, will it," said grandfather, scornfully.

"Maybe not - but what's in it might." Tarasch's mouth dropped open.

Jebal's wife leaned forward. "It's always guarded, night and day, and kept covered with a curtain of wonderfully woven cloth, in purple, blue and scarlet. And.." she paused, looking around at her audience. Tarasch, Hadad, Timnal, me... we all sat wide-eyed, hanging on her every word. "There's something very dangerous in the box." She sat back and looked pleased at the silence.

"What? What?" said Hadad.

" Jebal never saw. Nobody sees inside the box, except Joshua and the priests. But it's so dangerous, Joshua commanded the priests to carry it ahead. Then he told the Habiru people to follow - but they must stay at least a thousand yards away or..." She swilled the milk around in her bowl.

"Or what?"

"They will die." She drained the bowl then sat back and gloated over the effect her words had had. All of us waited for her to continue, even grandfather, though he tried to pretend he was more interested in picking lice from his feet.

"Joshua told his people they would move towards the Jordan, following the Levite priests with this box they call the Ark. Then, he said, they must stand in the water and..."

"They will know the Living God is amongst them," came a soft voice from the door. "The Lord will do amazing things. He will drive the Jebusites, the Hittites, Perizzites, Giraashites, Hivites, Amorites... and Canaanites before them." Rahab had been in the temple all day. The story had reached her first.

Her hair gleamed in the lamplight as she stood in the doorway. "Then Joshua chose twelve men, one from each of their tribes. And he said that as soon as the priests who bore the Ark set foot in the Jordan, the waters would cease to flow."

"And that's what has happened," said Timnal. "The Habiru are at the Jordan now."

"Nothing can stop them," said Rahab, moving

towards the fire.   "Their Lord sweeps all before them."

"No!" I leapt to my feet and faced my sister. "Our men are the bravest in Canaan. Our walls are the strongest. Jericho will not fall." Then I lowered my voice so no one else could hear. "Despite what you have done." Though she had betrayed us all, she was my sister and I had kept my silence. I could not be the cause of her death. For our King would have her stoned if he knew how she had harboured the spies. Besides, once they had gone, it was too late.

She took hold of my arm. Her nails stuck into my flesh. "I did what I did to save us all - you, Tarasch, Hadad..."

"You did what you did to slake your lust for the Habiru spy!" I whispered.

I reeled back across the room and fell to the floor, clutching my hand to my face. I could not speak for shock, not because the blow had been hard but because my sister had struck me. She had never once hit me before.

"What's going on here," called grandfather. "You two young harridans aren't too old to go across my knee," he quavered, not even attempting the effort it required him to drag his aged body to its feet.

Jebal's wife put down her bowl and scuttled to the

door. "I'd better get back to my man." She'd drunk her fill, had her moment of glory with a spellbound audience and now had no wish to get embroiled in a family row.

Rahab, still standing, her hair tumbling to her waist and streaked with copper as the last shafts of sunlight shone through the door waited till she had gone. I still sat sprawled on the floor, numb with shock. "Just remember," said Rahab, looking down at me. "I did it for you." Then she gazed around at our whole family seated by the fire. "When Jericho falls, your lives will be safe."

The last person on whom Rahab's gaze fell was Tarasch.

Chapter 6

Boy, am I glad to sit down. My feet are as sore as hell and I must've overdosed on museums. Still, at least it's not far back to uni. from the Rockerfeller and this exhibition of the Jericho finds was worth a few blisters. One of the skeletons even has a beaded headdress intact. I keep thinking those clay coffins might belong to people who actually knew Rahab and her family.

If only all the tourists would just bugger off out of this courtyard so I could dip my feet in the fishpond. I close my eyes and listen to the trickling of the water. I could stay here forever. It would be so easy if the only people I had to deal with were those bare-breasted women, dancing over the stone or the men who peep from the leaves on the Hiram's palace frieze. I suppose I should go back soon. I can't hide out here forever.

I sometimes wonder if I was born in the wrong era. I'm never happier than when I'm lost in some other place and time. Hardly surprising, I guess, when my own world is such a jumble of fear and confusion half the time. But then it's all too easy to romanticise the past when you're having a hard time in the present. I bet Rahab's sister would have given her right arm to swop places with me. My problems are pathetic in comparison.

I have another image leaping out of my pre-dawn terrors now. A dead boy limp in the arms of his

163

father veiled by a cloud of drifting dust. How many images of horror did she carry in her head as she ran from the ashes of that looted city, I wonder. How did she survive with all that mess in her head? A lot better than me. Why can't I cope with so much less. I wish I had a fraction of her courage.

   Here's me mooning around museums pretending I don't care that Ben hasn't called me for days, like some lovesick teenager who won't grow up. She had to , and pretty damn quick. Just because Ben's busy, it doesn't necessarily mean he thinks I'm a worthless slut. Even if I am.

   My stupid preoccupations are so trivial compared to the stuff I've seen in these Israeli museums. I find a couple of stale biscuits in my bag and crumble them for the fish as images from the Holocaust float through my mind, drifting to the surface like dead things from a wreck. Lampshades made from human skin, bars of soap from flesh. That children's memorial - one solitary flame, burning cold and bright, the names of the victims whispering and echoing across a mirrored hall. As I watch the fish rise from the depths of the pond, I wonder if those horrors of the past will forever lurk in the Israeli consciousness, like monsters that will never be appeased. Israel as Andromeda with Perseus standing her up.

   Maybe that's why they dig into their newly established homeland like some insecure kid clinging onto its mother, beating off others who are fighting for their space too. The fish jostle and snatch at crumbs. There are no more biscuits left. Before I flew out I read up on the modern history of Palestine; how Israel, not content with its UN allocated boundaries, scooped the Golan Heights, the Gaza strip and East Jerusalem into its borders too; seizing tracts of land from Syria, Egypt, Lebanon, squeezing out the Palestinians who had lived there for centuries. It's very ironic, I think, as I watch the fish nudge one another away, fighting for the last morsels of biscuit. After all the Jews have suffered, now they've finally achieved their dream of a homeland, it's at the expense of some other poor sods who now have to fight Israel for their land. Nazi hatred, Jewish fear, Arab rage. Where will it all end, I wonder, as the biggest fish devours the final crumbs and swims back down to the darkness at the bottom of the pool.

I really have no right to think I'm hard done by just because Ben has been busy. I'm going to remember all those funerals instead, Israeli solders dead in suicide bombings. Palestinian children shot as they walk to school. He's rushing from lectures, to meetings, to the dig, tearing down corridors, calling as he goes that he has so much work to catch up on, promising to make it up to me... He seems snowed under but he could be avoiding me. Maybe he's regretting that moment of weakness, when after the shock of staring death in the face, he dived for comfort straight into the arms of the nearest available woman. It's my own fault, of course. How could I have been so stupid. I wanted a new life free from traumas and tangled affairs. An

165

embarrassing fling with a work colleague drowning in family problems is hardly a sensible way of carrying on, is it. Why should he want anything more than a one night stand with me. Why should anyone want a relationship with me?

Well, I refuse to be a mug. There's no way I'm going to to sit around waiting for him to call, or mope alone in the flat, and I've filled every spare hour when I'm not working on the fragments with museum visits. It's all helped to increase my knowledge of the Canaanite world, and to take my mind off Ben. And I won't let myself dwell on those letters. Nor the vultures waiting to swoop on my work. Dead children are important. My worries aren't. I have everything going for me. Great job, great prospects ... if I can only keep away from the edge of that huge abyss which keep opening up in the darkness of my mind.

I have no right to be unhappy. None at all.

I have laid out a clean white cloth on the altar of my table. The door of my flat is locked, phone off the hook. I have arranged the taller things at the back, two bottles of coke, three loaves of white bread, two boxes of cornflakes and six packets of breadsticks fanned out in glasses. In front of them lies a pack of unsalted butter on a silver dish, a pot of strawberry jam, four packets of Jaffa cakes, one pack of almond cookies, a cheese and tomato quiche and a jar of green olives.

I stand in this temple I have created,

166

admire my handiwork and prepare to sacrifice myself to the food god. To conduct my ritual to the lords of binging and stuffing.

Then I attack.

Breadsticks first, three shoved into my mouth at once and washed down with coke straight from the bottle. I grab a loaf, rip off a chunk with my hands and smear it across the butter. I have no need for a knife. The Maenads have nothing on me. With bread-encrusted fingernails, I tear the lid from the jam, hurl it onto the floor and scoop up a great dollop with the bread. I stuff it into my mouth as fast as I can while reaching for the olives. What would they say at uni. if they could see me now?

Then the doorbell rings.

"Miss Charlotte. Open. It's me."

As I turn, I catch sight of my reflection in the mirror. A clown's face. Huge red mouth. No lipstick. Just a great wadge of strawberry jam smeared all round my lips. The food god, grinning at me from my own face.

"Miss Charlotte, I gotta talk to you."

I grab a cloth and wipe the jam from my lips.

"Hello Abdul," I say, opening the door with a smile. "What can I do for you?"

He's standing in front of my door with a cardboard box. "Just came to tell you I can't walk Cruiser tomorrow. We go take food to my cousins in Ramallah. Them bastard Israelis plough up their field yesterday."

I notice a bag of apples and some packets of rice in his box. It doesn't look much.

"No crops, no money, no food, Miss Charlotte. Bastards, them Israelis. Watta my cousins supposed to eat? You watch out for them, Miss Charlotte."

I glance up at the landing as a door slams and Abdul's mother appears, locking the door and dragging a sack as she heads down the stairs.

Abdul, wait." I rush back inside, scoop up everything on the table and deposit the lot in Abdul's box. He stares in surprise.

"Miss Charlotte, you been having a party or..."

"Take it, Abdul, for your cousins."

Abdul's mother doesn't speak English. She doesn't have to. I understand her beams and gestures horribly well. I don't deserve their thanks, Abdul and his mother.

When they've gone, I close the door and slide down with my back against it to the floor. My face crumples like a discarded serviette. Abdul is wrong. I'm not kind. Not kind at all. Then I start to cry, with great racking sobs, in place of all that food I would be heaving up from my guts.

Cruiser comes padding up, not understanding. He puts his paw on my knee and looks at me with his chocolate eyes, with all that love which I don't deserve.

Me and my vile self-pity. Me and my fractured world.

"Charlotte! I've been trying to get hold of you all day."

"I've been out."

"I gathered that. Look I'm really sorry, I've hardly had a spare moment since I got back from the States."

"Of course." Ben looks tired and strained. I'd love to reach out and touch those lines on his face, but I'm not going to. I've already made up my mind how I'm going to play it.

"Look, I quite understand," I say coolly, reorganising papers on my desk which don't need it. "I know you've got an awful lot on your plate. That night before you left... if you regret it, I understand, and if you want to forget it happened then..."

"Charlotte." He takes my hand and I have to clutch onto my resolve for dear life.   "That's not what I want." He brushes some straying tendrils of hair from my face and I feel like I'm going melt all over the floor. "Do you?"

"Not if you're sure this is what you want." I'm praying it is but self-protection's the name of the game. Play it cool and you won't get hurt. Maybe.

"I don't deserve you." He seems about to say something else then chancres his mind. "Come on, how about a drink in the Barracuda. We've got some catching up to do."

"Well, I was going straight home to take this back with me."

Ben looks at the wad of paper in my hands. "Your translations? You take all that work home with you?"

"For safety," I explain. "I never leave anything

in my office now. Not since my computer was hacked into and..." I bite my lip.

"And what?" Ben frowns.

"Well, while you were away, someone came into my office and photocopied my translation."

Ben's face darkens. "How do you know?"

"There was a smudge of photocopy ink which wasn't been on my original."

He lets go of me and turns his face away. "Are you sure about that?"

"Quite sure. I knew something had been moved the minute I came in."

Ben walks over to the window and stands there for a moment, with his back to me. Then he turns round. "How long have you been taking your work home with you?"

"The last few days, since it happened."

"Charlotte..." He paces up and down the office. He wears that worried frown too often. "Come on, bring your papers. Let's go for that drink."

Just as we reach the door of the central office, Ben pauses. "Do you mind if I have a copy of your latest work?" he asks. "I can go through it in the Barracuda. If you trust me, that is."

"Of course, I trust you."

"I could sell them to the Russians."

"I don't think so."

We return to the office and I make a photocopy for him, then saying *shalom* to the security guards as we leave, we head for the underground car park.

"Damn." Ben feels his pockets with his free hand. "I've left my keys upstairs. Look, wait for me by the car, I'll be back in a minute."

Most of the academic staff have left by now. AA group of cleaners pass me in the entrance as they tramp up the steps with buckets and mops, then the doors swing shut behind them and I am left alone in the concrete gloom of the car park. A couple of overhead lights aren't working and the bays are darker than they should be. I must remember to report it to the works department.

Suddenly there is a loud screech from behind. I spin round and feel my heart thumping. A thin weasely cat leaps out from behind some bins, sending a pile of cardboard boxes and empty tins clattering across the concrete. I relax as the animal races away through the pillars then I walk to the Landrover. It's one of the few vehicles left. As I stand by the passenger *door* and wait for Ben, I'm sure I hear a noise behind me, near the gloomy area by the bins where the cat leapt out. I peer into the darkness and... surely that shadow moved. I freeze. Someone's lurking behind that concrete pillar, watching me. Then I hear the door swing shut and as I spin round I see Ben walking towards me.

"Got them." He holds up his keys, his copy of the latest fragments still clutched beneath his arm. "Is anything wrong?"

"How do you mean?"

"You just look worried. Not

171

having second thoughts?"

"What?"

"About getting involved with a three times divorced, emotionallyretarded, walking disaster where relationships are concerned, debt-ridden archeologist from Denver?"

"Three times divorced?"

"Now you are having second thoughts."

"No." I kiss his cheek. "I knew about Maddy of course, I just didn't realise you had a couple of others tucked away in your past."

"It's not something I boast about. So what were you looking so worried about?"

"Oh, I just thought I saw someone hanging about by the bins."

"You did."

"What?"

Ben shrugs. "I saw him too as I came though the doors. Just some young guy, having a quick cigarette probably. A student, I expect. What's up?" He clicks open the doors on his remote control.

"Nothing. He just made me jump."

"Let's go," says Ben, starting the engine. " I'm looking forward to that drink."

"Do you mind if we stop off at my flat first?" I ask. "I need to feed Cruiser."

"That mutt?" says Ben, as the Landrover swings out of the car-park into the street. "Has he infested your flat with fleas yet?"

"No he hasn't. Though someone covered my floor in brandy."

"Sorry."

"I was only joking."

Neither of us mentions the death of the Palestinian boy which occasioned the brandy, but it hovers, unspoken but palpable, in the air between us. We both fall silent, and I know he's thinking about it too.

When we reach my flat, Abdul is on the landing. He comes racing downstairs as I put my key in the lock and stops outside my door to stare up at Ben.

"Hey, Miss Charlotte.This your boyfriend?"

"Abdul "

Ben grins and says something in Arabic which I can't understand.

Abdul does, though, for he gives one of his cheekiest grins.

"Where's he taking you, Miss Charlotte, posh hotel? King David?"

"Barracuda bar," says Ben.

Abdul pulls a face.

"Move out of the way, Abdul," I tell him. I need to feed Cruiser before we go out."

"I feed Cruiser for you, Miss Charlotte." says Abdul.

"You go to Barracuda, I stay in and keep Cruiser company for you."

"Don't you have a home to go to?" says Ben.

"Abdul points upstairs. "Yes, but I look after Miss Charlotte's flat and dog," he says proudly.

"You'd better check with your mother, if

you're going to stay with Cruiser," I say. "She might worry if she doesn't know where you are."

"I tell her." Abdul races up the stairs two at a time, yells something through an open door in rapid Arabic, then jumps back down, taking the stairs three at a time on the descent.

"I do that." He takes the scoop from my hand, dips it into the bag of dogfood then shoos me away. "Go, Miss Charlotte. I look after Cruiser. You go to King David's with your boyfriend."

"Barracuda."

"Miss Charlotte is very beautiful lady," calls Abdul, as we head back to the door. "You want to take her to better place than that."

"Cheeky monkey," says Ben. "He's right, though, you are beautiful."

If only.

We settle in a quiet corner of the Barracuda and order drinks. "Are you sure it's OK leaving that kid in your flat?" asks Ben.

"He's very good with Cruiser. I don't know what I'd do without Abdul looking after him. I'm always so late back. Anyway, it's quite nice to know someone's keeping an eye out for me."

Ben laughs. "He certainly does that. Perhaps I should have taken you to the King David's like he said."

"This'll do fine."

"Any more signs of our friends from Mossad?"

"No," but Doctor Schlott's keeping these

possible new investors close to his chest." The waiter brings us our drinks and I take a sip from my glass of chilled wine.   "According to him, nothing's definite yet, but he won't say who they are. I've been wondering if the Israeli government have decided to step in and back the project."

"I wouldn't be surprised. Schlott never talks finance with the academic staff, but I've been thinking along the same lines. If the Israeli establishment wants to keep a close watch on the fragments, what better way than to become a financial backer." Ben downs half his glass of lager. "That's better. I needed that."

"I'm sure they'll be even more interested once I give Dr Schlott a copy of Fragment 33."

"How much have you given him so far?"

"Up to Fragment 32."

"That much?" Ben's face darkens.

"I had to. I had them in my hand and he caught me on the hop. Ben, we're not going to be able to keep this to ourselves. I'm pushing my luck as it is."

"I know. Would you like another wine?"

"No thanks. I'm still going strong with this one."

Ben drains the rest of his lager and motions the waiter to bring him another.

"So what's going on with Fragment 33?"

"Put it this way, it'll make anyone interested in the Ark of the Covenant even keener to get their hands on these fragments."

Ben pushes his empty glass away and leans his arms on the table. "Tell me more."

I hand him my translation. "Read it for yourself.

When he's finished, he lays the translation on the table and looks thoughtfully into his beer, swilling the dregs round the bottom of the glass. I'm a bit disappointed by his reaction. I mean, we're talking about a map which showed where this great power from the ancient world was... is.. supposed to come from. I don't know if I expected him to dance a jig on the table or rip out his hair or what really. But he could show a bit more emotion.

"I see what you mean. Does Schlott have Fragment 33 yet?" "No. I only finished it today."

"This a bit... well... isn't it."

"Yes," I say coolly, watching him over my glass.

"Damn Schlott. If only he hadn't insisted on making knowledge of these fragments public so soon. Look Charlotte, I'm worried about you. If this gets out, if people start thinking there's some kind of map involved which shows the source of this... this..."

"Power?"

"For want of a better word, yes." He might not be tearing his hair out in clumps but he's running his fingers through it that way he does when he's stressed. No paddy throwing but definitely discomforted. It's nice to see the experts get their knickers in a twist.

"Did you find any kind of map when you dug up the fragments?"

"No, nothing. But that's not the point. If any of these nutcases get the idea that there's a map to go with the fragments, the waters could get seriously hot round here. I don't want you in danger."

This little frisson goes through me, not unpleasant actually. I don't believe we're going to get men in black chasing us round the streets of Jerusalem or any such corny stuff, but the idea that he might just care about me catches me in the guts a lot more than the dark thrill of danger hovering ahead. "Dr Schlott's already promised to step up security, after the photocopy incident."

"So he knows about that?"

"I had to tell him. I thought it might have been him at first." "I just want you to be careful."

"I'll be all right." I lean forward a little so the top of my shirt strains slightly open, and make sure he sees it. I can't believe that someone like him, or anyone for that matter, can really care about me. I've seen the way the girls in admin. sneak glances and preen and giggle when he comes in. Thank God I've got my eating habits under control. I couldn't stand him knowing the truth.

"What about that guy you thought was watching you this evening?"

I pause, the glass halfway to my lips. "You said he was a student."

"I thought he was. I mean, early twenties, dark, closely cropped hair, casual dress... I just assumed it at the time, but he could have been anyone." Ben reaches across the table and runs his hand down the side of my face. Something quivers inside me, but this time it's rather more the shiver of fear than the touch of his hand. "Just be careful, that's all. You mean too much to me to...

"I'll be fine. I'm surrounded by security at work and I never go anywhere where I could be in danger. Only museums, places swarming with tourists and shady bars with a three times divorced, emotionally-retarded, debt-ridden archeologist from Denver."

"I suppose that's all right then." He takes my hand in his across the table and kisses my fingers lightly. These fingers I use to shove down my throat. They shouldn't be kissed.

It probably was some student, as he says. After all, it is a flaming university, for God's sake. Nothing to worry about. I smile back at him over the table. It feels good not to be alone. Then I remember my encounter in the Cafe Malkha. I haven't told him yet about that.

"Something up?"

"No, why?"

"I thought you were going to say something."

I'm not sure if I should tell him. He's got enough on his plate. Plus a ready disposition to paranoia which doesn't need me stoking it up. Unfortunately, he keeps pressing. I'll have to be careful. He's a bit too adept at spotting things lurking below the surface. I shall need all the skills in my armoury to pull the wool over his eyes when I want.

"Well?"

When I tell him about being set up for that meeting with Islamic militants in the cafe, Ben falls silent. He runs his hand across his face and looks grey and strained, despite his tan. "This is heavy," he says at last. "I've never heard of this Hamad Zaid guy. Look, maybe you should... have you thought of going back to London?"

"What?" I laugh in complete and utter astonishment. This is something I didn't expect.

"I don't want you in danger. I feel..well... responsible for you."

He's making me feel like a kid being taken to kindergarten by its Dad. I still have this delicious warm glow at the novelty of someone caring about me and have to remind myself severely I'm a post-feminist, financially independent, female academic, who's well versed in Gilbert and Gubar, and should know better than to subject myself to male domination tactics and infantilisation. But it is kind of nice that he cares.

"Ben," I squeeze his hand. "I have no intention of walking out on this job, even if I could go back, which I can't. Do you really want me to go thousands of miles away?"

As if I could.

"No. I just worry that..."

"I can look after myself." Moment of weakness over. Germaine Greer and Susan Faludi would be proud.

"I wish..." Ben picks up his glass and looks away across the bar. "...that things

179

were different."

"You mean with Tony and everything?"

"Yes, and.. oh hell, life is never simple, is it?" he said, not looking at me. "Look if you've finished your drink, how about about a meal?"

"'That would be lovely. Especially if it takes your mind off imagining danger to me. You've got enough to worry about already. Ingrid reckons you know all the best restaurants - and the worst dives.

"I'll make sure I take you to the former. You hungry?"

I nod. "Starved."

"Good." Den picks up the translation and his keys then pauses. "You've really got it beat, haven't you?"

"I'm sorry?"

"Look, I never wanted to embarrass you and if I'd known before I'd never have forced those *friandises* on you that time. But I think I should tell you I know about your eating problems."

It feels like someone's slapped me across the face with a firebrand. He knows. My dirty little secret. I just want to run the hell out that door and I have to use all my concrete resolve to weld myself onto my seat. He's watching me, embarrassed, wondering what I'm going to say. For a moment, I'm about to force a laugh, to deny it, but I can see it in his eyes. He knows.

"How did you guess?"

"I'm a lecturer, remember, as part of my job. I have

to deal with endless girls in tutorials and their problems aren't just academic. Plus my sister suffered from an eating disorder when she was at high school. So I guess I can spot the signs pretty well."

"Oh. That obvious?" My guts are practising reef knots. What did I do? How did I give it away?

He shifts round to my side of the table and gives me a hug. I make sure my hair falls forward. I don't want him to see my face. I'm crying inside. I didn't want anyone in Jerusalem to know. I can't understand why he's sitting here, with his arm round my shoulders. Why isn't he out that door? Why would anyone want to be close to someone who vomits up food? Yet through this burning embarrassment, there's a part of me that's relieved; I don't have pretend. But I really wanted to put all that behind me, not carry it around with me still.

"No, it's not obvious at all. As I said, you seem to have got it beat. I really admire you for that. You might look like a porcelain doll, but there's a lot of strength under that brittle exterior."

I'm not strong, I want to scream. I'm weak and pathetic and have to fight for every last gram of my horribly deficient self control. Then he frowns and looks away across the restaurant. "I only wish..."

"You wish what?"

"Oh nothing." He kisses the top of my head. "Come on. Let's get that food."

I glance at my reflection in the mirror above the bar as we walk out, forcing myself to remember those childhood ballet lessons I was never any good at and hold my head high. I am so relieved to notice that my doppelganger in the glass is composed, every inch the professional, with hair and make-up perfectly in place. She still projects that steely veneer from the hard surface of the glass, sending out to the world the image I work so hard to forge from all those pots in the secrecy of my bathroom.

But inside the real Charlotte Adams, it's like my emotions are in some sort of tumble drier - and as I head for the door I remember that mirrors are so easily smashed.

"It says here the Primula Porter Corporation is going to build a new Health and Beauty Multiplex at Ein Bokek," says Ingrid, looking up from her copy of Elle magazine and biting into her baklava. It beggars belief how this girl stays like a toothpick.

"That's on the Dead Sea, isn't it." I take a sip of my coffee and hope she's not going to start on about slimming or diets.

"Mm. Down in the south. They're big on Dead Sea mud. They recently set up a new research lab to investigate its properties and they market it all over the world."

"I wonder if it would do anything for me." I know what it did for Caleb. I reckon I could use a bit of Old Testament magic.

Ingrid scoffs. "You? You don't need it."

"I don't know about that."

"Take it from me. You don't." She licks the honey off her fingers and turns over the page. If she knew what I was really like.

Across the table I look at the back cover where Krista Belhoff flaunts an impossibly perfect complexion and a bottle of Primula Porter Silk Sensation for Super Smooth Skin.

"I didn't realise Primula Porter was based near here."

"They're everywhere," says Ingrid. "Big multi-national. "Paris, London, New York, Geneva, it says here. They own three or four spa hotels on the coast. read Sea Mud treatments - for the rich and famous and lucky sods who can afford it."

"Have you ever tried the mud?

"At the sea, *ja*. I've never bothered to buy the packaged stuff." She shrugs. "Why pay those prices when you can cover yourself down on the coast for nothing?"

"Mm, suppose so." I study my fingernails and ask casually, "Does it work?"

"It makes your skin really clean and soft, but I told you, you look great already. If I had your... " Ingrid glances at her watch and closes her magazine sharply. "Better get back. I'm expecting a call."

I touch the skin of my cheek and wonder if Dead Sea Mud would really make a difference. But I want to get back to my fragments and quickly finish the last of my coffee then follow Ingrid out of the canteen.

As I walk through the swing doors of Archaeology I run into Ben. He smiles and lightly brushes my hand as we pass. Naff, but nice. So casual that no one will notice. Or do they?

Ingrid is watching from her desk, phone pressed to her ear, and I can't be sure if I'm imagining it or if I really did see the shadow of a frown flicker across her face before she swivels round in her chair and continues her call, with her back to me.

I put down my translation and take out a cigarette. This is really getting freaky. Fragment 35 tells how the actual tablets from the Ark were buried in an oasis near Hebron and even gives clues where they might be found. Not only that, it reveals the existence of a map locating the source of the Hebrews' mysterious power. This is really close to the realms of loony Ark hunters. They'd have a field day with this. And it's not only going to draw the attention of amateur sleuths, if it gets out. A lot of people would die to get their hands on this. I don't know what it'll do to my professional reputation, being linked with this kind of Indiana Jones stuff, but it could certainly attract some pretty heavy people. The cigarette tastes foul. I don't enjoy smoking and I don't know why I do it. I stub it out and reach for the phone.

"Ben, I've finished Fragment 35. I think you should come up and see this. Hello?" I frown suspiciously as a series of clicks disrupts his reply.

"Yes, I hear you. Don't say any more. I'm on

my way."

I put down the receiver then quietly open the door of my office. Ingrid is on the phone. But then she spends half her time on the phone. It's her job. It doesn't mean anything. Or does it? Those clicks on the line could have been static or a fault. But seeing as my computer's already been hacked, I guess it's hardly paranoid to suspect my phone line might be monitored as well.

Ben closes the door behind him and sits down. "So what's the latest? I gather it's something important."

"Read this." I hand over my latest."

"By the way," he says, taking it from me. "I think you'd better be careful what you say on the phone from now on."

"Just what I was thinking."

Someone knocks sharply at the door.

"Come in."

It's Ingrid.

"I just wondered if you'd like coffee?"

"No thanks."

"Oh, right, OK. Ben?"

"No." Ben doesn't look up from the fragments. "Shut the door on your way out, Ingrid."

Ingrid's eyebrows arch ceilingwards then she closes the door with remarkable restraint. I'd have shoved his head in it first.

"You didn't have to be so rude," I tell him. "I think she knows about us."

185

"So what?" says Ben, still intent on the page.

I look out of the window while he reads, and pick at my nails. Ben might not care, but I don't want any bad feeling between Ingrid and me. I've got quite enough to worry about as it is.

At length Ben puts the translation down on the desk. "Well, this is really something else. Not only does she claim to have stolen these socalled secrets of the Ark, but to have hidden them too. But it figures those tablets were written in Egyptian, seeing as Moses was the guy who most likely brought them to Canaan."

"Ben, what if she never made it back to that cave, or if it was completely buried after the earthquake?" I catch myself lowering my voice and feel a bit silly.

He takes his time in replying but I can see a kind of gleam in his eyes. I wonder if he's not as sceptical as he makes out. I think he's more than a bit excited about what we might find. If anything. Not that we will. Not that we're even thinking of looking, of course.

"Hey," he says. We shouldn't get too carried away..."

"Who's carried away?"

"No, nor me. It was a hell of a long time ago," says Ben. "Maybe she came back and managed to get them out. Or someone else might have found them between then and now."

"Or maybe..." If he'd only let me get a word in...

"Don't get your hopes up too high yet. If they

are still there ...it's a ridiculous idea, of course...
"Never thought it for an instant."
They could be buried under tons of rock," he adds.
"It's absurd to even contemplate the possibility.""

Wow! The secrets of the Ark of the Covenant, lying still buried today, somewhere in the hills south of Hebron.

Then I catch that glint in his eye and I twig. "You've got an idea, haven't you? Come on, Ben, don't keep me in the dark. You know where those tablets could be buried."

Ben looks up from the map in front of him. "I keep telling you, we shouldn't get our hopes up. They're probably lost under piles of rubble or stolen centuries ago without anyone realising what they were."

"Or might still be there. You can't kid me you're going to pass up the chance to look for them. Come on, where is it you think they might be?"

"Well, Ben turns the map towards me. "The girl travelled south of Hebron and we know from where the fragments were found that she didn't get to Egypt but ended up on the western banks of the Dead Sea. That means she travelled across this area here." Ben traces southern Judea with his finger. "Now what narrows it down quite considerably...," He picks up the translation and points to the end of Fragment 35. "...is this reference to a range of sparkling hills."

"And you know where they are?" It's a

ridiculous idea. Completely mad. Crazy people stuff. But that's not stopping this great stupid thumping of excitement from pounding away at my chest.

Ben turns back to the map. "There's a range of hills leading down towards the southern end of the Dead Sea about here. You see, she writes about plunging down towards an endless night..."

"So they start high inland and drop down to the sea?"

"Exactly. And in the area close to Sodom the lower reaches of the hills are crystal white because of the salt."

"In the flashes from the lightning, they would presumably sparkle as she described?"

"Yes. So I think we can safely assume that was the route she took. She would have reached the sea around what's now Neve Zoha or maybe Ein Bokek and probably travelled north from there to Ein Gedi where she wrote the fragments."

I peer closely at the map. "But the cave where she buried the tablets from the Ark must be up in the hills somewhere, around the present day town of Arad."

"Somewhere in that vicinity, yes. But obviously we'd have to narrow it down considerably before we could start digging."

"So you are going to dig," I knew it.

"Of course I'd take a look if we did find the site. Just remember, archaeology is full of empty caves and disappointment. Even if we do find the place, there might be nothing there."

"So what about this high place with an altar she mentions, near an oasis? It's obviously far older than the Hebrew invasion. There can't be that many of those around. Come on, Ben. You're the top archaelogist in Israel today. Don't tell me you haven't got an idea where..." He's grinning his head off, the sod!   "You have! Tell me, then."

Ben rubs his arm and looks thoughtful.

"Tell me!"

He folds the map and stands up. "I've got a phone call to make."

"You're not leaving without..."

"I have to ring the hospital. They may have found a donor for Tony."

"Hey, you can't..." But I find myself staring open-mouthed at the door as Ben gives me a wave and closes it behind him.

I'm on my way down the corridor when I hear raised voices coming from Dr Schlott's office and when I get closer I realise the loudest one belongs to Ben.

"I have a right to know who..."

"Dr Tavers," comes Schlott's voice through the door, sounding decidedly frosty. "I have no intention of breaching client confidentiality by revealing who the possible backers of any archaeological project undertaken at this university might be."

"Stuff client confidentiality! What about freedom of information? The American constitution..."

"We are not, you may have noticed, in the United States now."

I don't know why Ben has to be so damn belligerent. Sometimes it's better just to keep your mouth shut. I hurry on past. The last thing I want is for them to open the door and find me standing there like an eavesdropper. Sod it, I really didn't want to plunge head over heels into a relationship. Not right now. And especially not with someone like Ben. Cantankerous, three-times divorced and all that. If it had to be anyone, why not someone a bit more... well, predictable. I could use a bit of stability. Sometimes I feel like I'm standing in a desert while a whirlwind whips away all the sand beneath my feet. Nothing is steady. Nothing is sure. It's only my career that's kept me going. My work is the one sane constant, whatever other turmoil is spinning my world out of control, and it's really the most important thing in my life. But that crusty old devil is starting to get under my skin.

When we're alone he can be so gentle and caring, not like his public face at all. But I wish he wasn't so overbearing and tactless. I mean, Hermann Schlott is our employer. I just can't see the point of biting the hand that feeds you. Ben might be at the top of his field, but he could still find himself out of a job, which is the last thing he needs right now. Anyway, there's no way I'm getting dragged into this row with Schlott. I value my job, even if he doesn't. Honestly, sometimes I find myself sympathising with Maddy, this much maligned ex-wife I've never met. She's had years of his bolshy attitude, and she's probably only trying to do the best for her son.

The voices fade as I head down the corridor. Ben's been really tense and strung out since he got back from New York, hardly surprising, considering Tony might die. Maybe I'm not being sympathetic enough. I've never had kids. Maybe I'm a hard-faced cow. Maybe I've been so long out of a relationship I don't know how to act in one. Or maybe I'm just useless all round. Why couldn't I fall for some Mr Reliable? I don't seem to be able to get a thing right. Damn it, why is nothing ever perfect? I'm not very good at life. I'm such a bloody failure. I suppose I'll just have to learn to put up with Ben's moods and try not to get upset by that weird sort of distance he sometimes seems to put between us. But I don't see why he has to argue with Schlott. Surely it doesn't matter who backs the project, so long as someone does. Anyway, right now I'm far more interested in the fact that Ben obviously has a pretty good idea where the tablets are buried. I'll catch him later. There's no way I'm letting him get away without telling me. I think it's better not to let on I overheard the row. I don't want him to think I've been checking up on him or earwigging. But I know he'll be in his office for tutorials later this afternoon and I'll be damned if I don't corner him and prise out where he thinks the tablets are buried.

"All right, all right," Ben throws up his hands in defeat. "I wasn't bull-shitting you. I really did have to make that call and I wanted to check up on the archaeological records before we got too excited."

191

"So where is it?"

"There's a clifftop between Arad and Sodom with the remains of a Canaanite temple dating back to the 3rd millennium BC."

"Which would be long before her time, just as she said. How about the cave near a waterfall? Is there anything like that near the site?"

"I don't know the area that well. The terrain's still very wild and barren, much the same as it would have been then. I thought maybe we could go check out the temple area and see if we can hit on this oasis. If you could fit a trip into your busy schedule, Miss Adams."

"I think I could just about manage that." Try and stop me, Dr Travers.

"The question is, do we wait until you finish translating more of the story?"

"But you know how long it takes to..."

Ben grins. "I thought you'd say that. Got any plans for tomorrow?"

"I have now." Indiana Jones, eat your heart out.

As usual, I'm the last to leave the department. Talk about glutton for punishment. I lock my office and make my way down the corridor to the lift. I'm the only one inside. But when it's halfway to the ground it shoots back up again. Damn, the sodding thing's going right to the top. Someone must've pressed the button up there. But when the door slides open there's no one there. So I press 'ground' - and blow me if it doesn't stop at the

192

fourth. Someone's playing silly buggers. I jab the *ground* button, but the thing goes shooting up. This is really starting to piss me off. Some idiot must be messing around, pressing buttons and running off. I really can't be bothered with this stupid game. It'll be quicker to use the bloody stairs.

As I hurry down the staircase, I notice another set of footsteps besides my own. Probably someone else fed up with the eccentricities of the lift. I glance up. The footsteps stop. I can't see anyone. It's probably some daft student messing around, not worth letting them get to me.

I carry on down the empty stairwell.

Sod it, they are again. Footsteps, not quite in sync with mine. If they think they're going to frighten me....

I spin round.

"Who's there?"

Silence.

"Whoever you are, just piss off!" My voice comes out brave and angry but I'm running by the time I reach the bottom.

I hover for a while in the foyer, despite the porter in the office giving me funny looks, to see which joker comes out of the stairwell or the lift. But no one does.

When I finally step outside into the evening sun, I'm annoyed at everything and everybody, most of all myself in case it's my imagination going into overdrive again.

As soon as I reach my landing I know there's

something wrong. The door to my flat is ajar. Abdul never forgets to lock up. I step inside, and Jesus Christ! The living room is a total wreck. Drawers hang askew, their contents spilled all over the floor. The cabinet doors are wide open, the contents rifled. My books and letters lie scattered amongst cutlery and broken shards of glass. The sofa cushions have been ripped off and hurled to the far side of the room. My things, so carefully stored and arranged. My home, violated.

I step across the wreckage then stop to pick up Cruiser's toy duck. Stuffing is banging out of its neck. My stomach rolls over and over, and suddenly I notice how deadly is the silence of this flat. Nothing is the same. No barking bundle of fur hurtling out of the kitchen. No cheerful chatter from Abdul rattling down the stairs. Just silence.

I feel sick to the core, as I creep over debris towards the kitchen. I'm so scared of what I shall find. By now the neon from the bar across the road will start to flood the room with crimson. Is it only light that stains the walls tonight? I see red before my eyes, as slowly, very slowly, I push open the door.

Fragment 9

We saw the truth of Jebal's tales from the Habiru camp for ourselves. The Habiru were camped

on the bank of the Jordan. The city gate stayed

194

closed. No one could come in or out of Jericho. We weren't too worried. We could withstand a siege. Jars of corn, wheat, barley, lentils and peas were stacked in our stores and all our animals had been brought inside the city walls. We had goats' milk and wine in abundance and our springs gave forth as much water as we could need and made our trees heavy with fruit. The Habiru, after all, were just a wandering tribe, with a few sheep and goats. Nothing solid to their name at all. Except a new God who had promised them our land, and a mysterious box that none but priests could go near.

I didn't pay much thought to their Ark at that time. All the children talked about it, of course. When they took their goats to feed, they would set up a stone they pretended was the Habiru Ark. They would creep towards it, touch it quickly then fall down as if they were dead. The King discouraged the stories about the Ark. People whispered in groups how Moses had locked something dreadful inside which leapt out when their enemies were near. Some said it was a thousand headed dragon which scorched men to death with its fiery breath. Others talked of a cloud of locusts that devoured people instead of crops. Some stories told of a poison so strong it could kill from a thousand yards, unless you had special magical protection which only

195

the priests of the Habiru knew.

I thought the same as our King. It was just a wooden box, no different to the ones the people of the far countries beyond Mount Hermon had on their shrines. The stories were no doubt put about by Joshua to inspire dread in the hearts of those whose lands they sought to steal. Jericho hearts would not be melted by such tales, thought . Their magic could not harm us.

I can hardly believe how innocent I was then. The days when Jericho still stood seem like another life away. I never dreamt that I would learn so much about that cloth covered box, never dreamt what it could do, nor how I would be pursued across the earth, and into Reshef's own domain, for the sake of the secrets it contained.

It was easy for the Habiru to cross over. The Jordan was nothing but a dirty yellow trickle. The priests went first with their terrible Ark, and stood on dry ground in what should have been the middle of a torrent. They stayed there, Guardians of such a Power as I had never dreamed, while the whole Habiru nation passed across.

I later learnt that Joshua called together the twelve men he had chosen from each of the tribes and told them to take twelve stones from the middle of the Jordan, from where the priests stood with the Ark, and place them at the spot they would camp that night, as a sign that the waters had stopped before their Ark, so that all the children of the Habiru to come would remember forever the power of their God.

Those bastard children of the Habiru! May their name be ever cursed! And a thousand curses on their One God, who was no God of Jericho! May he be torn from the sky and devoured by the fire of Baal!

When they had all crossed the Jordan, Joshua told their priests to come out of the river with the Ark. No sooner had their feet touched the bank – our side of the Jordan, our land – the river began to pour forth in full flow once more.

The news soon spread and when the kings and people of the the Amorites and Canaanites heard how the One God had dried the very waters of the Jordan that his people might cross, their hearts melted in fear.

We could only watch from our hilltop fort, as forty thousand Habiru, armed for battle, made camp that night, on our side of the Jordan, so close, so close to Jericho.

Fragment 10

We threw dung from the walls as they approached, smearing our hands, not caring about the stink.

Joshua stood apart from the rest, too far for me to make him out clearly from where I stood. But when he held up his sword and cried, "Advance!" his voice carried, full of power, up to the very walls of Jericho.

An armed Guard, bearing spears, marched towards the city first. The soldiers looked as strong and fearsome as their weapons, fit and well trained, not a man out of step. The desert years, far from shrivelling the Habiru up in the blazing sun, seemed rather to have made them sinewy and robust, like men who have been through the fire, and emerged more powerful from the flames.

Yet still we never thought they could topple our walls.

Then came the priests, Astarte damn their souls! Seven of them, all blasting on trumpets and making a terrible noise. There was much pointing and chattering among we citizens up on the hilltop when we saw what followed the priests.

Little Hadad grabbed my arm. "Look," he cried. "The magic box!"

"Huh, nothing magic about it," said I.

Now we could see with our very own eyes the Ark we had heard so much about. It was carried by four priests, one at each corner, on two poles that gleamed in the sun. "See how it shines!" said Tarasch.

Despite myself, I caught my breath. Surely those poles were made of gold! The Ark itself was hidden beneath a cloth.

Then came another large gap. The Ark and its priests traveled well apart from the marching men. The rear guard came next - they looked as grim and formidable as their companions at the front - and behind them the whole rabble of the Habiru people, men, women and children, the old and crippled limping at the back.

The trumpets blew non-stop. We jeered from the walls.

But from the Habiru ranks came not a word. No one spoke. Except for the trumpets, they marched in silence.

When they came within a stone's throw of the city gate, they stopped then turned and marched with their Ark right round the walls of Jericho.

"What are they doing?" said Tarasch, by my side.

"They are mad," I laughed, and rejoined my

neighbours in hurling dung. We knew it would fall far short of the Habiru but it was fun to throw shit at our enemy, safe on our hilltop, within the highest, thickest walls in the land.

They walked right round the walls and then, to our surprise, they went straight back to their camp. Our soldiers lowered their spears and jeered. We threw more dung. Then we returned to our homes and sat round our fires, laughing and joking about the antics of the Habiru. They had obviously taken one look around our stronghold and given up.

Meanwhile, our men still watched from the walls. The following day the Habiru did the same. First came the armed men, then the priests, the Ark and its bearers, then the rear guard and all the people, round the walls of Jericho and back to their camp.

By the fourth day, we had grown bored of watching. Hadad spent more time with the goat boys than gawping at the "magic box" and Tarasch didn't bother going to the walls but stayed in her favourite tree, arranging her "house" in its branches. She would take flat loaves and a jar of water from the spring and serve guests whom only she could see.

"I don't want you going far," Rahab had warned them. "Make sure you stay close to home, for when the Habiru strike, our whole family must keep inside this house. And that includes you," she said, turning to me.

"Jericho will not fall," I said.

Rahab said nothing. She turned to the window and made sure the red cord was securely fastened.

"You, Tarasch, Timnal, Hadad, Grandfather and Grandmother, I want you all inside these walls when the Habiru enter. I shall tell them Grandmother and Grandfather are our parents, so they don't think I'm trying to squeeze everyone I know inside."

"Scheme as you will," I said, washing the remains of some porridge from a bowl. "I don't know how you can believe that rabble can possibly get past Jericho's walls. The outer wall round the foot of the hill is as thick as a man from head to toe and even if they got past that, they'd still have to climb the inner one. That's thicker than two men stretched out in a line. And there's our soldiers. Besides, our walls reach up the sky. The Habiru will never take the city."

Rahab said nothing but looked out across the plain towards the Jordan, and touched the red cord in the window.

On the seventh day, the Habiru paraded around the city. But they did not stop there. They circled the walls again, and again. I stood with my jar at my feet. I was on my way back from the spring and had stopped to watch this new break in the Habiru routine.

"What are they doing?" said a girl next to me. A woman beside her shook her head.

Seven times they marched round the city walls. Our men held their spears at the ready. The Habiru trumpets blasted.

Then silence descended. The Habiru had not spoken a word all the times they had circled the walls. Now our people fell silent too. Even the birds were still. I felt the morning sun hot on my face and the smell of donkey dung rose warm in my nose. Sweat trickled down my face.

It was quiet, too quiet.

Joshua raised his sword and commanded his people, "Shout! For the Lord has given you this city! Jericho and all that is in it are to be destroyed!"

Then came words which chilled my blood and turned my stomach over.

"Only Rahab the prostitute," yelled Joshua, "and all who are with her in her house shall be spared, because she hid the spies we sent!"

"No!" I backed away. The jar of water tumbled over at my feet. People nearby turned to stare as the jar crashed on the ground. Eyes grew wide with surprise then fierce with hostility as Joshua's words rang out across the plain and up to the city, so Rahab's treachery was exposed before all of Jericho.

"Rahab?" breathed a woman. "A traitor?"

"That's Rahab's sister!" yelled a man close by.

"Kill her!" shouted a cripple, raising his stick.

Others took up the chant. "Kill her! Kill her!"

I turned to flee but tripped and sprawled on the around, certain that my end had come. Dust and nausea filled my mouth.

But then came a sound that shall ring in my ears till the Gods are no more. The trumpets blasted. A great cry went up from the Habiru people assembled outside the walls. A terrible roar filled the air and the very ground shook, as though a great bull imprisoned below the hill were charging up through the earth.

"The walls!" came a terrified cry. "The walls are crumbling!"

I scrambled to my feet. No one bothered about me, the sister of Rahab the traitor. People ran in all directions.

Chickens squawked and flapped as they scuttled to get out of the way of trampling feet. Donkeys brayed at the commotion and fled. Cattle bellowed in terror as the around shook beneath their hooves, and stampeded through the streets, scattering jugs and baskets and trampling those who were too slow or frail to get out of their way. I saw the cripple try to drag himself clear, as a surge of women and children rushed from the walls, but he vanished beneath the racing feet.

All around me, dust rose into the air. Ignoring the fleeing crowds, I stumbled forwards unsteadily. I had to see the walls for myself. A great rock detached itself and rolled straight at me. I dived aside. Then came another and another. And all the time that huge invisible bull roared and stamped till I thought my ears should shatter, making the around beneath me heave so I could not stand. I could no longer see the sky. Great clouds of dust billowed above, turning the bright sunlit morning to dusk.

A shower of small stones pelted me round the head then the dust cleared, for an instant. Before me I saw the tower, the bastion of all the fortifications of Jericho, falling, crushing all who stood beneath. I ran to avoid a stream of rocks then tripped and sprawled on the around I stared in horror at a sandal and a piece of cloth protruding from beneath a boulder and a leg disappearing below the rubble. The walls, the great strong walls of Jericho that soared to the sky, the pride of Canaan, came crashing, crashing down. I ran.

Strong hands dragged me inside. Timnal.

He barred the door behind me. Everyone was there. Hadad, Grandfather, Grandmother, Timnal, Rahab...

"Tarasch. Where is Tarasch," I asked, panic rising like bile in my throat.

"She said she had quests for a party in her tree," announced Hadad, his face white and solemn in the gloom of the house.

"I'll go and find her," said Timnal.

But as he opened the door, a crowd of people surged down the street in terror.

"The Habiru!" came a cry. "The Habiru are coming!"

Timnal stumbled against the doorpost, as someone pushed him out of the way. He caught his head on the stone and crumpled, stunned, to the floor.

Rahab dragged him inside.

"I'll go," I yelled, and jumped over Timnal into the street.

As I raced towards the piece of land where Tarasch's fig tree stood, I heard screams from a nearby house. A man staggered out, clutching a sword at his chest which stuck out through his back. He crumpled to the ground and a pool of blood spread around him in the dust. Then came such shrieks from inside his house as I hope to never hear again.

I clapped my hands over my ears and raced for Tarasch's tree. But a horde of Habiru rushed up the road towards me. The blades of their swords were red.

"Tarasch!" I screamed.

Joshua's murdering band lay between me and my sister.

A great crack opened up in the ground where I stood and I fell, banging my head. I lay there, entombed in the earth, a trickle of something hot and sticky running into my eyes, unable to move. Above me, the Habiru swarmed and the very sky screamed in terror and pain.

Fragment 11

When I crawled out of that tomb which had saved my life the day was nearly gone. I walked like a ghost through streets stained with blood. Friends, neighbours, people I exchanged greetings with every day at the springs lay dead in doorways and dust. Doors hung open, revealing whole families slaughtered within. I do not know how many bodies I had to step over to reach my home.

When I arrived, it was empty. It must have been the only house in Jericho with no corpses strewn across the floor. My family were gone. I sank down and laid my head on the around. Cinders from the fire mixed with the mess in my hair. I was rank with blood, sweat and ash, but I cared nothing that I stank.

I saw many horrors that day, most blended into one bloody tableau of death, yet some remain before my eyes, staining my mind forever. I do not know how long I lay on the floor but I remember a terrible crying, like a child in pain. When I dragged myself up and went to see, I found the noise was coming from the house across the road. All the occupants were dead. Chickens were scattered across the garden with their heads cut off. Sheep lay in pools of darkening blood. Only one thing moved. A donkey, one of its legs lying severed at a distance in the midden, its body rent with cuts from a sword. Yet still it lived, and cried like a child, heaving, choking, sobbing. Those bastard Habiru had spared nothing. The old, the sick, the lame, women, babies, even our animals had been put to the sword.

I found a dagger sticking out of the chest of a young girl sprawled across her clay toys in the garden. I pulled it out, spattering myself with her blood, and sliced the donkey's throat. The sobbing ceased. The heaving flanks fell still.

Now nothing moved. Nothing made a sound. While evening drew down, Jericho lay quiet and still in its blood.

Suddenly a spark of hope flared in my breast. Tarasch. She had probably been up her tree when the Habiru struck. Perhaps she was still there, terrified no doubt, but safe in its branches. I cast the dagger aside and ran, leaping over the dead, towards the tree.

I parted the branches and peered up. But she wasn't there.

I searched, how I searched. Everywhere I knew she might be. The shadow of night was falling by the time I found her, beside the city wall, in a little field now strewn with dead sheep and trampled poppies. The flames had not reached it yet, though they licked the dry grass at the edge.

The city was burning. Great tongues of fire leapt into the darkening sky, streaking it orange. A serpent of smoke devoured the evening star. The moon could not bear to show her face. Little flakes of ash fell softly upon me like rain. The stench of death and burning made me retch.

And there, in that field of death, while Jericho burnt, I buried my sister.

Fragment 12

I spent that night in the lee of a rock, a short way from the Jordan. The <u>girl</u> who woke and stretched her cut and aching limbs to a blazing sun was not the one who had sung her way to the springs with a jar on her head just one day before. That girl was gone. She had died with Jericho.

Keeping out of sight under the cover of rocks and scrub, I crept as close as I dared to the Habiru camp. A small group sat on the bank of the Jordan, grilling fish over sticks on their fire. My stomach heaved. After all I had seen I was sick to the very core. I had not eaten for a day, but I could not even think of food.

"They say the gold and metals from the heathen temple have been stored," said the woman in charge of turning the fish. "Joshua ordered all the treasures to be taken out of the city before it was burnt."

"The first of many," grinned her husband, tweaking her cheek. "Now Jericho has fallen, we can march into the rest of Canaan, just as the Lord promised Joshua."

"Don't be so sure," warned a crone in black, washing out a bowl. "Things aren't always that simple. And you were the first to complain when we had to march under the midday

209

sun to the Jordan."

"Yes but..."

"Yes but nothing," snapped the crone. "Now hand me a plate."

I kept still as a mouse and while the Habiru scum broke their fast - I prayed to Baal they would all choke on a fishbone - I learnt more of what had happened in Jericho. Joshua had given orders that no one was to be spared, but the promise made to Rahab must be kept. Labor and Shechem had gone to our house and taken the family out before the city was destroyed. I bet my sister smiled to see her Habiru lover again - may Astarte tear his eyes from his head and feed them to the vultures! When the treasure from our temple had been taken to the place of the Habiru God, and the city burnt, Joshua was still not content.

The man, fish juices running down his chin, the pig, told the women what he had seen.

"Joshua stood on a rock," he declared, "and pointed to the city as it burnt. Then he said, 'Let any man who attempts to rebuild Jericho be cursed before the Lord. May he lay its foundations at the cost of his firstborn son. At the cost of his youngest, will he set up its gates."

"He knows how to turn a pretty phrase, does Joshua, Son of Nun," cackled the hag.

"And to make a city burn," laughed the man. He spat a fishbone onto the ground.

"And what of the Canaanite whore?" asked the woman, setting a bowl of corn porridge in front of her man. "The one who Joshua ordered to be spared with her family?"

"The bitch was taken out by Shechem and Labor, the ones who stayed in her house."

"And shared some of her Canaanite hospitality, I'll bet," sneered another man across the fire.

"They've been put in a tent outside the camp," said the first. "No doubt the whore is unclean."

I had heard enough. I wanted to ram the fish heads down their throats till they choked then burn the whole Habiru band as they had burned Jericho, but I dragged my sore and aching limbs away.

I cleaned myself up in the Jordan, safely around a bend in the river which hid me from sight, then made my way to higher ground.

From the cover of a rock overlooking the Jordan I had a clear view of the Habiru camp as they went about their daily business, grazing their flocks, washing their children, filling their jars, as though sacking a city and putting all that moved within its walls to death was an every day event. Perhaps for them it was.

I saw too the tent outside the main camp. I crept across the plain, from rock to rock, till I was near enough to see how many of my family still lived. I saw Rahab emerge and go to greet that viper, Shechem. Her fingers reached out for his. His lips sucked hers. My skin crawled. I gripped the rock which hid me. Then I could stand no more and rushed towards them. They turned in surprise as I approached.

Hadad rushed out of the tent and clutched me around the waist, burying his head in the tatters of my dress. Timnal, Grandfather, Grandmother - I saw them all through the flap of goats' hair slung above the entrance to the tent.

Rahab ran towards me, a smile of delight on her face. Her fingers were still entwined with Shechem's.

"We thought you were dead!" she cried. "And Tarasch?" Her eyes lit up with hope. "Is she come to join us too?"

I gently prised Hadad's fingers away from my waist. "Tarasch is dead."

The morning sun burned inside my head. My eyes were filled with red, red from the sun, red from the blood I had seen flooding the streets of Jericho.

"I would not join you, you traitorous bitch, if you were

the last woman left alive by the murdering Habiru God!"

I made claws of my nails and rushed for her face. Rahab screamed, raising her arms. My claws, broken and jagged from scouring a grave from rocks for my sister, made deep grooves in her palms. I glimpsed livid streaks of blood before Shechem grabbed my hands and threw me to the ground.

Hadad began to wail. Timnal came out of the tent, blinking against the sun.

I backed away. I could not see. Sun, tears and blood blurred my eyes. Always blood.

"Traitor!" I screamed, and my cries mixed with those of the vultures circling the crumbled walls. "Traitor! I will never live with Habiru scum! You betrayed Jericho! From this day on, I have no family. You are dead, like Tarasch!"

"Let her go," I heard the snake say, when I stumbled blindly towards the rocks, and as I made for the hills, Hadad's wailing rang in my ears.

Fragment 13

I made a shrine in the rocks of the hills. A blasted tree was my Asherah pole. I ripped shreds from my gown and hung them on the broken branches. Then I lifted my arms to the sky and swore to Astarte to remain true. The One God would never steal *my* soul. Any god who demanded the blood of an entire city - babes in arms, little girls holding parties in trees and gentle donkeys too - would never, never be a God of mine.

When I had finished, I turned my back on the blackened ruin of Jericho and headed into the hills.

I thought I would find water. Those great white giants of chalk glowered above the Jordan, marching on forever. Surely in that ghostly wilderness there had to be be other springs, like those which kept our date palms heavy with fruit and our water jars full to the brim.

But I had rarely travelled out of Jericho in the sixteen years of my life and knew nothing of the hill country. I soon found that our luxuriant city was a precious jewel set in a wilderness of chalk. Here nothing grew. Once I found some water in a cleft in the rock and a leaping gazelle led me to a little patch of scrub where a snake lay sunning itself. I had lost count of the time I had been without food. I knew by now I would probably die in this barren waste but death was preferable to living with murderers and traitors. I seized my chance. I picked up a rock and smashed it down on the head of the snake then, with a jagged edge of stone, I slit its stomach and slaked my thirst on its blood and my hunger on its raw flesh.

I slept in caves by night. There were many that pocked the chalk. They sheltered me too from the burning heat of the midday sun. The skin on my hands was cracking. My lips bled. If I had found a pool of water, I would no doubt have scared myself at the sight of my face. My hair was matted and my dress in rags.

One night, I had managed to suck the juice of a cactus to stave off death for a little while more, and was dreaming of floating in a pool of beautiful blue water, when something brought me sharply awake. I crawled to the entrance of the cave, crouched down and listened. There it was again. A strange whistling noise that chilled my blood. Then came a chattering and burbling, followed by shrieking such as I had never heard in my life. Demons. I cowered in terror. All the creatures of my grandmother's stories rushed back to make me tremble. Dreadful, red-eyed, sharp clawed furies that flew out the night to carry off wayward girls. I was not going to die of thirst after all. The demons would get me first. Surely my heart would stop in terror at just the thought of what they would do to me.

Dark shapes emerged from holes in the ground and crept towards me. Others scuttled out from rocks. One came within yards of the cave then stopped and twitched his nose.

I laughed and the dark shapes bounded away, still squealing, whistling and shrieking. Coneys. Once I started laughing I could not stop. It was the first time I had laughed in days and my lips cracked so badly that my mouth filled with the metallic taste of blood. My eyes prickled and I sank to my knees, laughing till I cried, and sobbed with the pain of my loss.

After that I remember little. Crawling, crying, laughing. Day. Night. Sun. Chalk.

Then a curve like a snake before me. Sunlight sparkling on water. Was that the Jordan? Was I dreaming, or already in the land of the dead?

I crawled and crawled. Jagged stones ripped my arms and legs to shreds. The glistening band was still far away. Too far. I would never reach it. I laid my head in the sand and while the sun beat down so hot I could not move, strange visions passed across my eyes.

216

A box, covered in cloth. A strange being, whose face I could not see for brilliant light, pulled away the cover and opened the box. A great silver cloud ascended from within. Screams filled the air and all around me people fell dying. I reached into the box. Water swirled about my hands, washing away the grime, healing my cuts. My skin was made new. An old man lay dying beside me. The being of light dipped a jug into the magic box and poured water over the old man's face. He sat up. His skin peeled back, wrinkles smoothed away, and when he got to his feet he was young again. The silver cloud returned to the box, leaving corpses strewn across the sand. I cupped my hands and tried to drink the water… water… water… then all turned black.

Someone was kicking me.

"Look! A girl! Astarte's answered my prayers!" A babble of voices.

The rags of my dress were ripped from neck to waist and hot sun burned into my breast.

"We're going to have some fun at last!"

"Get out of it!"

"I saw her first."

Scuffles around me. Blinding sun.

"Away!"

The scuffling stopped. The voices were still.

"Let's get a look at her beneath this dirt."

A foul stench in my face then cool water running down my skin.

"Yes, I thought so," came the same rough voice. It was my language, but as I had never heard it spoken before. "This is a pretty one."

"Let's have her!"

"I haven't seen a woman in weeks!"

"Give us our fun!"

"Be silent!" A whip cracked.

Cold stone at my mouth. Cool water on my burning lips.

"This one is not for such as you."

Foul breath again in my face. But I did not care. I had water. I opened my eyes. An old man leaned over me, his head covered with a coloured cloth, his eyes gleaming and skin deeply lined, burnt to the colour of tamarisk wood by the sun, It was his breath that reeked in my nose.

"This one will fetch a price that will keep us all in whores."

Thus began my new life, as a slave.

Chapter 7

Doesn't Schlott believe in fresh air or something? His office feels more like an Aga. I hardly got any sleep last night, I've had the police rummaging through all my most intimate stuff, my flat resembles Newark tip on a bad day, I can't find my *Genevre* perfume which I feel totally naked without, I have a cup of cheap instant coffee in front of me that tastes like dishwater, and I'm telling you, I feel like heading straight for the airport to get the first plane out. In the end, I can't stand the airlessness a moment longer and throw the sodding window open myself.

When I turn round, my boss and my lover are both watching me across the office. So far there's been no repeat yesterday's argument, but I'm not holding my breath.

"Charlotte, I can't tell you how sorry I am," says Hermann Schlott. "Nothing like this has ever happened before. We can find you another flat or maybe you'd feel happier with rooms in the mature students' residence. They're not so spacious as the flat but you'd have your own kitchen and bathroom and the benefit of the university on site."

"I think that would be a good idea," says Ben grimly. "I also suggest, Dr Schlott, that whoever your backers or prospective backers are, no further details of the fragments are released until

Charlotte's finished the translation."

Here they go again. Dogfighting, while this little blonde bimbo is supposed to play fly on the wall and let them tussle over their bones.

"That can be arranged, but we don't know that the ransacking of Charlotte's flat was anything to do with her work. The police have suggested the motive was robbery."

"Bah, without anything being taken?" scoffs Ben. "Someone has obviously been watching her take work home and decided to try and get their hands on it while she was out. She should be rehoused in secure university accommodation right away."

I can feel a throbbing behind my temples. Who the hell do these two think they are, planning my life for me, like I'm some piece of baggage to be dumped in a hall. I've really had enough.

I stand up and lean on the table, glaring. "It may have escaped your notice, but I am still here, and, believe it or not, I do actually have a brain with which to make decisions for myself." They are both taken aback. I take a deep breath. Opening the window has made not a jot of difference to the stifling heat. "Dr Schlott, do you mind if I go outside for some air and think about your offer?"

"Of course not." Dr Schlott jumps up and sees me to the door. Ben is still slouching crossly in his chair. "This must have been a terrible shock for you. I really can't tell you how sorry I am. I can assure you the university will do everything possible." He holds the door open as thankfully I make my escape.

"Charlotte!"

Why the hell can't Ben butt out? He tries to follow me down the corridor, but I wave him away without turning round. I just want a bit of time and space, for heaven's sake. Luckily, he takes the hint and returns to Schlott's office. I can hear him from the end of the corridor, still ranting on about bloody investors. As if I care right now.

I grab a Coke from the machine and take it out to the gardens where I find a shaded spot beneath a clump of acacia trees and at last I can sit and think, without that pair of chauvinists breathing down my neck.

I feel like I've been raped. Not my body, my life. My books, my letters from Susan and Sarah, my diary, my Vaseline, my Wonderbras, all scattered by strangers across the floor, then further tainted by the probing fingers of the police. Much as I hate to agree with Ben, I'm pretty certain that whatever the police might claim, this was no robbery. Nothing seems to have been taken but my flat has been completely turned over. Whoever they were, they must've been after the translated fragments. Someone knew I've been taking them home every night and decided to ransack the flat. In a bizarre way, I'm relieved to realise I wasn't just being paranoid all those times when I was sure someone was watching me. But stuff them, they were out of luck. Yesterday morning I brought the translations back them to my office. I could kick myself for thinking my work would be safer at home at night. But it could have been so much worse.

It sickens me to the core when I think what might have happened. If Abdul had been there, or Cruiser, alone in the flat...

How would I ever face Abdul's mother, or forgive myself, if anything happened to him? I saw an Arab funeral cortege pass by in the street last week. A young boy had been killed throwing stones at an Israeli guard post. I saw the sorrow carving lines on the faces of those women in black and heard their awful wail of grief for the dead. I tell you, I've never been so relieved in all my life as when I turned away from the empty kitchen and heard Abdul's cheerful voice on the stairs as he returned with Cruiser safely trotting beside him on the lead. Thank God they had gone for a walk when they did.

Of course, Ben came tearing round like Indiana Jones as soon as I rang him, the tyres of his Landrover screeching on the tarmac as he pulled up outside the block. His face, as he rushed into the flat, was white. I didn't take much persuading to stay at his apartment off Kalid ibn El Walid. The flat was a tip and the last thing I wanted was to spend the night alone. Ben treated me as though I were made of glass and somehow seemed more shocked than I was. He found a blanket for Cruiser and didn't even mention fleas.

And it was nice, to be all wrapped up his arms and have someone look after for me for a change, instead of having to be so damned strong. I know you're supposed to cope on your own without a man, but God, it felt good.

I watch a group of students sprawl on the

grass nearby, laughing without a care in the world. I used to be like them, not so long ago. But I must focus on what I'm going to do. Getting the first plane back to Heathrow is not an option. Do I clear up the mess in my present flat or let the uni. find me another? Cruiser's a real problem. Dogs aren't allowed on university premises so that knocks Schlott's suggestion of a Hall of Residence on the head. Anyway, I need my own space, just me and Cruiser, without being surrounded by hoards of students. It could take a while to find another flat and it would be so much upheaval. I'm really quite settled where I am. At least, I was. I pick at a broken cuticle and frown. I notice Ben hasn't suggested I move in with him. Of course, we're still finding out about each other. Our relationship is too new for that. I'm not exactly the world's most stable person and Ben's preoccupied with his problems. Hardly the best start for a relationship. Moving in together would be a disaster right now. But it would have been nice to be asked.

I chew at the cuticle, ignoring the pain. Maybe there's still something between him and Maddy. He's always on the phone to New York. Having me in his flat might cramp his style.

Damn Ben Travers and Dr Schlott. It was Schlott's idea to put details of the fragments out prematurely which has caused all this trouble. And the pair of them had the cheek to sit there discussing where I should live as though I wasn't there! No, I damn well don't want to live in the pocket of the university all the time. Neither do I want to be carted off somewhere else. Besides, I like having Abdul with his cheeky grin around to mind my dog and it's highly unlikely the intruders will come back, now they knew I don't leave papers unattended in the flat. Sod them all. No one's going to arrange my life for me. I'll clean up the mess and stay where I am. Schlott can damn well arrange to get me a stronger door fitted, with extra security locks. No one's going to force me from yet another home. Sod Jonathon too. No one is going to terrorise me again.

I'm on my way back inside when I hear a voice behind me.

"Miss Adams?"

I turn round, still bristling, but relax when I see a friendly face.

"Yusef, *shalom.*"

He glances around, checking that no one else is in earshot. "Miss Adams, I'm sorry to hear about what happened to your flat."

"Thank you. So am I."

"Look, I don't want to *worry* you, but..." He looks around cautiously again as a group of students come chattering down the corridor and waits for them to pass before he continues. "I was interested in why so many people were hacking into your computer and I've run a few more checks. I managed to get a trace on one of those locations in the States."

"You did? Who was it?"

"The site in Los Angeles. It took me a while to crack but I did it eventually. I thought I should warn you."

"Warn me?"

"Look I don't know what you're working on exactly. But as well as Mossad, you've been infiltrated by a U.S. arms dealer called Arms' R Us."

"Arms R Us?" I immediately think of kids with toys. "What a sick name."

"You could be dealing with some sick people as well. I mean, what kind of people sell guns for a living?"

I notice the CND symbol decorating Yusef's bag along with the Greenpeace stickers. This guy certainly has his colours nailed to the wall. "Yes, I suppose you're right. Look, you're sure about this?"

"Of course. Once I got in, I had no trouble finding out who they were. Does it make any sense to you?"

"Oh yes," I say grimly, and remember thinking of the white fire that destroyed the cities of Ai, Gibeon, Lachish. "It makes sense all right. Thank you, Yusef."

"No worries. Glad to help. *Shalom.*"

"*Shalom.*" I'm about to walk on when I think of something else.

"Yusef."

Yusef turns round again.

"Please don't mention this to Dr Travers. He's got enough on his plate and I don't think it's a good idea to worry him."

225

"Sure. And Miss Adams?"

"Yes?"

"Just watch your back."

"This is a crazy idea," growls Ben, dumping a new box of crockery on the kitchen work surface to replace the set which was smashed. "You could have let Schlott find a new flat or moved into a Hall of..."

"..or got on with clearing up the mess in this flat, as I'm doing."

"And what if they come back?"

"Why should they? They've found out I don't have unattended papers here and I'll leave my work at uni. from now on, where security can look out for it. Lightning never strikes twice and all that."

"That's a myth. There was this man in Colorado..."

"Ben." He's starting to get on my nerves. I mean, it's sweet he's so concerned about me, but I'm not going to chuck all my independence out the window and suffocate in cotton wool. I point to the new reinforced door. "Have you seen those locks and bolts? It would take half a kilo of semtex to get in now."

"Maybe that's what they'll use next time."

"There won't be a next time. Anyway, the local police are going to keep a check on the place." I fold my arms and glare at him across the kitchen. This is my home and I'm staying put." I'm not going to let anyone terrorise me from place to place. Not any more.

"You sure are stubborn. I suppose nothing I can say will make you change your mind?"

"Nothing."

"It's all that mutt's fault." Ben glares at Cruiser who sits watching him balefully from the kitchen floor. "You're putting yourself at risk just so that... creature can stay with you."

"Look, if you're going to get in the way and insult my dog, I can finish clearing up on my own."

"No," says Ben. "I'm staying here tonight, to keep an eye on you."

"You can't keep an eye on me all the time." I must admit the thought of him sleeping beside me all night is more than appealing. Quite apart from not having to lie there alone, tensing up at every sound. Dr Ben Travers in my bed does have certain attractions.

"No, but I can tomorrow."

"What's happening then?"

"Seeing as we had to postpone our trip to Arad because of the breakin, I thought it might help take your mind off things if we go tomorrow instead."

"That, Ben Travers, is the first helpful suggestion you've made all day."

"But," warns Ben. "We're going to watch our backs from now on."

I sink down on a stool, suddenly exhausted. It's been such an emotionally draining twenty four hours and there are times you just can't be strong any longer. That brief bubbling up of elation at the idea searching for the tablets dissolves like an Anadin in water. Yusef used much the same phrase. This is the second time today I've been warned to watch my back.

We leave early in the morning before the sun grows too hot and travel down the coast road along the western bank of the Dead Sea. We could have taken the inland route but because of the latest flare-ups between Palestinians and the Israeli army, Ben wants to avoid Hebron which is always a flash point for trouble.

Vegetable stalls and apartment blocks strung with washing line the route as we pass the Arab suburb of Et Tur then, as we leave the outskirts of the city behind, the road winds its way through the rocky gorges of the Judean mountains. Rusting tanks by the roadside serve as a reminder, as if anyone could forget, of Israel's turbulent past; a volcano constantly erupting into present day unrest. Ben taps his fingers in irritation on the steering wheel as we're held up at a check-point on the road. It turns out to be one of several, the current tension being what it is, and it's a good couple of hours before we pass through the resort of Ein Gedi.

We pass a sign in front of a health spar, proclaiming the virtues of Primula Porter beauty products and the latest Dead Sea facial. "You know, I fancy trying some of that mud"

"We haven't got time," growls Ben. "We need all the daylight hours we can get."

"I don't mean today. Just sometime.

Ingrid was telling me about Primula Porter's new..."

"You don't want to go *there!*"

"Why not?"

Ben scowls and purses his lips. His knuckles tighten on the wheel.

"And don't give me that line 'because you're beautiful how you are." (Though I really don't mind if he does. Even though I know how far from the truth it is.) "I'd just like to give it a go some time, seeing as we're so close to the Dead Sea."

"If you must cover yourself yourself in revolting gunge, go to the beach. But you wouldn't like the Primula Porter spas."

"How do you know?" Honestly, I can't believe him sometimes, but he does look sexy when he comes over all macho.

He indicates and turns into a service station. "I need some gas and some more bottled water." He gets out of the Landrover, slams the door and marches towards the kiosk.

I watch him storm across the tarmac. I can't for the life of me see why he has to be so tetchy about me trying Dead Sea mud. It's not as though I'm planning on dragging him along too. Maybe he's fed up with face packs and stuff after his years with Maddy. God knows what he makes of my bathroom.

Anyway, what I do is my business. He's not going to dictate anything to me. Still, maybe the mud has nothing to do with it. I reckon he's just on edge because of Tony and the break-in. Both our nerves are strung pretty taut right now.

The Landrover soon gets hot when it's
standing still and my shirt
is plastered to my back. Through the window I can
see that Ben's got stuck in a queue. He's huffing and
puffing, of course, glaring at that poor girl on the till. I
might as well get out of this greenhouse for some air.
I jump out and walk towards the strip of golden
sand, as shrieks of laughter drift towards me from
these weird looking humanoids who are smeared
from head to toe in black mud. Some steps lead
down to a sign in several different languages and I
spring onto the sand for a closer look.

Black Mud
Makes you feel young and full of energy,
relaxes tensions and soothes pains.
Application of mud stimulates the metabolism
and blood circulation. Keeps the skin young
and fresh. Can be applied to the entire body,
to painful parts, as a beauty face-mask, or as
a means for strengthening hair growth. The
legendary Queen Cleopatra is said to have
sent slaves here to fetch the mud for her.

Just like Joshua and Caleb did. But no one is
claiming this mud keeps you looking like Mel
Gibson when you're eighty, and turns you into a
one man geriatric fighting force.

At the bottom of the sign is a list of minerals
present in the mud.

Montmorilonite, Caolinite, Illite, Quartz,

230

Feldspars, Organic Material.

Organic material could be anything. Perhaps it was some special'organic' ingredient which gave the Hebrews' mud its unique rejuvenating qualities. But the big question now is could it still exist today?

"Are you going to try it?"

Christ, that made me jump. I spin round towards the voice, too close behind me for comfort. A tall blonde man with a toothpaste ad. smile stands at the bottom of the steps.

He grins. "You on holiday?"

"No."

"I'm from Texas, just staying for a couple of weeks. The wife and I are planning to take the mud today."

I glance back at the forecourt where Ben is loading some bottles of water into the back of the Landrover.

"Not sunbathing today?"

"Just sightseeing."

The man nods. "Going anywhere special?"

"Not really. I should be getting back to the car."

"Sure. Enjoy your trip." I watch as he disappears round the back of an ice-cream hut. He's probably just on holiday, but it's hard when you don't who to trust.

"Who were you talking to?" asks Ben, as I get back into the car.

"Just some tourist."

"You sure?"

"If he was following us, he'd hardly be likely

to come straight up and ask me where we were going, would he?"

Ben pulls a face. "You didn't mention where we're headed, did you?"

"Of course not."

"Good."

We pull out of the forecourt, followed by a number of other vehicles, then we're on our way down the coastal road to Ein Bokek and the southern reaches of the Dead Sea. The highway has rather more traffic than we could do with and Ben keeps tapping his fingers against the wheel whenever we have to slow down, especially when we get stuck behind a tanker. There are loads of them too, ferrying petro-chemicals from all the plants along the Dead Sea.

I let Ben stew in his impatience and gaze out of the window. It's just so weird. The further south we travel, the wilder and more desolate the landscape becomes. The mountains loom higher, complete devoid of any vegetation, crystal white slopes falling sheer to the sea like some sort of advert for Saxa. All the rocks are covered in salt so they form these twisted images of ghostly people. I wouldn't like to be alone out here at night.

The road to Arad is signposted ahead and I turn back in my seat to catch the last glimpse of human habitation at the spas and the glittering of the sea before we head up into the mountains. Then I notice there's another vehicle behind us, a Rover, I think. I can't be sure, but it looks like the man I met on the beach in the passenger seat, with another man driving. So much for taking the mud with his wife."

"Ben, don't look now but..."

Ben glances in his rear view mirror. "Oh shit, not again."

A large tanker pulls out of a slip road from a chemical plant and blocks the other car from view.

Ben swings the Landrover sharply into the Arad road.

I keep an eye behind us but to my relief, when the tanker disappears there's no sign of the other car. "They've gone. I thought it looked like the guy I saw on the beach, but maybe they weren't following us."

"Keep your eyes peeled just in case. The last thing we want is to lead someone straight to the possible site of the tablets. I've had my eye on the rear view mirror since we left Jerusalem but there's been too much traffic on the road today to tell if anyone's been on our tail."

We climb higher and higher, through sheer wastes of rock, where black shadows stain the ochre of impossible slopes. We're alone on this little ribbon of asphalt weaving through endless rock, two insignificant scraps of humanity in a world of desolation. Give me city pollution any day.

I peer out of the windscreen and watch a tiny speck of a bird that must surely be an eagle soar high overhead, yet it's still nowhere near the top of the mountain, and I wonder how any living thing can survive out here. There's not a single tree or plant in sight. Eerie columns twist out of the shale while gigantic faces seem to stare from the stone. We skirt a gorge and I shudder when I see rusted wrecks of cars lying in pieces at the bottom. Then my thoughts drift to the fragments and I wonder how it would feel to be there at night, with only the stars for company, knowing you didn't have a friend in the world. No wonder the poor kid cried herself to sleep.

I reach across to touch Ben's arm, thanking the gods who rule this harsh land that I'm not here on my own.

After climbing over a thousand metres into the mountains, we arrive in the modern town of Arad. At last, civilisation again. We've been driving all morning and I'm my legs feel really cramped. I've never been so glad to see shops and apartment blocks. .

We swing into the side of the road and Ben switches off the ignition. "Right, first things first. Food."

"Great, and I'm dying for a drink." I could also do with a loo and some cold water to splash on my face.

"Me too," says Ben. "I could murder a beer. Come on. Let's go find a restaurant."

True to form, Ben soon sniffs out an Arabic restaurant which is blissfully cool and has an array of lunch dishes even he can't complain about. After a large plate of couscous, almond rice, and the most amazing smoked aubergines with tahini, I sit back and sip my sparkling Perrier while Ben heads off to the gents.

The restaurant is crowded and noisy, obviously a popular venue with the locals. Ben definitely has a nose for these sort of places, like a police dog for cocaine. Now he's gone, a number of men are gawping my way. An Arab, with a paunch to rival Pavarotti, lets his eyes flick over my chest. I ignore him as he pulls out his mobile phone. Probably on the phone to his wife, dirty creep. I pick up the dessert menu to spoil his view. Then I notice someone peer in through the window. For a moment I wonder if it's that man from the beach again, but whoever it is disappears and I can't be sure. No point worrying Dr Paranoia.

"Ready to go?" says Ben,
reappearing by my side."

I push back my chair. "Yes,
let's be off."

Outside the restaurant there are only business people and shoppers strolling past. The movement at the window was probably just someone checking out the restaurant. I'm pretty sick of looking over my shoulder. I would really like just to enjoy a day out. And what a day out this could turn out to be. I know it's unlikely, but this surge of excitement keeps going through me every time I think of those tablets. Priceless artefacts which any archaeologist or academic would die to get hold of. Of course, they probably won't still be there, it's daft really to hold out too much hope, but there is a weeny, weeny chance, we might just find them. Ben can witter on about being cautious all he likes, but he's as worked up as I am. Let's face it, any archaeologist would be. I mean, not getting excited at even the slimmest chance of finding the secrets from the Ark of the Covenant, hidden for thousand of years? Who's he trying to kid?

We drive west out of Arad until we reach the site of the Canaanite settlement which is now in the middle of farming land, with. the mound of Tell Arad showing signs of recent excavations. Ben parks near the site and I follow him down the way to a pool with a sign that reads `cult basin.'

"This is where the Canaanite settlement of the 3rd millennium was," he says, crouching down and splashing his face with the water. "It was probably nothing but a ruin at the time of our fragments, but it was resettled in Solomon's time and a temple built. The excavations here showed traces of sacrificial animal fat which is consistent with the Hebrews building temples on sites of previous Canaanite sanctity."

"But there's nothing here to fit the description in Fragment 35." I shade my eyes and gaze out at the farmland eked from the desert. "I can't see any trace of a hilltop altar or an oasis."

"Yes, but this is our starting point. We know the Canaanites were around this area in the 3rd millennium BC. Plus you can see a long way from here and get a good overall picture of the landscape."

"We need to look out for that ridge of hills she headed for, during the storm. Where the Great Golden Lion Leapt on the Struggling Hawk, whatever that means."

"Exactly."

A coach draws up, spilling tourists across the Tell, and a helicopter whirs into view overhead.

"It's too flat to be the site we're looking for but I wanted to check out the lie of the land as this settlement fits the right time scale," says Ben. "Next we need to take the road down toward the hills of Sodom."

The helicopter circles lower.

Ben squints up at the sky and frowns.

"It's like rush hour on the New York subway round here. "Come on, let's get back to the Landrover and check out this ruined temple. I've got a pretty good idea where she means."

The road towards Sodom winds round sheer mountain drops and gorges and have to keep closing my eyes as the drops to the bottom make me feel sick. "I'm really glad you only drank one beer," I say to Ben, my nails digging into the dashboard as we swing round another of these scary hairpin bends.

"Don't you trust me?" he grins. He takes his eyes off the road for a second, which does nothing to reassure me.

"If someone comes round too fast..."

"All right, thank you very much for your vote of confidence." Ben glances in his rear view mirror and I nervously find myself doing the same. There is a glimmer of sunlight on metal and glass. We're not alone on this road.

"Once we reach the place I'm thinking of,"

says Ben, "I'm going to pull off the road so no one'll see us."

I can't help shuddering and offer up a little prayer to

Astarte. Well, why not. This is her patch after all. We need all the gods we can get on our side. This is the last place on earth I'd want any trouble.

There is a faint whir above us and a helicopter crosses the sliver of brilliant blue between two mountain peaks.

A tour coach suddenly looms up from around the next bend. I press myself against the back of the seat and scrunch up my eyes. Sweat has pooled in the pit of my back. We're going to crash, I know we are. I brace myself, but nothing happens and when I open them again, the coach has gone.

"Now I know you don't trust me," laughs Ben. "We turn off here. Hold on tight."

He spins the Landrover off the road and onto a rocky plateau where we bump along, hidden from the road behind a chain of enormous boulders. "If anyone is following us we should lose them here. It'll be ages before they realise." He turns off the ignition. "Come on. Let's get out."

"Ben! Is that it?" My God, that's it. I squint against the sun at a clifftop high above us where several standing stones lay prone. That's it! The altar on a high place!

"Ben shades his eyes from the sun and looks up. "I'm pretty sure this is the place. "It's so inaccessible it's never been properly excavated and very few people even know it's here. It was documented in the 19th century by a French explorer, and a team in the thirties managed to climb up and establish that it dates from the 3rd Millennium like the settlement at Arad. But no one's been up there since."

I look around at the rocky terrain. "If this is it, there should be an oasis somewhere nearby."

"Don't forget it might not be that simple. Oases sometimes dry up in the course of centuries. We might have to search for something that no longer exists. Don't get too excited yet. And the landscape may have altered after earthquakes."

But as I gaze up at the ancient stones I know this is the place. I can just see that poor exhausted girl, clutching her camel on the bumpy ride through the mountains, with the tablets stowed on its back. Here we go again, this butterfly feeling. Those tablets could be just feet away.

"Take some Evian," says Ben, tossing me a bottle from the back of the Landrover, and we set off through the rocks.

But although we search for over an hour, we can't find any sign of an oasis or a cave. My mouth feels full of dust and it's unbearably hot out here. The heat seems to suck all the energy out of you and despondency crawls in instead. Perhaps successive earthquakes have changed the landscape out of recognition since 1230 BC and the tablets are lost forever.

Ben sits down on a rock and takes a swig from his bottle of water. "I'm sure this is the place. There're the hills of Sodom," he points, with a frown.

239

"And there's the high place with the altar. I think we'd better assume the oasis doesn't exist any more and start looking for traces of old water courses."

I adjust my sunglasses and look around this bleak, burning mountain range. How a young girl on her own managed to survive in such a hostile place is beyond me. Never, even during the very worst times, have I felt as alone as she must have been. In her place I wouldn't just have cried myself to sleep in the darkness. I would have gone completely stark staring off my head.

I brought a copy of Fragment 35 with me and now I pull it out of my rucksack to search for links between the landscape of the text and this hellish terrain. I leave Ben sitting on the rock and climb higher to try and get a better view. Suddenly I notice something shining between the rocks. I grab an overhanging ledge and pull myself up. I'm now high enough to see, and shit! Our Landrover is no longer alone. A silver Citroen is parked by the roadside where we turned off and two men - I can just make out one has blond hair - are running towards the Landrover. Bastard. I knew he was up to no good. Back where the road snakes out of sight towards Arad, a smaller vehicle, I think it's a Metro, has pulled up.

I slide all the way down the shale to the bottom of the cliff and stumble back to where Ben sits studying his map.

"We're being followed!" I pant. "There's a car parked near the Landrover and two men are heading this way. I think one of them's the

American who approached me at the beach."

"Christ!" Ben leaps to his feet, stuffing the map into his bag.

"And there's another vehicle a bit further along the road."

Ben grabs my arm. "Look, there's no way I'm letting you get into danger. We can't get back to the Landrover without running straight into them, so we'll have to convince them there's nothing here to find." He thinks for a moment. "I've got some tools in my rucksack. I want you to take that animal track into the cliff. You'll be high up and able to keep an eye on them. Just stay out of sight. I'll start chipping at that rock face over there where I'll be in full view. I'll dig for a bit then give up, as if there's nothing there. When they see we haven't found anything, they'll probably back off. I doubt they'll harm us because they'll want to watch us until we do find something. As soon as you see them drive off, meet me back at the Landrover."

"But I can't leave you in danger."

"I won't be. They'll only be watching to see if I'm onto anything. Just make sure you stay safely out of sight."

"They'll wonder where I am."

"You've got a head start. Keep out of sight and I'll make out I'm going to give them something worth watching so they needn't worry about you."

"But what if...?"

"Go on, quickly!"

I don't like this one bit but there's no time to argue so I climb up to the narrow path which skirts the lower slopes of the cliff. It's obviously meant for gazelles or mountain goats, not city-lifers like me, but at least I'm screened from anyone below.

When I stop for breath I hear the sound of chipping from below and as I peer through the rocks I see Ben hammering away at a cleft. There's no sign yet of our pursuers. I've got sweat pouring off me like the Ganges in flood and my legs feel like rubbery toys, but I have to go on.

The path winds higher and soon I reach a ledge which gives a good view of the road and the terrain beneath the cliff. Crouching behind a large boulder, I peep out and... shit! The blond guy and his sidekick are hunched behind a rock, watching Ben. As I look towards the road, I glimpse three other men, Arabs, running stealthily between the rocks, some way behind the Americans. I pause uncertainly on the ledge.

What if they don't just go away when he doesn't find anything? This is a crackpot idea of Ben's. I should never have agreed to it. We're completely alone out here. There's no cavalry to come charging to our rescue if things go wrong. The blond guy suddenly looks up, searching the cliff face. I shrink back, my heart pounding now. He's obviously wondering where I am. Damn Ben Travers and his stupid, stupid ideas. The Arabs crouch behind some rocks, a short distance from the Americans who seem blissfully unaware that Ben is not the only one being spied on. The leading Arab motions the others to keep their heads down, and they wait.

Ben continues to tap, his back to them all. He must be roasting.

He's full in the sun with no shade from the rock face. Please God,

or Goddess, whoever's listening, let him be OK. He keeps chipping. Both sets of spies seem prepared to sit it out and wait until he finds something. Then I see the Arab leader look round, searching the terrain. Like the Americans, he must be wondering where I am. He whispers to one of the others who nods and... oh hell... begins to scan the desert with a pair of binoculars slung round his neck. I sink back against the rock. Please God, don't let him spot me.

Suddenly a hail of small stones showers down the cliff face from somewhere above me. The Arab with the binoculars swings round and trains them on the cliff. The others are all looking in my direction too. I daren't move an inch. Then a gazelle comes scampering down the path. It sees me and stops, its great brown eyes bulging with fright, then leaps back the way it has come. The men have obviously seen it too for they turn their attention back to Ben. The Arab swings his binoculars away from my direction. I breathe a sigh of relief and realise all my clothes are soaked in sweat. I smell of fear. As I look up to where the animal has vanished, I notice a fissure in the rocks and checking that no one is looking, I climb stealthily towards it and manage to slip inside. I'm now completely out of sight of the men. Why the hell did I let Ben have his own stupid way? I should have insisted he come with me, instead of exposing himself to danger. But it's too late now. And God knows how either of us will get back to the Landrover safely. I follow the tunnel of rock through the cliff, the sky just discernible as a narrow strip of blue, and I catch the whir of invisible helicopter blades.

I finally emerge on the opposite side of the cliff, on some scree which spills down the lower slopes of the cliff. I can't hear the tapping of Ben's hammer, or see any of the men. I've left them all well behind. But as I look down to the plain in front of me I see a small Bedouin camp, with no more than half a dozen tents, a few camels and a flock of sheep nibbling at a patch of green. An old man sits on a rock, hunched against the sun, watching the animals graze. Hang on, there's grass here. That means water. An oasis. And a sound, or am I imagining it? I stop and listen. Yes, there it is. Water, trickling below. Oh my God, this could be it. I stumble down the scree, sending a hail of small stones clattering down, and close to the bottom, I find a spring, fringed with ferns, gushing out of the rocks to trickle away though the Bedouin camp. Oh my God, this place is exactly as Rahab's sister described. Ben must have got the right clifftop but the wrong side of the mountain. I wonder how it's possible that the landscape has changed so little. But when you gaze out at those rough hide tents and the old man in his traditional dress, you realise that nothing's changed out here for millennia. If it weren't for the Arab music blaring tinnily from inside a tent I could well be back in Canaanite times.

But there could be more than one spring. I can't be sure this is the one near the cave where the girl stashed the tablets from the Ark, but taking a look around, the mountain on this side is much less stable than where I left Ben chipping away at the rockface. Large boulders and small stones litter the plain where the Bedouins have made their camp and I'm surrounded by loose scree which has tumbled down the mountain side like a rocky glacier. There are a number of gashes caused by past upheavals and you don't need a degree in geology to realise this is an earthquake zone.

I shade my eyes and look out across the plain past the Bedouin camp. A ridge of hills, smooth and rounded, quite unlike the jagged mountains at my rear, stretch across the horizon towards the invisible sea. I wonder if she stood here too. Then, as my eyes start to water from the sun, I notice a shape formed by the closest hill. It curves round on itself, golden in the sunlight, tapering into a line of dark rocks running down the side, like the mane of an animal, crouched in the landscape ready to strike. Oh wow, it's a giant golden lion, formed by the contours of the land. Then I notice a rock formation just in front of the lion bill, with jagged edges like the wings of a bird. I've found it! I grab the translation from my rucksack and check. This has to be the right place. It's here, right in front me! The Great Golden Lion which Leaps on the Struggling Hawk. But the cave. What about the cave? Please, Astarte, let it not be buried under tons of rocks. Let me find the cave.

Suddenly the scree gives way and I find

myself sliding in clouds of dust towards the bottom of the slope. I land unceremoniously and bruised on my back and when I look up, I'm staring at all these curious eyes. The occupants of the tents have come to see what the commotion is. The whole family must be here. I quickly sit up and try to regain a bit of dignity. The women are all in black from head to toe, from the littlest girl to a tiny wizened woman who must be her grandmother. The father wears *kiffeyah* and jeans and stands staring down at me with his arms folded, not looking terribly pleased, then the old man comes scurrying up to peer at the unexpected arrival. I feel a bit like a lab specimen, and at a decided disadvantage, having arrived here here on my bum.

"Er, *Shalom.*" I scramble to my feet and dust myself off.

The father scowls.

I could kick myself. A Hebrew greeting is probably not the most appropriate under the circumstances. Not when you're surrounded by a load of Arabs in the middle of nowhere. I wish I'd been over here long enough to have picked up some Arabic.

"Hello, do you speak English?" I feel so foolish. They must think I'm some particularly stupid tourist.

A small boy has been circling me curiously and now he points to my rear and begins to titter. I feel my Levis and oh shit! there's a dirty great rip where I slipped down the scree. His father cuffs him over the head and then, thank goodness, that very stern face breaks into a smile. His wife offers me some water from a goatskin flask which I take with a great show of thanks. Now they've turned out to be friendly I want to make sure they stay that way.

"Him," says the father, ruffling the hair of the little boy with the cheeky grin. "Him speak English."

"I learn at school," announces the boy proudly. "I am best in my class."

"Well done," I say, shamed at my lack of his language while this little boy has somehow managed to learn mine in an empty wilderness of rock.

"What's your name?" I ask, crouching down to his level.

"My name is Gemal. I am eight years old. I live with my mother and father. I speak Arabic and English," recites the boy, and we grin at each other.

He's so sweet, and turns out to be a right little chatterbox. Gemal is obviously determined to make the most of his chance to show off every word he's learnt. His parents nod proudly and the littlest sister looks on in wonder, with her finger in her mouth.

"Hey, your English is great, Gemal."

Gemal beams, then I think he must have repeated that in Arabic, for the whole family begins to talk at once and his father pats him on the back.

"Gemal," I say, crouching down beside him. "I wonder if you can help me. I'm looking for a cave."

"Cave?" Gemal looks puzzled. "What is that?"

I point to a nearby depression in the rock

face. "Like that, but bigger."

"Ah, yes. Come."

I hurry behind, followed by the rest of the family, as he marches over to the cliffside to show me a small cavity eroded in the rock. "This is cave?"

"Yes, that's right. Gemal, are there other caves here?"

Gemal points high up the cliff to where several small black holes gape in the rock, impossibly high and inaccessible. None of those could be the right one. I look around. Perhaps the landslide buried it too deep to find. Yet the scree near the bottom is loose. It would only take a violent spate of rain to wash it onto the plain. Judging by all the loose rocks lying near the camp, that's exactly what's happened. There's a chance it might be near the surface and if anyone knows of such a cave, it's these people.

I pull out my notepad and pen and draw what I hope looks like a cave set into the rockface with a spring gushing nearby. Gemal crouches beside me, watching intently. When I look up, I find the whole family are curiously peering at the sketch. Then I add some rectangles marked with squiggly lines. Art was never my forte. I don't know if Gemal understands what there're supposed to be.

The grandfather crouches on the ground, squints at my drawing then starts to chatter excitedly. The men discuss the map, with the old man persistently pointing to the mountainside. Christ, I wish I could understand Arabic.

"Grandfather say his father find them. In

cave." Gemal points to the blocks. "Writing on stones."

"Yes, yes. That's it, Gemal. That's what I'm looking for. Can you show me?"

Gemal speaks to the old man who hobbles over some stepping stones to the opposite side of the stream. I hurry behind, followed by the family, all pointing and chattering. I can't believe this is really happening. Please, God, let the tablets still be here.

The old man beats aside a clump of ferns with his stick - and there it is - a cave, the entrance full of loose stones. My heart is going like the clappers. I can't get the zip on the rucksack open, my fingers are fumbling so much, but I finally manage to pull out my torch. I can hear a faint whirring of that helicopter outside, but I can't be bothered with that right now. I want those tablets. The cave slopes down at the back, forming a natural cavity, perfect for someone to store their most valuable possessions. It's shrouded in darkness. I crawl closer, scraping my knees on the rock. Everything fits the description in Fragment 35. Oh God, I hardly dare breathe. Please let them be there.

I shine my torch into the cavity. It's empty. Suddenly I feel like a pricked balloon. I pick up a handful of sand and let it trickle through my fingers.

Ben. Where is he? And the men who were following us. He could be in terrible danger. How could I have forgotten him, even for a moment? He could be dying out there while I'm looking for relics that don't exist. What a selfish bitch!

I scramble out of the cave and look up in

alarm as the helicopter swoops low towards me. What if it's back-up for the men out here? Probably the Americans. An Arab helicopter would never get through Israeli air space. It hovers over the camp then, thank God, flies off. I have to find Ben. Please let him be OK. I'll never binge again, I swear. Just let him be safe.

"Grandfather say his father found writing on stones," says Gemal. "Long time ago. He sell them to a man in Jerusalem and make much money. He buy many camels."

"I see." I try to smile for Gemal's sake. His little face looks so hopeful that he's helped me find what I want. It's funny how often the poorer people are the more they try to give.

"Thank you very much, Gemal. You're a very good boy. Your English is brilliant. And please thank your grandfather too."

Suddenly, a loud bang whips through the desert air and the echo bounces off the rocks. No mistaking that. A gun shot. From the other side of the cliff. What if... No. I dig my nails into the palms of my hands. He can't be, he mustn't be. I take a deep breath and force myself into some sort of composure. If he's injured it's me who has to help him.

"Gemal, I have to leave now. Thank you so much for your help. No, really I can't..." I shake my head as Gemal's mother beckons me into the largest tent. "Sorry... I have to go."

I race around the cliff towards where I left him. I daren't waste time returning along the mountain track. I have to know what's happened. I stumble over loose rocks, and keep seeing these awful images of Ben lying bleeding to death. Please God, let there not be vultures hovering over the other side.

A gunshot echoes off the mountainside, and another, followed by a shout. Now I can see the cars parked off the road. I tear around the cliff - and crash headlong into the Arab with binoculars.

Winded, he doubles up and grunts, clutching his stomach then looks up with a scowl and lunges towards me. But there's no way I'm hanging around waiting for him to regain his breath. I kick him hard and carry on running while he writhes on the ground, clutching his groin. Good, I think grimly. Ahead a volley of gunshots cracks through the air. I'm headed straight for them, but I have to find Ben. Nothing else matters.

Suddenly a hand reaches out from behind a projection of rock and clamps across my mouth and before I know what's happening, I'm struggling and kicking on the ground.

Adrenaline is racing through my veins at 80 kilometres an hour, with terror hot on its heels. I wriggle and strain to see my attacker. Relief floods my body like a warm ocean current. It's Ben.

He takes his hand from my mouth and gestures me to keep quiet.   "What happened?" I whisper. "How did...?"

"Ssh. I'll explain later. Quick. We've got to get back to the Landrover."

He grabs my hand and we make a dash

through the rocks.

A shot rings out and ricochets off a boulder. I glance back and see the Arab, still bent over with pain, but managing to aim the gun in his hand.

"Run!" I yell.

Another shot rings out and this time the bullet whistles close by my head.

As we race for the Landrover, we pass the now empty Citroen. Such a little way to go now, but it seems like a marathon. My lungs are bursting and the heat is demonic. Flecks of light are doing some sort of dance before my eyes and my head feels like a mass of machine gun-blasted cotton wool.

We reach the Landrover at last. Ben fumbles for the keys and the engine revs into life. I'm wringing wet all over and my head is thumping like hell. My teeth jar as as we bump towards the road, and I can't see clearly for sweat running into my eyes. But I can hear shouting and the slam of a car door behind us.

They're not going to give up.

Fragment 14

First he made sure I was a virgin. It took five of them to hold me down. One at each of my arms and legs and the fifth to sit on my chest. Astarte knew, I was weak as a new born baby but I still managed to struggle and shout so much that he stuffed a filthy rag in my mouth, for he swore I'd pierce his eardrums. One of the men went to strike me a blow across my face, but the old man, Abilech was his name, stayed his hand in mid air.

"Be still, fool! If this one's as virginal as her face is pretty, she'll be worth more than all the camels we sold in Moab, in the right quarters. So I don't want a mark on her, understand? She's in a bad enough state as it is."

They obviously did understand. For aside from the men holding me down, no one made a move to touch me again - except for Abilech.

I tried to scream but choked into the filthy rag that bound my mouth as they forced my legs apart and I felt his bony fingers crawling inside my body. Heat rushed down my legs and my face burnt with shame. He probed me carefully, taking great trouble not to spoil his merchandise. I strained with all my might against the hands that held me down but in

253

vain. I retched into the cloth.

The fingers crawled out of my body. "Yes," he announced. "This one has never known a man. She'll fetch a pretty price. Take her to the river. Clean her up - and remember, don't try anything. I'll be watching."

Fragment 15

I stood naked in the Jordan, shaking with fury and shame while those rough men of the desert washed me down. True to his word, Abilech stood on the bank, his arms folded across the front of his multi-coloured robe, watching like a hawk.

I travelled with Abilech's caravan for several moons. They had a train of camels, laden with all kinds of goods. Olives, wooden combs, bangles in copper and bronze, cosmetic boxes, eye make-up flasks and hundreds of tiny statues of Astarte. Most of it, from what I could see sticking out of the baskets on the camels, was well crafted - though nothing compared to the treasures we had in our temples in Jericho, before the Habiru stole them. Some were copies of Egyptian designs, others were Canaanite while some were a mix of the two.

Abilech knew his business. He kept a careful eye on

his merchandise. Baal betide any man who dared to steal a single olive from a camel's back. He made sure everything was kept in perfect condition, so he could get the best possible price and not one of his men dared lay a hand on his goods. His goods included me. They cleaned me up, gave me a new robe to wear and made sure I was well fed and watered. They treated me even better than the camels. Abilech ordered that I was to travel on the back of one of the donkeys, so the skin of my feet would not grow hard. He said rich men don't like calloused feet scratching against their legs in bed. Sometimes he would rub olive oil into my soles and into my hair to make it shine. My cuts were kept clean and treated with juice from plants that grew beside the Jordan, and gradually, when I looked at myself in the water, I was more like myself again than the filthy bleeding creature that came down from the hills. At least, on the outside. Inside, I kept my tears bottled up and they concealed to form hard stones within me. The girl who ran carefree along Jericho's walls was gone. I would never be her again.

One day, after he had been away from our camp for a while, he returned, bringing a fine dress and some jewelry for me. He washed me himself and combed and dressed my hair with olive oil till it shone. He had brought back some faience and kohl and painted my eyes the

Egyptian way. Then he sat back to admire his handiwork.

I stared at the horizon while he rubbed his hands together and chuckled.

"Beautiful, beautiful," he muttered. "I shall get more for you, my lady, than all those ivory boxes and copper bracelets together."

The stones that once were tears lay hard and bright within me. I continued to stare ahead, like some temple statue.

"Fit for a king," Abilech continued, twisting his gnarled old hands together in glee. "King of Jericho."

Something stirred inside me. Our King was dead.

"Conqueror of Jericho, Canaan's curse," muttered the old trader. "And now a rich man with all that temple gold. My pretty, I'm going to sell you to Joshua himself."

Fragment 16

I returned to Jericho on the back of a donkey. Abilech rode by my side and the men followed behind, leading the camels. The Habiru had set up camp outside the ruins of the city, near the Jordan. The stench of burning still drifted on the air and the hilltop was black.

As we rode into the Habiru camp, I allowed myself to smile at the paltriness of their possessions. They obviously had no idea how to make firm houses of mud brick or walls of stone like ours they had destroyed. The whole tribe lived in tents made of goats' hair. The pots and jars I saw carried by their women as we passed, were rough and crude and their only good pieces of jewelry were Egyptian or Canaanite, no doubt plundered from us.

I held my head high. Abilech had made stylish work of his most valued possession. The linen of my dress was finer by far than anything worn by the Habiru women and my belt in scarlet, purple and blue was brighter than any of theirs. Many covetous glances were cast my way. The Habiru women had probably never even seen the purple murex dye before. Hundreds of sea creatures had to be gathered to make just one stripe of my belt. Those nomads had good reason to be jealous.

I forgot for a while I was just a slave and, for the first time, was glad that Abilech had made such a good job of me. I knew my hair glistened and shone from all that olive oil he had lavished on me, and now my body was healed, my skin gleamed in the sunlight too. The Habiru men stopped in their work and watched me pass. I rejoiced when a Habiru woman slapped her man across the cheek for staring too hard, though I kept my eyes firmly fixed on the air, not deigning to cast a glance at any of those murdering tribes. I held my head high and scorned the Habiru, with all my Canaanite heart.

Fragment 17

Who, in Dagon's name, did he think he was! The Habiru leader hadn't even come out of his tent to see what he'd bought! Fury burned in my belly. Abilech sold me off for a hundred shekels of silver and rode off, muttering he'd been robbed, without so much as a "by your leave" in my direction. Some minion had decided "The Egyptian Queen", as they called me, was too splendid a trophy for any but Joshua himself, and paid the lowest price that Abilech would accept.

As that vile old man scuttled away, grasping his shekels, I remembered what he had done to me on the banks of the Jordan, and when the Habiru's eyes were turned, spat on the around behind him.

I was taken by two of Joshua's men and escorted to a group of small tents. In the centre was a much larger tent. The goat hair flaps across the door were closed.

"That's Joshua's," said one of the men. I turned my head away and stuck out my chin. Fool! As if I hadn't worked that out for myself.

His companion's eyes slithered down my gown. "This one's yours," he said, his gaze fixed on my breasts as he lifted the flap of a very small tent, close to Joshua's. "I'm on guard duty here till sunset, so if you get lonely, just give me a call." He leaned over me, his face leering into mine. His hot breath stank.

"Hey," called his commander, the one who had bought me. "Watch yourself, Achan! You know what happens to those who trespass on the property of Joshua or the Lord."

Achan muttered something and scowled, but turned around and assumed his position as sentry at the door of the tent.

I was about to lift the flap and step inside, when another voice boomed out behind me. Despite my resolution to ignore all Habiru as far as I could, I turned around.

"Well, who have we got here?"

A tall man with glistening black hair stood leaning on his sword before me. Both his beard and hair were longer than most of the Habiru men's and he stood a good head and shoulders above the rest. His eyes gleamed black and shiny as jet and something strong and sensual hung on the

259

curve of his lips. He was a handsome man, I had to give him that, even though he were a Habiru. I wondered if he was Joshua, for though I had glimpsed the Habiru leader and heard him shout at Jericho, he had been too far off for me to see what he looked like.

He sauntered towards me, and grabbed my chin, studying my face as he would before buying a camel.

Finally he nodded. "Very fine, very fine." His breath didn't stink like the guard's. I noticed his teeth were very straight and white and none were missing, except for a noticeable chip off one of those at the front.

"She's Egyptian, sir," leered the guard.

"Hah!" The man laughed. "It's always a pleasure to see them made into slaves of ours. Especially such a beautiful one."

"Yes, sir. Yes, Sir." The man grinned and rubbed his crotch. I thought he would probably shoot his arrow all over his tunic the minute no one was looking.

"Keep your hands to yourself, you hear." The tall man, no doubt, was much of the same opinion.

The commander had come over to join them and cuffed the guard round the head. He held up the tent flap and motioned me inside. The voices faded away as the men walked off and I looked around.

The tent was not high enough for me to stand and just a few yards long. Goatskins were strewn over the floor and fortunately there were a few cushions to lie on. I made myself as comfortable as I could and stared up at the roof. The skins reeked. Even the Habiru goats stank worse than ours.

It had been a long journey and I soon fell asleep. I was woken up by a clatter beside me and sat bolt upright on the goatskins, startled. An old woman laid a jug of water in front of me, some rough flat bread and a bowl of something. She stared at me curiously. I picked up the bread, studied it carefully from all angles then flung it at her head, followed by the bowl. The bread bounced off her skull like a stone. Whatever foul Habiru mess was inside the bowl ran down her face. She cursed. They hadn't even learnt to bake decent bread or cook proper stew, those desert rats.

The hag shrieked. Her gnarled old fingers bent like eagle's talons and swooped for my face.

The guard hauled her out of the tent, taking care to have a good grope at my breast on the way. I reached for the bread and hurled it after him.

After that everything went quiet.

My mouth was dry and reluctantly I picked up the water jug. There was a bit left in the bottom which hadn't been spilt in the rumpus, and though the Habiru pottery was crude and rough on my lips and left a foul taste, my parched mouth received the water gladly.

When I had drained the last drop, I cast the poorly made jug aside, cursing the Habiru scum. They couldn't bake bread, they couldn't make pots, they couldn't build houses, they couldn't make anything beautiful or fine. They were nothing but vermin, murdering their way across our land, and I wished to Baal the desert had shrivelled the whole infernal pack.

Fragment 18

The sun set and rose three times. I hardly moved from my tent. A guard watched me always. A few times I ventured out and wandered around the nearest tents to stretch my legs, and to relieve both my bladder and the boredom of staring at the little food on my plate. The old woman now refused to enter and left it with the guard outside. I decided not to starve. I had nearly died of thirst in the hills and had no wish to endure a similar fate.

I spent a long time, thinking and staring at the roof in that tent. I had nothing to live for. My city was burnt, my friends and my people were dead. My family were dead to me too. Sometimes the thought of little Hadad, the way his

262

eyes lit up when he saw me approach their tent, and how his hands clutched around my waist as though he would never let me go „ wrenched at my gut. But they had all gone with Rahab, the betrayer, which I would never do, so I was alone in the world.

I thought of escaping, but I had nowhere to run. The nearest town was Ai, but vast ranges of chalk lay between Jericho and our nearest Canaanite neighbours, all uphill through those terrible waterless wastes which had nearly finished me off before.

I had nothing to live for. But deep inside me, a spark blazed still. I dozed, and waited, and burned. Once I overheard a conversation between two of the guards as they changed the watch. One of them was Achan.

"Too many accursed heathen," muttered the other. "Got better things to do than watch over some Egyptian slut. And there's them Canaanite filth just beyond the camp. Joshua should kill 'em all."

More footsteps approached. "Joshua's a man of his word. He doesn't break an oath, not even to heathens." I recognised the voice as the commander's. "He promised Rahab he'd spare her family in return for hiding our spies."

"That miserable Labor," muttered the other. "And we all know why Sechem visits the Canaanite tents so often, don't we."

Achan sniggered. "Good on him. I'd have a piece of that Canaanite whore, given half a chance. Have you seen her..."

"That's enough."

"Big as melons!"

"I said that's enough. Now change over the pair of you, before I break both your heads."

Two sets of footsteps tramped away and all was quiet except for the murmur of chatter from the nearest tents.

After a while, Achan stuck his head through the door of the tent.

"How are we today, my pretty Egyptian Queen," he leered. His tongue ran over his lips. Small beads of saliva glistened at the corners of his mouth.

I glared.

"Listen," Achan lowered his voice. He glanced behind him to make no one was near and crept into the tent.

I picked up my water jar.

"You come any closer and I'll crack this over your head. Then I'll scream so loud that you raped me, all Joshua's men will come running. And you know what happens to those whose trespass on the property of

Joshua and the Lord," I sneered sarcastically, wondering, as I repeated the commander's words, what actually did happen.

Little did I know then that both I, and Achan, were soon to find out.

Achan held out his hand. "Whoah, there, my pretty." He stayed where he was, but his face leered closer. "I just want to know something."

I gripped the jug harder.

"Tell me." His eyes were fixed on the front of my dress. They bulged like a frog's. More saliva frothed at the sides of his mouth. "In Egypt, do they do what the Canaanites do, in their temples? You know, the rites of Baal, where the men can have a priestess?" He crept closer, rubbing his hand against his groin. "How about it? You and me? You be the priestess and I..."

I hurled the jar at his skull and he retreated quickly out of the door, tangling himself in the goatskin flap in his haste.

"Egyptian whore!" he yelled from outside.

"Habiru hog!" I picked up some dates and sat back on the cushions, knowing he wouldn't risk any more commotion that might bring his commander running.

Later that evening, Achan had gone and a different

guard stood watching me as I strolled round the camp. A group of men were gathered near a camp fire. One stood head and shoulders above the rest. As he turned slightly to speak to his neighbour, I caught sight of his face. His skin gleamed in the firelight. It was the man I had seen on the day I arrived.

At first I had thought he must be Joshua, but later I realised he couldn't be. I knew from the tales that were told in Jericho, that Joshua, together with his friend, Caleb, had been sent to spy on Canaan *before* their forty years in the desert. So if Joshua was a young man in his twenties then, he must be at least sixty now. That would explain why he had never come to my tent. He must be a shrunken old man after all those years under the blazing desert sun. No doubt his private parts were just as wizened as well.

I turned to my guard. "Who is that tall man over by the fire?"

The guard looked across. "That's Caleb."

"Caleb?" I frowned. The Caleb of the stories was surely just as old as Joshua. It had to be another of that name.

"Is he named after the one who was sent out by Moses to spy on Canaan?" I asked.

The guard laughed. "No, he's one and the

same."

"But... that cannot be. More than forty years has passed. He would be an old man by now."

I stared at the man by the fire. He laughed and joked with his companions, his body firm and strong, his face barely lined by the sun, a man in the prime of his life.

The guard laughed at my confusion. "He barely ages from one turn of the sun to another. He's one of the Holders."

"Holders?"

"Holders of the Secrets of the Ark."

"And they don't grow old?"

"Hardly at all. The Holders have long, long lives." "And the people?"

The guard laughed. "The secrets are barred to all but the few. Those who have tried to steal them have been blasted and shrivelled, for the Ark can destroy as well as give life. Believe me, not one of the people dares go near."

I stared in astonishment, wondering, what, for the love of Astarte, was in that magic box.

Fragment 19

The following evening I was taken to meet Joshua.

Some women came for me late in the afternoon and took me to a much larger tent where a shallow oval tub filled with water awaited. When they had bathed me and combed out my hair, they smoothed sweet oils into my skin. I was surprised these nomads had such civilised luxuries. I supposed they must have stolen them, or bought them from traders like Abilech (I shuddered at the memory of that disgusting old man) with the proceeds of our looted temple. I steeled myself for whatever lay ahead. No doubt Joshua would be as vile as Abilech. I was still a virgin, and could not help but fear the coming night.

They dressed me in clean robes and even produced a box of kohl to freshly line my eyes the Egyptian way. I had not bothered to enlighten them I was Canaanite. It suited me to let them believe I was Egyptian. That way no one would tell Rahab there was another Canaanite woman in the camp. I never wanted to set eyes on her face. Anyway, the old me was dead and gone. I might as well be Egyptian as any other. But my heart, I knew, would be Canaanite till the day it stopped beating.

None of them spoke to me. I knew what they

thought of me. It could not match what I thought of them. I imagined Rahab's life outside the camp. They must treat her much the same. No one would speak to her. No one would come near her. She would have no friends to gossip with, or to bring her news. They would whisper behind her back, or perhaps throw things at her when she went to the well, if Sechem wasn't near. Jericho bitch. Canaanite whore. Her life, which she had sacrificed her whole people to save, would be spent in loneliness, reviled, spat upon. Well, I was glad. I resolved to never approach the isolated tent where they dwelt and to put her and the rest of my family who had chosen that path out of my mind for ever. Henceforth, they were dead to me.

When the women had finished, they put back all the fine jewelry Abilech had adorned me with and took me to Joshua's tent. I realised I was shaking. This was no more than the priestesses at Jericho did every day at the temple, I told myself. I had already completed much of my training before the city fell. I had heard it was only the first time that hurt. After that, they seemed to enjoy it. Perhaps it would not be so bad. But still I shook.

As I stood before the closed flap of goats' hair, I felt a shove in my back, then holding my head up high, and steeling myself for what I knew must lie ahead, I walked inside.

No one else was there. Just Joshua. He was exactly as Jebal had described. Neither tall nor short. Black hair and beard neatly cropped. Not as long as Caleb's, more like the other Habiru men. He had nothing of Caleb's height or even his handsome looks. But I could not take my eyes off him. He sat on a stool, polishing his sword and looked up as I entered. The muscles in his arms were strong and powerful, the veins standing out in the lamplight as he smoothed down the sword. I stood, fascinated, like a rabbit caught in the stare of a leopard. It was not the light from the oil lamp that burned in his eyes. It was something else. I understood then what Jebal had meant. "They say he is a man filled with the spirit..." I kept my head high and met his gaze with mine, vowing, whatever happened, to dedicate my virginity to Astarte, they way I should if I had finished my training at the temple in Jericho. But I swallowed and hoped he didn't see. In that moment, as my eyes met his, for the first time in my life I saw and feared the Habiru God.

He put down his sword. He stepped forward and walked all around me, appraising me with his eyes. But he was not as other men. He didn't leer like Achan, nor take my chin in his hand and study me like a camel, as did Caleb. He was like no man I had ever seen. Something, a kind of power, radiated from his body. I was sure I could see it, a golden ring surging out all around him. That light did not come from the oil lamp. I felt a pulsing, that was either the beating of my own heart, or came from him.

I realised then why he was the leader of all the Habiru tribes. And how that bunch of vagabonds had taken my city, scattering its gigantic walls down the hill. And why all of Canaan trembled before him and his God.

He did not touch me. When he had finished looking at what the women had brought him that night, he nodded, as though he was satisfied with his new possession. Then he called to a guard at the entrance and told him to take me back to my tent. The guard looked surprised but escorted me outside.

The first stars of evening glistened in the sky. The sweet air of Canaan caressed my skin with a soft warm breeze. The scent of wild rosemary filled the gathering night.

As I left Joshua's tent behind, I suddenly realised that he looked no more than forty at most. Yet, like Caleb, he had to be sixty if he was a day. Surely more, judging from the time which had passed between Moses sending them out to spy and the final conquering of Jericho, over forty years later.

I remembered the conversation I had had with the

guard about how the Holders barely aged. If Caleb was a Holder of the Secrets of the Ark, then Joshua, as leader of all the Habiru, undoubtedly was.

I looked up at the Star of Astarte which sparkled above the distant hills, and in her name, I swore I'd learn those Secrets too.

Chapter 8

"I've had enough of this," says Ben grimly. "Hold on tight. We'll show them what Landrovers are made for. He spins the vehicle onto a flat piece of land and I offer up prayers to the Virgin Mary, Astarte, Britney Spears and anyone else that springs to mind as we weave through some gigantic, boulders which screen us from the road. Between screwing my eyes tight shut and opening them wide in horror, I catch a glint of metal as the Metro races past. The Arabs have fallen for it but there's no sign of the Americans.

Ben slams on the brake. "We need to know where that Citroen is before we can get back on the road. And quick, before the other guys twig and start heading back."

He leaps out, then crouches behind a rock. It's like cops and robbers this. Honestly, I'd laugh if I weren't so damned scared.

"Can't see them," he calls. "I'm going to climb up a bit higher.

I wait, and the seconds seem like hours. Now the engine is silent I can hear a dull drone overhead. I squint up at the sky. That helicopter again. What's their game?

Ben jumps back inside and starts the engine. "No trace of them. But we can't stay here in case the Arabs turn round. I'm going to head back the way we came. We'll just have to take our chances. But get ready to duck."

As we bump across country to regain the road I hang onto the dashboard and thank God for my seatbelt. How did I get into this situation anyway? We approach the place we originally turned off and I catch a glimpse of the Americans through the rocks. "I see them! They're still parked in the same place!"

Ben accelerates and we speed past the turning. The two Americans are crouched by a wheel of their car. One of them springs to his feet and I catch sight of my rucksack in his hand.

As we race along the narrow mountain road, we both keep an anxious lookout behind us and it's not until we reach the coast road, that Ben's hands relax on the wheel.

"It's odd how the Citroen didn't come after us," he says cautiously, looking in the mirror.

"I think they had problems. I saw them looking at a wheel."

"Maybe the other guys slit their tyres," says Ben. "To stop them running off with anything we found before they did."

"But how did they know we were looking for the tablets? No one but us has seen Fragment 35."

"Perhaps they didn't," says Ben. "They've obviously had instructions to keep an eye on us. That young guy in the underground car park that time..."

"The one you thought was a student?"

"Yeah. He could have been spying on us."

"But there are two separate cars." Maybe it's the stress and the heat but I can't get my head around this. "The Arabs and the Americans weren't working together."

"No. It looks like we're attracting interest from at least two different quarters."

My head is spinning and I feel like I'm in some low budget movie, with bad guys taking potshots at every turning. I'm just waiting for Vinnie Jones to pop out from the nearest rock. "So what happened while I was on the cliffside?" I ask. "I thought something awful had happened when I heard those gunshots."

"They won't risk anything here, even if they do catch up," he says, ignoring my question. "There's too much traffic on this stretch of road for them to try anything stupid. I'm pretty sure we've lost them." He runs his hand over his face. "Look, I'm dead beat and it's a long drive back to Jerusalem. Let's pull over at that hotel and grab a coffee before we go any further. Then we can fill each other in on what happened when we were separated."

Night is starting to fall and the lights of Ein Gedi blink on alone the shore outside the large glass window of the Tiberias Hotel bar. I sip at my coffee and glance around. The place is crawling with men in lounge suits and women in cocktail dresses. Ben and I, let's face it, are looking pretty rough. I am dirty, sweaty and dishevelled, with a broken strap hanging from one of my sandals. Ben has dust in his eyebrows, a torn shirt and a cut above one eye. He doesn't seem bothered about our tattiness in front of the smart set, but then he still manages to look pretty sexy. It's so different for men. It's just not fair. I wish I didn't have to work so hard at looking even remotely fit for anything other than a scrap heap.

"So I chipped away at the cleft for nearly half an hour, making out I was hard at work," explains Ben. "But then I really did find something."

"You did?" For a moment I imagine a hoard of ancient tablets hidden in the rock.

"Yeah, a load of junk," Ben laughs. "An old tobacco tin, an empty whisky bottle and the remains of an antique matchbox. They could have been left by the 1930s expedition." He knocks back his coffee and grins, but he doesn't kid me. It'll take a bit more than that to cover up bow stressed he is. "Anyway, I acted like it was something really special. I carefully lifted out each piece of garbage, put them into a bag, labelled them up, and made a great show of marking out the whole area like a dig. Then I left the bag in full view of our buddies back there and walked away. I managed to lose them in the rocks and headed up the cliff after you. When I looked down, blondie was peering into the bag."

"I bet they weren't too happy when they found it was full of junk, instead of the secrets of the Ark."

"Actually, they hardly had time to notice," says Ben. "I had a good view from up on the cliff. As soon as they picked up the bag, the Arabs started creeping up on them but one missed his footing, sent some rocks crashing along the ground and bingo - they started taking potshots at each other."

"You were lucky you weren't shot."

"I was well out of their sights by that time. Then I saw you pelting hell for leather round the base of the mountain. Luckily I found another track down the cliff and managed to get down to you. You don't get rid of me that easily."

I'm sure Ben's attempting to stay upbeat for my sake. For fuck's sake, we could have been killed. In the reflection of the window opposite I catch sight of my tangled hair. Talk about Medusa's daughter. My lips are all dry and cracked and of course, all my gear was in the rucksack, hairbrush, lipsalve... Oh no!The rucksack!

"What's up?"

"The rucksack. It had copies of those latest fragments, about the tablets and map."

"Where is it?"

"When we were running for the Landrover, it snagged on a rock and the strap broke. I had to leave it there. The Americans have got it."

"Hell!" Ben sweeps the cup and saucer off the table.

I half jump out my skin. I look at the smashed crockery on the tiles, then at Ben, in astonishment.

"Great. Not only did we fail to find the tablets, but now some trigger-happy mob have got their hands on the latest fragments. Nice one, Charlotte."

"Ben, there were bullets whizzing straight past my head. I had no choice, I could've been killed." I've never seen him like this before. Perhaps he cares more about the translations than me.

He tugs at the collar of his shirt, glances at the bar, then takes my hand across the table. "I know. I'm sorry, sweetheart. I couldn't bear it if anything happened to you. I guess I'm just bushed. Finish your coffee and let's get back to Jerusalem. I've had enough for one day."

"Don't you want..."

"No." He stands up. I mumble apologies to the waitress who has scurried over to pick up the pieces, but Ben grabs me by the hand and nearly drags me outside. Talk about caveman tactics. But honestly, I'm too tired to care. I really don't know what's going on any more.

It's nearly midnight by the time we get back to Jerusalem. After Ben drops me at the flat, I yank off my shoes and crash out on the sofa. You know, I'm glad he's heading back to his place. I'm shattered and just want to be on my own.

I dump my filthy clothes straight into the wash and start running the shower. If only the water could wash away memories and fear. Then I wrap myself in my dressing gown and go to make some tea as I'll never sleep if I go to bed now. My mind is racing faster than Damon Hill and there are things I need to get straight. Cruiser curls up beside me on the sofa, as cradling the mug in my hands, I run an action replay of the day's events in my head.

I reckon the Arabs must belong to the same group as the ones in the Cafe Malkha. The Americans, from what Yusef found out, could well be from Arms R Us. But I don't understand what that helicopter was up to. Ben just shrugged when I mentioned it, and said it was probably back-up for the Americans. But how come it didn't help them when the shooting started, or even warn them the Arabs were creeping up? I'm certain the blast which killed that Arab chasing after me came from the helicopter. But just whose side was it on? Ours? It buggared off once Ben and I were safe in the Landrover. I wonder if we have a mystery ally. Someone who's prepared to kill to keep us alive. And what's their game anyway? Waiting to for us to find something probably, then Charlotte Adams and Ben Travers conveniently disappear.

And then there's Ben. I mean, what am I supposed to make of his behaviour? Over the top or what? I saw another side of him this evening. OK, so the translated fragments have fallen into the Americans' hands, but at least neither of us was killed. What on earth possessed him to over-react like some spoilt schoolkid, knocking his coffee onto the floor? But he's been under terrible strain, what with one thing and another. It's not fair of me, of course he's bound to snap. I should be more understanding, I shouldn't expect so much. But it's just that this horrible little voice keeps asking me how well I really know Ben Travers.

I stare into my tea and swill it around in the mug. I came so close to finding those tablets today. Right place, wrong time. God only knows where they are now. It seems like the secrets of the Ark of the Covenant have already been found - by someone who had no bloody idea what they even were. They're probably in some private collection or lying unrecognised somewhere, possibly even in the British Museum, unlisted in the basement. It wouldn't be the first time.

The telephone rings and I nearly trip over the coffee table in my haste to grab the phone. There's only one person it can be at this time of night. I make myself count to ten before I pick up the receiver.

"Hello?"

"Charlotte. I've just got back to my flat. There's a message on my answerphone. Maddy rang when we were out."

Now why does that not surprise me?

"The hospital have found a donor for Tony. He's set to have the operation the day after tomorrow."

"That's wonderful, Ben." I'm such a bitch. I know I should be happy for him and Tony but all I can think of is how alone I am, and sod it, I just feel guilty, like I'm Glenn Close and Maddy is the good little wife.

"I have to be there for him." Ben's voice sounds far-away. "I'm going to the airport and catching the next available flight back home."

"I hope the operation's a success," I hear myself say. "Take care in New York, yes I'll be fine, hope Tony is too...." All the things you're supposed to say. Poor kid, I hope he is OK, but it's hard to get worked up about someone you've never met. At least it is for me. Other people are kinder, have more sympathy. I only think of myself.

The second I put down that phone, I'm swamped by a sea of emptiness. Here I am, alone again, in an alien country, surrounded by voices I can't understand; I have no idea who's leeching my secrets and I'm watched by people who shoot to kill.

Of course, I can't sodding sleep properly tonight. I throw off the covers in an effort to find some cool, but the hot Jerusalem night presses down and the sheets are soaked in sweat. At last I fall into some sort of fitful state that reassembles sleep and I'm plagued by dreams where I'm running through an endless waste of rock along a sheer drop to a gorge, where stone swords stick up from the ground, with other foolhardy travellers impaled on the blades. I can't stop running. I have to find a way though. There's someone behind me. I can hear their footsteps and feel hot breath at the back of my neck. I slip and almost plunge down to the waiting swords, but I manage to pick myself up. I don't know who's behind me, but I sense it's someone I've met before. A small cave opens in the rock ahead and I crawl inside. It's pitch black, reeking of damp. I grope through the darkness, my fingers sliding on slime and ice. Someone is panting, hoarse, rasping breath, drawing closer.   Then I'm confronted by a warren of caves, lit by a dim glow from the walls. I look around, frantically, not knowing which way to choose, but the ground gives way and I hurtle down into the darkness towards invisible water, and I know I will never see the sun again.

Ben has taken the first flight of the day from Tel Aviv. He called me from the departure lounge before take-off. I sat in my office and listened as though it were some stranger on the line and heard myself speak like I was someone else too. I was glad when he said he had to go. I've drunk four cups of coffee but I still feel half asleep. It's left a foul taste in my mouth but I can't stop drinking the stuff.

I'm not going to let myself look at the clock. I shan't torture myself by gauging the exact moment when Ben's plane is taxiing down the runway, and I refuse to watch it in my mind eye, as it shoots through the brilliant Israeli sky, towards a world in which I have no part. I try to concentrate on my work, but I'm so tired the cuneiform signs keep swimming in and out of focus, and no matter how much coffee I force down it doesn't seem to help. The traffic drones outside and I can hear children's voices singing. The sounds only accentuate the quiet of the office and make me realise just how alone I am in this strange city. I think about going for a chat with Ingrid, yet I really don't know if she's a friend or not. Someone copied those translations. Someone's been watching every move I make and reporting back to God knows who. Ingrid knows everything that goes on in Archaeology. I might be imagining it but I keep thinking she's been a bit.. well... nothing I can put my finger on. Just a bit funny with me lately. Ever since I started this relationship with Ben. Oh bugger.

I'm not going to cry. I'm just tired, that's all, exhausted with the strain of of it all, and hours spent poring over small cuneiform script. Self-pity is a luxury I can't afford right now.

I gather my notes together and try to look on the bright side. I mean, at least I'm not pregnant, like that poor girl. I can't begin to imagine how I would coped in her situation. Probably not very well, knowing me. No midwife, no doctor, no epidural, all by herself in a cave. No thanks, I'm far too squeamish for that.

Actually I don't feel so bad as the day wears on. The harder I work on the tablets, the more I forget my own problems. I reach for my packet of sesame snacks and browse through these latest fragments. I'm really glad Ben took me to the Dead Sea and the Mountains of Sodom. Now I've seen for myself those weird shapes in the rock and ghostly salt banks it's easy to visualise her, all alone out there, plunging on her camel down the mountains to the sea.

Fragment 37 is by far the strangest, and even though I feel shattered and really pissed off about Ben leaving me on my own, I can't help getting excited about this. I mean, the tablets from the Ark are probably lost but it could be that the actual source of the Ark's power, the Cave of White Fire, is still out there somewhere. The white fire's probably long gone out, but I could be the one to find the site and what a coup that would be. It would certainly make my career. Christ, I deserve a break. I can't risk someone else finding it first. I'm going to make damn sure no further translations fall into anyone else's hands.

Of course, it's highly unlikely, but just supposing, the source has remained active, forgotten but still potent. Jesus, if I found that... And I know how to read the codes in the texts. When I first came across that reference to the Great Golden Lion and the Struggling Hawk it seemed pretty obscure but now I know it refers to land formations. The Canaanite's world view was essentially pagan, where every rock and mountain could embody the spirit of an animal or God or whatever. It was natural that Rahab's sister should view the land in those terms. Now I can do that too. And I know her. I work with her every day. I see the world through her eyes. I turn back to Fragment 37 which describes the path to the Cave of White Fire. If that other cave was anything to go by, I could find this site by locating the correct landscape features. It must lie near where the mountains of Sodom meet the banks of the Dead Sea. I reach for a pen and draw a black line beneath every clue. *The Lizard's Tail, The Army in White* and *The Seraphim with Wings Outstretched.* Sod Ben for going off. His Landrover's just sitting there, useless. I really wish I'd applied for an International Driving Licence before I left England. I can't search without a vehicle.

I dust the crumbs off the desk and you know, when I pick up my notes it's like a wave of exhilaration breaking over my head. Despite being swept along on a white water raft of emotions, one second up, one second down, I'm really glad I took this post.

Honestly, these fragments are incredible. There are professors who've spent years in the field without ever getting a chance like this and they'll be tearing their hair out with jealousy when my work comes out. It makes abandoning my PhD to escape from London's memories all worth while. Up yours, Jonathon. You did me a favour. This could really catapult me into the top bracket. An honorary doctorate maybe, a top post in any Ancient Semitic department I choose, head-hunted by the Louvre, a salary running to weekends in Primula Porter Beauty Spas... But would I even need a beauty spa? Of course, it's crazy, but the secret of eternal youth? Imagine it, no cellulite, no wrinkles, no saggy skin. Wow! Kate Moss eat your skinny little heart out.

Even if the Cave of White Fire is lost, like the tablets from the Ark, these fragments are explosive. They shed more light on the characters in the Book of Joshua and the Ark's powers than anything ever discovered. When this is published...

You know, I can understand what motivated the Canaanite girl to seek out the Cave of White Fire. It wasn't just revenge that drove her. I bet she felt just as excited as I do now.

She found it. The question is, will I?

Let's have a look at this passage again.

I had found the secret place of the Habiru leaders: the place of the fire that could kill from afar and the mud that gave life to keep men - and women - young. People would kill for a secret such as I possessed.

285

My heart is going like the clappers and it's not just the coffee. Now I'm holding that secret in my hands.

A picture of the Arab lying in a pool of blood on the ground flashes into my mind. Some things haven't changed in three thousand years. For power like that, there's people who won't think twice before sticking a knife in your back. Let's face it, the murder of a Canaanite orphan or an English translator doesn't rank that high in the scheme of things, not compared to achieving the means of destroying cities, or staying young for a century.

Oh so what if Ben's gone off. It's his loss. I've got my own life to lead. My Canaanite friend didn't allow life to drag her down. If she could keep battling on in the face of adversity, after all she went through, so can I. Me and my piddling little problems.

There's a knock on the door and Ingrid comes in with the post.

"Some stuff here for you," she says, handing it over.

I flick through the envelopes and notice one with an air mail label and a London postmark. Then I look at the handwriting and smile as I recognise the familiar scrawl. Things are definitely looking up. A letter from Sarah, at last. I'll take it home to read, give myself something to look forward to later. I'll make myself a really nice salad this evening - maybe get some avocados from the market - then catch up on the gos.

On my way home, I stop off at Faruk's to buy some freshly ground coffee and have a bit of a wander through the market. I love the smell of cinnamon and nutmeg from the spice stall, and all those dazzling yellows of saffron, turmeric and paprika, explosions of sunshine in the souks. Then I make for the veg and go a bit over the top. Artichokes, avocados, kohl rabi, peppers, mangetout... you name it, in the bag it goes and I end up staggering home, down a narrow side street, full of kitsch shops selling icons near the Damascus gate. At the far end is a crowd of women in black and in the middle, a group of men, holding a coffin on their shoulders, which sways unsteadily while wails of grief drift down the street. The last thing I want is to get in their way.

As I go to turn around, an Arab, only about seventeen years old, blocks my way. He growls something in Arabic, then seeing my incomprehension, comes a bit closer.

"You American?" He stares at my hair and I feel suddenly selfconscious of how blonde it is. He glances at my shopping bag.

I look down too. It has a stars and stripes logo on the side.

"No, I'm not American," I say hastily.

He grabs my bag and stares in disgust. I tug it out of his hand and back away.

Then he stabs a finger at me and yells, "You fucking American!"

The funeral cortege is nearly upon us. He yells

something in Arabic and a murmur swells from the crowd. The coffin, draped in the claret, white and blue stripes of the Palestinian flag, sways precariously above their heads. Christ! I've got to get out of here. But the kid grabs my arm and his fingers dig hard into my flesh. I drop my shopping and avocados and oranges spill into the gutter. He points to the coffin and screams.

"You know him? Ahmed Shikaki! Fifteen years old, shot by Israelis! Israeli bullet, fucking American gun! "

I can't get away. His fingers are claws in my arm.

"A1 mauwt la Israliyeen! A1 Mauwt la Amerikiyeen!" Shit! I've heard that before. "Death to Israel! Death to the USA!" I've got to get out, but I just can't escape his grip on my arm.

Only a few yards away now, the men take up the chant. Their fists punch the air, anger flares in their eyes, and their hatred pours down the street.

"Al mauwt la Israliyeen! AL mauwt la Amerikiyeen!

Something vile and ugly is swelling into life in this street.

The boy shakes my arm. His eyes blaze into mine. "Fucking Israelis! Fucking America!" He spits onto my bag in the gutter and kicks at the stars and stripes logo. I am so scared now I feel like my stomach's about to drop through the ground. Pounding the air with his fist, he eggs on the crowd in Arabic to greater heights of fury.

"Al mauwt la Israliyeen!
Al mauwt la Amerikiyeen!"

288

There's a side alley into
which I could escape but this kid
won't let go. I tug at his fingers,
feel sweat prickling its way down
my back, but he just keeps
yelling in my face.

I yank his little finger back and he squeals,
letting go my wrist. I'm about to race down the
alley - then a shot rings out.

A look of astonishment passes over
his face. He crumples to his knees,
clutching his back.

"Run, Charlotte!"

The cry comes from the end of the street.

As the boy falls onto his face, a dark stain
spreads across the back of his shirt, and I catch sight
of a figure with a gun drawing back behind the
corner, then I dive into the alley and run.

I slam the door and slide the bolts into place,
closing my eyes and leaning against the door. When
I've caught my breath, I fling open the drinks
cabinet and pull out the brandy. I pour myself a
glass and gulp it straight down.

All his anger evaporated when he fell. He just
looked astonished. Completely astonished. That's
another young life destroyed before my eyes. Now
those poor women will have another coffin to
follow; another wasted life to mourn. All that futile
death.

But this time it wasn't down to some Israeli
bullet, or skirmish with occupying troops.

This is my fault. He was killed because of me. I down another mouthful of brandy but it can't block out the hatred in those eyes which blazes before me every time I close mine. I can't blame him for hating me. Americans, British, to him we're all the same. We don't have to live in occupied land. We just stand by while Israel, like a giant cukoo, shoves them out of the nest. He wasn't to know I understand terror too. Back there in the street, I felt that hatred bloating like a maggot gorging on blood. I never realised before how hate has a life of its own. But no, I don't blame that boy for hating me.

Now he'll be reduced to one more statistic; one more Palestinian death in the fight against Israel's oppression.

Except he wasn't.

Whoever fired the gun knew my name. But I just can't place the voice. This is the second time someone has been shot before they could harm me. Who is prepared to gun people down in cold blood to save me?

I curl up on the sofa and loose all track of time. Then I realise I haven't eaten anything and my shopping is lying in a gutter. God, I feel guilty. How can I be hungry when, for fuck's sake, I've just seen someone die? I skipped lunch and I've gone the whole day on coffee. But that's no. excuse. I'm a bad person. I deserve everything I get.

I go into the kitchen and open a cupboard. Not much there. A box of dates, a few tins of tomatoes and sweet corn, some rice and pasta, two packets of honey and almond halva, a jar of crystallised figs and some apricot *bouchees* which I bought on a whim. No fresh vegetables at all. They're all squashed in the gutter, mixed with the blood of that boy who was shot because of me. Guilt makes me hungry. I felt guilty when Sally-Ann died; guilty because I wasn't there to stop her getting into the car; guilty that she was the the golden girl, and if there was any justice in the world, it should have been me, and not her, whose brains were splattered across the M25. But we all know life's not fair. Who said death should be?

I am ravenous with guilt. I tear open the packet of dates and stuff a great handful into my mouth, then twist at the lid of the figs. Damn, it's stiff and won't open. It slips out of my hand and glass smashes all over the floor. Syrup, glass and figs splatter everywhere, running together like blood and juice in the gutter. I rip open one of the packets of halva, break off a large piece and cram as much I can into my mouth, but it's dry and I can't swallow it. I chew it slowly, look out of the window and suddenly this flat, this great city racked by violence and division, is such a lonely place. But honey halva and dates are not much comfort. Right now what I wouldn't give for a giant bar of Galaxy or Cadbury's Dairy Milk. I tip a load of apricot balls into my hand then tilt back my head. It's so easy. I can always throw them up later. But I see Susan Hewitt's sympathetic face and hear her voice in my head. *It wasn't your fault. None of it was your fault. Don't punish yourself for something you never asked to happen.* The almond *bouchèes* are full of sugar and taste disgusting. Why am I doing this to myself? Susan Hewitt's voice is soft and soothing, motherly but insistent, as my own mother's never was. *You've suffered enough. Guilt is a completely wasteful emotion. You don't need to do this to yourself. It helps no one. Nourish, don't torture, yourself.*

Then I feel a pawing at my leg. Cruiser looks up at me with his head tilted on one side so his ears go all floppy and he whines. I've forgotten to feed him, poor thing, and it's growing late. I'm cruel and mean. No wonder he's hungry. I deserve to be punished, but he doesn't.

I look at the mess on the floor and the sweetmeat in my hand, then chuck it into the bin, followed by all the other sticky, gooey things. Then I start to clear up the glass before Cruiser cuts his paws.

"Come on, boy. You poor hungry thing. Let's get your dinner, shall we?" I hug him tight and bury my face in his fur.

While Cruiser's tucking into his Happidog, I take a look in the fridge then start to make myself some pasta with a few left-over vegetables I find in the bottom. Later I sit down on the sofa, turning on the TV where an old edition of Dallas is showing, and settle down with Cruiser curled up beside me, to watch Sue Ellen drunkenly slugging it out with J.R. It's load of rubbish, but it's company and a relief to lose myself in someone else's world. Though Sue Ellen isn't so far removed from me.

It's only as the credits start to run that I remember Sarah's letter. Fortunately my handbag stayed on my shoulder when my shopping ended up in the gutter, and the letter's still inside.

I turn off the TV and fish it out of my bag, then settle on my sofa with my feet up. I'm so looking forward to forgetting about all the heavy stuff and dying to hear a bit of uncomplicated gossip. I look at the Mill Hill postmark and homesickness wacks me in the stomach with all the force of a Beckham free kick. We did have some good times, me and Sarah. Maybe I should go back to London. Do I want to stay here to be killed? As Jonathon's in jail, there's nothing really to stop me going back, only the memories, but I think I could deal with them now. At least there I'd have my friends, unlike in this beautiful alien city where, apart from from exciting, sexy and totally unreliable Ben Travers, I have no one. Anyway, I'm probably just a fluffy little bit of entertainment to him, and I wouldn't be surprised if he eventually goes back to Maddy. Whenever I need him, sod it, he isn't there. I surprise myself at how bitter I feel.

I haven't drawn the curtains yet, and get up to block the encroaching dark, to shut out the nightscape of this exotic city which doesn't belong to me. As I throw myself back on the sofa, I could just sit here and blub for London. All those little things, I've left behind. Pigeons scrapping over left-over sandwiches in Russell Square; double decker buses advertising Next and the London Dungeon as they clog up Oxford Street; fettucini with black olives and chilli in Dino's on Greek Street and watching through their large plate glass window the Soho boys on the pull; reading The Guardian on the tube and wondering if the train will get stuck at that point in the tunnel at Camden Town where trains have to pass; and the rain over chimneys on a black November skyline at Waterloo.

I rip open the letter and begin to read.

When I finish, I fold it carefully, in the same creases that Sarah made, and lay it down on the table.

I'd expected Sarah to be writing about some bloke who is yes-reallythis-time - The One, her boss's extra-marital affair or Darren's latest scrape with the law - anything, in fact, but what I've just read. I curl up on the sofa, hug my knees and stare at the voile as it gently sways in front of the window. I never expected this. A year and a half, he should have sodding been in jail, and that was far too little for all he put me through. Parole. Good behaviour. Remission. Early release. The words mean nothing to me, except injustice, insult and mockery. My fingernails dig into my palms. He deserves to be in jail. He should rot in jail. Sarah's news has turned my insides to steel and ice. There's no way I can return to London now.

Jonathon is free.

Fragment 20

I left my small tent the next day, on Joshua's orders, and was taken into his large one to serve. I was glad to have more room to move around and even for the tasks I was set. It made life more bearable to have something to do, and serving as Joshua's handmaid was not arduous. Other women, common Habiru, with coarse skin and rough hands, did the heavy unpleasant jobs, like turning the enormous stones to grind flour or beating the goatskins clean with stones. I didn't even have to bring jars of water from the springs.

I held the jug to him when he drank, tidied away the bowls after meals and made sure I looked down my nose when I handed them to the Habiru women at the door of the tent. I smoothed the skins and shook the cushion after he rose from sleep. He only had one for his head. I had had more in my tiny tent. His quarters were Spartan, his possessions few. He rose with the sun and the first thing he did was pray to his Habiru God. I knew, because I peeped through the curtain and saw him on his knees, head bowed and hands clasped to his breast, and I heard him ask his God for strength to lead his people.

Astarte knew, he needed it. I do not know how he put up with his pack of desert rats. They were always muttering, always complaining, always wishing they were somewhere else. Such a tribe of moaners I had never come across in my life. Of course, in Jericho, we sometimes complained about the heat, the cold, the untimely wind that blasted the crops, but mostly we were a happy people. We knew we lived in a rich and fertile land, flowing with fresh water, milk, and honey. Ours was the City of Palms where the springs never failed and the date trees, laden with sweet fruit, splashed the wilderness with green. A jewel beside the Jordan. An oasis in an arid waste. We knew we were fortunate and thanked our gods for our beautiful fertile land.

But not those Habiru. They weren't happy even after all they had stolen from us. Now I was Joshua's handmaid and they were not concerned I would try to run away, I had much more freedom. I moved amongst the Habiru and though I did not speak with them unless I needed to, I listened. The women moaned about having to carry jars to the wells, about the flies round their food, about their men, their sheep, their goats... The men grumbled their feet were sore, their milk was sour, their women did not do as they wished.... And all of them whined about how good life had been in Egypt. How they had had so much to eat and drink, all kinds of delicacies brought in from across the empire, how Egypt was rich and they never lacked for this or that... Baal believe me, how they went on! And I knew that none of them, except Joshua and Caleb, had even been in Egypt. They had only heard the stories from their parents or grandparents who had died in the desert before they invaded my land. I knew the stories too. How they had been forced by the Egyptian slave masters to make mud bricks from dawn to dusk, backbreaking work in the burning sun, harshly whipped if they slacked. Yet Egypt was the land of Habiru luxury, to hear them talk, while Canaan was the cess pit of the earth. I marvelled at such a bellyaching bunch of vagabonds, who had probably never had it so good, and wondered how in Astarte's name, Joshua put up with the lot of them.

Twice a day, Joshua would go to the Ark. I was burning to see it, but it was kept in a pure white tent made of finest cloth in a sacred part of the land. I could see the tent, shining in the sun from afar, but I was never allowed anywhere near it. Nor were the Habiru people, only the Levite priests who served the Ark of their God, and they kept apart from the rest.

I did not know why Joshua wanted me to serve him. Perhaps it was because he thought I was one of the Egyptians who had made slaves of his people and, like Caleb, he liked to see the roles reversed. Yet he was not unkind to me. At first he barely spoke to me, just nodded, or curtly gave a command. He was like that with everyone, except Caleb. It was only when the two of them sat deep in discussion by the fire or around the camp that he spoke at any length. He puzzled me. I kept reminding myself, that this was the man who had slaughtered my people. His were the orders that cut my neighbours' throats. His commands put every man, woman, child and beast to the sword. He killed Tarasch. It was my duty to make sure he paid for what he did that day. Yet he never touched me once.

Guards were never far away. Two of them stood sentinel while he slept. I watched and waited. There would surely come a time when I could quietly slit his throat. Revenge for Jericho. Revenge for Tarasch. But I first I would await my chance to learn about the magic box. I wanted Joshua's secrets to come spilling out with his blood.

Fragment 21

I was with Joshua in his tent when he sent a couple of men to spy on the town of Ai, up in the hill country to the north east of Jericho. I did not really have anything to do, except stand there and look like the Egyptian Queen, while he gave commands.

As time passed, Joshua would beckon me over more and more to accompany him on his missions around the camp or to stand behind him during his councils of war. I did not understand him. Most of his men would have ravished me in seconds. I had been several moons in Joshua's service and I was still as virginal as when Abilech sold me. Perhaps I served as a reminder that the Habiru were slaves to Egypt no longer, a good morale booster for his troops to have me on constant display. Whatever the reason, he seemed to like me around.

"I want you to go up and spy out the region," he told the two men. Caleb was there as well.

"About time we gave the Canaanites more dead to bury," said Caleb.

I stared at the wall of the tent and around my teeth.

"The Lord promised that all the Land of Milk and Honey shall be given over to us," said Joshua. "So shall it be."

"First Jericho, then Ai," said Caleb. "Then we sweep across the whole of Canaan."

"I want a report on everything we need to know to take the city," ordered Joshua. "Their fortifications, how many men they have, their links with Bethel, and how the land lies all around."

"Yes sir."

"I also want an estimate as to how big an army we will need to take the city."

"Yes sir."

"Go now. May the Lord be with you."

The spies left and Joshua turned to Caleb. "Come, my friend, let us go to the tabernacle. We shall need to renew our javelins in the Ark before we take Ai."

"And ourselves," added Caleb.

I was all ears.

They fastened their tunics and strolled towards the door.

"Master." I stepped forward quickly.

"Ho! Your pretty Egyptian Queen wants something."

Joshua turned round and frowned.

"Master, take me with you."

"That is not possible. Women are not allowed."

"Master, I would come wherever you go."

Caleb folded his arms and grinned. "I wish I had such a pretty slave that would follow me everywhere I go. You could follow me, my pretty, anywhere, anytime, especially to my bed."

"Shut up, Caleb." Joshua pushed open the tent flap.

"So what's she like?" I heard Caleb say, as they left.

"A good handmaiden. Does her work and keeps her tongue."

"That's not what I meant."

"I know what you meant. I serve the Lord. You know I do not follow the lascivious ways of Baal."

"She's wasted on you, Joshua," laughed Caleb. Then he stuck his head back round the tent flap. "Remember, Egyptian Queen, you can follow me anywhere, anytime."

Joshua's strong arm reached in and hauled him out.

I will, Caleb, I smiled to myself. But not where you think.

Fragment 22

When they returned with their javelins a few hours later and sat down on the skins for their meal, they both looked different. I glanced at their faces as I handed them their bread. They shone. Even their javelins glowed. That radiance I had seen around Joshua the first time I saw him flickered like a cloud of fireflies around both men. They looked younger. The lines which had marked Joshua's face as he plotted to take Ai, were wiped away. His brow was smooth and radiant. As he took the bread from me, I noticed that a small cut on his hand, which he had caught on a broken shard only that afternoon, had gone. The skin was

301

completely unmarked.

"Hah. I feel a new man." Caleb stretched his arms above his head.

"Hey, pretty Egyptian." He grabbed my wrist and pulled me towards him. I nearly dropped the rest of the bread. "Feel that." He flexed the muscles in his arm. They were hard as rocks and his skin gleamed smooth and bronzed.

"I was forty years old when Moses sent me out from Kadesh Barnea, with this dour master of yours, to explore the land of Canaan. The Lord and his Ark have kept me as strong and alive as the day we left, and that was forty five years ago."

"Your boasting will be end of you," said Joshua.

"Hah, my end and yours will be long in coming."

Caleb picked up his javelin. He held it out in a way I had never seen a javelin held before, outstretched, instead of at his shoulder, then as true as Astarte shines from the heavens, I swear a stream of white fire shot out from the point and a heavy pot on the far side of the tent smashed into pieces, though no one was near.

"Caleb, that's enough. The power of the Ark is not for party tricks. You know what can happen.

Joshua grabbed the javelin and set it on the floor. He handed him a jar of wine. "Now eat, drink, and don't

302

be a fool."

Then he turned to me and took my chin in his hand. "Girl, not a word of this."

I nodded. I could not at that moment have uttered a word if I tried. Perhaps the Habiru God had stolen the thunderbolts of Baal himself and trapped them in that Ark.

My hands were trembling as I served them the stew.

Fragment 23

The spies returned from Ai.

"Well?" said Joshua.

"Sir, the city lies on a plateau of the hill country," began one of the men.

"About ten miles from Jericho," said the other. "High up at the far edge of the chalklands. There are stone quarries some way outside the city gates."

"Their people are allied to Bethel. About two miles west of Ai."

"Is Ai well fortified?" asked Joshua.

"Not like Jericho, sir."

"How many men will we need to capture it?"

One of the spies laughed. "Sir, you will not need all our people to go up against Ai. They only have have a handful of men to guard the city. It's ours for the taking."

"Send two or three thousand, sir," said the other. "There's no need to exhaust the rest of our troops."

"You're sure about that?" said Joshua.

"Sir, it'll be a pushover."

"Very well. Uri!"

"Sir." The commander stepped forward.

"Take three thousand men and march on the city of Ai. The remainder can rest in preparation for the next stage of the campaign."

"Yes, sir."

"And Commander, spare no one."

"Yes, sir."

"Girl!"

I stepped forward. "Yes, master?"

Master! It made me want to spit to call a Habiru that, but I played the docile little slave to the best of my ability. I was desperate to know how Joshua and Caleb stayed young and what the Ark could do to make a javelin shatter a pot without even being thrown. I wondered why the Habiru people didn't try to get the secrets too, but they all seemed terrified of the Ark.

"Hand me some wine."

As I poured the sweet red wine from Canaan's grapes into the Habiru leader's cup, I wished my curses could turn it into deadly poison. So Ai was next. Those people were Canaanite too, and they would suffer the same fate as my people in Jericho. It appeared that Ai did not have had a Rahab. The entire town would be slaughtered, with not even one family of traitors spared.

But the campaign to take Ai did not go as planned. The three thousand Habiru troops were routed by the men of Ai. I rejoiced in secret when I heard that thirty six Habiru were killed and the remainder chased away from the city gates to be struck down in the stone quarries. Few returned to tell the tale.

The Habiru shrank together in fear. People muttered in huddles. "The Canaanites will slaughter us all."

"This is a disaster," said Caleb, as they stormed into the tent. "What in the Lord's name were those spies thinking of? Three thousand men? Ours for the taking? Commander, put them to the sword."

"Sir, they are dead already. The vultures peck at their bones in the quarries of Ai."

"Along with nearly three thousand others of our people." I had never seen Joshua so grim. "As soon as the other Canaanites get to hear about this, they will no longer be afraid of us and will surround us and wipe out our name."

"Our whole entry into the Promised Land depends on our enemies trembling before us and our God," said Caleb.

"Do you think I don't know that?" snapped Joshua.

"So what are you going to do about it?"

"Just go." Joshua waved the men away.

Caleb opened his mouth to say something else, but Joshua gestured for him to leave too. And when Joshua's eyes were burning, no one, not even Caleb, argued.

Once the tent was empty, Joshua sank onto a pile of skins on the floor and put his head in his hands. Then he looked up at the roof of the tent.

"Oh Sovereign Lord, why did you ever bring our people across the Jordan to deliver us into the hands of these heathens?"

I stood and watched him, uncertainly. I had never seen Joshua like this before. He had always been strong, so full of faith in his God. I never dreamed I would see him doubt or question the God who had led his people through the wilderness for more than forty years. I did not know what to do. I bent down and picked up the dregs of the wine. Quietly I turned to the door. But Joshua must have heard me move, for he looked across. His face was tired and strained.

"No," he said. "Don't go."

I stood there, wondering what I should do, the pitcher in my hands.

"Come here."

I went towards him slowly.

"Put down the wine."

I did as I was told. My heart began to thump in my breast.

Joshua caught my wrist and pulled me down on my knees on the skins before him. "You have been a loyal servant to me," he said. "You are a very good girl, I see it in your eyes."

I swallowed. I prayed he could not read my soul; that he would not really see what lay behind my eyes. What if he had the power to know my thoughts? That I waited to destroy him the first chance I got? He would kill me in an instant. But he looked so tired. I was confused. I did not like to see him this way. He killed Tarasch, I told myself. He slaughtered the children of Jericho. But still my heart beat as though it would burst.

"Oh Lord." Dark curls of hair pushed through his fingers as he held his head in his hands then looked up at the roof of the tent.   "What can I say to the people, now Israel has been routed by its enemies? When the Cannanites move in for the kill, what of your great name then?"

Slowly, as though they did not belong to me, my fingers reached out, hovered in the air, then gently touched those springs of dark curls.

Joshua looked up. His face looked sad, noble and beautiful to me then. You killed Tarasch, I said to myself. You made the walls of Jericho fall. You killed Tarasch.

Joshua took my hand and held it in his. It was three times the size of mine, yet there was gentleness there. My blood surged through my veins. A sudden rush of heat swept though my belly and my legs. You killed Tarasch. You slaughtered Jericho. You killed Tarasch. His face was so close to mine. My lips parted. I ran my tongue over my teeth. If I had been standing, I swear my legs would have given way beneath me. I did not understand what was happening to me. Moistness clung to my body and I felt as I had never felt before. You killed Tarasch, I repeated to myself, in desperation. This man is your enemy. Kill him. I was dimly aware of the knife at his belt. Take it, screamed a voice inside me. Slit the bastard's throat. But I could not take my eyes from his. His fingers pressed against mine. I wondered if he would do to me then what the men did with the priestesses in the temple and I felt my breasts turn hard and force themselves against the fabric of my gown.

Then he let go my hand and stood up. "I must go to the Ark," he said. "I must ask the Lord my God what I should do."

He turned his back on me and marched out of the door, leaving me kneeling still on the goatskins.

"Damn your Ark. Damn your God." I hurled the pitcher across the tent, then flung myself on the skins and cried bitter tears, though I was not sure why.

That night, in the secret dark of my bed, all alone, I did to myself what I knew the women did who had no man. Then I cried again.

Fragment 24

The next morning I rose with the sun and went into the camp to stretch my legs and greet my Gods. I walked to the spring, splashed cool water on my face then closed my eyes and prayed to Astarte, silently, in my heart, taking care that

309

any prying Habiru eyes would think I had come just to bathe.

As I walked back, I heard men's voices behind a rock. A fire crackled and the smell of grilling fish drifted on the air. I pressed myself against the rock. I had no wish to be discovered alone by a band of Habiru men.

"See where Joshua's God has brought us to," muttered one. "The Canaanites will all be down upon us, when they hear about Ai."

"I say we should dump the One God, before it's too late."

Cautiously, I peeped out from behind the rock at the small group of men by the fire.

"Hush, such talk is treason. Do you want to get us all killed?"

"Naphish is right. We should appease Baal and the other Gods, seeing as we're in their land."

"I agree. Besides, the One God only tells us what we can't do."

"I'd willingly serve Baal," growled another. "The Canaanites have a lot more fun than we do. They're always sacrificing and feasting, and I hear their priestesses are more than willing."

As a burst of raucous laughter went up, I decided to go and crept away from the rock, but my foot dislodged some small stones which tumbled down the slope towards the men.

"Ho! What have we here?"

I was about to run, but a hairy arm grabbed me around my waist and dragged me to the fire.

"I'll show you what we could do in the service of Baal, with this." The man ripped open his tunic and showed his manhood to the rest, still gripping me round the waist with his other arm.

The men began to stamp their feet, urging him on with bawdy gestures and yelling. Some of them chanted, "Baal! Baal! Baal!" I screamed and kicked but could not get free.

"What's going on here?"

The men fell silent.

Achan strode into their midst. The hairy man let go my waist.

"This is Joshua's airl. Let her go, or I'll tell our leader what has gone here."

No one stopped me as I ran towards the camp. But before I had gone far, Achan stepped out from a rock in front of me. I pulled up short. He must have cut across the wasteground to intercept me.

"What do you want?" I tried not to sound nervous.

He sauntered towards me. "Is that the way to thank your rescuer?" He grinned, and picked up a strand of my hair. His fingers were blackened and greasy. I tried to pull away but he wound my hair tighter around his hand. Then clapping his free hand across my mouth, he muffled my cries and pulled me towards a nearby tent. Still keeping his hand across my mouth, he dragged me inside. The tent stank of sweat. Achan rolled back the goat skins from the floor. To my surprise, a beautiful robe, such as the Babylonians make, lay underneath. I knew instantly he had stolen it. There was no way a humble soldier could afford a a robe like that, and I knew Joshua had declared that all the plunder from Jericho was to be devoted to the One God and taken to their holy place.

"See that, Egyptian?" he smirked, his hot breath in my ear. "If you perform the pagan rites with me, I'll give you it to wear? And I'll fill your pretty hands with gold, if you put them here." He pulled open his robe.

"Have this instead!" I kicked him, hard.

He yelled in pain, clutching his groin, and I scrambled out of the tent.

"Pig swill!" I yelled. Then I ran for the safety of Joshua's tent, smiling. So he had gold as well. I would get my revenge on that Habiru filth.

Joshua had returned from the Ark with the fire burning within him.

I stood behind him when he addressed the Habiru people later that day. He had called all the tribes to stand before him, his most trusted guards at his back.

"On your knees!" he yelled.

The whole Habiru nation sank down on the _around.

No one dared mention Baal now, I noticed, with scorn.

"Israel has sinned!" Joshua's voice boomed across the assembled heads. "You have violated the orders of the Lord!"

A soldier shuffled behind me.

"Israel has taken some of the things devoted to the Lord; they have stolen and lied; they have put the Lord's treasures with their own possessions!"

Not a soul spoke amongst that whole nation gathered there. Not a soul moved.

"That is why the Israelites cannot stand against their enemies!" raged Joshua. "The Lord will not back a people who steals from him!"

The silence was only broken by one soldier's nervous coughing in the troops at our back.

Joshua turned to the Levite priests who stood in a group to one side. They were dressed in turbans, and blue robes fringed alternately with golden bells and purple, blue, and scarlet pomegranates, with sashes to match.

"Go, consecrate the people," he commanded the priests. "In preparation for tomorrow." Then he turned back to the tribes.

"In the morning," he yelled. "Present yourselves, tribe by tribe! The tribe the Lord takes, shall come forward, clan by clan. The clan the Lord takes, shall come forward, family by family. The family the Lord takes, shall come forward, man by man."

Again, from behind me, came that nervous cough.

"He who has stolen the devoted things shall be destroyed!" roared Joshua. "And all that belongs to him! Israel shall not stand against her enemies until this is done! For he has violated the covenant of the Lord and done a disgraceful thing in Israel!"

Joshua turned away and while the priests made ready to consecrate the people, we of Joshua's household followed behind him. Among the assembled guard, I caught a glimpse of Achan's face.

He wasn't smiling now.

Early the next morning, the tribes assembled. Again, Joshua went before them, his loyal guard at his rear, the priests in their brilliant robes to the side. I stood just behind him, as usual.

He called out the names of all the Habiru tribes, Manassah, Ephraim, Gad, Benjamin, Simeon... until all the names were called.

Silence fell upon the assembled hoards.

"The Lord takes Judah!" shouted Joshua.

I heard Caleb curse under his breath. He was of the Tribe of Judah. He stepped forward.

Several others of Joshua's trusted guard stepped out of the ranks as well. Among them was Achan. I noticed his knuckles were white as he gripped his spear. The whole tribe of Judah came forward and assembled before the rest. Caleb held his head high.

"I call the clans of Judah!" shouted Joshua, and called out the names of the clans. Tension crackled on the air as the Habiru waited. I noticed Achan's legs were trembling.

"The Lord takes the clan of the Zerahites!"

The other clans of Judah, including Caleb's, fell back relieved. Except for the Zerahites, who came together in a huddle.

"Now let the families of the Zerahites be called!"

The families came forward, one at a time, men, women, children and babes in arms. Some of the little ones began to cry. Remembered wails of frightened children rose unbidden in my ears.

I swallowed and forced down the lump in my throat.

Achan's wife, a thin miserable looking woman and three scrawny children, one a boy of no more than six with a club foot and sad expression, huddled by his side. I could almost smell their fear.

"I call the family of Zimri!"

Achan's wife's knees buckled. Achan stood rooted to the spot. Other members of their family pushed them forward.

Then there was silence. The whole of the Habiru people waited to see who would be called next.

Joshua's voice boomed across the hillside. "I call Achan, son of Carmi!"

"No!" Achan's wife screamed. The children looked around, bemused. The little boy with the club foot began to

316

whimper and tripped over. A guard prodded him back with his sword. Another took Achan's spear.

Then Joshua said to Achan, "Tell me what you have done."

Achan flung himself to his knees and clasped his hands before him.

A murmur went up from the crowd.

"How did Joshua know?" whispered someone close by me. "Surely the Lord himself must have revealed the sin to him."

I smiled.

"Why have you brought this trouble on us?" boomed Joshua. "You caused the Lord to desert us at Ai. Now the Lord will bring trouble on you today."

I watched as Achan's face crumpled. Joshua nodded to his men and several stepped forward, two of them seizing Achan by his arms.

"Stone him," said Joshua.

A stream of liquid ran down Achan's legs and pooled in the sand. "Mercy, sir, mercy, sir," he babbled.

"And stone all who belong to him."

Achan's wife clutched her children and screamed.

The little boy with the club foot stuck his thumb in his mouth and cried for his mother when the guards dragged him off, not understanding.

Joshua turned away and all of us in his household and his guard, save those taking away Achan and his wretched family, followed him across the slope.

That evening, Joshua called me to him. He took my chin in his hand and tilted my face towards his. "You have proved yourself a loyal servant to me and my God," he said. "You have been more faithful than many of my own people. Including that treacherous Achan, who was one of my most trusted guard."

Hah, I thought to myself. If only you knew. I hate you and your One God. I serve Astarte and the true Gods of Canaan.

And if I can stop you doing to Ai and the rest what you did at Jericho, I'll put a knife in your gut.

"Do you have a family," he asked suddenly.

He caught me off guard. I had to force hot tears back behind my eyes. "No, master. I have no family. None but you."

He looked deeply into my eyes. Again I remembered the Ark and feared his powers. "You have served Israel well. I needed to show the people why we lost at Ai. They must learn that the Lord demands obedience - and that deception such as Achan's leads to death. You have well earned my trust. I shall not forget it."

Nor did he did forget he trusted me - ever. And, in the moons to come, great would be his rage when he learned that I betrayed him too.

Chapter 9

I feel like I've just hit the bottom of a cliff. Sweat is flooding my bed and my hair is waterweed. The dream has sucked me down again like I've been drowning. It's been the same night after night since Ben left. Each time I'm falling, falling through blackness, and though I can't see anything, somehow I know that at the bottom of this void lies water, dark, cold water, and that I'll never see sunshine again.

The telephone is ringing. Ben. It must be. He doesn't realise the time. It's probably midday in the States. I snatch it up it quickly, sending my clock-alarm crashing to the floor, but to hell with that. An Israeli voice gabbles down the line. Wrong number. I slam down the receiver, and disappointment cuts through me so hard I feel like I've been stuck with a bayonet. Ben, or the lack of him, has turned me into another Sharon Tate.

I chuck aside these horrible, wringing wet sheets and haul myself out of bed. I shan't get any more sleep. Might as well make some coffee then stagger into the bathroom, inspect my battalion of pots and prepare to do battle for yet another bloody day alone.

I keep staring at the final phrase of Fragment 38, trying to listen as she speaks, but there are other words screaming through my head. *You bitch! I only wanted you to love me. I'll make you pay for this!* Curses are slashing through the veils of my memory, and through the rents I see his face across that courtroom again, twisted, full of pain and hate. *"How could you do this to me! You fucking whore!"*

I lean on my desk and clap my hands over my ears but nothing can shut out screams engraved on my brain cells. If I could only have had the satisfaction of hurting him back. Hurled stones at him or something, as she did. If I could only feel that I had done something, anything, instead of sitting passively in the courtroom like some pre-Pankhurstian simperer, while the lawyers argued and twisted the truth, probing with intimate questions about my relationship with Jonathon. They made me want to curl up and die with shame for something I didn't do. But me, poor pathetic me, I just sat there, didn't I. Never stood up for myself. Answered their stupid questions, put up with cameras flashing in my eyes and reporters hounding me every time I left court. *Miss Adams, Miss Adams, just one moment...*

Why did I let them? Why wasn't I like her? She didn't take any nonsense. She twisted her most powerful enemies round her finger, chewed them up and spat them out. Why aren't I like her, instead of this snivelling heap of self-pitying garbage. Look how she dealt with Achan. Why didn't I pick up the first thing that came to hand. A bag, a camera or the Bible I'd sworn on, to tell the truth, the whole truth and nothing but the truth. I should have hurled the thing at his head, and to hell with the consequences. I would have been punished for contempt but at least I'd have had the satisfaction of knowing I'd done something, anything, to show them all that I wasn't just some spineless victim, waiting to be trod on as he kicked me every step of the way. That stone faced judge decided everything in place of me. No, better to be held in contempt of court than contempt of myself.

Eighteen months at Her Majesty's Pleasure. I hope Her Majesty got some pleasure out that sentence, for I damn well didn't. Eighteen months, after all Jonathon did to me. Now not even that. He was a good little boy in jail, I'm sure. No doubt he smiled at the guards and did as he was told. I can just see it now. *Yes sir. I'm really sorry, sir. I've seen the light. I'm rehabilitated now, sir. A credit to your system. I'll never do it again.*

Now he's out, a free man, with a third off his sentence for 'good behavior.' How much 'gooder' do I have to be till my sentence is over?

I've snapped my pen in half. I hurl the pieces into the bin. Anger surges though me like a cleansing tide, sweeping away the driftwood. Anger is pure. Anger is sweet. How dare he make my life a misery. Why let him turn me into a pale reflection of all I can be, a wretched creature who jumps at shadows in the afternoon? This isn't what I want for myself.

I search my handbag for the Marlboro. One thing's for sure. If I ever come face to face with that creep again, it won't be lawyers and judges who give him what's he's got coming. I flick on my lighter, take a few puffs, but I don't need this cigarette after all. I snuff out the glow and grind it into my ashtray, hard.

It must be growing late. I can hear the buckets of the Filipino women clanking down the corridor. The rest of the academic staff have left. But I'm still sitting here, poring over these fragments. The cleaners must think I'm a really sad case. No home worth going to. But I don't want to go anywhere. All I need is here. This story is like a drug to me. I want nothing more than to inhale the smell of old clay, breathe in the fragrance of ferns around the oasis and immerse myself in tales of Canaan. These aren't just lines on dead tablets to me. Since I left England and the cool marble halls of the British Museum, this hot tormented land of Palestine and its people has sprung to life for me. When I look at these fragments I don't see squiggles on stone. I see her, slogging up its hills and running down its valleys, tying tributes to the trees for her gods. Her world never truly existed for me before, not when it was filtered through London smog, but now I understand how Canaan had a life of its own, how Palestine lives and breathes through its people.

I turn back to the beginning of Fragment 39. Radiation sickness. It has to be. The power of the Ark must have involved some sort of harnessing of a radioactive substance by the ancient Hebrews. Maybe someone discovered the cave by chance, a goat boy perhaps. They seem to have found half the treasures of antiquity. Some kid who followed an animal inside the earth, and ending up discovering something that's fascinated people ever since. From Moses' to Spielberg. It's pretty incredible - destruction and renewal, blazing side by side.

It's such a shame this girl got too close to the fire. She had no protection as her enemies did, with their strange silver suits. I'm so sorry that her courage couldn't save her, that the secret of the Hebrews destroyed her and her child in the end.

I go to the window to watch liquid gold melt over the city as the sun sets over Jerusalem, and questions flicker across my mind as the lights begin to come on. Did she take her revenge on Joshua and his Hebrews for the rape of Canaan? Was the location of the cave lost along with the map? Or might it still be found today?

I am hungry for that map. It's not so important for Ben. He's already at the top. I'm nothing. No one's heard of Charlotte Adams outside the two establishments I've worked in. All that must change. But I want to find that cave for her too. Somehow I feel her struggle has been mine. I want her to see the secret of the Hebrews exposed and for her to scream through the centuries again against Joshua and his murdering God.

If the white fire burnt in some inaccessible place, and only a handful of select people knew where to find it, one of whom was already dead, she might have succeeded. The Hebrew elders would have made sure it was kept a very closely guarded secret. Maybe her breaking the chain caused it to be lost altogether. My research has failed to reveal any sign that exceptional longevity and youth was handed on after Joshua and Caleb. Perhaps the location of the cave vanished along with Rahab's sister. I hope she got her revenge.

I could be on the verge of finding her secret again.

I go back to my desk. I can barely keep my eyes open, but I must take another look at that final fragment.

I shall hide the map where they shall never find it. The secrets of the Ark of the One God shall be lost to the Habiru forever. But forever is a long very time. When I was a kid, I read in a fairy tale that a secret only stays hidden for so long. Maybe now's the time for it to come round again.

I can hear the banging of mops by my door. I really don't want to leave the fragments but exhaustion has got me by the teeth. I can't do any more today. But I'm desperate to know more and as I arrange my desk, every little thing in its place, my mind is a whirlpool of possibilities and questions. The glorious Professor Charlotte Adams could sit in her high level Hall of Learning and gloat over Claudia Schiffer's wrinkles and Jodie Kidd's double chins. I have to find out. Has the White Fire continued to burn in secret through the years, and where could she have hidden that map? I don't want any of those power-hungry blokes to have it, anymore than she did. There is a sisterhood in secrets.

I owe it to myself - and to her - to find it first.

*I am plunging towards the water. Men
dressed in black are shaking their fists from
above. Furious voices tear holes in the darkness.
But they can't hurt me now. I have what they
want and it's way beyond their reach. I clutch it
to me as I fall. They shan't have it, unless they
want to follow me into the realm of Reshef. Their
faces disappear. I leave them far behind. The
water is waiting, for me and my secret.*

I sit up and turn on the light. My sheets are
soaked again and I feel like I've done ten rounds
with Tyson in my sleep. But I don't care. I've found it.
Illumination in nightmare. Elation is streaming out of
every sweat-filled pore.
I know where the map is.

"Charlotte, fax me the final fragments, as
soon as you can." Ben's voice is terse and
strained.
"What about Tony? How is he?"
"What? Oh, yes, he's doing as well as can be
expected. The donor
marrow's being prepared. There're just a few
er...formalities to tie up
before the operation can go ahead. Look,
Charlotte, the fragments."
"Are you sure you want to be bothered with
work at a time like this?"
"Charlotte, I really need...
"Everything's fine here. Why don't you just

concentrate on..."

"Charlotte, just fax me your final translation, as fast as you can."

"O.K., O.K. Don't worry. I'll sort it."

"Here's the fax number of the hotel where I'm staying."

I scribble down the number. I don't mention anything else. This isn't the time. When I put down the phone I go straight to the
fax machine and send Ben the final fragments before I forget. If I was in his place, I don't think I'd be bothering about work, even it did involve the secrets of the Ark of the Covenant. Still, maybe he needs it, to take his mind off the fear that Tony mightn't pull through. I find it hard to focus on Ben and the son I've never met. I suppose I should feel guilty, but my mind is a minefield of caves and maps. Anyway, I think I've done enough guilt. I tap in the number and the final fragments are winging their way to New York.

Well, if he's not here, all the more glory for me. Plus the beauty treatment of all time. If he misses out on eternal youth, that's his loss. I'll be on at least an equal footing as the illustrious Dr Travers before long. But I'm damn well going to find that cave for her as well. Her men in black are my men in black. Only the century's changed.

There's a message from Schlott. He's itching to see more of my translation. I'd love to know for sure about his investors, but I don't trust him, or them, whoever they are. The increased security at the university hasn't stopped me from being followed nor my flat being ransacked. It's his fault I've been in danger. If he hadn't insisted on releasing details of the fragments so early, no one outside the university would even know about their existence yet. Maybe I'm being stupid. He is my boss and the university pays my salary. But somehow my loyalties don't lie here any longer. I can't help myself. They belong more with a spunky young girl and her people who lived over three millennia ago, and maybe their descendants, who knows. Somehow I feel my destiny's linked to this land - but not here, not in Israel, this Hebrew world. I put the minimum of work I think I can get away with in an envelope, mark it with Schlott's name and stick it in the internal post. That should keep him off my back while I get the chance to search for the cave.

      I wish I had a car of my own in Jerusalem. I can just imagine the time and the red tape I'll have to wade through to get my International Driver's Licence. I need access to the caves. I pace up and down my office. Now I know how King Richard felt. A car, a car, my queendom for a Kia Shuma five door hatchback. Ingrid knocks and sticks her head around the door. No, I say, I don't want coffee, not just yet. She retreats but I call her back, for she has a Renault Megane. Oh how the hell can I ask Ingrid to come on a quest for the secrets of the Ark. I don't trust her any more. I witter some remark about stock and let her go.

      Ben's never here when I need him. Is any

man?

I suppose I could just take a car and drive, but I could have stopped and I really don't fancy trouble with the police, not here.

But I'm getting lightheaded. I Haven't eaten today. I can't afford to lose my grip. I decide to go after Ingrid to say I've changed my mind about going to the canteen but she's out of the office. I go on my own and as I sit down with an freshly squeezed orange juice and a sesame bagel, I see Emile stride through the door. He gives me a wave and starts heading this way. Eureka, I've found the solution. Seeing as Harrison Ford's tied up, who better to join me on my quest than Ben's right hand man, the very person who's now leading the excavations at Ein Gedi, and this charming Frenchman has all the uni.'s digging equipment at his command. I give him my very best smile and prepare to win him to my cause.

I haven't been able to reach Ben on the phone since I spoke to him yesterday. Some bored sounding receptionist told me he's in the operating theatre with his son. With Maddy too, I bet. Jealousy is an especially vicious emotion. Its deepest cuts are reserved for the person it's coming from. I'm disgusted at myself that I can be so selfish while that little kid is fighting for his life. Perhaps I'm bad inside, like a rotting peach, and I deserve everything that's happened to me. But sod it, why should I think like this? There's no need for it, not any longer. It's about time I stopped running like some clockwork mouse backwards and forwards along the tracks of my own negative thoughts and started to put into action all those things that Dr Hewitt made me see. Feelings, however horrible they may be, are natural, and at the end of the day, Tony is nothing more to me than a name and a face on a battered photograph. And its his father who's battering my heart.

Ben won't mind my going it alone with Emile. He'll be excited too, when he gets back, if things go according to plan. Most kids are pretty resilient. Tony will probably soon be running around as though he'd never been ill. Then Ben will return and we'll finish this quest together.

The alternative is too awful to contemplate.

I've arranged to meet Emile on Derekh Yerikho, in the shadow of the Mount of Olives, so no one will see me drive away from the university. To make doubly sure, I'm going to work as usual today, but I know where the cleaner's overalls are kept and put one over my clothes then cover my head with an awful garish scarf which I bought from the Armenian stall in the bazaar on some ethnic whim. I wouldn't be seen dead in it normally.

I keep my face hidden as I wait for Emile by the Yusefiya cemetery and watch anxiously as the cars speed by. God, I hope my precautions have worked. My nails are going to end up in bits. I was never cut out for this Charley's Angel's stuff. The rush hour traffic pours on. I don't think anyone's been following but as Emile's Volvo pulls up and I jump inside, I still watch my back. No doubt they've been keeping an eye on the dig but as far as we know, no one has bothered to shadow Emile. Oh God, who am I trying to kid? If someone is determined enough, they'll be out there somewhere, waiting.

I like Emile. His hair keeps falling into his eyes and he tosses it aside as he drives. He plays CDs of Jean Michel Jarre and some French rock band I've never heard of and fills the car with music. I put on my sunglasses, lean back against the seat and try to relax, as the buildings give way to Jerusalem pines and the hills of Judea in the distance. It's early yet. We wanted to have as much daylight as possible to dig. I keep glancing behind. It doesn't seem as though any cars are tailing us, but you never can tell.

This is backbreaking work. We've been at it for bloody hours. Now I know why I'm a translator not an archaeologist. All this humping rocks and soil around is not my scene. Especially not in this heat. I wouldn't last a week. Emile did suggest roping in the rest of the team as well. We could have excavated much faster, but I managed to persuade him otherwise. I can't afford to take chances. The less people who know about this the better. Emile was a bit uncertain at first. He thought they'd already found everything there was to find in the cave when they dug out the fragments. But I know there's something still in there. The final fragments tell of something they've missed. I pull out some of the rubble that fills the back of the cave and roll it aside. My fingers are cut and bleeding. I'm filly with dirt and sweat. Emile hands me another bottle of Evian and I take it from him gratefully. Then we set to work again, clearing the rocks. The roof must have collapsed several times since the Canaanite era, for the cave goes back much further than Ben's team had originally thought.

"Are you sure about this," grunts Emile, yanking a boulder aside. I know he's wondering if I've made a mistake and all this effort will result in nothing but wasted time and aching muscles.

"Of course," I say, without looking round, and take the next rock in my hands and tug. A shower of small stones and earth rains around my head. I choke and sit back on my heels. Sod this for a game of soldiers.

But I have to find it.

Emile looks anxiously up at the roof. "Come on," he says. "We need to put up some more posts. The roof is loose here. The last thing we want is to bring it down round our heads."

We drag some wooden supports from the clay pit and bring them to the back of the cave. Emile manoeuvres them into place then glances at his watch.

"If we don't find something soon, we'll have to leave it for another day. We'll lose the light before long."

"Just a bit more," I plead. "We must be getting close now."

Suddenly the rubble in front of me gives way. I fall forwards and my hands are clutching at nothing. But nothing means something here. I've nearly reached the end. I scrabble away the remaining stones. Please, let it be there.

"Emile! Here! I've found it!" My voice echoes triumphantly off the the walls and back at me through the cave and hell, I just feel like I want to cry.

Emile, crawling on his stomach like a snake, joins me at the rear of the cave. He turns on his torch and lying on our fronts, we stare into the void beneath. A small trickle of sand drops from the roof. Silence rises up to engulf us. The smell of ages lingers on these walls. The taste in my mouth is of cold and stone. This is the place of my dreams.

Emile lets a pebble drop. But there's no splash as it reaches the bottom. Nor can I hear any sound of a spring near the top, as the last fragments describe. This well has long run dry. But it is the place, I know it is.

"So," says Emile. "You were right."

"We have to go down." I have to know what's down there. My heart is bashing away like there's one of those Trafalgar Square pigeons trapped in my chest.

"I'll fetch some climbing gear," says Emile.

When he's gone, I glance up at the roof. It doesn't look very safe.

Emile returns with a harness and a long coil of rope which he loops securely round a boulder in the cave and tests with his weight.

"Let me go." This is my project. No one else is going till I've seen what's down there.

Emile looks unhappy but I manage to

persuade him it'll be safer if he stays on the surface to fetch help if anything goes wrong. Poor man. He looks like he's dying to play the macho hero but doesn't want to be politically incorrect. But this is my discovery. This is the place where the girl whose life I've spent every working hour resurrecting ended her days. I feel like a tigress protecting her young. This is her place, and now it becomes my place too. I shall not have a stranger intruding on our hallowed ground.

The descent is very different to my dreams. I lower myself down I bump and crash against the rock. I never was much good at this sort of thing. And God it hurts when you skin your knees on the rock. It's a slow, jerking process, quite unlike the smooth plunge through the darkness of my dream, and, I suspect, so different to how my friend from Canaan made her descent. But it's still the same place. I am afraid, as I slowly lower myself into the dark. And I have Emile up there, dependable and solid, ready to help if anything goes wrong. I can see the glow shining his torch from the top, and I too have a lamp tied around my waist which throws jagged shadows on the tunnel of smooth black rock. She had no Emile. No light. I know I could not have done what she did. I wish I was brave like her.

I start to wonder if this pit goes on forever. That pigeon which has taken residence in my heart is beating its wings for England and I wonder how many women in their twenties die of a coronary. My mouth is Sahara dry and I start to kick out in panic as

I remember that in my dream I knew would never again see daylight.

I should have seen it as a warning. I should never have come here.

What if the rope breaks? What if Emile walks away, or...

Suddenly my feet hit solid ground. The rope goes slack and I drop to my knees. The harness has cut into the skin beneath my arms. My palms smart from rope burns.

Ignoring the pain, I take off the lamp at my belt and flash it around the bottom of the well.

I see her. Face to face at last. Though the flesh is long gone, she is almost intact. There was water when she fell. She would have sunk slowly as the well drained away, its source dried up. She would have floated gently to the bottom till she came to lie where I find her now. I reach out towards the whiteness of bones in the lamplight but I do not touch her. Her head is turned towards me. There are cold tracks on my face. I think I have tears on my cheeks. It's as though I have found a long lost friend, at last.

Then something else catches my eye on the far side of the pit. A clay tablet. The only remaining one which she took to her death.

I loosen my harness and scramble towards it. All those long hours of tugging at rocks are made worthwhile in this moment. Fear and exhaustion are swept away by an incoming rush of adrenaline. This is it. A tablet from the very Ark itself. A holy of holies. The map which will lead to the Cave of White Fire, destroyer of cities and the secret of near eternal youth.

Now I have it in my grasp. The clay is cold, so cold. I turn it
over.

I can't believe what I see.
The tablet is blank.

<u>Fragment 26</u>

While the Habiru were stoning Achan and his family, they took two other men and killed them too. I did not understand, for they had done nothing more than our men of Jericho did, who favoured other men instead of girls. They had not stolen or deceived as Achan had done. Their only crime had been to perform the rites of love, as men did with the priests in our temples of Canaan.

I asked Uri, the commander, who was one of the few Habiru worth talking to, why they were killed.

He seemed as surprised at my question as I was by their deaths.

"Why? They have sinned, of course. For men to lie to with men is an abomination and our God forbids it. It is the way of heathens and the followers of Baal.

If anyone is found to be doing evil acts which are against the ways of the Lord, they must be purged from our people and put to death."

I still did not understand. But the more I heard of the ways of the One God, the more I hated him.

Joshua was full of fire now the reason for the defeat of Ai was found. I heard him speak of how his God had promised that Ai was now his.

"Do not be afraid; do not be discouraged!' This is what the Lord said to me," he told his people. "The Lord said, 'Take the whole army with you, and go up and attack Ai. For I have delivered into your hands the king of Ai, his people, his city and his land.'"

A great cheer rose up from the people, who were much heartened since the stoning of Achan, and the guards raised their spears in salute to the One God who promised them all.

"'You shall do to Ai and its king as you did to Jericho and its king," said Joshua, "except that you may carry off their plunder and livestock for yourselves.' This is what the Lord has said."

That's good of him, I thought. At least the animals will be spared this time and only men, women and babies put to the sword. I wondered what had happened to my king.

I was crouched in the shadows when Joshua chose his best fighting men and sent them out one night.

"Listen carefully," he told Uri. "Set an ambush behind the city. Don't move far and be on the alert. I and all those with me will advance on Ai, and when the men come out we will flee. Then I want you and your troops to rise up from the ambush and take the city. The Lord will give it into your hands. Trust in him."

"Yes sir."

"Then Ai shall be set on fire."

Joshua remained with the people while Uri's men headed for Ai, and the place of ambush, west of the city.

I schemed and plotted all night, trying to think of a way to warn the citizens of Ai, but I was all alone amongst the Habiru. Even if I escaped and set off through the hills, I would never reach the city before Uri's men.

I went with Joshua to serve him when he took Caleb and the other leaders of the tribes to set up camp, north of Ai. They pitched the tents with the valley between them and the city. That night, Joshua took his fighting men into the valley. I stayed with the servants and the others who were left behind in the camp. Under cover of darkness, I planned to sneak out and run to the gates of Ai, to warn their king that Joshua would ambush them from behind, but when I raised the flap of my tent, I found that guards swarmed all over the camp. I would be captured in an instant. I cursed and withdrew, hugging my knees in the darkness, wishing, burning to warn the king of Ai. But morning came and I was still trapped in the camp, helpless to warn Ai of its fate.

As soon as the sun came up, revealing Joshua's troops before the city, the gate opened and the men of Ai poured out. All the Habiru in the camp stood on the hillside, watching. I seized my chance and ran down the hill towards Ai. The city gates were open. All the men had come out. A great cheer rose up across the land. The men of Ai were rejoicing at the prospect of another routing of Joshua's rabble. I tore down the hillside, sliding on stones and cutting my knees on the harsh terrain. My breath stabbed at my chest. The city gates lay wide open. I had to warn the king.

But I should have known I would never succeed. I had gone but a short way down the hillside when something happened that stopped me in my tracks.

I had a good view across the valley and saw Joshua come out at the head of his army. He held out his javelin. His men fell back. Joshua stood alone. Then the men in the ambush rose from their hiding place and rushed forward on the city.

Joshua raised his javelin and aimed it at Ai. Then - I swear to all the Gods in the heavens that this is true - white fire streamed from his javelin and struck a tower which rose up from the walls of Ai, and set the city ablaze.

Someone shouted behind me and as I turned, I saw some of the Habiru had cowered in a nook of the hillside when they saw the javelin fire.

"The power of the Ark of the Lord has set the city alight!" called someone close by. "The Lord has delivered Ai into our hands, as Joshua promised he would."

"Never mind that!" yelled another. "Pray to the Lord he doesn't strike us down too!"

I sank down on the stony slope and watched, helpless, as the men of Ai looked back and saw their city on fire, coils of black smoke staining the sky. Then Joshua's men, who had been pretending to flee into the desert, rushed back and attacked the men of Ai.

Uri's ambushing troops closed the gates of the city, trapping all the citizens inside while it burned, then rushed on the men of Ai from behind.

The Habiru cut down them down. Not a man of Ai was left alive, save one.

Joshua remained before the city, and he did not draw

back the hand that held the javelin until that stream of white fire had made a blackened ruin of Ai.

His men had driven the livestock away and removed the plunder. The animals were saved this time for themselves, as Joshua had ordered.

The only man of Ai to be spared the sword outside the gates was the king, who was taken alive.

Joshua had him hung from a tree. When the sun went down, his body still swung. Joshua commanded his men to take it down and throw it at the entrance to the ruined city's gate.

And so I learned what had been the fate of my king too.

Fragment 27

Joshua laughed when he heard that five Amorite tribes were marching against him.

The kings of Jerusalem, Hebron, Lachish, Eglon and Jarmuth joined forces when they heard the people of Gibeon had made a peace treaty with Joshua. They moved all their troops into position near Gibeon then attacked the city.

The Gibeonites sent word to Joshua, back in the

camp near Jericho.

"Do not abandon your servants," pleaded the
messenger, on his knees at Joshua's feet.

I rolled my eyes to the sky. Snivellers and cowards
were a disgrace to Canaan and our Gods.

"Come quickly and save us! We beg you, help us,
because all the Amorite kings from the hill country have
joined against Gibeon!"

Joshua was in excellent humour that day. He had
returned from the Ark with his face aglow. The few grey
hairs that had crept into his beard were gone. He shone with
power.

He picked up his javelin, caressed the shaft and
smiled. "Have no fear. The Lord will give the Amorites and
their kings into our hands."

I looked across at Caleb. He was smiling too. He
looked as handsome and strong as ever. I could scarcely
believe he was more than eighty years old. He was as robust
as an ox and more virile than all his soldiers put together, if
the stories that ran round the camp were true. Not a grey
hair stained his hair or beard. I wondered if he and Joshua
themselves were Gods. Did that Habiru Ark have the
power to make men immortal? It had already crossed my mind
that Joshua might be invincible. He certainly acted as if he

were. He was no more worried by the five kings moving against him than by a fly brushing past his nose. More than once, I had tried to put a blade to his throat while he slept, but I always failed. A guard would enter, Joshua's eyelids would flicker open or even my own hand would stay in mid air, refusing to do the deed that would end the slaughter of Canaan forever, as though his God protected him while he slept.

Once he woke while I crouched by his side, the knife I used to cut his bread concealed in my gown. He grabbed my wrist. "Oh, it is you." Then he let go my hand and sat up. "What is my Egyptian queen doing here in the dark?"

"Master," I whispered, "I often sit beside you at night and would chase away the evil spirits that bring bad dreams."

Joshua laughed. I felt his breath on my face in the darkness and grew hot. "My God will protect me from lesser spirits in the night." His hand reached out and stroked my hair. "But I thank you, little Egyptian, for your care. You are a good and loyal servant to me. I trust you more than many of my own people, who are forever complaining, conspiring and turning to Baal."

"They do not deserve such a leader," I whispered through the dark. I could feel heat surging through my belly and filling my limbs with fire. I sank closer to him. My breasts pressed against the thin fabric of my gown as they strained towards him. I moistened my lips with my tongue. If I could press my body into his, catch him off guard, feel the hard strong warmth of his chest against mine, I could take my knife and sink it into his back.

But the moment was lost.

"I shall sleep no more," he announced, firmly putting me from him. "I shall take a walk beneath the stars and commune with the Lord."

"Curse your Lord," I muttered, as he strode away.

I was fed up with moving. The Habiru never stayed long in one place. Joshua used the camp at Gilgal near Jericho as his base, but they seemed incapable of putting down roots. It was nothing to them to pack up their tents, load their paltry possessions onto their camels or mangy donkeys and head off some place else. I had lived in our little house in Jericho all my life. I detested the nomads and their wandering ways.

So once again, Joshua left a few people at Gilgal then marched through the wasteland, right up into the hill country and on to Gibeon. I rode on a donkey most of the way, and sulked, even though we did start out at night and

344

avoided the burning heat of the sun. I hated those desolate hills and the strange sounds that pierced the night. My backside soon grew sore from that ass. How the creature's bones stuck into mine. How I wished I were back at Jericho, in my home, and Tarasch would come running in through the door, laughing with a pile of flax in her arms.

The Ark, of course, came with us too. It was always kept under its cloth and guarded by the Levite priests. But the main army travelled apart. Though the Ark had a guard of the best fighting men both in front and behind, they never came within a thousand yards of that box. Once I let my donkey lag back, but there were always soldiers to make sure that I, like the rest, could never come close.

"Why can no one except the priests and Holders approach the Ark?" I asked Uri once.

His face turned grim. "If you had seen how it blasts those who do not know its ways, seen their flesh shrivel from their bones, then watched those bones crumble to naught, you would not ask."

I could get nothing more out of him. But I noticed how none of the Habiru people tried to get near. They were afraid even to speak of it. Still my curiosity burned.

But it was not long before I saw again how strange were the powers of the Ark.

When the sun came up the next day, Joshua took his army and marched on Gibeon.

Those of us who were left, remained at a safe distance on the top of a hill. The Ark stayed too, but the priests took it to the summit of another hill, then retreated back down the slope and disappeared, except for two. These were not dressed in their usual robes but wore strange garments of silver which covered them from head to toe, even their faces.

I made tunnels of my hands and watched as they removed the cloth and lifted the lid of that magic box. Then they hurried down the hillside to rejoin the rest of the priests. I thought it exceedingly strange that the Habiru had left their treasured Ark alone on a foreign hill.

I couldn't see the battle at Gibeon from those distant slopes, but the stories were told for a long time to come. Joshua took the armies of the five kings by surprise. He defeated them at Gibeon then pursued the survivors all along the road to Beth Horan, cutting them down as they fled, till the road ran red with blood.

But I did see what part that Ark played. The stories do not tell of the cloud that rose up from the box. At first I thought it was an ordinary rain cloud forming above the hill, but as I watched, I realised it was coming from the Ark itself.

It was not plain *grey* like a normal cloud, but specks of silver sparkled from within. It grew bigger and bigger and floated off till it covered the sky on the other side of Gibeon. They said in the stories that giant hailstones fell on the Amorite men as they fled, and more were killed by those than by the Habiru swords. But no hailstones I have ever seen came from a cloud such as that.

Joshua had taken the Amorites by surprise but his rabble were nothing compared to the whole combined armies of five of the most powerful cities of Canaan. He was outnumbered by far and the Amorite soldiers were far stronger than his. They had chariots too, with blades slicing from the wheels as they drove. Joshua's Habiru band would not have stood a chance were it not for the Ark.

Before the cloud moved over to Gibeon I saw it pass over an oryx which had come out to feed. A giant ball of silver - no hailstone - fell from the cloud and that beautiful creature fell dead on the ground. Its antlers turned to dust, its white coat shrivelled and in minutes there was nothing left but a pile of ash. I stared, amazed, then shuddered and bugged my arms around my chest.

The Habiru in my camp had by now all retreated into a cave on the hillside and sat there, huddled together. I decided, turning away from that

charred stain on the landscape which had been the
oryx, that they had the right idea, and ran to join them.

"Hush" urged a man, as I sat in the mouth of the cave
and tried to speak of what I had seen. "It is dangerous even
to talk of such things."

They say in the stories that the sun stood still that
day and the moon did not move across the sky until the
Habiru had avenged themselves on their enemies. But I saw
what really happened. The silver cloud *grew* so big it
covered the whole of the sky. It stayed like that till the same
time the following day, covering up the sun and the moon, so
the night never came. When it finally faded away, it seemed
as though those two bright spheres had stayed where they
were for a day, but had started to move again.

The two priests in their silver garments, closed
the Ark, covered it up, and carried it down the hillside.
None of the Habiru would speak of it, save to say the
Lord rained hailstones on their enemies to help them,
but I saw what really happened - the day the sun stood
still.

Fragment 28

Joshua did not need the Ark to deal with the five Amorite kings. When they knew their armies lay dead on the road from Gibeon all the way down to Azekah, they fled to Makkedah and hid in a cave. The Habiru sealed up the entrance with rocks and posted a guard.

After the battle was won, Joshua and his men returned to his camp at Makkedah. He said, "Open the mouth of that cave and bring those five kings to me."

Hebron, Jarmuth, Lachish, Ealon and Jerusalem. How I wept to hear how the men of those cities lay dead and broken at Joshua's hand. But I dared not let anyone see my tears. Five of the strongest cities in Canaan. Joshua and the Ark of his God had murdered their men and captured all their kings.

It was when I saw what happened at Gibeon and the fate of those kings I truly began to fear Joshua. I had hated him when I found Tarasch, yet he had never been cruel or even angry with me. But now I knew fear to the bottom of my soul. I wondered where were the Gods of Canaan? Could the One God really be more powerful than they? The

Habiru said he could see into the soul of all people. I cowered in the tent, and feared he had seen me creep into the sleeping place of his Chosen One and take the knife I would plunge into Joshua's heart. Perhaps it was the One God who had stayed my hand. Yes, it was then I truly knew fear.

But I left the tent in the dark and turned my eyes to the evening star, to the brightness of Astarte, and begged her to keep me from the One God's wrath.

Joshua summoned all his men to see the five kings brought brought before him. He called Uri and the other commanders. He still had the fire in his eyes and I shivered when I saw the javelin in his hand.

"Come," he said to the commanders. "Guards! Force these wretches to kneel on the ground!"

No one would think they were kings to see them now. Their hands were bound behind behind their backs and their heads hung low.

"Put your feet on the necks of these kings."

The commanders hesitated. I was surprised to see they were afraid too.

"Come, be strong," said Joshua. "Watch. This is what the Lord will do to all the enemies you are going to fight."

Uri stepped forward. The other commanders glanced at each other then came forward too.

Each commander placed a foot on the neck of one of the kings. Uri looked unhappy but did as Joshua commanded.

Then Joshua took a club and struck each of the kings on the head. Their skulls cracked and blood, mixed with a whitish grey substance, oozed onto the ground. The last one tried to look up when he heard the blows and managed to scream into the dust, before he too fell silent.

I almost choked, swallowing back my own vomit. I was determined not to be sick in front of the Habiru, though some of them turned green.

Joshua had the bodies hung on five trees. They swung there, with the vultures circling, the braver ones swooping down to peck out an eye or tear off a strip of flesh before feasting in the safety of a nearby tree.

At sunset, Joshua ordered his men to take down the corpses corpses and throw them into the same cave in which the kings had hid. Then he had the entrance sealed with large rocks.

The city of Makkedah was next on his list. Joshua did not hang around. He wanted to return to Gilgal. He did not need the Ark this time. The people had heard what had happened at Gibeon and even their strongest men's hearts turned to pulp. He put every man, woman and child to the sword. No one was left. Then he killed the king of Makkedah in his favourite fashion.

I was in the camp at Makkedah when the city fell. I saw the Habiru clean the blood from their swords when they returned. I saw them wash it from their arms, even their shoulders stained red. I heard the screams rise up from the city walls. I smelt the horror on the air.

I saw Joshua's face, smiling through blood and grime and dust, and as I heard him plan to rage through the remaining cities of Canaan... Libnah, Debir, Gaza, Hazor and the rest... I knew I could remain no longer with him and his murdering God.

Fragment 29

I was determined to escape, but not without taking revenge on Joshua for what he had done. He had killed my sister, my friends, and everyone I knew. Because of him, my family were aliens to me. He had destroyed my home and my city, and now would wreak the wrath of his God on the whole of Canaan. I would make him pay.

Joshua grew more and more distant from me. He busied himself with his commanders, forever scheming, forever planning, believing he could not lose. But I knew how to hurt the Habiru leader most. I had long ago spotted the weak link in the chain.

Libnah fell. So did Lachish. Joshua dragged us all along with him and his army. Only a few were left in the camp at Gilgal, including Rahab and the remains of what had been my family. They were not permitted to mix with the Habiru.

I had to up sticks and follow with the rest as Joshua slaughtered city after city, him and his Ark. He could never have defeated Canaan without the white fire and the silver cloud which rained destruction wherever the Ark was taken.

It came just before Ealon was taken. Joshua had advanced on the city with the main part of the army, leaving the rest of his rabble in the camp, a good distance away. Caleb stayed behind too. He had been injured at Lachish, where a sword had pierced his right thigh, and much to his annoyance, he was having to rest until it healed.

I waited till Joshua and his army were gone. Then I combed my hair till it shone, washed myself in a large bowl of water and made up my eyes with fresh kohl. When I was happy with what I saw in the reflection on the water, I put on a clean fresh gown, tugging it slightly lower at the breast than I would normally wear it.

I knelt and poured a libation onto the ground then closed my eyes. I had never given my body to a man. But although I could never now become a priestess at Jericho, I would still serve the Goddess as I knew how, and I dedicated what I was about to do to Astarte, vowing to her whom I loved, that by this act, I would bring those hated Habiru down.

Then I took some grapes, sweet dates and wine to Caleb's tent.

Caleb was polishing his sword. It gleamed so much I guessed he had been at it for most of the day. He scowled and rubbed furiously at the metal. He hated to be idle and stuck in his tent. His leg was still strapped and swathed in cloths.

The bowls and the jar of wine clinked as I laid them on the floor. Caleb looked up.

"Ah!" His face brightened in an instant, as I had hoped it would. "The lovely Egyptian Queen! To what do I owe the honour of being served by Joshua's maid?" His eyes dropped to the front of my gown. I poured him some wine, taking care to bend forward, revealing more of my breasts.

When he managed to look up, I fixed my eyes on his and drew closer towards him.

"Sir," I said. "It must be tedious for you, stuck in this tent, while the men go to war. I wish there was something I could do to help pass the hours."

Caleb smiled. He ran his tongue over his chipped front tooth. His smile could be devastating. I could see why so women had succumbed to his charms. They did not impress me. But I was glad he was falling such easy prey to mine.

"Sir, does your leg pain you greatly?" I reached out and stroked the part of his leg which was not under wraps. Despite myself, I marvelled at the strength of his muscles and the smooth skin unblemished by time. This man was over eighty years old, yet as youthful as men less than half his age. Many would kill for such secrets as he possessed.

"Not so much that it would stop me appreciating rare beauty like yours." Caleb placed his hand on the back of my neck. I quivered. His eyes dropped again to the front of my gown.

I let my fingers run a little higher up his leg. This was even easier than I thought it would be.

Caleb traced the outline of my breasts above my dress, then stopped. "But you are Joshua's maid. I do not wish to anger him, and he is my friend."

I leaned a little bit closer.

"Sir, Joshua does not have to know. He is away at war. Besides, he does not care for me. He only cares for his God."

"That figures." Caleb's eyes were still on my breasts. Now so were his hands.

"I am often lonely, sir. I have no family and no friends amongst your people. The women will not talk to me, sir."

"And no wonder," said Caleb. "They are jealous. Such loveliness puts our women to shame." He pulled my gown off my shoulders. For all Joshua was his leader and friend, he could not help himself.

"I thought Habiru men only cared for the Lord," I said, with a smile. He was like clay in my hands.

"Only a few," said Caleb, pulling me down on the goatskins. "The rest of us have a fancy for a pretty face."

"A little more than a face, I fancy, sir?"

I   He loosened the front of my gown.

"Sir, "Joshua is cold to me," I whispered in his ear. "He has never touched me once. Nor has any man."

Caleb could not resist that. His eyes gleamed. "Well, we'll have to do something about that."

"What about your leg, sir?"

"You let me worry about that." He pushed me back on the skins then ripped open the front of my dress.

"Got you." I thought to myself. As I closed my eyes, and felt my body shudder beneath his hands, all I could see was that Habiru box.

I cared not I had never been with a man before. He was falling right into my hands, and with him the secrets of the Ark.

Fragment 30

I continued to visit Caleb's tent while Joshua and the rest of his army were at Ealon. It made my task much easier that the bulk of the men were gone. All the same, I was careful to avoid anyone seeing me enter and made sure I always took wine and food in case anyone did, so I had an excuse. It would not do if word reached Joshua's ears.

On one occasion, I was surprised to see Caleb without the bandaging and as I knelt by his side, I noticed his injured leg was covered with green mud. Yet it was unlike any I had ever seen. Tiny flecks of silver sparkled in this strange clay. I tried to look closer but Caleb pulled me to him, wound his fingers around my hair and greedily sought my mouth with his own. I pulled away from him and looked at the leg. "Sir, your wound," I said in surprise, for the gash had been deep. "It is nearly healed."

"I'm never out of action for long," he boasted. "Mine and Joshua's wounds heal quicker than any man's."

"What is that on your leg?" I said, and scooped some of the sparkling substance onto my finger.

Caleb grabbed my hand and wiped it off. "Don't ask questions. Some things are not for all men to know."

"I am not all men," I said, pressing my body into his. "I would be all women to you."

Caleb pulled me against him. "And you are."

I let it rest, for then. But I was determined to find out more. I knew Caleb's wound could not possibly have healed so much in the short space of time which had passed. I wondered if this was part of the secrets of the Ark. Could it heal as well as kill, and keep old men young?

Although I had never been with a man before Caleb, I had nearly completed my training in the temple at Jericho. For it was always intended I should follow her of the hated name on the path of temple priestess. Women talk and whisper in corners. So I was not entirely ignorant of the ways of the God and Goddess. I knew how to bring a man to his knees or take him to heights that only a priestess could give. The Habiru women knew nothing of the rites of Baal and Astarte. Not a woman in that nation could do to Caleb what I did to him.

Little by little, I squeezed more of his secrets into my hand. Once I noticed some of the sparkling mud in his beard and traces at the side of his neck. I scooped it onto my finger and pretending to caress him, smeared it onto a fine line at the side of one of his eyes. Later, as I kissed him, I surreptitiously rubbed the mud away. The line had gone. The skin was smooth as the day he was born.

I waited till all his passion was spent, which, Caleb being the man he was, lasted till the sun came up. Then before he fell asleep, I asked him about the mud.

"Shh. It is time to sleep," he murmured against my hair. "Let the powers of the Ark be at peace, and I too."

He was soon asleep. But I lay wide awake. So the sparkling mud was part of the powers of the Ark. I had guessed as much. Was this how Joshua and Caleb stayed so strong and youthful? I would put up with this Habiru scum asleep on my breast until I had milked every drop of his secrets, and I swore to Astarte I would not rest until I had them in my hands.

Chapter 10

Schlott wants to see me, so I have to sit here in his office, drumming my what's left of my nails on the desk and wait while he answers the 'phone. My translation's on his desk, beside a letter with an Israeli government crest at the top. Schlott stands up, the receiver tucked under his chin, and walks to a filing cabinet. Then while his back's turned, I pull the letter towards me.

Just as I suspected. It confirms that the Israeli government is extremely interested in the fragments, and offers a guarantee of financial support. They are now my paymasters.

I replace it quickly before Schlott turns round and smile at him sweetly.

He sits down, begins to talk, and I play the dutiful employee. I make sure I beam when he says he's very happy with my work, murmur the right noises in the appropriate pauses, say how glad I am that he wants to renew my contract... you know, all the things you do to play the game.

"Our backers," he says, "are looking forward immensely to the completion of the fragments."

I grit my teeth and smile. I bet they are.

I'm so glad to get out of there. In fact, I could do with getting right out of the university for a bit. I think I'll go for a coffee outside. I'm sick of the politics. All this bowing and scraping to the people who put up the cash. Now it's Mossad and their bosses, who order mortar attacks on twelve year old kids, who are keeping me in work.

This project has changed. Now I know who's calling the shots. The question I have to ask myself, knowing the devastating power the fragments could uncover, is am I prepared to deliver something capable of destroying whole cities straight up into Israel's hands?

I find a seat in a half empty brasserie, order an expresso and make dunes in the sugar. An Ethiopian woman with a child on her hip is going around the tables with her palm held out. The cafe owner shoos her away but I manage to give her some loose change. Despite that blank clay tablet, I'm sure the map still exists and I have a strong gut feeling that I'm very close to finding it. I just can't understand how I was wrong about it being in the well. I'm missing something, I know I am.

The coffee arrives, thick, steaming and sweet, more Turkish than Italian. Just what I need after a close encounter of the third kind with Schlott. I glance guiltily at the mess I've made with the sugar but the waiter doesn't notice.

If the fragments and the map, assuming it still exists, do lead to this energy source, the ramifications of them falling into the wrong hands are horrendous. I mean, Israel has ignored every single U.N. resolution condemning its invasions of its neighbours since 1967. They don't give a toss what the rest of the world thinks. And why should they, when they're backed by the U.S.A. with its strong Jewish lobby and military might, and the rest of us quite content to eat their oranges and let them bully Arabs as it's-not-on-our-doorstep-thank-you-very-much? Why should Israel care? Even America's unhappy with the missiles they're directing from helicopters against Palestinians on the ground with their stones and guns. The discovery of radioactive white fire could add an appalling new dimension to Middle East conflict; a terrifying new weapon which could be a secret and sinister way of swatting the irritating Palestinian fly once and for all. In my opinion, the Palestinian people have been oppressed far too much already.

But then there's another scenario. That same power falling into the hands of some of these radical Moslem groups, like Hizbollah or Hamas with their suicide bombers would be equally horrifying. If the white fire could wipe out Gibeon what would it do to Tel Aviv? Thousand of innocent Israelis dead.

As for the uses to which Arms For Us would put it - some unscrupulous arms dealer willing to flog the white fire to anyone willing to pay... Shit, I'd rather see the map destroyed.

This is scary stuff. I could hold the whole balance of Middle Eastern war and peace in my hands. In fact, not just the Middle East. I gulp down the rest of my expresso and I'm tempted to follow it with a double brandy but it's only eleven a.m. This is heavy stuff for a bulimic translator of obscure linguistics. All I can do for now is to make sure no one but Ben sees the final fragments until I find out whether the cave still exists and if the white fire is still active today. If it isn't, then great. The fragments will whip up an academic and theological storm and my career will sky rocket. If it is, there could be genocide.

Schlott has no idea how hard I've worked and how much I've really translated, so I've bought myself some time. Of course I know Ben will guard those faxes with his life. He's the only one I can trust. Emile is sweet, but I can't let him be drawn into something which might put him at risk and anyway, the less people who know anything the better. No, I'm on my own here. I have to make sure no one gets to the there before me. I must find that map first, and destroy it if necessary, even if I have to tear every boulder in that cave aside single-handed. I'd better get back to work. Emile and the team are going to start to catalogue the bones of the girl in the well. I'm glad it's Emile on the job. I know he'll treat her with respect. Now I have to find a way of searching the cave again before anyone from the archaeological team stumbles on the map. I'm sure it's there. I just don't understand how I could be wrong about her taking the map to her death. There must be something I've missed. I know it was dark but I searched every inch of that well with my lamp and only found that one blank tablet. I persuaded Emile to let me take it away, despite university regulations. I told him I wanted to compare it with the tablets in my office but really I thought maybe there might be a map outline which had become too eroded to spot with the naked eye. Yet I've run it under a microscope and haven't found a thing.

The map must still be in that cave.

I love Jerusalem nights. A velvety blackness drifts down on the city as it mirrors the stars, alive with thousands of lights. I stand on my balcony a while, cradling a glass of Muscadet in my hand, and gaze out at the hill of the Garden Tomb, a black silhouette against the skyline. Golgotha, it's called, the place of the skull. A red glow hangs over this ancient city and neon signs flash out their messages, above the lines of traffic which crawl like tiny grounded fireflies in long winding columns through the night. The bar opposite my flat thuds with music from the juke box and bursts of laughter ripple across the street while the towers of churches and domes of mosques press up toward the moon. Its name means 'place of peace.' It is anything but.

I take a sip of my wine, leaning on the coolness of the wrought iron railing, and breathe in the scents of the night. Fish and roast lamb from the Minazar down the road, falafel and hot pitta bread from Rafi's stall, cardamom, mint, and occasional wafts from some sweet blossom drifting from the gardens of Golgotha, jasmine perhaps, or linden.

The smells of food are making me hungry so I decide to go down to Rafi's and pick up a pitta bread salad. I leave my glass on the coffee table by the bottle of Muscadet, pleasantly full for when I return. Also on the table is that bewildering blank tablet. I still haven't managed to work out why that was in the well. Mind you, I don't feel guilty in the

364

slightest about bringing it home. My loyalty to the N.I.U.J. has worn thinner than a supermodel's waist. I don't know why the Canaanite girl went to her death with this, but I feel it belongs with me, in my home, not locked in a case, labelled with some anonymous catalogue number. This is anathema to the academic establishment I know, but heresy's the path I seem to be treading these days. I pick up my purse and my keys from the table. Cruiser is asleep in his basket and barely twitches his ears as I click back the safety latch and head out into the night.

After a lot of indecision, I hit on fetta cheese, spinach and kalamata olives in my pitta bread, along with a portion of finely shredded cabbage coated in olive oil and toasted sesame seeds. Then I cross the street, thinking of the bottle of Muscadet.

Then just as I reach the doorway to my building, I freeze. The back of my neck is tingling. Hidden eyes are boring so hard into my back it hurts. Someone is behind me, watching.

I spin round. A young Israeli couple, stealing kisses as they go, head away from me down the street. A family of Arabs ambles away from Rafi's and a mangy cat runs off with part of a burger. No one pays me any attention. But I know that in the shadows of this street, someone is watching every move I make.

I push open the door and run upstairs. When I reach the landing, I hear a sound below. I'm not the only one on the stairs. My building is quiet. Muffled canned laughter and melodramatic shouting matches from Israeli soaps seep through the walls from TVs in the flats. This is my home, damn it. I'm through with running from shadows. So I stay on the landing, my hand poised on the stair rail, listening. Soft shoeleather squeaks as someone comes slowly up the stairs behind me. Sod this. Bravery's one thing. Stupidity another. My nerve flies out of the window and I thrust my keys in the lock. As I open the door, Cruiser comes rushing past me and stops on the landing, bristling. His bark is sharp and hostile. He knows it's not a friend who is coming up these stairs.

"Cruiser!" I tug at his collar but he doesn't want to budge and carries on barking. I manage to pull him back but my hands are full of wriggling fur and though I try to kick shut the door, the latch doesn't click. I drop my pitta bread on the table, shove Cruiser in the kitchen then run back to shut the door.

Too late. Someone is already standing in the doorway, with a gun in his hand.

Jonathon.

"Hello, Charlotte."

He steps into the flat, pushes the door though it doesn't quite close, and stares at me over the sights of the gun. He's wearing 501s and a faded denim jacket. His hair is much closer cropped than I remember. He looks older. There are lines around his eyes which weren't there before and a hardness tightens his mouth. We stare at each other across the gun. Neither of us speaks. I can hear muffled Arab music from a nearby flat. A tin can clatters and a cat yowls outside. The gun trembles slightly. He's nervous. With a shock, I realise that insecure little boy from a Luton council estate, who came home from school most days to find his mother drunk in a chair, is still looking out from those deep set blue eyes. Jonathon has found no place for himself in a hostile world. Now this psycho has me in the sights of his gun.

For a moment I am raw unadulterated terror and silent screaming fills my head. But the moment fades and I become diamond and steel.

This could be my last breath, but it doesn't matter any more. I have peace, deep inside me. Jonathon, though he has the power to kill me, does not.

He steps forward, walks around me, circling, watching , never taking his eyes from my face.

"You betrayed me, Charlotte. You told lies about me in court."

I try to squeeze out one of my well practised semblances of a smile. It doesn't come so I force myself to speak. "No Jonathon." My voice is a croak. This is not how I want to sound. I must try to talk him round, to make him put down the gun. "I was sorry when they put you in jail." I can hear myself sounding calmer now, more in control.

His eyes narrow. His lips press together. Something mean and twisted crosses that little boy face. "You hurt me, Charlotte."

"I didn't want to hurt you."

"You hurt me!" He yells in my face, presses the gun against my stomach. The metal is cold, and

I suddenly I realise how warm is my flesh, and how delicate. Jonathon has power over me. One tiny movement of muscle, one drawing back of his finger and my skin will be ripped apart.

"I didn't mean to hurt you." My voice is a whisper now. I can't take my eyes from his.

He circles me again, slowly. He's playing with me, cat staring at mouse.

"I loved you, Charlotte." He picks up a strand of my hair and raises it to his lips. There are tears in his eyes. They are more frightening than his anger. "I really wanted you to love me too."

"Jonathon, I do. Maybe we could start all over again. Just put down the gun and..."

"No!" He claps his hands over his ears. The gun is pointing to the ceiling.

"No! No! No! It's too late for all that!" He dashes the tears from his eyes and realigns the gun.

"Jonathon." I try to sound reassuring and this time succeed in getting my lips to sham a smile. "We can talk."

"Shut up!"

I jump, but I must keep still. I mustn't tip him over the edge.

"I've seen you," he hisses. "With that... that man. Getting into his Landrover, his arms around you, kissing you." Jonathon wipes his hand over his mouth. His face is contorted with disgust. "I've watched you, followed you, on the stairs, in the lift, home from work. And I've seen you with other men too. In cafes. And I've seen them follow you. You didn't know they were there. But I did."

Iciness spreads through my stomach. It was him, following me from the Cafe Malkha, spying from the underground car-park, his footsteps on the stairs, his hand playing games with the buttons on the lift. And he knew about the others who were watching me too.

How dare he do this to me.

"You're a whore, Charlotte." He draws back his finger. The safety catch clicks. "You deserve to die." The gun quivers in his hand.

I stand quite still. I'm not afraid of death, but fury is spreading right through me, like I'm Vesuvius ready to spill. I am livid that Jonathon decides when my life ends. He forced me out of my job and the places I loved, claimed power over my life, and now he wants power over my death. Well, there is no way I'll let him this time. I will reclaim my life.

"Let's sit down and talk, Jonathon."

Jonathon does nothing. He continues to stare. I don't think he wants to kill me. Once I'm dead he'll lose his power over me. He won't be able to torment his weak little Charlotte any more.

"Did you ever love me?"

"Yes, Jonathon. Of course, I did. I still do, but I can't talk to you while you're pointing that gun at me."

He stares. He says nothing. That bloody Arab music is still playing through the walls. Then a picture flashes though my mind. I can smell the goatskin as vile, scheming Achan stretches his lecherous fingers across the tent. She wouldn't let anyone get the better of her. She defeated her enemies even in

369

death. Quickly, think. What would she do?

Now I become her. Her fury is mine. I take a step towards him.

"Give me the gun and we'll talk." I'm scared, but my anger is stronger. He's not going to do this to me, not any more, this frightened little boy.

Jonathon wavers, uncertain.

There's movement on the landing and a face peeps round the door. Oh no! It's Abdul.

I have no time to shout a warning for Jonathon sees him too. He spins round and a bullet splinters the wood.

I snatch the first object to hand and in my mind's eye I see Achan's face crumple as a jug hits his skull. I hurl the clay tablet at Jonathon. It strikes him full on the back of the head and he drops to his knees. As the gun clatters from his hand, I rush forward to grab it, then back away, holding it towards him with both hands. Power rushes up through my spine and illuminates every cell.

Jonathon lifts his head. A bright stream of blood is running into the back of his shirt. He looks confused. "Charlotte, give me the gun."

"Shut up!"

Abdul's frightened face is peeping round the door.

"You could have killed a child!"

He tries to crawl towards me.

"Don't move!" My anger burns with a pure bright flame. Fury is a joyful candle in the night.

He looks as though he has never seen me before. "Charlotte, this isn't you. You're so gentle and..."

"Meek? Timid? Afraid? Was that why you picked on me? Well, was it?"

Jonathon is shocked, confused. "Charlotte, You're not yourself."

"This is me!" I yell at him, gripping the gun. "This is me *now*, Jonathon! I'm not that scared little girl afraid of your shadow disappearing behind street corners!"

"Charlotte, don't hurt me," he whines. "I love you, Charlotte." He lowers his voice and a sly expression comes into his eyes. "I've killed for you."

It takes a moment for what he says to sink in.

"You shot that boy at the funeral cortege." The gun is no longer cold in my hand. The heat from my hands is spreading through the metal and I feel the fire of my anger will burn this whole city down.

"He would have hurt you, Charlotte."

"It wasn't his fault."

"You're mine, Charlotte. It wasn't up to some stranger to decide what should be done with you." He tries to crawl again. I stamp on his fingers. Jonathon squeals and cowers on the floor, cradling his hands.

"You killed someone? For me? You're sick Jonathon. Really sick! You disgust me!"

Jonathon looks up. "But I didn't kill your dog."

I frown. Suspicion is tainting my anger. I grip the gun tighter.

"I could have killed him." Jonathon tucks his wounded fingers between his knees. "I nearly did. I knew you loved that creature, but you couldn't love me. And the boy. I could have killed both of them, together."

"When was this?"

"Any time. I've been watching your flat. I got in once, when it was turned over."

"It was you? You raided my flat? You did all that?"

"No, Charlotte. Not me. I was watching, looking out for you. Like I always do. But I saw them, two Americans. I heard them burst in the door and I hid."

"You're lying."

"Never, Charlotte. Not to you. No secrets between us. When they left, the door was wide open. I knew you'd be unhappy. I just looked at your things. I held your clothes against my cheek. And all I took was a little bottle of perfume, *Genevre,* to keep under my pillow, so I can dream of you and breathe in your scent through the night."

"You're disgusting." I look down at Jonathon, grovelling on the floor, as I would at some foul mess in the gutter. The feel of this gun in my hands is more of a thrill than anything I felt in bed with Ben. I am reclaiming my power.

Jonathon doesn't move He is frozen. He knows I'll pull the trigger. I know it too. Exhilaration is rushing through my veins. Power is freedom. My anger is a liberation.

I crouch down and look into his eyes, his frightened, little boy eyes. I grab his hair and pull back his head. As he freezes at the gun on his temple I see tiny veins snaking the whites of his eyes.

"Now listen to me. This is the last time you see my face. You're going to run down those stairs, take a taxi to the airport and get the hell out of my life forever. Do you understand me? If you try to come back, I'll have this gun. And I'll make damn sure that next time, you won't escape with a few months in jail. I'll give you something to remember me by for the rest of your life."

He nods. Flecks of saliva appear at the edges of his lips.

I stand up and motion towards the door.

He clutches his head, staggers to the door and crashes heavily onto the landing.

I shan't call the police. I want to do this my way. I've succeeded. I know Jonathon won't return. His Charlotte is gone. He'll never find her again. Neither will I. That pathetic, self-obsessed little girl who tottered on unstable high heels down the gangplank at Ben Gurion does not exist any more. She has moved on, and that ugly little caterpillar has become a bold bright butterfly, toting a gun.

Someone must have dialled 100, maybe when they saw him enter
the flats with a weapon, or when they heard the shot, for heavy footsteps are crashing up the stairs and the landing is suddenly full of uniformed men. I hand over the gun. Jonathon doesn't look behind him, as his arms are forced behind his back and he's

thrust down the stairs. I know for certain this time, I shan't see him again.

"Hey, Miss Charlotte," Abdul claps his hands. "You were great, Miss Charlotte! You know what? Holding that gun, you looked like Uma Thurman!"

I laugh and ruffle his hair, then his mother drags him away. God knows what she thinks of me.

I hear tramping on the stairs below. The police are coming back. There's something I must do; something they mustn't find.

The clay tablet has broken in two. I pick up the pieces and shove them in Cruiser's basket beneath the blankets. I don't want the police to take them away. I snatch up a heavy hardback edition of Kathleen Kenyon's investigations into the ruins at Jericho, and place it in the splashes of Jonathon's blood by the door. Now the police can ask me questions all they like.

When they've gone, I drain the rest of my Muscadet then take the broken pieces of tablet from under the blankets. Not only have I removed an ancient relic from a university dig without proper authorisation, bashed someone over the head with it and concealed it from a police investigation, but I've smashed the thing to bits. Emile has categorised it already so it's in the system. I won't be able to keep this from Schlott. But the trouble I could face from him is a piece of cake compared to what I've managed to deal with tonight. I feel like I could take on the world.

The top layer of clay has fallen off one of the pieces and as I hold it up to the light, I realise it's not the same material as that underneath. Someone has overlaid the original tablet with an extra coating of clay. Only one person is likely to have done that. I grab a knife and scrape away more of the top layer. Cruiser turns his back, thoroughly pissed off at me for shutting him in the kitchen.

I keep chipping, little by little, terrified in case I cause any more damage, then a chunk falls away and oh my God, I see the outlines of the map. I sit back and hug Cruiser to me then begin to laugh and find I can't stop till I end up having to dab my eyes with the bottom of my shirt.

"Jonathon," I say, out loud. "You've really done me a favour."

Fragment 31

"Caleb, take me with you," I murmured into his ear. His leg had healed and strapping on his sandals, he had announced he was going to the Ark.

"Women are not allowed."

"Please, I would see the magic mud for myself."

He grabbed my wrist. "If you tell anyone about..."

"I will not. I swear. But take me with you, let me.."

375

"No. Not a word."

I waited until he had left, then pulled on my clothes and followed him, taking care not to be seen. He entered the sacred precinct. The priests stood back to let him pass. I climbed up into some rocks until I could see the tent which housed the Ark. At the entrance, a priest handed him a silver garment, like the ones I had seen the two priests wear near Gibeon. Caleb put it on and disappeared inside. I was furious. I could see nothing. The Ark was always surrounded by priests. How was I ever going to find out what lay inside.

My chance came one day when I was at the spring outside the camp. A young boy came riding out of the desert, furiously driving his camel towards the camp. The animal was tired, and as it approached the spring it stumbled, sending its rider headlong onto the around. A wooden box slipped off too, and smashed apart on a rock.

As I ran up, I saw that amid the the shattered splinters of wood, oozed thick green mud, flecked with silver. The boy was badly injured. Blood ran from a gash on his head. His mouth lolled open. I slapped his cheeks. He groaned and his eyes rolled upwards again. I hit him harder. "Awake," I cried. "What is this mud?"

"Can't...tell."

I grabbed his little finger and pressed it back until he squealed with pain.

"Tell me! Where did you get it?"

"Must not tell..."

I pressed the finger back harder.

"Tell me!"

"Cave... aah! Sea of Arabah..."

Furiously I flung his body down. The wretch had died before I could wrest more from 'him. I sat back on my heels and played with the silver flecked mud. But I had learnt something.

The mud was now drying in the sun. I stood up and left the boy to the vultures. I had other means of finding out more.

I knew I had to act swiftly. Any day now Joshua and the army would return, Caleb would join them on their next foray of destruction, and my chance to find out all I could from him would be gone.

I tucked a knife in my gown, went up to the hills and scoured the land until I found what I was looking for. Finally, after hot hours searching the sun-blasted slopes, I came across one small precious plant. Carefully, I parted the leaves then smiled when I saw the red berries, dangling like droplets of blood from a stem. There were only a few, but a few would go a long way. I closed my eyes and offered a prayer to Reshef, for such plants were sacred to the Underworld and its God. Then I cut some leaves and the stem with the berries and carefully stowed them inside my gown.

That night I around the leaves to a paste and mixed them with the wine I took to Caleb's tent. The berries I saved. I was careful to drink just the right amount myself. Too much and I would fall into deep sleep, unable to remember the dreams the next morning - if I woke at all. Too little and I would not be able to accompany Caleb on his nocturnal wanderings. I knew from my training in the temple, the mixture had to be just right so I could direct him where I wanted him to travel, and see through his eyes his world of dreams. My hands shook as I stirred the wine and I prayed as I carried the jar to his tent that night, I had made the measure right. Mistakes, with such a plant, cost dear.

When Caleb had finally taken his fill of both me and the wine, I lay down beside him and sank into the darkness, waiting for the sacred leaves to let me share his dreams, and prayed I had used the right amount.

Fragment 32

Caleb was walking towards the sacred precinct. I followed behind. Our footprints left no trace in the sand of the dream world. The priests on guard came forward to meet him. He uttered a sacred word and they let him pass. It was neither day nor night in that realm. The tabernacle which housed the Ark was shrouded in a strange kind of twilight. A covering of pure white linen lay over the tent. A curtain of blue, purple and scarlet yarn and finest twisted linen hung over the entrance. Caleb paused.

"Go on," I breathed. For I could only direct and follow where he went. The dream was his. "Caleb, enter."

He seemed to sway on his feet. Then a priest appeared and handed him a silver garment. He put it on, pushed aside the curtain and went inside. I kept close behind him, seeing through his eyes. A strong smell of sandalwood, cedar and myrrh overpowered me, making me reel. Keep awake, I told myself sternly. Keep awake in the dream.

Curtain after curtain, tent inside tent. We passed through them all. Rams hide, goatskin, sea cow, goat hair linen. The incense grew stronger. Coils of thick scented smoke stung our eyes. Curtain after curtain. I began to wonder if this was some trick of the night demons that preyed on travelers who entered the world of wakeful dreaming, and if I would ever see the sun again.

Then the final curtain lifted. Before us was the Ark. It stood on a table of acacia wood, lit by the light of seven lamps on one branched stand, made of solid gold. The magic box gleamed, for it too was overlaid with gold. Gold rings shone at each corner. Two winged cherubim, their wings outstretched, faced each other above the Ark. My breath hurt my chest. I had never seen such a thing as this. Even in Canaan, our finest craftsmen had never produced workmanship like this. Nothing I had ever seen come out of Babylon or Ugarit could match. Every feather of their wings, every curve of their cheeks, those cherubim looked as though they breathed and would at any moment, soar through the roof of the tent and carry the Ark into the star-spangled sky.

But I was not going to stop there.

"Open it, Caleb," I commanded.

He began to sway again. The dark pressed in around me. I was losing him. He was falling into Reshef's realm. His dream was fading. "Open it!" I would have kicked him if it were not a dream. To my relief, the oil light grew brighter. Caleb raised the lid.

I peered over his shoulder, wishing I could elbow him aside. But the dream was his. I could only watch where he watched.

Two chests of tamarisk wood lay inside the Ark. There was also a number of clay tablets, the top one covered with markings that looked like a map.

Caleb lifted the tablets then called out. A boy appeared from the shadows, took them from him and stepped back into the darkness. A boy, yet again, I noticed.

Then Caleb opened the box on the left.

It was full of sparkling green mud.

The light began to fade again. I could barely see Caleb swayed and let fall the lid of the chest.

"Open the second box!" I whispered urgently.

His figure blurred. I knew I could not hold the dream much longer.

"You are mad," came a faraway voice. I did not know if it was his. "Do not open it. The light will kill you."

I forced myself to the edge of the Ark and again commanded, "Open it." The lid lifted. I peered inside. The darkness swirled around me and Caleb faded. But before both he and I were lost in Reshef's realm, I saw that chest was bubbling with white sparkling fire.

Fragment 33

I rose before first light. I had to be swift. Joshua had already stayed away longer than expected. I had to act before the army returned.

Caleb was still snoring like a pig. I crept out of the tent and quietly headed for the precinct of the Ark. No one was about. Just one lone billy goat stared balefully at me as I passed. The star of Astarte still shone over the distant ridge of hills.

First I climbed into the rocks to check the guard. As usual, two stood sentinel at the entrance to the sacred precinct. Another pair guarded the tabernacle while two more pairs watched the far end. The remaining priests were still asleep in their tents.

I checked inside my gown. The precious berries were still tucked inside. The leaves of that little plant gave waking visions of the night, but the berries were more powerful still.

Then I hurried back to the camp. The star of Astarte was sinking behind the hills. The moon would soon fade and it would not be long before the first rays of the sun pierced the sky. I grabbed a jug and went in search of a goat. The animals were stirring now. I grabbed a nanny by the horns and soon had a full jug of frothing milk. Carefully, I placed the jug in some sand so it would not overturn, then squatted on the ground and took out my berries. It was a fiddly task to pick off the skins. I kept looking around, in case any any early riser spotted me and became suspicious.

But I had to get rid of every bit of red peel so only the white creamy pulp of the berries remained. Any tiny piece of red and my plan could be discovered.

Finally, my nails full of red pith, I finished the last one. Grinding the little white balls between two flat stones I mashed them to a creamy pulp and emptied it into the jug. Then I stirred the mixture round with my hand and headed for the precinct.

"Your goatsmilk for the day," I called to the guards as they approached.

"Good," said one. "We have been here all night and I could do with a drink."

"Me too." His companion produced two bowls and held them out.

"Not all of it," I said. "Some is for your companions inside."

"Who do we owe this pleasure to?" said one, as he held out his cup. "We don't normally get goatsmilk till the sun is risen."

"My lord Caleb." The lies came easily to me now. "He sent word that the guardians of the Ark are worthy of great honours and a little drop of milk is just the start."

"Sounds good to me." They drained their cups and I moved to serve the rest of the guards. The last one, one of the pair at the far end, proved more difficult than those at the entrance and by the tabernacle. I thought for one horrible instant my plot would be discovered.

"Milk?" he growled. "I could do with a flagon of wine after being up half the night." He pushed me scathingly aside.

"Sir," I said anxiously. "It is a special boon from my Lord Caleb. He told me the guards of the Ark must be treated with honour. I would not have to return and tell him his gift has been turned down. His temper is much to be feared."

"Bah." The guard let me serve him from my jar and swallowed the milk in one go.

Soon all the guards lay sprawled on the ground. A

glow had appeared above the hills and I looked around anxiously. Dawn would soon be upon me and the rest of the priests would rise from their sleep. I had to hurry.

A box outside the tabernacle contained a pair of silver garments. Hastily I put one on, making sure every part of me was covered as I had seen Caleb and the priests do before they entered. Then I lifted the curtain and stepped inside.

The incense had not yet been lit but the curtains of the tent were heavy with the scent. I pushed curtain after curtain aside until finally I stood before the Ark itself. The waking dream had shown me the splendour of the Habiru's most precious possession but I was not prepared for the awe which struck me as I stared at that gilded chest, protected by the outstretched wings of cherubim. My hand shook as I lifted the lid. The two closed chests lay inside. I dared open neither. I knew what the white fire could do. My fingers closed around the clay tablets. As soon as I pulled them out, my heart leapt in triumph. I knew this was the real value of the Ark. I had no need for what lay in the chests. I now possessed the map which showed where the secrets of the Habiru lay; the very source of the sparkling clay which kept men young, and the fire that killed from the sky.

Fragment 34

I made my escape on the back of a camel, dressed as a boy in stolen clothes, just as the first rosy streaks of dawn lit up the horizon. I drove the beast as fast as it would go, into the hills, with the precious tablets loaded in a tamarisk chest on its back. I did not know how long I would have before they discovered their secrets were gone, and Joshua's handmaid too. I kept to the tracts of stony ground or sparse lands, where the camel tracts were less likely to show on the around and kept looking back behind me, my hair streaming on the wind, expecting to see at any moment, an army of Habiru racing towards me.

However, none appeared. Perhaps the guards kept quiet, embarrassed at finding themselves asleep on their watch, or perhaps no one actually looked inside the Ark till much later. Or it may have been that my care to leave no tracks paid off and they did not know which I way I went. All I know is that I rode all day, seeing no one, and escaped with the secrets of the Ark.

Towards late afternoon, I came upon a caravan of travellers, Anakites on their way to Hebron. I kept my head covered and my garments were loose so they had no reason to doubt I was just the boy I appeared to be. Whole families, women and children too, were travelling across the hill country, in search of safety from Joshua's marauding hordes.

Bad news travels fast and word of what Joshua had done at Makkehdah and Libnah had put the fear of the Habiru God into everyone. I heard from the Anakites that Eglon had fallen too and tales were rife of a dragon that breathed white fire and a magic javelin which killed from afar. They were too fearful for their lives to pay much attention to a nomad boy. So, deciding that if the Habiru turned up in pursuit, I could blend more easily into a crowd, I travelled with them towards Hebron, keeping myself to myself.

But when we were drawing close to the city, word reached the Anakites that Joshua was already marching on Hebron, swearing to wreak destruction there as he had at the other cities of Canaan. Panic swept through the tribe as the word spread from mouth to mouth, and after a long discussion, the tribal elders concluded that the One God must have rendered the Habiru invincible. So rather than risk certain death at Hebron, they decided to flee Canaan altogether, and ordered the whole caravan to turn south and

387

head for Egypt.

I travelled south with them for a distance. Their plans suited mine for I needed to find a place where I and my cargo could be safely hidden from the vengeance of Joshua and Caleb. I could well. imagine their fury when they found what I had done. I had seen the sword of Joshua's vengeance. The fate of the five kings of the Amorites would be nothing compared to mine if I were found.

But I began to feel strangely tired all the time, and several times my head spun, so I had to dismount and sit down till the dizzy spell passed. This happened often over some days until finally one such bout of giddiness overwhelmed me so much I had to lie down in the lee of a rock with my camel tethered close by. I must have passed out, for the next thing I knew, the sun had moved high into the sky and the caravan was nowhere in sight.

I jumped to my feet, but immediately the dizziness came over me again and flecks of light danced before my eyes. I clutched the rock for support and heaved the leaven bread and goatsmilk I had earlier consumed onto the ground.

When at last I felt well enough to travel, I walked over to my camel - but as I took his reins in my hands, I realised I had no idea where to go. Without the caravan I would not reach the safety of Egypt. I did not know where I was. I had only the sun and the stars to guide me away from Hebron. Hebron and Joshua. I decided to keep that fated city at my back and keep heading south towards then sun. Perhaps if I rode fast enough I would meet up with the Anakites again.

But although I travelled until the sun went down, I never saw them again. When I came upon a spring trickling from some rocks, I threw myself down on the ground and thankfully drank the sweet waters, leaving a strip of my robe on a shrub in thanks to Astarte for this unexpected gift. She had kept me safe so far. She would not let me down. I had a package of bread and broke some off, but I dared not eat it all, hungry as I was, for I did not know when I would come upon food again.

That night I wrapped myself up as best I could in my garments and laid on the around, looking up at the stars. How far away they were and how cold was the nighttime sky. Yet even those stars had each other for company as they sailed across their shiny celestial sea. I had no one. I lay all alone in the darkness. Some creature howled a long way off. It was answered by another. Even the wild beasts were not as solitary as I was, and if they should devour me in the night, there would be no one to pile up a cairn for me. The stars shimmered and blurred as tears welled up behind my eyes then flooded down my cheeks, and though I had tried so hard to be brave, my whole body heaved with sobs I could not stem. Finally all the stars blinked out, and I was glad to let Reshef draw me down, down into the waiting dark.

Fragment 35

The next morning I woke with the sun and sat up. My stomach rebelled at once and I thought I would retch till my guts spilled onto the ground. When the sickness passed I put my head in my hands. I did not know was happening to me. If I had a fever, I could die in these hills and no one would know that all the Habiru secrets lay lost beneath this southern sky.

I do not know how long I travelled. That time remains in my memory as a blur of heat hazed hills and burning desert stones. All I know is that I hauled my traitorous body onto the camel and headed into the sun.

It was my camel who found water in the desert scrub, from small oases which offered what little sustenance that harsh land gave. He came to a halt near a high place, where the remains of an altar stood on the hill, its fallen stones a testament to gods and people long before my own. A small cave in the cliff gave me shelter, and the water from the spring which gushed from the rocks was sweet. I eked out the last of my bread and managed to find berries in the ferns which fringed the waterfall.

I remained there for some days, adding to my meagre diet with conies I managed to trap in a gully, hoping the sickness would go. But it didn't. Every morning was the same. Thankfully it would pass as the sun rose in the sun. One day I looked down at myself and realised I was becoming quite plump. I wondered what was in the water, for the food I ate was barely enough to feed a rat.

While I stayed in that little oasis, I took out the clay tablets I had stolen, hoping to learn the secrets of the Habiru. But to my dismay, the script was unknown to me. It was written in the language of Egypt which I had not learnt. As I stared at those glyphs of birds and eyes and symbols etched in clay, I thought bitterly how I probably held in my hands the secrets of the white fire that burnt whole cities - but they were barred to me. Perhaps if I found my way into Egypt, I could learn their script and one day unravel the code.

But the map I could understand. I kept it on the top of the pile and spent many an hour studying the curves of the sea until every feature of that land was as well known to me as the palm of my hand. As soon as I was well, I decided, I would continue south and try to find the land of the Pharaohs. Then when I had learnt their language and the secrets of the Habiru, I would return to seek out the cave at Arabah. If I could control the fire as Joshua did, I could destroy his murdering tribes and return the land of Canaan to its own.

I kept the chest of tablets in the cave and let my camel graze unburdened till I felt able to continue my journey.

But I did not get well. I still felt sick and tired and when the next moon passed without a sign, I grew fearful.

Then disaster struck. Baal raged against what the Habiru had done to his land. First the conies fled. Then I saw a herd of gazelles racing away across the land. The birds were silent. My camel grew restless and tugged at his tether. He showed the whites of his eyes and stamped the ground. The evening turned too swiftly into night and I trembled lest the vengeance of the One God was upon me, or Joshua was drawing near with the powers of the Ark ready to punish his thieving runaway slave.

Then as I tried to calm my panicking camel, Baal unleashed his rage from the altar on the bill and hurled his thunderbolts upon the land. The sky flashed white. The earth trembled beneath my feet. A stream of small stones, followed by larger rocks, tumbled down the slope above the waterfall and partly blocked the entrance to my cave.

"No!" I screamed and rushed to the cave, clambering frantically over the fallen stones. I grabbed the map front the top, but, with a sound like a thousand horses, the very earth beneath my feet shook in terror at the rage of the God. A rain of stones showered the cave mouth. Sobbing in despair, for I could never carry them all before the cave mouth closed, I cast one last look at my precious clay tablets, then, clutching the one with the map, I raced for the entrance, lest I too should be buried with the Habiru secrets.

Climbing onto my camel, I held on for dear life and let the beast go wherever he would.

The sky split asunder and torrents of rain beat down as we raced towards the topmost ridge of the hills where the Great Golden Lion Leapt on the Struggling Hawk and when I looked back, I saw the cave was gone, buried behind a sea of rocks. Then we plummeted down from the ridge and when the fire of Baal lit up the sky, I saw an endless range of hills before me, sparkling strangely like crystals, plunging down towards an endless night.

Chapter 11

The first rays of sun are striking the garden tomb as I take my coffee onto the balcony. I'm not at my best first thing but last night's adrenaline is soon kick started again by the caffeine. I quickly down a second cup and head for the bathroom. I don't have time to drool over a picturesque sunrise. There's stuff I need to do.

I want to make a copy of the map before anyone else arrives for work and I've got to make sure I don't run into Schlott. No doubt word will soon get back to him about another little 'incident' at my flat and Emile will have told him all about our discovery at the well. I must get in and out as quickly as possible then arrange some transport. Maybe I can find a willing official I can bribe to sort the paperwork.

The back entrance into uni. from the underground car-park is open and as I pass the cleaners' cloakroom I catch a glimpse of the Filipino women hanging up their overalls at the end of their shift. Apart from security, and the caretaker who gives me a nod as I head for the stairs, the building is deserted. Arye and Binyamin, the two guards in the corridor outside Archaeology are leaning against the wall and bid me 'shalom' without surprise. I suppose they're used to people coming and going at all hours.

The main door to the department is locked

but I have a copy of the key. The silent office feels pretty weird without the staff, like The Marie Celeste, and there are still faint smears of wet on the tiles from the cleaners' mops. There's no time to waste. I head straight for the large Xerox by Ingrid's desk, whip out the broken pieces of tablet and arrange them on the glass. After several takes, I manage to get a good A3 copy. In fact, some of the original features have come out clearer with the enlargement. I roll it up and sit down for a moment. I've got to hide the original somewhere no one will find it, whatever happens to me.

Got it. The door to *Art and Illustration* is open. What better way to hide the map than by disguising it again, just as Rahab's sister did. I hurry to the cupboard where Janice keeps the liquid clay she uses to restore broken pots, search for a colour match, then grab a spatula. I've got to hurry before anyone finds me here. By the time I stick together the broken pieces and smooth a layer of clay back over the map it looks much as it did. No one will know it's there. I hope.

I replace everything exactly as I found it, clean my hands on some kitchen towel and carry the tablet carefully into my office. The safest place is in the case with the rest. No unauthorised person will get past security unless they come in with all guns blazing, and they'd certainly be hard pressed to get out again. I lay the tablet carefully inside the case then replace the lid. It shouldn't take long to dry, and if Dr Schlott does start asking where it is, I can quite truthfully point out it's in my office with the rest. Unless something happens to me. I stuff the copy into my bag. I can't think that way. But if it does, I doubt anyone will think of breaking the tablet up to search for a map they don't even know is there. I have to consider all possibilities. There's too much at stake, and, let's face it, there's a chance I may not come out of this alive.

The Avis office on David ha-Melekh is my first port of call.

The man behind the desk stares at me coolly as I walk in. The doors have only just opened and I'm the first customer of the day.

"Yes, Madam?" His voice is full of polite insolence. He has me sussed, obviously English or American, before I even open my mouth. Somehow I don't think he's the sort to take bribes, not from a woman.

Do you have your English Driving Licence?" he asks, in response to my query.

I hand it over and he checks it quickly before giving it back.

"There is no problem. What kind of car would you like?"

"So I don't need an International Driving Licence?"

"No madam. We are permitted to hire out cars if the driver's licence is in English or French."

"Then I can take out a car today?"

"If Madam so wishes."

Brilliant. I leave the office clutching keys to a Saab 900 and head for the parking lot. I didn't think it would be that easy. Now I have to get on the road.

I stuff the paperwork into my bag - and shit! The photocopied map falls out.   I stumble after it, in a panic, but slip and end up sprawled on the pavement. Any other time, I'd die of embarrassment but, thank Christ, I've got the map. The street is bustling with people hurrying off to work, making an early start on their shopping or sightseeing. I clamber to my feet and aside from the odd funny look, no one pays much attention. A bit like Monday morning on the tube. You could drop dead on the Central Line and they'd carry on reading the Express.

I doubt anyone's been tailing me today as I left the flat long before my usual time, but just to be sure I go up and down the escalators and several times round the hardware section of the Maccabi Department Store, glancing behind me. Then I head for my Saab and get started for Ein Bokek.

I keep checking my rear view mirror but the roads through Jerusalem are so clogged with rush hour traffic it's impossible to tell if anyone's following me.

I still can't believe everything's gone so well. Traffic permitting, I should be in Ein Bokek shortly after midday. I switch on the radio and fiddle with the tuning till I find a music station playing eighties hits and sing along to Tears For Fears, trying to forget I'm up against some of the most dangerous people in the world.

By the time the great pinnacle of rock which houses the fortress of Masada comes into sight I'm ready for a break and pull over to a tourist viewing point on a quiet stretch of road near the ruins. There's a stall selling drinks and snacks nearby and I could kill for a coffee. Another couple of cars pull in behind me. I watch them in the mirror. No one gets out. I wait for a while, my eyes on the rear view mirror.

Then a very attractive black girl in a low cut top and skin tight 501s gets out from the furthest car and slinks past me towards the stall, and a fat man in a ridiculous floral shirt hauls himself out of the other. He waddles to the barrier and sneaks a good look at the the black girl's bum through his binoculars before focusing on the ruins.

Just tourists, of the worst kind. I grab my bag and make a beeline for the stall.

I drink my coffee in a small patch of shade by the rocks. I need to stretch my legs a bit after being cramped in the car for the past couple of hours but the overhang offers little protection from the sun and I soon decide my air-conditioned Saab is a much better bet. The man behind the stall is engrossed in his Arabic newspaper and doesn't bother to look up as I toss my cup in the bin. The fat man's disappeared. It didn't take him long to melt in the heat. A pair of long denim-clad legs slides into the far vehicle and the slam of the door bounces off the rocks. Jesus, it's hot.

I get back into the Saab and turn on the ignition, noticing as I check the mirror, there's no one in the fat man's car. There's a click behind me and something hard presses into my head.

In the mirror a fleshy face emerges, several floppy chins and hard tiny eyes. A sweaty arm slides round my throat and the stench of BO makes me want to retch but all my muscles are frozen.

"Don't move."

Another face slides into the mirror: a face I've seen before, on the beach and up in the hills near Arad. He pushes away his blonde hair. His eyes are laughing at me, grey, and sardonic, beside his companion's gleaming piggy ones.

"So, we meet again." I can feel his breath on the back of my neck, smell the aftershave.

The fat man's arm clamps harder around my throat. The gun presses into my skull.

"What do you want? My Visa card's..."

"You know what we want."

My mouth has gone dry. The desert landscape beyond the windscreen is a red ochre blur. The fortress ruins are shimmering and breaking up. Only the barrel of the gun is solid at the back of my head.

"Tut, tut. Very careless. Rushing out to hire a car and scrabbling in the gutter for something you obviously don't want to lose. I wonder what it could be."

My bag's beside me on the passenger side. I daren't take my eyes off the mirror but I hear the swish of fabric as an arm reaches down the seat. Sod it, the map.

Suddenly the pressure on my head from the gun is released. The faces vanish from the mirror.

"Not a word!" the fat man hisses. "Just act

normal or you're dead."

"Hi!" A bright smile at my window and a gleam of impossibly white teeth. The black girl leans her slim arm along my open window and tosses back a glossy curtain of hair. "Can you tell me how to get to the Qmran caves from here?"

I don't know what's going on, but I bet that gun's now pointing at my back. "Just carry on up the road and turn off at the sign." Christ, even I can't believe how normal my voice sounds. I must be so used to lies and facades it's engrained in my nature. The heat in here is stifling. In the short time the car's been stationary the sun seems to have sucked out all the air. Sweat is coming off me, in bucketfuls, and I can hardly breathe.

"Well, hi there," smiles the girl across my shoulder at the men. She leans forward, exposing a large expanse of cleavage and in the mirror I see the fat man's eyes bulge. "Are you guys on holiday as well?"

The piggy eyes go blank. He falls forward and there's a thud at the top of my seat, but I daren't turn round. The black girl's smile disappears as she opens my door, a pungent, chemical smell hits the back of my throat, up through my nose, and suddenly I'm gasping for air. A wave of nausea and a rip tide of stars rolls by then all my confusion is drowned in an ocean of oblivion.

There is softness engulfing my head and my

feet and I think I'm floundering in cotton wool. I try to stretch out my hand and my fingers touch something silky before a flash of pain whips across my forehead and I sink back into stillness.

I've no idea how time is passing or where I am. I'm drifting, gently on the swell of some heaving sea, up and down, through blackness and light. I manage to move my head a little and realise there's a foul metallic taste in my mouth and my tongue feels like one of those large fuzzy things used by TV sound technicians. I open my eyes to find myself staring at something black whirling its arms and legs above me, a helicopter or a giant spider. Shit, I can't see clearly. Something's wrong with my eyes. Then the pain starts up again and bugger this, it's better to keep them shut.

I think I've been unconscious for some time. I'm staring up at a high white ceiling and the giant creature has turned into the blades of a an air-conditioning fan. Cool wings of air are beating against my face. I look at my hand which doesn't seem to belong to me and notice it's resting on a pure silk cushion. Where the hell am I? I push myself up on one elbow and discover I'm lying on the largest white sofa I have ever seen, like something out of one of those features on celebrity homes in *House and Garden*. What's going on here? I swing my legs to the floor and put my head in my hands. I'm a wreck and badly in need of some water. The room keeps lurching around me.

When everything stops spinning I take a look around. I'm in an enormous living room, furnished in

white, like a drug dealer's paradise on a James
Band set, and on the whole of one side of the
room, these amazing white curtains sweep from
floor to ceiling. The floor is polished pine. The walls
are simply but very tastefully decorated with a few
well placed paintings. The blaze of sunflowers,
cypress and wheatfields nearest me looks like an
original Van Gogh. One graceful white vase
containing a single bird of paradise flower stands
on a pine coffee table, alone except for a large
leather bound book. There aren't any windows.

My bag, with the map, isn't here.

I get to my feet and test out my legs. They
feel like I've borrowed them from someone else but
I manage to reach the white curtains and push
them aside. A ball of orange sun hits me with the
force of an exploding bomb. Pain shoots behind my
eyes and I retreat from the the ferocity of colour
and light. I sway and reach out for some support,
but there isn't any, only the soft white curtains,
which, like the cushions, are made of silk. As I sink
onto my knees I catch the glittering of the sea and
realise the curtains are shading the living room from
a large sun terrace. I stare stupidly down at the tiles,
red terra cotta, Italian style, inlaid with a simple
floral design which floats in and out focus before
my eyes. The cool of the tiles revives me a little and
I force my head up from the floor. The terrace is
simply furnished with a wicker table and chairs to
match. I drag myself to my feet and lean on the
table for support. The sea glitters way below. I am
high, high up. This is a penthouse suite. A

champagne cooler stands beside the table on which is an empty bottle of Dom Perignon, two champagne flutes, and a gold cigarette lighter. I pick up the lighter and as it catches the sun the flash hurts my eyes. I still have difficulty focusing. I notice an engraving on the gold and squint in an effort to force my eyes to stop acting like a zoom lens gone mad. *With Love to a special friend, Donatella Versace.* I put the lighter down and notice a lipstick case, also gold, lying on a chair. *Primula Porter, Rose of Ice.* The two champagne flutes give off the scent of Dom Perignon. I notice *Primula Porter, Rose of Ice* doesn't leave a mark on glass. I wish there was some ice left in the cooler. My lips are cracked and my mouth feels like baked cotton wool. I'm desperate for a drink.

Then I hear a sound that freezes me to the spot. A low, bloodcurdling growl. The floor comes rushing up to meet me but gritting my teeth, and crouching on hands and knees, I manage to stop myself passing out again. Slowly, very slowly, I force myself to crawl round.

Two great amber eyes are so close I can see the irises, flecked with green and gold. Pitiless eyes. A sleek back arches and distinctive black and gold diamond patterns shimmer on fur. Pointed ears and long whiskers twitch. The jaguar arches its back and snarls. My last second has arrived. I didn't expect it to end this way and distantly remembered Hail Marys stick in my throat. The jaws draw back, revealing a bony palate, a long pink tongue - and nothing else. My relief soon curdles into horror and disgust. Its teeth and claws have been pulled. The jaguar prowls up and down the terrace then sinks into a patch of shade. It doesn't even condescend to look at me again and closes its eyes.

I creep away and retreat behind the curtains, pulling the glass doors shut. There's a door to my left which thankfully leads to a kitchen and - oh bliss - water. I grab the nearest glass and swallow great gulpfuls of to relieve this bitter thirst and dried out mouth. Then I splash it onto my face and chest and start to feel human again and notice that this is the most incredibly expensive fitted kitchen I've ever seen. Even the taps and unit fittings are gold. Then I wander back into the living room and try the door which I assume leads out of the suite. It's locked.

There's some kind of screen on the wall, a flicker of movement. and when I draw closer I find it's a monitor. Three security men in black suits are patrolling the corridor outside, then the black girl looms close up to the camera, holding a clipboard, and says something to one of the guards before moving out of view.

I turn away, despondent. My chances of escaping from here are zilch. I go back to the sofa and sit down, uncertain what to do next. My brain is still fuggy, too tired and dull to even start to work out where I am and who's brought me here.

I pick up the leather bound volume and find it's a photograph album. To my astonishment the first picture shows me, running up the steps to the university. In the next I'm standing with Ben at Jericho, as he points out the foundations of an early Bronze Age house. I turn over the pages and see myself sipping mint tea in Cafe Azziz; struggling through a crowd of students outside the main lecture hall; wandering the souks in the Muslim Quarter; pulling a face in the Via Dolorosa at a hideous picture of the Virgin; getting out of the Landrover as Ben and I stop for a coffee en route to Ein Gedi. I feel sick as I turn over page after page. Someone has been keeping track of everything I've done, everywhere I've been. The pages fall open at a series of blurred distance photos, where the camera's obviously moving. The Landrover weaving through the hills; me shading my eyes from the sun beside the cult basin at Tell Arad; standing by the Bedouin camp; crouching by the entrance to the cave with Gemal, and racing away round the rocks. Then I realise. These shots were all taken from above. Whoever controlled that helicopter is responsible for having me watched, twenty hours a day, for shooting the Arab by the cliff, and keeping me prisoner here, for I assume that's what I am, albeit imprisoned in luxury.

My head still feels too dull and fuzzy to make sense of any of this. Is Arms R Us behind it all, or Hamas or Hizbollah? I gaze around at the rich simplicity of the decor, the Van Goghs and Monets, the single bird of paradise flower in what is no doubt an extremely expensive vase. Somehow I don't think this is their style. I would more likely have woken up in an underground bunker or shack on some deserted hill on the Golan Heights Anyway, I remember the champagne glasses. Devout Muslims don't drink alcohol. I put my head in my hands and run my fingers through the tangled mess of my hair. I'm so confused and have this awful throbbing pain behind my forehead. I don't understand what happened back there in the car. Nothing makes sense.

Suddenly I want to go home, to Cruiser and my flat. I don't want to be here and I start bawling my eyes out. I make a dash for the door, but my head is spinning and I end up a snivelling heap on this beautifully polished pine floor. Half-blinded by tears, I pick myself up and stumble across the room, crashing heavily into the door before hauling myself to my feet and *tugging* uselessly at the handle. I turn round and slide down the wood, collapsing with my legs stuck out in front of me and head on my chest like some stupid rag doll, and cry with great heaving sobs till I'm lost in stupor again.

When I finally drag myself to my feet, the apartment's in shadow. I've no idea how long I've been here. It could be two hours or two days for all I know. My mouth tastes like elephant dung. I catch sight of myself in a mirror and see that my eyes look like something out of a Boris Karloff movie and my hair from a storks' nest safari. I feel so bad I don't even care. I need more water.

After downing a couple of glassfuls in the kitchen, I find another door close by and try the handle. It opens to reveal a large study, panelled in mahogany, impeccably tidy. An Intel Pentium sits on the desk. Next to it lies a folded copy of the

Financial Times. One wall is covered with certificates and framed photographs.

Primula Porter Certificate for Achievement 1998. New York Centre of Commerce. European Federation of Trade. Certificate of Excellence. Awarded to the Primula Porter Corporation, 1999. World of Health and Beauty, September 2000, Special Achievement Award, Primula Porter Ice Blonde Range.

Well bully for Primula Porter. I squint through my poor vampiric eyes at a cluster of photographs. Business people in suits and gold jewelry are gathered on a rostrum where a young woman is receiving a trophy. She has Vidal Sassoon blonde hair and is wearing a beautifully tailored suit with stiletto heels. Next to it is a close up shot, showing her lips are smiling as she displays a shield engraved in silver with the words *Excellence in World Beauty Products,* but her eyes are not.

I stare at the wall. It's all award ceremonies and certificates. There aren't any personal pictures here. No children, no lovers, no husband. The cool blue eyes stare into mine beneath that immaculate blonde crop. It's the woman I saw at Dr Schlott's office and the fashion show at the King David Hotel.

Suddenly I hear the opening of a door and I jump, guiltily, though there's no reason why I should. I never asked to be brought here, did I. There's a murmur of voices in the apartment outside and heels tap across the pine. I try to catch my breath and find my chest feels like it's bound with straps.

The door of the study swings open and in stalks my captor, followed by the black girl holding a file. She's more beautiful than she looks in the photographs. I realise how dry and cracked my lips are when I see how glossily hers are made up, her own brand, of course, *Rose of Ice*. We stare at each other across the study, sizing each other up, like lionesses about to fight over a kill - well, I'm more of a run-over tabby half squashed in the road. Her make-up is subtle, giving her a disgustingly natural-looking glow and defining cheekbones I'd die for, the bitch. Her eyebrows are haughty arches, no doubt shaped in some salon who wouldn't let riff-raff like me even empty the bins, and that Chanel suit makes me feel like a Buy-Lo reject. Primula Porter makes me sick.

"Sit down." She takes her high-backed seat at the desk and gestures towards the opposite chair. The body language is clear.

"I'll stand." I grit my teeth. I am dying to give my jelly baby legs a break but I'll retain my ground if it kills me.

"As you wish." She crosses her legs, elegantly, and I see she's wearing the sheerest grey stockings, despite the heat. I suppose she lives under constant air conditioning. In another era she'd have a slave on call, wafting a peacock feather fan. I've never disliked anyone so much. I bet she doesn't forget to put on sunblock as I do, or buy hers in the effing Body Shop. She's never had to battle with bulimia to keep her figure, or deal with psychos, I'm sure. Of course she bloody hasn't. No doubt a personal trainer and those burly security men fight all her battles.

"I expect you are wondering why you are here." She has a slight French accent and has learnt her English in the States. "Zandra, would you go and check the rota with Andres?"

"Yes, Mademoiselle Porter." There's nothing of the vamp or the casual tourist about the black girl now. She too is wearing a suit and her hair is neatly twisted into a far more elegant chignon than I could ever achieve, though, of course, she doesn't upstage her boss. She takes her folder and leaves. The perfect lackey.

"I want to know where I am and how I got here."

The carefully pencilled eyebrows arch. "You are in my apartment, of course, and I had you brought here."

"I want to go home, now." I sound like a sulky child. No doubt I look like one as well, compared to this paragon of Swiss Finishing School style. It's hard to keep up a front when you know you look like something the jaguar's mauled. But I'm trying.

A saccharine smile. "We have business to discuss.""I have no business to discuss with you. I insist on leaving." I force my voice to keep steady. "Or are you keeping me prisoner here?"

"Prisoner? That is a rather strong word."

"Then let me leave."

She leans back in her chair and lightly rests her hands on the arms. "That will not be possible."

"I'll call the police."

She stretches a manicured hand to stop me dialling. I never expected to reach the phone and I'm more annoyed by the fact she has not one solitary chip on her scarlet nail varnish. Another Primula bloody Porter product, no doubt.

"Please, Miss Adams. I have been informed you are an intelligent woman. Don't disappoint me."

I walk over to the wall and stare at a photograph of the Primula Porter Corporation headquarters in Geneva. "I suppose you *inherited* your business?" I say, trying to muster some scorn into my voice which feels like it's going to crack any minute. I'm surprised how much I can dislike someone. I never thought of myself as bitter. I suppose it takes a crisis to really know yourself.

"When my father died, I inherited a mediocre drugs company with limited appeal and falling share prices. I turned it around till it grew into the multi million dollar health and beauty corporation whose products you see in top stores across the world today. I built my company, Miss Adams. I am very proud of my work, as I am sure you are of yours."

I've got nothing in common with you. Nothing at all.

"Which, of course, is why I'm here."

It's hard to maintain dignity when you feel like something off the refugee camp rubbish tips. How do you deal with someone who not only looks like she's just stepped out of Vogue but who owns the company that makes her lipstick? Then I remember she holds my life in her hands, and suddenly ironing board abs and Cindy Crawford lips are wholly unimportant when you're staring at death in Chanel.

"What happened to me back there near Masada?"

"You were about to be abducted until we stepped in and rescued you."

"So if you 'rescued' me, why won't you let me go?"

"Miss Adams, we have business to discuss."

"I want to know." I lean my hands on her desk. "Those two men,they're from Arms R' Us, right?"

"They *were* from Arms R' Us."

I stare at those cool green eyes and a chill goes through me. "You had them killed?"

The eyebrows go up again. "Miss Adams, please. Such an unpleasant notion. The overweight gentleman was 'taken out of the equation.' We couldn't let him carry you off as he was about to do. As for the blonde gentleman, Stevens, well, Arms R' Us thought he was a loyal worker, but..." she shrugs. "If the price is right, loyalty proves a cheap commodity."

"So he's been working for them but passing information on to you."

The door swishes open behind me and the jaguar pads in. He arches his back and rubs his head against those sheerest of stockings, which would no doubt, implode before they laddered. She caresses his fur with her long slim fingers and he purrs.

"Come," she stands up. "I will show you the bathroom. You will feel better once refreshed. Then you will dine with me this evening. Perhaps food will make you more amenable."

"I don't want to eat with you."

"Miss Adams, you have no choice."

I feel a bit less like something from Aliens now, since I've taken up her offer of a bath. You should see the bathroom. It's the size of my living room, completely tiled in marble and glass, with real fur rugs strewn over the floor and this enormous shell-shaped sunken bath with jacuzzi and headrests. I try not to luxuriate as I soak my aching body in Primula Porter Ice Temptation Bubble Bath, and think instead about the animals who died to make those rugs. But when I haul myself out of the scented water and rub myself down with the hugest softest bath towel I've ever seen, I feel almost normal again. My stomach's rumbling and though I have no wish to sit with that cow at her table, I won't gain much by keeling over through lack of food, and I do need to keep my wits about me, if I'm ever to get out of this. So I perch on a large wicker chair by the bath and consider my options. I'm safe only until Ms Porter has what she wants, and I bet she didn't build a multi-million dollar enterprise by dishing out compassion. Let's face it. She keeps a jaguar for a pet, but has dead animals in her bathroom. She buys off employees of large American arms companies and makes them disappear like David Blane. She has a team of private security thugs paid to execute her every command. The disappearance of a solitary English translator would be chicken feed. I start to shiver and pull on my clothes.

When I come out of the bathroom I catch the tail end of a telephone conversation.

"Stupid people. Put out a press release denying we test on animals and get on to Norbert. A little 'firework' beneath a car at the Geneva HQ will soon discredit the protesters."

Now that really makes me feel a whole lot better. I'd say my chances of surviving this rich bitch's claws are diminishing by the second. She lays down her mobile and glances up.

"Ah Miss Adams. You look fresher. I hope you are feeling better too. We have much to discuss."

She's been watching the news on her gigantic TV while I've been in the bath. Debris from an Arab car bomb strews a settlement in Hebron and a Jewish community leader swears revenge. It might as well be a world away. I bet she cares more about her lipstick smudging than kids lying dead in a street, and with a pang of shame, I realise, so did I, once. She aims the remote and the picture disappears.

Shalimar the Jaguar wolfs down his carefully minced steak while I steel myself to dine with this jet-set queen on the balcony which is lit up by soft concealed lighting as the moon rises over the sea. The sky is purple and two bright stars have come out. Below us the sounds of laughter rise up from a barbecue on the beach, people having fun, oblivious to all the dramas unfolding in every inch of this beautiful deranged Palestine. This lovely whore who is tearing herself to bits. The menu on the table is from the Trocadero Hotel, which, according to the blurb on the back, is part of the Primula Porter chain. It boasts its own swimming pool fed by spa water, and the most exclusive health and beauty treatments under the sun, specialising, of course, in Dead Sea mud. I assume the food has been sent up from the hotel which must lie beneath this penthouse suite.

I help myself from the selection of dishes she's ordered, and try hard not to look too enthusiastic, though I'm starving now. It must be hours since I ate. She eats *Larks Tongues in Wine Jelly* and *Escallopes of Veal with Pigeon Imperiale,* daintily, without smudging her lipstick, of course. I pick at mushrooms and artichokes, watching her eat, and think of calves packed into crates and song birds blasted from the sky. I refuse her Dom Perignon and drink Perrier instead.

"My dog." I suddenly remember Cruiser. He'll be all alone in my flat, unfed.

"I am sure your little Arab boy will look him while you're away."

I put down my fork and stare at her over the table. This woman knows everything about me. She's had me watched for weeks, just like Jonathon. I remember Jonathon's note, cut out of newsprint. *EVERY STEP OF THE WAY*. This spoilt cow's

414

been playing the same game with me too. She's every bit as bad as Jonathon. Maybe worse. At least he has the excuse of a deprived childhood. It my fault? Do I attract persecution? Get right off that track, Charlotte. Keep your head together. You need all your wits to stay alive. No room for stupid obsessions at this inn.

I have to get out of here somehow, away from this woman. When the meal is over, she has Zandra bring some coffee to the living room then goes into her study and returns with a sheet of A3. She smoothes it out on the table and smiles. It's my map.

"Now let us talk."

I watch her across the table. She'll find that cave over my dead body, and I think, grimly, it might just come to that.

"You realise of course, the Primula Porter Corporation would be extremely interested in finding the source of the substance that preserved Joshua and Caleb well into their eighties."

I say nothing and don't allow myself to even glance at the map.

"You will pass the night here in my suite and tomorrow you and I will go in search of the Cave of White Fire. Just the two of us. The less people who know of this the better."

"I'm not helping you do anything."

"I am not giving you a choice. I know the fragments on which you have been working describe how the girl found the cave. I think you can find it too."

I frown and run through the order of the fragments in my mind. There's something wrong here. The finding of the cave didn't occur until Fragment 37.

"I understand you found the other cave where the tablets from the Ark had been buried, although they had unfortunately long been removed." She watches me coolly. "No doubt you were rushing off today in your hire car to search for the Cave of White Fire." Her green eyes narrow slightly. "I am sure you know the meaning of the the Army in White, the Lizard's Tail and the Seraphim with Wings Outstretched."

This is all wrong. She shouldn't know about that. The names of those features aren't given on the map. They appear in Fragment 37, and there are only two copies of the final fragments. One is in my guarded office and the other in New York.

She's noticed my confusion and smiles. "You are wondering how I am in possession of your final translations. Let me show you."

She stands up and goes into her study. My mind's racing faster than Formula One. She must've bribed the guards on duty outside Archaeology. One of them's got hold of a key and sneaked into my office. Or Ingrid's sleeping with the Head of Security...

When she comes back, she's carrying a sheaf of papers. She stands beside me, so close I catch a strong drift of her perfume, and flicks through them to show me. They're all there, every one, from Fragment 1 to the final Fragment 40. Then she holds out a separate sheet of A4. I pause, then take it, unwillingly. It's a fax. From New York. The message reads;

Please find enclosed the final fragments of Charlotte Adams' translation, as promised. I trust you will find them of great   interest and look forward to the transfer of funds to my account   as agreed.

"Schlott." I look up at her in desperation. "It has to be. You're his sponsor for the project, not the Israelis."

She looks at me, pityingly. "No, I offered, but he declined my financial backing. He seemed to think the Israeli government would consolidate the position of the university, and his own, of course, and establish it as a prime academic force. He wanted these fragments to have the same international repute as the Dead Sea Scrolls and decided the Israel government, who administer The Shrine of the Book where the scrolls are housed, would give more academic respectability than a cosmetics house." She bends down to stroke Shalimar who is rubbing against her leg. "Silly man, he could have saved everyone a lot of bother if he'd accepted my offer. Still never mind, I always get what I want in the end."

I don't want to see the name at the top of the fax. She's watching me, her eyes glinting unnervingly like Shalimar's, waiting for a response. I swallow and force back the tears, for I will not give her the satisfaction. Then I stare at the name of the sender.

"I told you, if the price is right..."

Ben.

This hurts worse than anything I've ever felt before. He's wounded me to the core. My trust is a passionflower and it's folded up in shock, desperate to repel the damage he's caused, to return to the bud, before all the bad things happened. But somewhere in New York City is a man with a sword who's cutting the petals to shreds.

Passiflora meets Attila the Hun.

Oh Ben. Why did you do this?

"How much did you pay him?"

I want to know how cheap is the price of betrayal.

"Bone marrow transplants do not come free in the United States."

The sword twists in my guts.

"We start out tomorrow at nine."

Fragment 36

When the sun rose, the steep hills were behind us. The sky was as blue as faience and the world washed new by the storm. I reined in my camel. We were both exhausted by the long ride through the sparkling hills and ready to drop. Before me lay a strange sight. A shore littered with pillars of ghostly figures and banks of crusty white salt rising out of

418

the morning mist; a mist which the rising sun soon burned away to reveal none other than the shimmering Sea of Arabah.

I clutched my one remaining tablet to me. But I did not need to look at it to know where I was. Those curves, which. I I had pored over for so long they were etched into my mind, now translated themselves before my very eyes into the bays of the salty sea. By some strange quirk of the Gods, my runaway camel had brought me to the shores of that very place, not a thousand cubits from the Cave of White Fire.

Fragment 37

As soon as I spied a cave, I hurried towards it, tethered my camel to one of those strange salt-encrusted pillars and laid down, thankful for the coolness of the earth. For the early morning sun blazed through the sky as though the rain had washed a veil from the air, leaving it free to burn the very salt from the sea.

I was not sick that morning. A peacefulness I had not known for many moons enveloped me as I lay on the earth and let my eyelids close. I put my hands on my belly. I could ignore those swollen curves no longer. The moon had not lied. I knew I was with child.

I slept till the sun reached its zenith and began its slow descent across the distant hills. Then I sat gazing out at that shimmering shore, all its rocks and peaks encrusted with a creamy whiteness that glistened in the rays of the sun around the still blue Sea of Arabah. The surface of the water water barely stirred. Not a shadow of a bird flew across to tremble its surface. Not a creature moved to disturb its solitude. Only a hazy bank of little clouds above the hills marred the blue of sea and sky. I felt the peace of that strange and desolate place seep into my bones as I sat in the cave mouth, wondering, and it seemed that something in my soul was healed.

As the sun curved down towards the bills, a little breeze rippled the surface of the Sea and gently touched my face. I stood up. It was time to go. I had not eaten or drunk anything that day, yet I was neither hungry nor thirsty. It seemed the spirits of that salty land had nourished me with all my body and soul could desire.

It did not take me long to find the Cave of White Fire. The map was true. I had to climb high up the cliff to reach the Lizard's Tail. The twists and turns that led through the pillars of the Army in White would have defeated me for sure without the map. That strange path would have defeated anyone who did not possess the key.

When I reached the Mouth of the Lizard, I could see the Seraphim with Wings Outstretched and feared for a moment lest that terrible being should come to life and swoop down on me with the vengeance of the Habiru. But I stood firm, paused in the gateway, and offered my humble plea to the guardian spirits of that most strange place to let me pass in peace and squeezed through the rocks.

I soon discovered why the Habiru leaders always sent boys. The fissure in the rocks as it led down towards Reshef's realm was too narrow for a full grown man. Had I been longer with child, I could not have passed myself. As it was, I had to squeeze between the rocks in places. I did not need fire to light my way for the rocks glowed with their own strange light, leading me down into the earth until I finally found myself on a rocky ledge, staring down at a cavern below, filled with a pool of white fire. A path led down to that bubbling spring, steeply shelving and as black and smooth as obsidian. But I dared not go down.

A spray of white fire shot out of the pool and I recoiled in horror, terrified in case that terrible radiance blasted me like the victims of the Ark. I decided at once to get out of that forbidden place but as I made my way back

421

up, I noticed another passage whose entrance had been hidden on my descent behind a jutting edge of rock.

I knew what it was from my map. Sure enough, it led straight into the second chamber. The floor dropped away so sharply that in the gloom, lit only by that ghostly glow from the rocks themselves, I almost fell into the pit; the pit that heaved as though some strange creature from long forgotten times stirred that liquid mess with its tail; the pit that churned with sparkling green mud.

Cautiously I reached down and scooped a tiny bit on my finger, then smeared it onto the rough worn skin of my heel. I left it, as I had seen Caleb do. Then the walls of the chamber suddenly seemed to bear down on me and I thought if I stayed there longer, I would surely bear the screams of demons, and I fled.

When I squeezed back through, the fissure, I realised I was trembling. I sat down in the welcome embrace of the afternoon sun then rubbed the mud from my heel. The skin was as new and smooth as the day I was born.

A sudden surge of exhilaration swept over me. I had found the secret place of the Habiru leaders; the place of the fire that could kill from afar and the mud that gave life to keep men - and women - young. People would kill for a secret such as I possessed.

Then I felt hungrier than I had ever been in my life. I turned back towards the Sea. I knew I could not stay there. There was no drinking water anywhere that I could see and not a living thing from which I could eke a meal. I made my way back to my camel and decided to travel north up the shore, for I knew that somewhere on that western side of the Sea of Arabah were Canaanite settlements where I could find shelter and sustenance for me and my child.

My child. Half Canaanite, half Habiru. Conceived when I dedicated my virginity to Astarte, swearing that act of love and hate would help bring down the Habiru and wreak Canaan's wrath on the people of the One God. When I placed my hand on my swollen belly and felt that tiny life quicken beneath my touch, I did not know what I felt. Tenderness and fierceness to protect the helpless child within, a child born in sacredness to Astarte, a child to be nurtured and loved, as I had loved Tarasch. Or the child of one of those beasts who had murdered my sister, the child of my most hated enemy, a child who should be ripped from my womb and hurled into the most accursed pit of fire for monsters to devour.

Chapter 12

We leave at daybreak, in a black Mercedes Benz, driven by one of her security lackeys, which sweeps out of the drive of the Trocadero Hotel. She sits in state at the front, in a headscarf and Armani sunglasses while I'm shoved in the back with another of her thugs, who seems to have an unhealthy obsession with stroking his gun. I think I could be forgiven for wondering if all men are psychos or traitors, but I'm through with bitterness. What I feel right now is bruised, really bruised, deep inside, and raw, like I've taken a such a battering if you turned me inside out I'd look like I'd stood in Central Park at midnight swathed in Rolexes and yelled out "Mug me!"

But I'm not beaten yet.

I can see now through these darkened windows that the Trocadero is situated right on the beach. Tourists are strolling through the grounds with their rolled up towels and bags stuffed with suncream, kids are playing football and there are plenty of heads bobbing in the sea already. Another sunny day in paradise! Unless you feel like Trevor Reece Jones straight after the crash.

Traffic rolls past on the freeway as the Mercedes waits to pull out of the drive. I don't have any choice except to go along with this. If I refuse to search for the cave, Cruella here will simply have me shot, or worse. But I do have one Ace in my hand. She needs me to interpret the meaning of the features named in the fragments. The map alone's not enough, and she knows it. She doesn't understand the relationship of the girl to the land as I do. The Army in White and the Seraphim with Wings Outstretched are obscure references to her, as they once were to me. Yesterday she told me the search for the cave would involve just the two of us. Charming prospect, I must say. I think I'd rather spend a day with Harold Shipman. But there's a chance she might ditch her security men as we move closer to the vicinity of the cave and perhaps then, when it's just the two of us, I can watch for a chance to escape. The way I feel right now, I'd happily shove her over a cliff. Let's see how much good Primula Porter Products would be at filling in cracks in her skull.

It's so weird, driving down this road with all its memories of Ben, but I keep my eyes fixed ahead and won't not allow myself to wallow in the cess pit of misery he's caused. He betrayed me and led me into this snare, but I've wrapped those raw wounds inside me with razor wire.

We speed past the long strip of sand where holiday makers lounge with ice creams beneath parasols or chase each other across the sand. Their laughter and freedom is a mockery as I sit with a gun at my back.

We drive into Ein Bokek, at the southern end of the sea, its hotels standing directly on the bleakest of shores, devoid of any vegetation. The landscape is lunar; dead, like that abortion which used to be Ben and me. Beyond the spas lie the mountains of Sodom, the sparkling hills of the fragments, which tumble into a lifeless sea. Crusts of salt float like a foamy scum. No seabirds strut on this shore and there's not a single plant or tree. The sky is hard as sapphire, the rocks bleached and skeletal. What better place for a grande finale to a love affair.

We reach a place where a forest of salt-encrusted pillars rises behind the road and although I don't want to share my secret, her secret, with this bitch, I don't really have a choice.

"We need to go on foot from here."

She takes the gun from her lackey and instructs the driver to park off the road. A few solitary spa hotels rise up from the shore and behind us lies the burning mass of the mountains of Sodom. She stays close to me, the gun concealed behind her bag in case we meet anyone, but this is still a desolate spot, three and half thousand years on.

We leave the hotels behind us as we trudge along the shore and I find myself alone with my enemy and her gun, following in the footsteps of the Canaanite girl through an empty world. We don't speak. No birds shatter the stillness and no waves lap at this silent shore. In fact it's so quiet I'd give anything to hear a sea gull squawk. We walk on, and this vastness of sky and rock makes her Armarni labels look pathetic.

A number of caves pock the cliff. Any one of them could have given shelter to Rahab's sister and her unborn child. Mademoiselle Fur Coat and

No Knickers is content to let me lead. She doesn't seem to like this peculiar stillness, which makes me feel decidedly better. I bet she's wondering if I've brought her to the right place. Well, tough. You've got no option but to follow me.

Under different circumstances I'd have been like a kid at Christmas at the prospect of finding the cave, hoping in spite of the centuries that Santa Claus has left me something to find. Mind you, there's no way I'd go down as far as Rahab's sister without being protected from radiation. Now though, I just dread the thought of the white fire falling into Cruella's manicured hands.

I stop to look at the map. She watches me closely through her sunglasses and cradles her gun. I scour the cliffs for any features which resemble a lizard's tail but I can't see anything and continue down the sand. We round a headland and, at last, there's a path snaking up through the rocks. I check the map again. This must be the one. It's the only way up the cliff so far and as far ahead as I can see is a smooth, impossible ascent.

I start to climb and she follows.

"Merde," she curses, causing a clatter of stones as she slips on the path. I spin round, hopefully, but she hasn't dropped the gun, or broken her neck. She waves her hand imperiously. "Va! Carry on!"

As we climb I can hear her panting. The sun's behind us, the glare blinding on the rocks, scorching the air so it feels like we're baking in

Satan's oven. But I grit my teeth and fortify myself with malicious pleasure, knowing that the sun is roasting her pig-delicate flesh. I hope her lungs will burst.

I climb on, grimly. I don't care if this kills me, but I'll make her drop first.

Suddenly the terrain flattens out and turns into a forest of pillars, like a great tribe of people frozen in salt. Time for another look at the map.

"Qu'est-ce qui se passe?"

I ignore her. She's in my hands now. We're at the Army in White, rank upon rank of soldiers of stone. No one could find their way through this maze without a key. I'm amazed and full of admiration at how Rahab's sister made this same journey weighed down with her unborn child. She was made from a tougher mould than mine. I know it's nonsense but I can't help feeling her spirit is close to me now, among these rocks which she struggled and sweated through too, and I feel some of her strength is steeling me for this climb. I'm delightfully, malevolently pleased, that I'm not the one who's heaving for breath and clutching a rock for support.

"Comment? Pourquoi...Why are we stopping?"

Good. Foundation can't hide her livid red cheeks, and her terribly expensive eyeliner's making little black fans of the edges of her eyes. She's also lapsing into her native French, despite the flawlessness of her English. But she's still clutching that gun.

I pause and listen. Something's

changed. It's not as still as before. A low grinding noise growls through the pillars.

I take the path through the Army in White as shown on the map, careful to proceed exactly as it shows, closely followed by Cruella de Chanel and her gun.

Suddenly there's no army of salty pillars any more. The mountainside falls away into a great gouged out pit. The growl in the air becomes a roar.

"Comment?" Her hair is dishevelled. Her face is shiny with sweat as she adjusts her sunglasses on her nose. *"Qu'est-ce...* What is going on here?"

Suddenly I'm laughing my guts out and I don't care about that gun. For there's no Lizards Mouth, no Seraphim with Wings Outstretched. Only a huge quarry hacked out of the mountain, full with funnels and giant kilns, while bulldozers and articulated trucks crawl and scream across this naked earth. The roar is deafening as conveyor belts and machinery grind at the Dead Sea Mineral Works. There's no narrow fissure in the rocks leading to the Cave of White Fire. It's all gone, the cave's destroyed, finito, caput. Nothing but yawning wasteland remains as minerals are ripped from the earth and processed, before being hauled away in containers to Ashdod or Eilat.

"Give me that map." There's fury and a really gratifying disbelief, in the eyes of this rich bitch who always gets her own way. Well, not this time, honey. Nothing can restore the ultimate in anti-wrinkle treatments now. Nothing can salvage your dream of selling the world's greatest beauty treatment ever to the jet-set elite. Rahab's sister stole it from Joshua, and The Dead Sea Mineral Works has robbed it from you. My heart bleeds. Here lies your Cave of White of Fire. R.I.P.

"C'est pas possible!"

"Oh it is." I fold my arms and lean against a rock. The dregs of Joshua's secret power are buried somewhere in a canister of potash.

She snatches the map from my hands, stuffs the gun into her bag and runs down into the mineral works. Someone yells. A man in a yellow safety helmet turns round then strides towards her, shouting, but his words are lost in the roar of the bulldozers. She looks at the map then stares wildly around before running through a tangle of machinery to a conveyor belt where large skips full of chemicals are rolling towards the waiting trucks.

I stand at the edge, watching. I know I should get the hell out of here while I have the chance for she's still got the gun, but I have to admit, I'm mesmerised by the sight of this epitome of style and wealth who's really lost it big time, along with one Gucci sandal which lies abandoned by a skip.

She clutches at the map, turns it this way and that, then runs towards a deep vat in the ground which is filled with mud. Above it is a kind of cable car, equipped with huge moving buckets which run mechanically over the vat towards the processing plant. Several men in safety helmets are now hurtling towards her. She whips round and fires a shot from her gun. They duck behind any available piece of machinery then she races off again. She stops at the mud vat and hovers, a dishevelled figure on the edge, frantically consulting a torn and crumpled scrap of paper.

With a kind of fascinated horror I see one of the enormous buckets slide down the cables towards her. She's still engrossed in what's left of the map. I shout. The men shout. They leap out from cover and yell but the noise of machinery is deafening. The map falls from her hands as the heavy bucket strikes her in the back. Then I don't see her any more. Primula Porter, multi-million dollar corporate figurehead, is lost, in a giant vat of rejuvenating Dead Sea mud.

Fragment 38,

I rode northwards along the shore on my trusty camel, my only companion on that solitary journey, until just as the sun was sinking in a blaze of orange fire below the western hills, I came to a settlement. Springs gushed forth from the cliffs and beautiful ferns fringed the path of the stream as it tumbled down the rocks towards the sea. Birds wheeled and circled overhead, and as I approached, I saw a herd of gazelles springing across the land. I dropped to my knees and gave thanks to Astarte, for by now my mouth raged with thirst and I was so hungry I could have eaten an ibex whole.

The people there were simple Canaanites who lived off the land. Some dwelt in the many caves that pocked the cliffs. Others had huts in the lush green tract that surrounded the springs. They gave me food and showed me a cave I could use for my own, offering me goatskins to keep me warm at night, then left me to myself.

I made myself comfortable on the skins and feeling more peaceful than I had at the end of any other day since I fled the ruins of Jericho, I slowly sank into sleep, smiling, as though I had come home.

I stayed there for many moons. From the day I arrived, I did not bother to try to keep up my boy's disguise. I told them I was from Eglon and had fled after all my family were killed in Joshua's raid. I knew my growing child would soon be impossible to hide and besides, I would need the skills of their wise women when my time came.

While I was there, I heard rumours of Joshua's army. True to his word, he had destroyed Hebron, killing all who dwelt within the city. Then he had headed south-west to Debir. There were rumours of a strange white fire which blasted Hebron from afar and tales of the Ark grew more extravagant with every telling, until it was as big as a house and full of dragons that devoured a thousand men a day to satisfy their ravenous needs.

I was disappointed to hear Joshua still had his white fire. But I supposed the chest I had dared not touch was still in the Ark. If it was as full of the magic fire as I had seen in my dream, it would last him for the destruction of another city or two. And there were probably boys who had visited the cave before who might be able to find their way without the map. Though anyone would surely be hard pressed to weave their way through the Army in White without the key. I could only hope that without the writings on the tablets or the map, the knowledge the Habiru kept in the Ark would slowly die with its priests. But how long, if at all, it would take for their power to diminish I could not tell. I could only hope I had struck them a mortal blow.

One day, I caught a man in my cave. I had just returned from the springs with a jar on my head when I heard the sound of scuffling inside. I laid down my jar and quietly crept to the entrance. I peered around the rock and saw a small weasel of a man, so thin his ribs showed through, with a mess of untidy black hair, rummaging through my things. He stuffed his mouth full of some dates I had stored in a bowl then lifted my goatskins. As he picked up my precious clay tablet, I rushed inside and beat him about the head.

"Aiee!" He dropped the tablet and covered his head with his hands.

"Filthy pig! Thief! Leave my things alone!"

He scuttled towards the entrance, shielding his pathetic head from my blows. It was fortunate for me he was such a scrawny thief, for by now my belly was growing heavy with child. As he turned to flee, I caught a glimpse of his eyes. They were narrow and beady like a snake's, and so full of hatred I was nearly caught off my guard. But I picked up a handful of stones and flung them at his head as he slid down the slope, squealing like a pig.

When he was out of range of my stones, be stopped and shook his fist at me. Something in his eyes, still pouring venom, made my stomach turn.

"She-wolf! Sow! You little bitch!" he cursed. "You'll pay for this one day!"

Fragment 39

I began to grow sick. My skin peeled off in shreds, leaving raw patches on my legs and arms that itched and burnt till I wished I could tear it off. Blisters came up on my feet and hands and several boils erupted on my back. The people gave me herbs and cooling plants at first, before my condition grew worse. Then they threw me out.

They turned me from my cave and burnt the skins on which I had laid, holding herbs across their mouths and taking care not to touch me or anything of mine. It was all. I could do to to grab the map and a jug and flee.

"Leper!"

The screams rang in my ears as I fled up the cliff path, a torrent of stones ringing on the ground behind me.

But I had seen leprosy in Jericho. I knew this sickness was nothing had known before.

I had to continue higher up in the cliffs, despite the heavy burden I carried inside me. For my way along the shore was blocked by the people below and the only path I could take led up. My breath heaved in great gulps and my legs shook, on the verge of collapse, by the time I glimpsed the opening to a cave, almost hidden by ferns. I only discovered it because a startled gazelle leapt out of my way and disturbed the ferns as it fled.

Gratefully, I squeezed inside the opening. Once past the narrow sill, it was bigger than it had seemed from without, and I sank down, sick and exhausted, onto the coolness of the ground.

There I made my sanctuary. Goats came by from the settlement and I was able to get some milk. Olives grew a little way up and with a makeshift sling, I was able to bring down birds and small animals. At the rear of the cave, was a well, so deep I could not see the bottom, but I was able to lower a jug into a shallower spring which gushed down a short way from the top.

There was a clay pit nearby and some broken tablets were left scattered around. As I picked one of them up, an idea came to me I had time on my hands and nowhere to go, even had I the strength to travel. While I waited for my baby to born, for he grew at a pace which mocked my weakening body, I would write my story. So here I stayed, passing many days, scratching my tale into the tablets. The memories spilling onto the clay drove away my pain.

One day, by some unlucky turn of fate, I saw the thief again. The people knew I still dwelt high above them, for occasionally a goat boy came upon me while I gathered berries or plucked olives from the trees. But no one came near. Until I saw the thief, standing on a rock some way down the path. He was too much of a coward to approach and risk catching my disease, so he yelled at me from a distance.

"You filthy sow!" I know where you are! Joshua's on his way to these shores with al his army! They say he's raging about a girl who ran off with some tablets of his! Says he'll search all of Canaan till he finds her, then flay her alive till the skin is whipped from her bones and blows in the wind from Egypt!"

A cold chill passed over me as I recalled how he had pulled back my goatskins and seen the tablet with the map.

"Wouldn't it be a shame if someone went to Joshua and told him about a little bitch with a clay tablet hidden beneath her goatskins?"

Then he scuttled off down the path, laughing all the way down.

That night, the fever took me. If I had had any hope of escape before, it left me now. I would never have the strength to go further up the cliff, and if I went down the people would stone me for sure. I could only lie there while the fever burnt my face, and wait for the vengeance of Joshua to seek me out.

Fragment 40

I hear they are coming for me. I fear my child may never see the light of day. But they shall not get back their precious tablets from the Ark. I shall hide the map where they shall never find it. The secrets of the Ark of the One God shall be lost to the Habiru forever.

I shall cheat Joshua of his vengeance. He will not flay what is left of my skin from my bones. They will not take me or my baby, for I know what I must do.

I have done everything I could to take revenge for Jericho, after the Habiru took all I had. I do not understand all the secrets of the Ark but I know those clay blocks required an armed guard, day and night, without cease. Joshua's rage is enough to tell me I have dealt the Habiru a blow which, I am sure, will echo down the ages and sap at their might. They will never find them again.

I shall hide my story, and commend what is left to Astarte who has always lent me light on my solitary journey. My heart shall always lie in Jericho, and I can only wish that one day my bones would lie there too.

These are the last scratchings I shall make on the clay before I hide my tale.

Perhaps, one day, in time to come, someone will find my story and sing again the songs of Jericho.

Chapter 13

It's still early in the morning and only a few dedicated tourists, clutching guidebooks and cameras, are wandering round the ruins. The town below lies shrouded in mist but closer to the Tell I can just make out the palm trees, where golden red date clusters shimmer. The hum of traffic seems far away and the voices of my fellow early risers don't disturb me as I gaze out across the hillside. This is the place I love most in the whole of Palestine; the mound of Tell- es-Sultan at Jericho. I sit hugging my knees on this sunbaked ground with the ruins of Jericho's ancient walls stretched out before me, and the sun burning away the mist to unveil the valley of the Jordan, I feel time is unfurling with the dawn and it's like all those long dead Canaanites are still here. It's silly I know, a pyramidiot dream, but they feel so close I can almost stretch out my fingers and touch their robes. If I shut my eyes, I can hear those women laughing at their own lewd Joshua jokes as they harvest their wheat, and glimpse their husbands returning from the hunt with their kill on a pole, scorning mountain lion and Habiru with a single breath; and on the still desert air their gales of laughter ring out as they mock a raggle-taggle band of landless vagabonds who believe in a single god.

In this place anything seems possible. I can

drift beyond the present to hear the chatter of flax-clad children as they play with wooden toys in dusty streets, and catch the hot reek of animals as the goatboy boy yells at his straying herd. I can smell fresh baking from the stall where the crone sells barley cakes; and from Rahab's house drift whispered tales of Joshua's might, from hushed voices around the hearth.

This is truly a place of beginnings. I open my eyes and look out across this ancient mound which started as a flat piece of ground, and remember how the earliest people made this their home, and thrived on the springs and the dates, the carob and corn that burst from the land. It's amazing how settlement after settlement crumbled, until Jericho grew, and became this hill of multitudinous layers of history, and the final one is where I sit today. From my perch high on the Tell, I can see the fence which encircles the foundations of a small round house, like a Bedouin tent in stone, which is nine thousand years old. This is the oldest city in the world, and its antiquity awes me.

This is where the story which brought me to Palestine began, where three sisters sowed seed in the fields and drew water from the wells. This is where Rahab let the spies down from her window and her sister clawed the ground to build a grave, before turning away to begin a solitary journey, which ends with me today. She left behind her, at the world's oldest city, a small heap of stones, and at its strangest, lowest shore, a chronicle of her fate. Her story survived the centuries, but not her name.

This is also the place where I first came with Ben, but I don't waste any thoughts on him. He's an irrelevance, someone who let me down. Love without trust is seeds on stony ground. I've learnt my lessons. No more Ben. No more Jonathon. No more torturing myself for the sister I never was. I've left them way behind and I've gained a hard bright sparkling strength deep inside. There's only one person I can ever truly trust, and that's myself. Whoever may enter my life in the future, and tap at this brittle and beautiful shell in which my passion and my pain are sealed, I'll always keep that inner strength which poured into my veins as I scaled the hills of Palestine.

So here we are, at Tell-es Sultan - the beginning and the end of a trail of footsteps left more than three millennia ago, as this new millennium unfolds.

There aren't any flowers on this barren mound and it might seem soppy, but next time I'll bring roses, sharp thorns, beautiful petals, and hope, my nameless heroine, that somehow, over the centuries and the grave, you'll know I lay them here for you.

Chapter 14

I stand up and dust the grit from my jeans. I've come here not just to to remember the past, but to think about the future. My contract will soon be up at the International University and Dr Schlott's desperate for me to renew. Well, he would be, wouldn't he. Since the fragments have been released and extracts published in newspapers and magazines across the world, I've never been so much in demand in my life. Talk about a boost to a girl's self-esteem. Not only international academia but the press as well are clamouring for articles and the most prestigious universities and museums are chucking contracts at me like they're going out of fashion. Chicago, Munich, the Israeli Museum - it seems they all want the translator of the Ein Gedi Fragments on their staff. It's taken off in a way which has far surpassed anything I imagined. The fragments are even going to be serialised in the international press. I had a letter from Mum, she's so proud, and I didn't even think she'd be interested. It was always Sally-Ann whose name was going to appear in The Times, but I think my sister would be proud of me too.

I needed to come back here, to this place of beginnings, to think, and in that small dusty town below, there's one more offer I've yet to hear.

I glance at my watch. The sun has nearly burnt away the last traces of mist and it's time for me to return to the town, to Jericho, where I have a meeting which may change my future forever.

Well! I had no idea he would be there! I nearly died when Dr Ali Zaid, - he's the Cultural Representative for the Palestinian National Authority - told me the President himself was fascinated by my work and wanted to meet me. I mean, me? Meeting him? I only had time to open to my mouth in astonishment when Dr Zaid opened the door and right there in front of me, sat at his desk with a Palestinian flag draped on the wall behind him, was that grizzled face you see so often on TV beneath that famous red and white checked *kiffeyah*. I was so gobsmacked I hardly remember what he said, but by the time I left his office, I knew where my destiny lay.

Epilogue

The fax machine hums and a sheet of paper slides out. Yet another one from Ben. I chuck it straight into the bin with the rest. Then I return to my desk and sit looking out towards the mound of Tell es-Sultan. This is the most unexalted post I could have accepted and the one which pays the least, in financial terms, that is. But it's the one I really wanted, in fact, the only one I could have chosen and still remained true to myself.

Sometimes I can hear gunshots from this window and Israeli shells exploding not too far away. It makes me sad when I see the hate etched onto the faces of my students as they speak of the oppressors of their land; and when I see on the news the collapse of yet another round of talks, I honestly despair that this most ancient, most revered territory on earth, will ever know peace.

But never once, have I had a single regret. I love this place and its passionate people who can alternate between love and hate as fast as I can flick a switch.

I can make a difference here, in a way I never could at those illustrious museums or universities in Chicago, Munich or Jerusalem. The walls may be pitted by snipers' bullets and damaged by Israeli shells, but something new is growing here out of the carcass of ancient hatreds. Young Palestinians don't have to travel to Cairo or

Jordan to gain a degree. The tower block of this university rises up like a phoenix among the ashes of the old refugee camps. The funding has come from a UN aid package, designated exclusively for education, and gives a glimmer of hope to those bright youngsters playing football in shell-pocked streets, and I like to think that it sends an academic and intellectual challenge to institutions far better funded and equipped, on the other side of that Green Line. Of course, the Israeli establishment was livid that the Ein Gedi translator jumped ship to the enemy but I know my decision gave a much needed boost to Palestine's quest for autonomy, and I'm valued here far beyond anything I could find elsewhere in the world.

My lecturing load is fairly light, my academic work a constant joy and fascination. It leaves me plenty of time to gather notes for this book I'm burning to write, for a story which is craving to be told. It's a story of Canaan and its early people, before Joshua's plundering army stormed their walls, slayed their children and drowned their city in blood; Scriptural sages turned invaders into heroes and reshaped old myths into brand new tales of war to legitimise the emerging world of the conquering god. Well, my story will do the reverse. My inspiration comes from Canaan and its people, both present and past, and somehow, despite all the odds, when I see that passion on the faces of my students, I don't think the Hebrew army will ever succeed in crushing Canaan's flower a second time.

I stand up and go to the case in the corner of

my room. I still don't know how I ever persuaded Dr Schlott eventually to hand over this precious relic. Perhaps in the end it came down to guilt that his lust for funds nearly got me killed, or it may have been that fate stepped in and smoothed the road to return. At any rate, I now have power and prestige of my own. I pestered and persisted and finally my demands have been met.

I run my hand over the glass and gaze at the bones which lie inside - so delicate, so strong. It's not yet been decided where exactly she will rest but damn it, I fought my guts out to ensure her last wish was fulfilled. She's come back to lie at Jericho.

I know she'd like the book I'm writing. It'll tell the story of her city, her journey, and make the world remember that the forgotten, conquered people have their songs to sing down the paths of history too.

I crouch on the floor, press my fingers against the glass and whisper a promise to the spirit that once animated these ancient bones. I've drawn meaning from the figures in clay which your fingers forged. I've deciphered from strange symbols an understanding of how you loved your family, your Goddess, and your land. I've climbed the same paths through harsh and endless rock, and suffered the onslaught of that same blazing sun. I too have been pursued and terrorised for those secrets which you stole, and I have made your struggles mine.

I know your sisters, I know your story, and I shall make damn sure that Joshua's is not the only tale to be told down through the years.

About the Author

Cara Louise has been writing stories since she was six.

She is a graduate of Manchester Metropolitan University's BA Honours Degree in English and Writing and has an MA in Writing For Children from King Alfred's College, Winchester.

She has published many novels for children and won 2nd prize for fiction for readers of 12 plus at the Annual Writers' Competition, Winchester in 1999.

BETRAYED is her first adult novel and won 2nd prize for First Three Pages of a novel at Winchester in 2000.

She has also taught English as a Foreign Language and trained teachers in the UK, Japan, Taiwan, Austria, Spain, Madeira, Bulgaria, Finland and Malaysia.

Her research for BETRAYED led her to campaign in support of the people of Palestine. She is also an ardent supporter of animal rights.

Cara currently lives in Devon.

Published Children's Paperbacks

The Boy From the Hills
The Serpent of the Woods
The Guardian and the Goddess
The Lady of the Rock -
Biffy and the Barrow
Annie and the Dragon

Published E-Books - Children's Fiction

The Demon's Secret,
Raven Jack and the Fire of Doom,
Cannis Major Mystery. .
The Beast of Biddersley Grange
The Stones of Power,
The Lords of Time.
A Posy for Poll,
Stars Upon the Ceiling,
The Silent Pool.
Sorceress
The Hounds of Darkness
Annie and the Dragon -
Myths of the Xingu Indians
The Mystery of Deepderry Down
12 Bedtime Stories for 3-7s.

Published Talking Books on CD

Biffy and the Barrow
The Serpent of the Wood
The Guardian and the Goddess
Feng Shui and Babylon
The Lady of the Rock
Annie and the Dragon